INFERNAL CHAOS

The Apocalypse : Episode Three

DAVID O. BULLOCK

Black Rose Writing | Texas

ISBN: 978-1-68433-694-4
PUBLISHED BY BLACK ROSE WRITING
www.blackrosewriting.com

Printed in the United States of America
Suggested Retail Price (SRP) $20.95

Infernal Chaos is printed in Calluna

*As a planet-friendly publisher, Black Rose Writing does its best to eliminate
unnecessary waste to reduce paper usage and energy costs, while never compromising
the reading experience. As a result, the final word count vs. page count may not meet
common expectations.

To my beautiful daughters, Amy and Amber
You are the lights of my life
always have been
always will be
I love you with all my heart
Dad

They called to the mountains and the rocks,
"Fall on us and hide us from the face of him who sits on the throne and
from the wrath of the Lamb!
For the great day of their wrath has come, and who can withstand it?"
–Revelation 6:16-17 NIV

Then the seven angels who had the seven trumpets prepared to sound
them.
–Revelation 8:6 NIV

She sat alone in the luxurious suite that had been her home for weeks. It was hers, all hers, with everything she could ever want. She received the best care anyone could hope for, but had not been out of the room since the day she arrived. It was extravagant, but it was also her prison. Worse, no one knew where she was, and there was no escape.

When she looked in the mirror, she now saw herself again. Not Kelly Davis, Humanitarian Aid Worker; Beth Jennings Thompson, Smyrnian, believer in Jesus, reporter, wife of Blake Thompson. Her hair was growing back. No one had cut it since Ally and Kathie gave her a makeover that day at the Shelter to disguise her identity. The brunette had faded, and her natural blonde was returning.

She thought of Blake and wept... again. They were so happy since being married following the Rapture.

Then came the trip to Iran and their second meeting with the believers in Tehran. They could have left, but wanted to meet with them once more before leaving the country. Their minds had been on Ally alone with a monster, whose plans for her that night were evil. They prayed for her and heard news that she escaped, whisked away by Ollie and Amelia. It was a miracle!

Where was *her* miracle? Jesus had done so much for the Smyrnians since they put their faith in him. Why not now? Why had he left her alone in this prison with the same monster from whom he freed Ally?

Her mind raced back to that evening after she and Blake returned to the house to meet with the believers again. Knocking. No answer. Begging to leave; Blake refused to go. Opening the door and walking inside. Darkness shielding their eyes from what lay before them. Blake tripping. Her slipping. Eyes adjusting to the light. A gruesome scene meeting their sight. The entire group slaughtered. Fear. We *must* leave! A flight out of the country. The Shelter. The team. *Home!* Blake holding her, promising they would go right then.

The door bursting open. AMPP men running in. Handcuffs. Blindfolds. Dragged outside. Shoved inside a vehicle. Rough ride. Abandoned building. Separated from Blake. Longing for him to rush in and save her. From behind... something placed over her nose and mouth! Fighting to stop it; she could not. A mask! Inhaling. Sleep. Awakened by the pungent odor of ammonia. *Who was that?* Messai! Evil... Alluring. Chilling... Charming. His mansion. Her new home. Hopelessness. Tears. Blake, where are you? Save me! Jesus, why have you left me? I need you! No escape. She collapsed onto the bed, weeping. *Get ahold of yourself, Beth.* She needed a plan, but no plan came. She must be strong. A key turning in the lock. Someone was coming in. *Be strong, Beth.*

Blake knew where Beth was, or at least who had her. The AMPP men said their orders came from the top. That meant they came from Messai. He had searched for her in Tehran, but was certain he would not find her there. She was in Belgium. He knew it. His first impulse was to fly there, take on Messai and his men and rescue her himself. But wisdom and the calm, yet forceful voice of Ben Abramson had convinced him to fly to Ozark and let the Smyrnians join him on that mission. He knew Ben was right. Messai wanted to draw him into his web and destroy him, to show the world he would not tolerate the behavior of the *Smyrnians*. All in the name of peace and prosperity.

He could not allow Messai to eliminate him, so he returned to Missouri, even though he did not want to. He and Beth were aware times like this would come during the Tribulation, but not now. He was not ready for this. The weeks had been grueling as the team prayed and sought a way to overcome the most invincible force in the world and set Beth free. But there was no way. He sat in the Shelter this day, broken, alone and longing for his wife when, out of the blue, it hit him. She needed his help. She was in trouble! He could wait no longer. If the team would not act now, he would go alone. Evan's voice jarred him to his senses, calling to him from the living room of Bunker One.

"Blake, you need to see this."

INFERNAL
CHAOS

CHAPTER 1

The door opened. Messai walked in, guards by his side. Why did he need them every time he came in? Even if she tried to escape, the mansion was so guarded that getting away was impossible. She sat and waited for him to speak.

"Beth, you are looking in the mirror. You must recognize the same thing I see; that you are gorgeous again. Not that you weren't before, but now you are once again the beauty I fell in love with in the UN building when the council nominated me for Secretary-General. I have loved you from that day until now and waited for this moment every day since."

She did not move or lift her head, refusing to look at him.

"I come bearing wonderful news. You and I will become husband and wife this Wednesday, September 11."

Married? No! Three days! Her face revealed the shock. Failing to acknowledge it, he continued.

"Mid-week may seem like a strange day for a wedding, but it is also the anniversary of the disappearances. The world needs a pleasant memory of that day, don't you agree?"

Still no response.

"I'm sure it will make you happy to learn that I called a press conference today to announce our upcoming marriage to the world. Try to cheer up, my dear. We will marry at noon in a beautiful ceremony, then go for an elaborate honeymoon in Jerusalem, where I will combine business with pleasure. We will stay at the King David Hotel in the Presidential Suite. I assume you are aware of what happened the last time I was there. That did not turn out so well, but I realize now, she was not the right one; you are. And when *we* go, you will be my wife."

"You can't do that; and I *won't* do it. I will never marry you. I am Mrs. Blake Thompson."

"You fail to understand, dearest Beth. There is no option. You *will* stand beside me and become my wife. Look around; you are the most fortunate woman in the world. Trust me, you will get used to the idea and fall in love with me."

"I will *never* fall in love with you, nor will I become your wife and go with you to Jerusalem."

"Now my dear, you didn't believe you would come to me here in my mansion either, did you? Oh yes, you will fly with me to Jerusalem, either awake or sleeping. That part will be your choice."

She sat silent once again, refusing to give him the pleasure of seeing her lash out, reject him or cry. In her mind, she was praying, asking Jesus to show her what to do. But again, Jesus seemed far away, not hearing her pleas for help. The hopelessness returned, and she fought against it as it sought to claim her mind. He was right; she was powerless before him. If he forced her to become his wife, she could not stop him. He would anesthetize her again and fly her to Jerusalem. She could not prevent him from doing that either. She may attempt to fight him there, but he would drug her or force himself on her. This time he would have such a security patrol that she could not escape, no matter how hard she tried.

Jesus, help me, she whispered in her mind.

"Now I must go. The press has gathered for my announcement. No one knows yet what I plan to say. I am sure it will shock the world. And I am just as certain your little band of Smyrnians will watch, including your soon to be ex, or perhaps *late* husband. Oh yes, he will come and try to rescue you. I hope he brings the others so I can rid the world of all of them once and for all. But you, only you, will survive, and you will be my wife. Smile, Beth; the future is bright!"

He turned and walked out. The door locked again, leaving the guards standing outside to ensure she did not escape. Once he was gone, the tears flowed again. *Stop it, Beth. Be strong. You must be strong, regardless of what happens. Please, Blake, come and rescue me, my knight in shining armor. No, don't come! Jesus, where are you? Why have you left me here alone?*

Blake dashed into the room to find the others already gathered. Fear clawed at his mind. Evan had paused the television and rewound it to the beginning of the press conference. Aissa Messai was his usual pleasant self on camera with a smile revealing something made him jubilant today.

•　　•　　•　　•　　•

"Ladies and gentlemen of the world," Messai began. "It is my distinct pleasure to stand before you today to make a very important announcement. I never imagined this would happen, but it has, and I am ecstatic!" He paused, as if for effect, allowing his listeners to crave his next words.

"You have seen and heard much about Beth Jennings, the news reporter, turned Smyrnian. Beth joined the rebels in their attempt to interfere with our efforts to bring peace and prosperity to the world. Now she has defected, escaping them and coming to join us in our mission! She has been with me for several weeks, and the relationship between us has grown into something special."

"So, today I stand here to inform you that this Wednesday at noon she will become my wife! It makes me the happiest man in the world knowing the beautiful Miss Jennings has come to accept our agenda and chosen to unite with me in marriage! I would never have dreamed such a perfect scenario was possible. I trust you will welcome Beth as your new first lady and also give her your unwavering support, as you give it to me. That is all for today. Please make plans to tune in Wednesday for this simple, yet most wonderful wedding of all time! I love you and am honored to serve you as the Secretary-General of your United Nations."

Blake leapt to his feet. "No! That will not happen! Beth neither defected nor agreed to become his wife. We should have already done something. I will not wait any longer!"

"Blake is right!" said John Baldwin. "I'm ready to take off for Belgium. Who's with us?"

"Count me in!" said Evan. "Let's pack up and go right now!"

"Let's do this!" shouted Anders. "I will not allow that monster to own Beth!"

"Me too!" said Malachi. "I'm sure we can figure something out when we get there."

"Let's all go!" Ollie was ready. "We need all of us for this one. Amelia and I proved twice that we specialize in rescue efforts like this."

Ben calmed things down again, as difficult as that was with emotions at fever pitch in the room. He took charge, as you might expect from the former producer of a major news network. This moment called for someone to do that.

"We cannot all go. This requires a small group, and those who go must be careful. You can't allow your emotions to control you because that would play right into Messai's hands. We need a team of five at most. Let's select that group, then get a move on. Blake will go; that much is certain. And I agree that Evan, Anders, and Malachi need to go. That leaves one. Ally, you can't go, for obvious reasons. Neither can Ollie and Amelia. You are all wanted criminals. Trey, the same is true for you. John and Kathie, you're supposed to be dead, so you can't show your face in Messai's territory. And Rickie, we need you here. None of the rest of you need to go, but I want to suggest someone, if all of you agree, and if *he* will agree."

They looked at each other, wondering who remained that Ben could have on his mind.

"Bruno Fromm lives closer to Beth's location than any of us, and he craves getting in on the action. Well, this is his chance. We need the big man for this one."

"Call him!" Evan knew Ben was right on with that suggestion.

"Daddy will be ready!" said Ally. "But you need to keep a close eye on him. He can be a loose cannon sometimes."

"Don't worry, Ally; I can handle that. He likes me and says I am like another son to him."

"You're right, Evan. If daddy will listen to anyone, it's you."

John appeared to be somewhat hurt that he would not get to go, but he also understood.

Ben placed the call and put his phone on speaker so everyone could join the conversation. Bruno did not even take time to say hello.

"Ben, we just watched the news. Something has to happen! We can't sit back and let Messai follow through with this sham of a wedding. Somebody has to stop him!"

"That's why we are calling you, Bruno. We're assembling a team of five to go at once. Blake, Evan, Anders and Malachi are in, and…"

"Say no more!" Bruno interrupted. "I'm your fifth! Just tell me when to be there and I'll be ready!"

"You realize what a dangerous mission this is, don't you, Mr. Fromm?" asked Evan. "Our chances for success, and even survival, are low. It is possible they'll capture or kill some, or all, of us."

"I do, but Beth is depending on us. I'm ready to fight and die to save her, if that is what it takes!"

"Bruno, this is Blake. We'll leave tomorrow morning, if we can get a flight. I haven't talked to the others about this, but my opinion is, we need to fly to your place and drive in from there. Messai will expect us, or at least me to come, and have AMPP patrols on high alert at the airport. If we fly to Germany, then take a car from there, we should be able to get in without being noticed. Am I right that it is only a four to five-hour drive from where you are?"

"Yep, that's right. I'll be ready and waiting for you and will pick you up at the airport, so we can hit the road. Any idea what time you'll get here?"

"I'll call you as soon as we book a flight. Thanks, Bruno. I sure am glad you are on our side."

"No happier than me, I assure you. The big man's time has come to shine! I've been waiting for this moment for almost a year!"

Ben raised a question. "Before you go, Bruno, do you foresee any problems at the border crossing? It's hard to imagine Messai beefing up security at the checkpoints. He won't expect you to drive in, will he?"

"I wouldn't be too sure about that. He will cover all his bases, and that may include the borders. Those border guards can get testy and like to push their authority. They will be a problem, if they're watching for us. But I have crossed many times. Don't worry; I know how to handle them."

"I'll help you out with that too," said Anders. "My parents were Dutch immigrants, so I speak fluent Dutch and look the part. It just happens that Malachi is fluent in Dutch too, and he looks as Belgian as I do. He and I are going back to visit relatives and bringing along a few American friends and a German bloke who is driving us. How does that sound?" He looked around the room.

"I like it." Evan was sure the idea would work, and the rest were in agreement.

"We need some things first, though," said Blake. "We don't have a lot of time, but Evan, I need a new ID. Messai's men know me as Ryan Davis. I need to change that and carry a passport with a name they won't recognize. They've seen me too, so ladies, I also need another quick makeover. It's too late to shop for supplies, so we'll work with whatever you have. Any suggestions?"

"If you can give us two hours, we'll fix you up."

"Let me book a flight. That will tell us how much time we have before we leave."

He called and got a flight for the next day. The other three men went to pack while he entered the makeshift *salon*. "Okay, give me the weirdest style you can come up with."

"You just sit back and let us do the work. This will take two hours max, but when we finish, nobody will recognize you!"

He was at their mercy, but the mission was too urgent to stop them. He sat down and let them go.

•　　•　　•　　•　　•

In Belgium, Aissa Messai was meeting with the director of AMPP and his senior officers.

"I am sure Thompson will come after my little announcement. We need to be ready for him when he does. He is coming right to us, so we cannot allow him to get away. We must capture him. What preparations are you making?"

"Well, sir, we are covering the airport so he and the others can't get past us there. I will station a hundred men to cover every square inch of the place. AMPP is aware of what he looks like now, and of the alias he uses, Ryan Davis. He can't escape us. And there will be more troops than you can imagine surrounding this place 24/7 until after you, and she, are on your way to Jerusalem. Don't worry, there will be ample coverage there too."

"Outstanding job, Director! Something else comes to mind because I don't want to leave any stone unturned. What about the border crossings?"

"Excuse me, sir?"

"The border crossings. What if he tries to sneak in through one of them?"

"Sir, I doubt he would do that. It would require him driving or walking across, thus he would need to fly into another airport and travel from there to here. I doubt he will take time for that, because he will be in such a hurry. I can't fathom the need to heighten security in those areas."

"I do not care what you can or cannot *fathom*, Director. These Smyrnians are very elusive, so I do not want to take any chances. Do I make myself clear? Please secure the borders, too."

"Yes, sir. I will make that happen. We will station additional men at each crossing."

"Good, good. Get choppers in the air, boots on the ground, whatever it takes to be certain no one gets in here, or that they do not escape if they try."

"Not to worry, sir. This place is impenetrable."

They carried out his orders at once. The mansion was one hundred percent inaccessible. Even if Smyrnians somehow entered the country, they would not enter the property. That much was sure.

•   •   •   •   •

Blake's new image was finished and ready to unveil to the team, not to mention to him. They used what they had left over: Amelia's carrot-top red. His hair was much shorter, with the messy look, which would require time and effort to maintain. The ladies groomed his beard and mustache to perfection, although it made him look rather evil. Gone were the sideburns and scraggly beard. In was the Van Dyke, complete with mustache, soul patch and goatee. Everything, from the hair to the Van Dyke, was carrot-top red. He did not even recognize himself when he looked in the mirror. Would Beth like it? He hoped he would get the chance to find out. It was time for him to pack. Evan took a quick photo for his new passport, so when they left, it would be ready to go. His name was Shawn Smith.

The four of them planned to talk and prepare during the flight and share with Bruno when they arrived in Germany. The rest of the team would pray for them as they did. Evan, always on top of things, printed a detailed map of Messai's mansion and property, including the surrounding area. He also found an aerial view which gave a bird's-eye glimpse of the place, revealing one thing. It was impossible for anyone to get into the mansion, and just as impossible for someone to get out, that someone being Beth. Blake became distraught when Evan showed them the images. But he remained determined to try everything possible to get inside and get her out. However, he knew in his heart there was nothing they could do.

Beth did the only thing she could do... pray. The more she prayed, the farther away Jesus seemed to be. *My prayers are not even reaching the ceiling*, she thought, *much less heaven*. Her destiny was to be the wife of the Antichrist for the remaining six years until Jesus returned. Would Jesus forgive her? Would it mean she had allied herself with Messai? Her mind could not grasp that thought. She prayed, "Jesus, please forgive me for what I am being forced to do. It isn't right for me to take my life to avoid it, because I trust in you. But it doesn't feel like you are here with me. I'm not even sure you are listening to me. If this is what I must do, please use it somehow to help the Smyrnians fight Messai, and help more people turn to you."

It was past the time to lie down and try to sleep. If only she had a Bible to read, but there was none. Beth had never been so alone and helpless in her life. While she lay in the huge, elegant bed and closed her eyes, a sound came. A voice! But it was not the voice of the guards outside her door, or of Messai. It was a still, small voice, soft and gentle.

The words came to her: *"In peace I will lie down and sleep, for you alone, Lord, make me dwell in safety."* She did not know those were the words of Psalm 4:8 in the Bible, or who spoke them to her at that moment. Tomorrow, she may not even remember hearing them. But tonight she fell into a deep, peaceful sleep that lasted until morning.

•   •   •   •   •

Blake, Evan, Anders and Malachi boarded their plane to Germany. They needed rest, but there would be no sleep on this flight. There was no time to spare and no answers for how to find and rescue Beth. The more they talked, the more discouraged they became. Malachi would try his best to find a way into the mansion, but even he did not believe it was possible. Their only option was to get there, then stay nearby, trying to identify some way to open a door and get them in.

But what if they got in? There was no way to get past the AMPP forces stationed everywhere in the house. Even if they did, how would they locate the room where Messai held Beth prisoner? Time flew by as they talked, and before they knew it, the plane landed in Germany. True to his word, Bruno waited for them with Mila by his side, accompanied by Hans and Heidi Meier. The four Smyrnians met Hans and Heidi for the first time. Mila introduced them. The introductions were special, but brief. Bruno and the four men drove away for Brussels on an impossible mission, unaware that an AMPP patrol awaited them at the border crossing from Germany into Belgium.

•   •   •   •   •

Messai awoke in a gleeful mood. In two and a half days, Beth Jennings would become his wife. And as yet, there had been no sign of Blake Thompson or any other would be intruders. The man must not love his wife as much as she believed he did. He smiled as he imagined his wedding, but even more, as he fantasized about the honeymoon he would share with his beautiful bride. It was impossible to contain his joy. Before retiring for the night, he needed another glimpse of her. He ascended the grand stairway and made his way to her room. The AMPP men unlocked the door and opened it for him, then stood guard as he went inside. When he entered the room, there she lay, curled up in the bed, hugging a pillow, fast asleep. He stood for a few minutes gazing at her. Her beauty captivated him. She must have surrendered to her future as his wife. That would explain why she slept so well and appeared so peaceful. He watched a little longer, then turned and left the room. He could wait two more days, but it would not be easy.

•   •   •   •   •

Bruno approached the border crossing and found it more active than normal in the early morning hours as darkness began giving way to daylight.

"Guys, give me your passports and prepare to answer any questions they ask you. Just remain calm and let me do the talking."

He stopped at the checkpoint and handed the passports to the guard.

"Beautiful morning, isn't it?" he asked the man in German.

"Put down the windows so I can get a look at your passengers."

Bruno obliged, and the guard peered at the men inside. He took the passports to another guard, allowed him to check them too, then returned.

"Sir, please pull over to the side, and ask all of your passengers to step out of the car."

"I appreciate your diligence, but we have a tight schedule and are running behind."

"Sir, pull to the side and exit the car, please!"

Bruno obeyed his order, seeing no other option. "Anders, you talk when we get out," he said.

Three armed guards, plus the one in charge, strode over and led them away from the car.

"We have orders to check any suspicious automobile coming through here. And I have reason to not trust you men. What is your purpose for coming to Belgium?" Anders spoke up in fluent Dutch, trying to put the man at ease.

"Sir," he said with a smile, addressing the man in charge, "my name is Steffen Janssen. I grew up in the United States, but my parents were Dutch immigrants, so I still have many family members in Belgium. I came to visit and brought a few friends along for the week. It's a holiday for them."

"My buddy here," he pointed to Malachi, "is also of Belgian descent and has relatives here, too."

Malachi also addressed the men in perfect Dutch. "Gentlemen, please don't give our friends a bad first impression of the country. Steffen and I told them so much about the hospitality here. I beg you to prove us truthful and give them a warm welcome." He was chipper, too.

"You," he pointed at Blake... "Mr. Smith. What is your purpose for coming to Belgium? And why are you driving across the border from Germany instead of flying into an airport?"

"Yes sir, my name is Shawn Smith. As my buddy Steffen said, he invited me to come with him while he visits his family. I've never seen your country, but I hear it is amazing. I plan to get in all the sightseeing I can while we are here."

"And you?" He nodded at Evan.

"Same thing. These are my friends, and I came on vacation with them. I'm excited to be here!"

"Mr. Fromm, you are German. Why are you driving these men?"

"I am well acquainted with them. They wanted to visit Germany too, so I volunteered to drive them if they were okay with that. They jumped at the chance. You can see so much more from a car than a plane."

"Mr. Smith's passport looks different from the others. It would not be fake, would it?"

Evan froze. Had he done something wrong? He was in a hurry when he created it.

"Sir, that's the passport they issued me. It is the correct one, even though it's new." Blake was perspiring now. Evan was trying to get his attention, nodding his head back and forth. "No!"

"If it is new, Mr. Smith, can you tell me why the expiration date occurs in less than a year?"

Evan realized he had forgotten to change the date to ten years ahead. If it was new, the date had to be close to that, but it was not. Why did Blake have to say it was new? That gave him away!

"It is obvious you are trying to hide something. There is no other reason for carrying a fake passport. Seize him!"

The guards moved fast. Two of them grabbed Blake by each arm and pulled his hands behind his back. The other held Evan, Anders, Malachi and Bruno at gunpoint.

"Nobody moves, or someone dies," shouted the man in charge.

Bruno flew into action even faster than the guards. If this was his time to shine, he was up to the challenge. Before the one with the machine gun trained on them had time to move, Bruno took him out with a single blow. The commander was next. Blake jerked away from the grasp of the two holding him and fell to the ground, clearing the way for Bruno's next victims to fall. Before either could draw his Beretta, he grabbed them, one with each hand, and slammed their heads together. They collapsed in a heap, one on top of the other.

"Quick, grab our passports and let's get out of here," he yelled. "It will take a while for them to wake up or someone to find them. We need to get as far away as we can before that happens. They know what we look like. They'll describe us to AMPP, who'll pass that on to Messai."

Passports in hand, they ran to the car and sped away, leaving the four security men lying unconscious on the ground. They took off for Brussels, still clueless about what to do when they got there. They would need to stay even more undercover now that AMPP may recognize them.

"Bruno, I've never seen anyone move with such precision and take out four guys like that," exclaimed Blake.

"I don't know about precision, but I did rather enjoy it. This is the big man's time to shine, and I plan to make the most of it! I'm always up for a good fight anytime Mila's not around to stop me." He grinned.

"I am so sorry for not changing the date on your passport, Blake." Evan was almost in tears.

"No use worrying about it now, Evan. We can't go back and change it. But I'm sure this word will get to Messai as soon as those guys report in. Every AMPP man in Belgium will be on the lookout for us. Has anybody come up with an idea yet? We need to find a way to get Beth out of there. But this changes everything, if there ever was a way."

Anders' faith came out again, as it so often did. "Blake, we can pray for her and ask Jesus to save her. That may be our only option. But I promise you, it is our *best* option."

"I'm not sure I want to hear that, Anders. It's hard to believe it right now." Jesus seemed almost as far away to Blake as he did to Beth. Despair overwhelmed him as all hope faded.

He called Ben and told him what happened, his despondency coming across over the phone.

"I understand it seems hopeless, Blake," Ben told him. "We feel the same way here. I wish I had some advice for you, or a word of wisdom. But I can't come up with anything right now. We're praying for Jesus to keep all of you safe; even more after what just happened."

"Don't worry about us!" Blake was almost screaming. "Pray for Beth! She is about to face a living hell on earth. I don't care what happens to us. What happens to *her* is all that matters!" He apologized right after those words came out. "I'm sorry, Ben. I didn't mean that." He broke into tears again.

"I understand, Blake. We are praying for her, too. Keep us updated."

"We will. I just want my wife and need her. I promised to always be there for her and never leave her. And now I am powerless to help when she needs me most."

The tears poured now. Anders put his hand on his partner's shoulder. He wished there was something he could say or do that would help him. But he could do nothing for him, or Beth.

CHAPTER 2

Beth awakened. The thought hit her mind the moment her eyes opened. *Two more days and I will marry Messai.* That could not be! She married Blake! Or did she? The state did not recognize their marriage because they performed it themselves, with the help of the other Smyrnians. They were not *legally* married, but they *were* married in the eyes of Jesus. To them, nothing else mattered, but to the world, and to Aissa Messai, their marriage never happened. She was sure he confirmed that before capturing her.

The day passed quickly. She willed it to slow down, but the hours continued to fly by. Night soon came again, and she lay down to sleep. Tomorrow would come and go. The following day, Messai would force her to stand beside him and agree to be his wife. Thinking of that repulsed her. She longed for the gentle voice of the previous night, but it did not come. Neither did sleep.

The five Smyrnians arrived in Brussels mid-morning. They spent the rest of the day trying to get close to the mansion, hoping to scope it out and find a way inside. But those attempts proved futile. Messai kept the place locked down like a prison. The abundance of AMPP's presence blew them away. No one could get anywhere near this magnificent structure without being seen.

Nightfall came, and they tried again under the cover of darkness. But the vast security presence still made it impossible. The other four held Blake to keep him from charging headlong for the front door. It would be utter foolishness, but he would rather die than see the wedding take place. It sent him into a rage every time he envisioned that. They would not sleep this night. Instead, they would spend every minute searching for a way, some way, any way to get in and rescue Beth. Exhaustion overwhelmed them, but they maintained their vigil through the night. Morning arrived, bringing with it no more answers than the day before. There was only one positive to this point; they had avoided being seen or captured.

At the Shelter, the team waited for someone to come up with a plan and call the men before Wednesday came. They now expected a plan to come in situations like this, but it did not happen this time. Despondency gnawed away at their faith. Their thoughts were on Beth and what she would go through tomorrow. They sat together, consumed by their anxiety, none of them saying a word. But each understood the thoughts of the others. Their faith which had been so strong for the past year was now very weak.

Tuesday morning. Beth once again longed for the hours to drag by. But as happened the previous day, they passed at warp speed. She stopped praying. It did no good, anyway. Sitting in shock, she struggled to resign herself to what would happen the next day at noon.

There was no choice but to accept it. She understood that. To fight it would be futile. How she would face it and go through with it, she did not know. It was the worst day of her life. The only thing that would save her now was the Second Coming of Jesus. And that would not happen for six more years. Fear clamored to take over her mind, and faith did not return to prevent it.

Blake and the four men with him gave up too. Despair overcame them. They had nothing more to give and saw no possibility of success.

"I wish I had come straight from Tehran the moment I realized Messai took her," Blake moaned. "Security may not have been on such high alert then. I could've gotten in and saved her. Why did I listen to Ben and go back to Missouri? I wasted my opportunity. This is my fault... all my fault."

"You would be dead if you had tried that," whispered Evan. "There's no way you could have survived. Then Beth would've lost her husband too."

"Well, now I've lost my wife," he said. "One year. One year into the Tribulation and I let this happen. We loved each other so much. But we didn't even get to enjoy being married for a year."

"Tonight and tomorrow, we'll get as close as we can." Malachi brought the conversation back to the matter at hand, hoping to give Blake a glimmer of hope. "I don't have a plan, but the one thing I've learned through the years is to stay close because you never can tell what may happen. Bruno, park the car somewhere we can get away fast if we need to, and we'll hide out nearby. We need to stick close to each other. Where can we stay that is close enough to the mansion to get in, if we see an opening, and close to the car, in case we need to escape?"

"That grove of spruce trees across the street, if we can park the car in there without being seen. Security is tight, but we can try to get in it from the back side, park, then hide just inside the front line of trees. From there, we can see what is going on outside."

"I'm not sure I can take it. After noon tomorrow, let's catch a flight to Jerusalem."

"We can't do that, Blake," said Evan. "It isn't wise. Besides, what will you do if you're there? How do you think you're going to stop anything?"

"None of you have to go if you don't want to. I'll go by myself. No hard feelings. I just want to be there. Maybe I can..." He stopped mid-sentence, again realizing the hopelessness of the situation.

"It will be dark soon," said Malachi. "We need to park the car before then so they can't see the lights. I found a spot behind the trees where we can hide it. From there, we could get away fast."

The car hidden, they got out of sight, holing up in the edge of the trees. It was 10:00 p.m.

Beth lay down again, knowing she would not sleep, but determined to try. She watched the time pass on the majestic grandfather clock in the corner.

11:00 p.m. In thirteen hours, she would stand beside her future husband and utter her vows, not meaning a word she said. She refused to cry. She would be strong. Her mind returned to this time one year ago. At midnight in America on September 11, 2029, the entire world changed in the blink of an eye. The Rapture took every follower of Jesus home to be with him, including her parents. Beth wished again she had been ready to go with them. But then she would not have married Blake. Neither would she have fought for Jesus during the seven years before he came again to bring it all to an end. But now that would all be over, unless she discovered ways to fight from within. Perhaps she would replace Ally as a Smyrnian spy. She must get up and move.

11:30. She walked the floor. Maybe it was nervous energy. She could not sit still, no matter how hard she tried. She longed to go out for a midnight run. But she understood that was not possible. The door stayed locked from the outside, and the guards never left their post.

11:45. She got dressed. Sweats, a comfortable shirt and tennis shoes. She prepared for a night run, fully aware there would not be one. Perhaps it would help to envision herself running. She remained in good physical shape, despite weeks of inactivity in the mansion. She had walked and run in place in the extensive suite. It provided plenty of space for that kind of activity. Now she stretched, as she always did before a run. She almost felt the cool night air blowing in her face. *This is crazy*, she said to herself. *Beth, you are losing your mind.*

11:55. She needed to lie back down, but that was not happening. She was wide awake, her body and mind ready for action. Without sleep, she would be a wreck tomorrow. But who cared? Not her, that much was certain.

11:59. She felt something. The floor swayed under her feet. Her imagination was playing tricks on her again. Sleeplessness and fatigue manipulated her mental faculties. *No, wait! This is real!*

12:00. Midnight. The mansion shook violently. *Earthquake!* John said it would come. The earth was convulsing not only in Belgium, but throughout the entire world at the same time. She knew it! Things crashed to the floor, and the door to the suite flew open. Messai's guards lay nearby under a pile of rubble. The ceiling above them collapsed and crushed them where they stood. The mansion quaked so much she could feel it falling apart. But calm surrounded her. The floor beneath her did not shake as the mansion crumbled around her. That made no sense! By some miracle, the staircase remained intact.

Darkness blinded her, concealing any potential means of escape as the power shut down. From out of nowhere, a ray of light illuminated the stairs, forming a glowing pathway to the front door. She realized it shone for her. Seeing no other signs of life, she descended the steps and found them as solid as when Messai's guards led her up them the first time. She followed the path to the door and found it open, hanging to one side, held by a single hinge.

Once outside, she broke into a run, sprinting toward a grove of trees across the street where the path led. *Follow the light, Beth*, she heard in her mind. She dashed along the path, praying as she ran. "I'm sorry for doubting you, Jesus. I should have known you would come through for me. I gave up hope, but you were right on time."

The men hiding in the trees saw the shaking, but did not feel it. They would not have believed it if they were not living it. When the quake began, Blake yelled, "Earthquake!" The noise prevented the others from hearing him. They watched as the mansion crumbled bit-by-bit while AMPP men ran for their lives. Most did not make it. Falling debris crushed them as they ran. Darkness enveloped the five men, obscuring their vision. "Beth!" screamed Blake. "I have to get to her!"

They all saw it at the same time: a light in the darkness. An illuminated pathway leading to where they stood. Anders grabbed Blake's arm. "Wait!" They saw her. She raced through the door and dashed on the path toward the trees. They did not need a plan! Jesus brought her out of the mansion and was leading her straight to them. They stood and watched as she sprinted toward them at full speed. Blake stepped out, arms outstretched, to receive her. He did not look like himself, but she recognized him. She leapt into his arms, and he held her as she sobbed. He wept with her.

"Let's go!" Bruno yelled. They darted across solid ground and made it to the car. The lighted path pointed the way and ended there. The six of them crammed inside and sped out of Brussels. Bruno drove like a madman, as destruction raged around them. They saw only what the car lights made visible. Sounds of collapsing buildings permeated their ears. The roadway shattered into pieces behind them. The noise roared, deafening them to each other's voices. This was no normal quake, and it showed no signs of letting up.

Meteorites blazing through the earth's atmosphere and crashing into the planet joined the convulsing earth. The falling balls of fire crushed buildings, leaving blazing infernos in their wake. Bruno swerved right and left to avoid cars crushed by them, too, or gaping holes in the pavement. It felt like the earth was splitting apart and appeared that heaven itself became visible, as if someone flung open giant doors between it and the planet. But Bruno and his passengers had no time to notice that. Their focus was escaping Brussels and getting to Germany.

On the outskirts of the city, the car's high beams exposed men and women running for their lives. But their attempts to evade the falling debris proved futile. They ran to the hills, trying to escape from that which was inescapable. Their eyes stared at the heavens, as strange terror overwhelmed them. The loud din drowned out their screams as they fled.

Bruno's mind was on Mila, the boys, and Ally as he drove. They all thought about their teammates at the Shelter. Were the bunkers destroyed? But fighting for survival left little time for reflection. The road shook so badly Bruno struggled to keep the car on it. Everything around them crashed and crumbled. Away from the city, on the open road, he drove at wild speeds as the car bounced and swerved in all directions. None of them cared. They only wanted to make it to his house.

When they came to the border crossing, he did not slow down. Blasting through it, they saw the earth had opened and swallowed the entire checkpoint, along with the guards. He dodged the gigantic hole at the last minute. The quake continued for a solid hour. They tried to imagine the scene that would meet their eyes when daylight came, knowing it would not be pretty. They finally arrived at Bruno's house. It still stood, although it had sustained extensive damage. Hans and Heidi were there with Bruno's wife and sons. They stayed safely inside, but feared for their lives. Bruno held his family for what seemed like forever.

In the Shelter, the group was praying for Beth, when the quake hit at 6:00 p.m. The earth trembled, lightly at first, then rapidly increased in intensity. John yelled, "It's the earthquake! I knew it!" They sprinted up the steps out of the bunkers and into the cabin to avoid being trapped underground.

From there, they ran outside into the large open area, away from anything that might fall and crush them. With no light, they stood in a tight huddle listening as the quake raged all around the property. It shocked them to find the ground calm where they stood. Jesus put a hedge of protection around his property and his people.

They clung to each other's hands and found their way back to the tiny house. When they walked inside, they stood on a solid floor, also unaffected by the quake. The loud din raged beyond the property, but inside they discovered peace and safety. After waiting an hour until they heard the quaking stop, they descended the steps, investigated the bunkers, and found everything unharmed.

"The quake hit the entire earth," said John. "I am certain of that. The world has changed again in a single night."

"What about Beth and the others?" asked Miriam.

"All we can do is wait and hope to hear from them..." Ben whispered, "...and pray." They did.

Flashlight in hand, Aissa Messai frantically climbed the stairs, which leaned precariously to one side. He ran to Beth's suite, longing to find her safe. But more than that, he had to make sure she did not escape. That must not happen. The wedding would go on tomorrow as planned; nothing would stop that. She would become his wife, but also his prisoner. He would be the master from whom she could not escape, controlling her and forcing her to do his every bidding. The world would not see that, but she would understand and realize she had no choice but to obey.

He saw the door open, hanging by a hinge. The AMPP guards lay crushed beneath a pile of rubble. That did not matter; they were expendable. She was not. He entered the room and found it untouched by the destructive force of the earthquake. How was that possible? What he did not find was Beth Jennings Thompson. She was gone. He ran from the room, searching everywhere, inside and outside.

He threw his head back and let out a howling shriek. Flashes of light darted around him, emanating from every part of his body. The quake had devastated his security teams. He realized it was useless to look for Beth, knowing he had lost her, and this battle. But he would *not* lose the war. "I will prevail!" he screamed. He would ramp up the pressure on the Smyrnians. They could not hide forever. "My men will find them and return Beth to me," he growled, his body pulsating with light.

The group in Germany racked their brains to find a plan which would allow them to get out of the country. They needed to get to the United States, Ozark, Missouri, and the Shelter. But with airports in shambles, no planes flying and phones useless, the impossibility of that happening hit home like a door slamming in their faces. They could not contact the team, nor could the team contact them. Once again they searched for an answer when there was none to find.

At the Shelter, Ally read her Bible and prayed. Acts Chapter 12 is the story of Jesus' freeing his disciple, Peter, from prison. The night before his trial, Peter faced a certain death sentence for preaching and teaching about Jesus. His situation seemed hopeless. He sat in a prison cell between two soldiers, bound with two chains, and sentries standing guard at the entrance. Escape was impossible.

But an angel appeared to Peter as a light shone in his cell. The angel told him to get up, and the chains fell off his wrists! The angel led him out to the gate of the city. It opened by itself! When they reached a certain point, the angel left him. He walked straight to the house where the other followers of Jesus gathered and prayed for him. The next day would have sealed his fate, but Jesus set him free at the last minute!

Wow, that is just like my escape from the King David Hotel in Jerusalem, Ally reasoned. She took a moment to thank Jesus for helping her escape that night and for putting Ollie and Amelia there right when she needed them. *You always come through at the right time, Jesus.* She smiled as she recalled those events.

A soft voice whispered, *Not you... Beth.* It took a moment to sink in, then it hit her. *Beth!* Jesus had set her free from Messai's prison at the last minute! The realization hit her mind like a missile! The earthquake! The timing was not accidental. Not only did it occur one year after the Rapture, but hours before Messai would force Beth to marry him! She sat stunned for a moment, trying to process what Jesus had just revealed to her.

She was certain the earthquake opened Beth's prison door and allowed her to walk free! And as Peter was told to dress in preparation to leave, the same thing happened for Beth. As a light shined in Peter's prison cell, a light had also shone for Beth. Jesus did not reveal to her how that happened. But she understood that Beth walked straight to the guys, in the same way Peter walked to the place where the group met, praying for him. And all six of the Smyrnians left the city and escaped to safety.

She jumped up as if ejected her from her seat. Racing to the living room, she yelled for the group to join her. She ran from Bunker One to Bunkers Two and Three where they stayed, then sprinted back to the first, gasping for breath as she did. The rest hurried in to hear what was going on. Older John and Mary ran so fast they made it before some others. When all of them arrived, she took a moment to catch her breath, then spoke much louder than she intended.

"Beth escaped!" It burst out with such excitement it caught them by surprise.

"How can you know that?" asked John. "We haven't even heard from them."

"Jesus told me!" she exclaimed. "I was praying and reading the story of Peter being set free from prison in Acts Chapter 12."

She told them everything she read and explained how the voice spoke to her. "The same things happened for Beth, in the exact ways they happened for Peter! I know they did!"

"I believe it!" said Ben. "We've seen that happen again and again. Remember how Jesus spoke to your parents in Germany saying you needed them? And that is only one example. He speaks to us most when we read the Bible."

"So, what do we do now?" asked Amelia. "If you're right, we need to get to her."

"We need to get to *them*," Ally said. "They all escaped together. I'm not sure where they went, but I am positive all six of them are safe, for now."

"They flew to Germany and drove to Brussels. Do you think they made it back to your mom and dad's house?" Ben asked.

"I guarantee you they did," said John with absolute certainty. "They didn't stay in Belgium. I wish I could say the earthquake killed Messai, but we know it didn't. He will be alive until the end of the Tribulation. No one can destroy him but Jesus."

"No, but I'd sure like to!" Kathie exclaimed under her breath, sitting next to him. They all heard her, and none of them disagreed. Each of them had thought the same thing during the past year.

"We need to get there, but how?" asked Ollie. "Every airport in the world must be closed. They can't get out of Germany, and there is no way for us to get to them."

"I have an idea," suggested Rickie.

"Are you thinking what I'm thinking?" asked Trey. They were military buddies, so their thoughts often moved in the same direction. Both had been through similar crises during combat missions.

"Without a doubt. You and I are both still in the Reserves, so they can call us up for national emergencies. We can take advantage of volunteer activation. All we need to do is go to the base and volunteer. We have connections there. They've called us to fly emergency missions in the past. U.S. citizens trapped on foreign soil and in grave danger constitutes an emergency, wouldn't you agree? If we can get clearance, we can fly to Germany and bring them back."

"But we have to be sure it's safe for takeoff at the base. The runways must be a mess after the quake. Then we have to be certain there is a place in Germany where we can land. How are we going to get that info before we get there?"

"We aren't. I hope we can land in Ramstein and drive to Bruno and Mila's house from there."

"But what if we fly to Ramstein and can't land because their runways are a mess?"

"Rickie is right," said Ally. "Jesus wouldn't have shown me this unless he wanted us to go after them, so I know he gave Rickie this idea too. I say you must take the chance."

"Ally is right, gentlemen," Amelia interrupted. "And I'm not saying that to agree with another woman in the room. If we believe this came from Jesus, you must go and trust him to take care of everything else. If he has done it before, I see no reason he won't do it again."

"That's easy for you to say." Trey rolled his eyes at Ally and Amelia. "I have a ton of questions. First, we can't be sure they'll let us volunteer. Then the question becomes, can we get a plane from the base? If we can, it has to be at least a C-130 like Bradley flew you guys over in. But we'll take anything that will cross the Atlantic without refueling."

"Oh, and we need to get clearance to go, too. I doubt that will be a problem because of our connections and the emergency. And last but not least, if we can't land at Ramstein, we're goners. What goes up must come down!"

"We have to try, Trey. If we don't make it, at least we died trying. Leave no man behind, right? Are you with me?"

"Okay, man, I'm in. Let's do this thing. Leave no man, or woman, behind."

This appeared to be one that required a lot of miraculous intervention to pull off. But Rickie was ready, as was Trey, after talking it through.

"Okay, it's a done deal. We'll head over to the base tomorrow morning and volunteer. I'm sure they'll agree to that. It would be rare for them to refuse a mission to rescue American citizens trapped on foreign soil and in danger. Not to mention, they know us and trust us. If everything works out, we'll fly out under the cover of darkness and land in Germany the next day."

Blake and Beth enjoyed a glorious reunion. They needed to pinch themselves to be sure it was happening. The group had been up all night and driven almost six hours in the middle of an earthquake, but Mila insisted on whipping up a hearty breakfast for them. While they waited, she provided choices of coffee, tea, hot chocolate and juice. The smell of freshly baked bread filled their nostrils and drew them to the table. Soft butter, jams and honey accompanied the bread, along with eggs, sausage, cheese, fresh fruit and milk. Cereals and yogurt rounded out the menu. They ate more than they should. It hit the spot and made them realize how much they needed it.

After eating, they sat and shared stories. Blake told of Bruno's heroics at the border crossing. Mila smiled. She had seen her husband in action, but not to that extent since he met Jesus. She now understood how important his skills would be during the Tribulation. He was more valuable to the Smyrnians than she realized.

Anders, Evan and Malachi talked about their harrowing trip to Brussels and the hopeless task of getting near Messai's mansion. But most of all, they wanted Beth to tell them about her experience. They pressed her for details of everything, from the day Messai took her captive to the previous night when she escaped. She described imprisonment in a luxurious suite, admitting most would never call it imprisonment. Messai gave her everything she wanted, and more. It mesmerized them when she told of the gentle voice speaking to her, giving her sweet peace and allowing her to sleep through the night. She now recalled the words, even though she heard them for the first time that night. *"In peace I will lie down and sleep, for you alone, Lord, make me dwell in safety."*

The resident theologian for the Smyrnians spoke up. "Psalm 4:8," Anders said with a wide smile. "I learned that verse months ago. It's better than any sleeping pill you can take!"

"I'm blown away by how much of the Bible you've memorized, Anders," Blake marveled.

"I'm trying to do what it says. Another verse, Psalm 119:11, says we are to hide his word in our hearts. I take that literally, and it has made a big difference for me!"

Beth continued her story of getting dressed the night before as the clock neared midnight. She wasn't aware then why she did it, but she understood when the earthquake struck! When she told them about the quake and lighted path showing her the way of escape, they were awestruck. It seemed weeks removed, but in reality, it had only been hours.

They all agreed they would do their best to trust Jesus in every situation for the next six years, regardless of how dire the circumstances may be. That would not be easy, but if they learned anything from this experience, it was that he would never let them down. They would encourage each other to remember that in the tough times.

The conversation returned to their present circumstances. It ended with an agreement to wait for things to clear up before searching for a way to get back to the Shelter. Until then, they would go help anyone in any way they could. Needs were extreme after the quake. When they did, they would seek opportunities to tell people about the one who changed their lives and eternities. That excited them above all else. But for now, they needed sleep. Even though it was morning, their bodies reached a point of exhaustion that prevented them from staying awake any longer.

The sights that met Rickie and Trey's eyes traveling to the base blew their minds. Devastation caused by the quake was worse than anything they saw in war. The word *catastrophic* described it best. Only piles of rubble remained of many homes. Demolished businesses and cavernous holes dotted the landscape. Broken and buckled roads greeted them at every turn. Even with no traffic, the drive was slow. They were off-road much of the way, just so they could keep going.

When they arrived at the military base, they found it in poor condition, too. The base commander met them, and they took time to renew their friendships and share memories of combat. Both served with him and remained part of his loyal *band of brothers*. He owed his life to them because of their actions, which saved him during one particular skirmish.

He would do almost anything for these two men, but this request stretched the limits of what he could do. He enlisted them into voluntary active duty for a limited time. That was no problem. But he took some time to consider their request before agreeing to let them fly to Germany. They pleaded with him, making sure he understood American lives hung in the balance.

"Trey, aren't you a wanted man by AMPP, with a bounty on your head?"

"I am, Paul. I can explain that to you when we get back. But we need to go. Lives are on the line, and every second counts. I can tell you those charges are bogus. You will understand when you hear what happened."

"I'll be eager to learn all about that. I may be out of my mind, but I'm going to let you take a plane. No questions asked, but you need to go before I change my mind. And guys, please try to get yourselves, those citizens and that plane back here all in one piece."

They made no promises, but assured him they would do their best. He allotted a KC-10 for the mission. Too large? Sure. But they needed something that would make the flight without refueling, and this baby would do it. Without cargo and the 300,000 pounds of fuel it normally carried when refueling fighter jets in mid-air, it could easily travel there and back without running out of fuel.

The cargo it would haul on the return flight would be the most precious of all. No one other than Commander Paul Johnson and a few of his top people were aware of this. Even he was unaware of who the passengers would be or what led to their predicament. His only knowledge was of American Citizens trapped on foreign soil, endangered, and in need of rescue. And he trusted Trey Butler and Rickie Cruz, two decorated combat veterans, reservists and comrades in arms.

It took the day to get everything arranged. By late afternoon they flew from Missouri, bound for Germany. Their mission: rescue their comrades in the army of faith, their *spiritual* band of brothers and sisters. They had no guarantee of success but would give it their all.

War is brutal, but this one would soon take a turn that neither they nor the world could imagine. They would need to be ready when it came. Loss of life would be greater than during any war in history. People had been expecting it for years, but it would still shake them to the core when it came. Even the Smyrnians did not dream it would finally happen. Yet, it loomed ominously on the horizon.

CHAPTER 3

Other than the property outside Ozark, Missouri, where they entombed the Shelter underground, the quake spared only one other place. The nation of Israel felt a slight tremor, but did not see the devastation and destruction endured by the rest of the world. The glorious Jewish temple still stood atop the Temple Mount next door to the Dome of the Rock Mosque. Neither sustained the slightest damage. Temple worship continued, and Jews and Muslims walked the Mount together. Peace reigned in Jerusalem. At least, the people of the world believed that to be true.

Messai intended to return there the next day. But this trip would not be for another ceremony or announcement. He would celebrate his honeymoon with his beautiful wife, Beth Jennings, or that was his plan. Neither the wedding nor the honeymoon happened. But he stuck with his plan to spend a few days there. This unfortunate turn of events would not stop him. He was flying there in his private jet. Nothing or no one could prevent him from doing that. They would get the plane off the ground, despite the damage caused to his airstrip by the quake.

He would travel alone. Appearances on the Temple Mount, around the Old City, and in modern-day Jerusalem remained a priority. The fastest way to recover his self-esteem was to stand before his adoring public and receive their accolades. He refused to spend days or weeks licking his wounds and pouting. He must keep his image untarnished. People needed to see the powerful world leader, undaunted by a sudden change of plans.

He also planned to meet with the Israeli Prime Minister, who now supported him. His support would be beneficial in years to come. The man may not have time for others, but he always made time for *him*. Deep down, Messai hated the Jews, but now he hated the Smyrnians more. His forces would hunt them down like animals and terminate them. But they would capture Blake Thompson and Beth Jennings and bring them to him. They would experience his fury.

He relished the thought of seeing Blake's head severed from his body, and Beth belonging to him. Things would not be so easy for her this time. They would both regret making a fool of him, each in distinct ways. So would the other Smyrnians when he found them. And he *would* find them.

He must decide how to spin the story of his fiancé's disappearance, forcing him to cancel his wedding. No simple task, but he would do it in typical Aissa Messai fashion. And the world would believe him, as they always did. Yes, they would continue to believe him, and believe *in* him.

At the Shelter, the team deployed the generator. It supplied the bunkers with electrical power. No one else around them had power and would not for several days. But in the bunkers, the Smyrnians had stocked up on everything they needed to survive. They anticipated the return of their teammates and planned a welcome home party for them when they arrived.

Ben spent his time recording videos for people to view online once humanity got the world powered up and running again. It was time to unleash his teaching on his people, the Jews, and tell them about the real Messiah, Jesus Christ. He had two people in mind who may play a huge role in that process: Alexander and Elizabeth Ben Ezra. He and Miriam became well acquainted with them via video conferencing. They conversed often, as they had done since the night the duo put their lives on the line by helping Ally, Ollie and Amelia escape from AMPP. Best of all, they believed in Jesus because of it.

Ben and Miriam taught them and prepared them to share with their fellow Jews what they experienced for themselves. They would need to be as covert as possible while they did that. But Jesus called Alexander and Elizabeth to be co-leaders of the Jewish movement, both in Israel and around the world. He intended to set up a secure branch of his own network to speak to the Jews in Israel. They would have their own *smyrnians.com* email address, allowing them to communicate one-on-one with people. Ben was eager to speak with Alexander again. But he had to wait like everyone else for connectivity to be available. He prayed for that to happen soon.

Alexander and Elizabeth still flew under the radar, hoping AMPP did not monitor their activity or view it as suspicious. They were well aware of their connection to Oliver and Amelia Barton and Ally Fromm. If they became suspicious, they would be all over them, watching their every move.

Disaster almost struck the night Alexander returned from driving the trio to the airport so they could escape the country. AMPP forced their way into their home and threatened to kill Elizabeth in front of him, if he did not tell them where he took the trio. But their fear disappeared after they watched Ben's video that same night and believed in Jesus.

They still did not fear for their lives. But Ben warned them, as leaders of the entire movement in Israel, they must stay safe and alive. They tried to heed his warning. But despite that, they still began talking to friends and neighbors who may be open to hearing about their experience.

Elizabeth chided Alexander for not being as careful as he needed to be. But he avowed he was not sure about waiting to hear from Ben. If they didn't restore communication soon, he would start, regardless. She reminded him, all it took was one person turning him in to AMPP. If that happened, their work in Israel would be over before it started.

He was an exemplary man, but also a very stubborn man. She struggled to rein him in when he set his mind on something. Alexander became the first Israeli Jew to believe in Jesus during the Tribulation. Ben's help was needed to stop him from being the first Jewish *martyr* of the Tribulation. She prayed they would soon restore the worldwide web, while he plodded along talking about Jesus to anyone who would listen. It was very dangerous, but he laughed in the face of danger. She hoped that boldness would not cost him.

Rickie and Trey enjoyed a seamless flight, with very little turbulence and made great time. They opted to fly earlier than planned and closed in on Ramstein Air Base in Germany at 7:00 a.m. local time. Rickie flew low over the tower to ensure they saw them and allowed them to land.

After the second pass, bright floodlights shone from the tower and personnel lined the only runway that appeared safe for landing. Even from the air, they saw it was in disrepair and knew it would make for a rough landing. Both hoped it was not enough to career the plane off to the side or blow a tire. They had endured rough landings but wanted this plane safe on the ground, rough or smooth.

Rickie circled back around and began his approach. When the tires of the huge plane touched the runway, it felt as rough as the roads they had driven on yesterday. The aircraft bumped and bounced, making them feel like they were on a bucking bronco. It lurched from side to side. Rickie maxed out the reverse thrust, trying to keep it on the buckled asphalt and bring it to a stop. That was not happening, so he yielded to the inevitable and looked for the smoothest route.

The ground on the right appeared smoother than the runway. He chose that route, then had to pull hard back to the left and steer away from the border fence. To crash through it would propel them into the trees. They would not survive that. If they kept the plane on the rough ground, it would function as an additional brake. It worked as they hoped, slowed them down, and made continuing forward more difficult. He steered the plane left just enough to get the front tire back onto the edge of the runway and came to a stop. When they exited, the men on the ground ran to meet them, making sure they were okay.

"What are you boys doing flying today? The military is on shutdown everywhere. Why in the world would you fly from the U.S. to Germany on a day like this?"

"We had no choice... top secret mission. Here are our orders from Base Commander Paul Johnson in Missouri." Trey handed over the paperwork Paul sent with them, as Rickie spoke up.

"Look, a group of American citizens are trapped here and in imminent danger. If we don't get to them in time, they will all die. We hope to rescue them and bring them back here. Then it's urgent that we get them out of the country as fast as possible. Fuel the plane, check everything, and have it ready to go when we get back. Hopefully, we will make it in four to five hours tops."

"If we run into trouble and don't make it, contact Commander Johnson when you can and let him know. But I feel certain we'll survive and accomplish what we came here to do. So when we get back, we have to load the passengers and be in the air fast. Keep an eye out for us and be ready to help if we need you."

"Yes, sir. We'll arrange everything and have it ready when you get back. A unit can go with you, if you need them. None of us have seen action in a while, so that might be fun." He grinned.

"I appreciate that, but we have to go alone. Too many men may arouse suspicion if they spot us. But it would help if you provide us with a vehicle large enough to transport up to twelve people."

"We have 15-passenger vans here that can handle that. We'll let you take the newest one we have."

"Where is it? We need to get on the road right now. We can't afford to waste any more time."

"This must be urgent. I'd think it would be okay to take a few minutes after that long flight. You know regulations prevent you from doing this and flying back so soon."

"I am well aware of regulations, but these are extenuating circumstances. There are two of us. I flew over, and my buddy will take her back."

"Whatever you say. We can't confirm anything, so we'll have to accept these orders."

He waved the paper around and said, "Let's get you on the road. But before you go, do you want weapons in case you need them?"

"That never hurts. If you don't mind, give us a few handguns and M4 Carbines. I hope we don't need them, but at least we'll have them if we do. You can't ever be too prepared."

Within minutes the men brought the van and stocked it with enough weapons and ammo to blast their way out of just about anything. They located the address and were on the road, headed to the Fromm house. The drive should take a little more than an hour. They hoped beyond hope the six Smyrnians made it back there. Otherwise, they had flown to Germany in vain.

The group at Bruno and Mila's had slept through much of the previous day. Now they were preparing for a trip back to the states, thanks to a challenge from Beth. She warned them to be ready when that time came, reiterating her prompting to be ready to run from the mansion, not knowing what would happen. Preparing after the fact may have kept her from escaping before Messai found her that night. They did what she said, not having much to get ready, anyway.

She also insisted that Bruno, Mila and the boys have their things ready, and that Hans and Heidi do the same. The latter two stayed with the group. Their house sustained enough damage to make it uninhabitable. All of them got everything together and were back in bed at midnight. They slept well again. The bodies of the men and Beth remained in dire need of rest.

Mila rose at 7:00 and cooked another amazing breakfast. Even the smell of food did not awaken them this time. But at 7:30 a loud banging on the front door startled them and brought them out of bed. They all sprang to their feet and threw on the clothes they took off before lying down for the night. A voice rang out.

"This is AMPP. We have the house surrounded. You cannot escape. Everyone in the front room. Now! We're coming in from every door. You have one minute to be in the room."

"How?" asked Blake as they congregated in the kitchen. "How did they find out we are here?"

Looking out the window, Bruno said, "He's right. They have the house surrounded. It looks like they brought an entire army. A bunch of them came, and I can tell they mean business. What are we going to do?"

"We sure can't fight our way out of this one," said Malachi. "We have to do what they say."

"They're *not* taking us back to Belgium! I will *not* allow Messai to get his hands on Beth again!"

Blake meant business too. But he also knew they were powerless against an armed AMPP patrol.

Malachi was not backing down. He couldn't let Blake get them all killed.

"We *can't* take them on. We don't stand a chance. If we try, we'll all die." Then his mind changed in a millisecond.

"But they'll kill us, no matter what we do. Except for you two." He pointed at Blake and Beth. "They'll save Beth for Messai and take you alive, Blake. I'd guess Messai will kill you on live TV. He'll want to show the world he's serious about the *danger* of the Smyrnians. Then he'll force Beth to marry him, and it will be worse for her than ever. So, I suggest we try something! What do we have to lose?"

"I would rather die here fighting to the end. They'll kill all of you anyway, and capture us, so why not go down swinging? We'll take as many of them out as we can. Bruno, do you have any weapons in the house?"

"I have plenty! Come with me and we'll grab them! Maybe we can hold them off for a little while."

He turned to run to the next room. The voice from outside yelled again.

"Time's up!" The front and back doors exploded open and the patrol rushed into the house, guns to their shoulders. It was an enormous group! They came and came, in an endless stream, until they packed the house. They had eleven of Messai's most hated targets in one room with no possibility of escape. He would be ecstatic when word reached him of the demise of nine of them, and the capture of Blake and Beth Thompson.

"In here... now!" the captain yelled.

They stumbled into the living room as armed men surrounded them in the kitchen, pushing them forward, nearly knocking some of them to the floor.

"Check the rest of the house. Make sure there are no others hiding anywhere." Several men dashed into the other rooms. Two climbed into the attic.

"Some of you check around outside too. Because we didn't see anyone doesn't mean they're not hiding out there. Leave no stone unturned. We don't want to miss anyone. And I sure don't want somebody out there to come in here causing trouble."

Even with all those who went into the other rooms and outside, a sizeable company remained in the living room guarding them. Blake found his mind returning to hopelessness as questions bombarded it. Why hadn't he done something? What happened to his willingness to fight to the death only minutes earlier?

How could he let them take Beth? He let her down once and couldn't bear the thought of doing it again. They came this far and celebrated their freedom. But there was nothing he could do. Malachi was right. These men would take Beth back to Messai and kill all the others, except him. They would not return to Messai without him, too.

All the men returned, now packing the room with Aissa Messai's Peace Patrol. They would prove once again they had nothing to do with peace.

"We secured everything, Captain. No others are in here, or out there."

"All of you sit right where you are. Ladies on the furniture, men on the floor." When they obeyed, he said, "Not you, Beth Jennings. You come over here."

Blake made a move toward them.

"Come on, Blake Thompson. I'd love nothing more than to put a bullet through your skull right here. You've caused me a ton of headaches. But we have to save you for the boss. However, we can and will incapacitate you if we need to. A bullet in the leg ought to do the trick. That would give me great pleasure. I served as a sniper, so I assure you I can handle that."

Blake stopped. Beth did not move.

"Miss Jennings, get over here, now! Move, or I will put that bullet in your boyfriend's leg in five seconds. And for every second you hesitate, he'll get another one. First, the other leg, then one shoulder at a time. And we'll deliver him back to Mr. Messai like that."

She saw no option. She took a step toward him.

"That's a good girl. The boss will be happy when we bring you back home to him. That is your home, isn't it, Beth? It appears he'll have that wedding after all!"

He reached out and grabbed her by the arm, pulling her to his side. "Cuff her, boys." They did. Memories of that day weeks ago in Tehran flooded back to her mind, and tears crept from her eyes.

"Don't cry, Beth. The boss will take excellent care of you. And you will take wonderful care of him, if you know what I mean."

His grin was evil.

"I suppose you want to hear how we found you, because you thought you got away from us. But even though there's no power, there's a battery-operated security camera at the border crossing. Guess what we saw when we checked it? That's right, the car that's sitting outside this house. We couldn't run the license plate, so we searched all day. I still can't believe we got so lucky."

"We've had the entire patrol out hunting everywhere. Then one of our men drove by here, and there it was in plain view! This will make the boss happier than you can imagine. And you can bet he will reward us big time. He takes good care of people who do their jobs."

The group sat in silence. They knew it would do no good to rush the men. There was no escape. If only an aftershock strong enough to drop the men to the floor would hit right then! But the earth remained calm.

"How would you like for me to kiss your girlfriend, Blake? I think I'd like to do that!"

He grabbed Beth's hair, drew her in and kissed her. She struggled against him, then turned her head and spat on the floor. Blake made a slight move again. His eyes flashed anger, which was about to lead to a foolish decision.

The man turned his gun toward him, and Blake sat back down. When he did, the gun barked and a bullet tore into the floor inches from where he sat, causing all of them to recoil.

"Do you believe me now, when I say I was a sniper? Try that again, and I'll show you the amount of pain I can inflict. Now, sit and watch like a good boy."

He grabbed Beth again. "I like it when they play hard to get."

"Captain, if the boss finds out what you're doing, he'll kill you! And I guarantee you, she'll tell him. I mean no disrespect, sir, but you need to stop."

The captain glared at him, then stopped. "You're right. She's not worth losing my career or my life... or that hefty reward I'm going to get. Count your lucky stars, woman."

He seized her arm again.

"On second thought, maybe you are worth it! You sure look good! No, I'm not taking that chance. But it doesn't mean I wouldn't like to."

He shoved her back, watching Blake's anger boil, knowing he was powerless to do anything about it. His smirk showed he loved playing this little game.

"What are we going to do with the others, sir? Should we take them all in?"

"No way. That would be too much trouble. We could let them go if they promise to keep quiet."

He grinned again.

"Just kidding, folks. I'm so sorry, but we must kill all of you. What a shame. Don't take it personally, we're just doing our jobs."

This time Bruno raised up.

"Go ahead, big man. Nothing would please me more than to make you the first one to die. Or perhaps it should be these boys. I assume they belong to you and the missis there."

"You leave them alone," Bruno growled.

The dream he had almost a year ago came racing back into his mind. Messai and his men stopped him, Mila, the boys. Messai ordered the boys shot before their eyes. Bruno recalled waking as he heard the first crack of gunfire. Now it was happening in real life. He must protect his sons! How? What could he do? He glanced at the clock. It was 8:15 a.m.

"Captain, we don't have time to wait. We need to get Thompson and the boss's bride-to-be back to him. Let's do what we came to do and get out of here. It's going to be a rough ride, and we need to make it back before dark."

The captain sneered at the group.

"Blake and Beth, allow me to introduce myself. I am the captain of Mr. Messai's special forces. I remember a scene just like this several weeks ago. You don't remember me, do you? Let me refresh your memory. It was at a house in Tehran."

He needed to say nothing more. The shock and fear showed on their faces as it all came back to them. Their recollection gave him obvious pleasure.

"Do you remember walking into the house and finding dead bodies all over the floor? How about being cuffed and taken away? Blake, do you recall that bump on the head? I'm sure you searched for your little Beth and couldn't find her. I wish I had been there to hear you yelling for her, getting no answer and blubbering like a baby. Well, this is about to end the same way that ended, except this time you're coming with us too. It is time we get on with it and get out of here."

One of them held up a rubber mask with a tube attached to a tank.

"Does this look familiar, Beth? It is time to go beddy-bye again."

She cringed at the sight.

The others moved into position to fire on the captain's command. The group steeled themselves, preparing to give their lives after one year of the Tribulation. Some of them prayed that Jesus would raise up others to replace them, while it filled others with fear.

Rickie and Trey neared Bruno and Mila's house. Trey threw up his hand. "Stop!"

He caught Rickie by surprise until he said, "Look," and pointed toward the house. It had just come into view. Military looking vehicles sat everywhere, accompanied by two black SUVs.

"AMPP!" whispered Rickie, as if they were close enough for the patrol to hear them.

"They must have found them! That means they're here, and we have to do something! Now!"

"Let's move!" Rickie had stopped the van and was already getting out.

"What are we going to do?"

"How am I supposed to know? Let's get to a window and see what's going on."

They ran as fast as they could, then when they neared the house slowed and tiptoed to a window. Inside, they saw the horrifying scene about to unfold. AMPP was getting ready to murder the group in cold blood and take Blake and Beth captive.

"We have to act now!" Rickie whispered, this time with greater urgency. They had both been in similar situations together in the military. "The van," he said. "Let's go!"

Sprinting back toward the vehicle, Trey, out of breath, asked, "What now?"

"You grab weapons, and I'll take the van. I'm going to ram the thing right through the side of the house into that room."

"But you might hurt or kill some of our own, or maybe even yourself!"

"Do you have a better idea?"

"No, but..."

"Go!"

Trey ran for the house, an M4 on his shoulder, and a Beretta in each hand. Rickie fired up the van and jerked it in gear. He started out slow, then picked up speed until he pegged the speedometer. Just as Trey got to the window, he heard the van approaching at breakneck speed. He turned and ran backwards to avoid debris, but ready to charge in with guns blaring.

"Well folks, it's party time. We get to take out a bunch of *Smyrnians* at one time."

He said that word with disgust in his voice.

"And we get to take the boss's little woman back to him. And Mr. Thompson will come along for the ride. The boss will want to make an example of him for the world to see. Ready, boys?"

The men raised their guns.

"Ready... Aim..." The group sat without saying a word. Bruno took Mila's hand and pulled the boys close. He saw the fear in their eyes. Hans and Heidi wrapped their arms around each other. Evan, Anders and Malachi sat looking the men in the eyes. Anders spoke in a soft voice.

"Dear Jesus, please do not hold this against these men. We forgive them and pray they will turn to you and accept you as their Savior, as we did."

The captain whirled about at a loud sound coming from the outside. When he turned to face the window, and the others rushed to join him, Beth ran toward Blake and dove beside him. The van slammed through the side of the house with such force it knocked it off its foundation. It plowed into the AMPP patrol at top speed, mowing them down like a subway train speeding into a station.

The Smyrnians threw themselves backwards and onto their faces, trying to avoid flying glass and pieces of wood. The captain and his men who had gotten near him were dead, their bodies lying mangled under the van. Some behind them had survived but were on the floor wounded. A couple reached for their weapons, but by that time Trey was in the room.

"Drop them!" he demanded.

They complied.

"Are all of you okay?" he asked his friends.

"We are now!" Evan exclaimed. "I wanted in on the action. I guess I got it, didn't I?"

"Find whatever you can and tie them up," demanded Trey. "Make sure they don't escape. Get the keys from his body," he pointed to the captain, "and get those cuffs off Beth."

Rickie was out of the van now, his head bleeding and limping. He stumbled toward the others and collapsed to the floor.

"Quick, help him!" yelled Anders.

They went to work on their fallen comrade, as efficient as any medical team in an emergency.

"His leg is broken," said Beth. She was glad to be alive and free, as were the others. But they forgot about everything that had just happened. They had a teammate's life to save. Rickie's nose was pouring blood, signaling he broke it. He was clutching his side and moaning, meaning broken ribs too. Who knew what other internal injuries he had suffered? He put his life on the line to save theirs. That is what a comrade does. Now they had to help him.

"No man left behind," he uttered, just before he blacked out.

"We have to get him out of here and find help," said Malachi.

"Hans studied medicine at the university, and I am a nurse," whispered Heidi. "Everyone get back and let us tend to him."

"Boy, are you going to come in handy on the team," said Blake.

Mila brought warm water and clean cloths. They cleaned and bandaged his wounds and stopped his nose from bleeding. Trey was standing over his fallen partner.

"Shouldn't you wrap his broken ribs? I've seen them do that in the movies. It seems like the first thing you should do."

"No!" Hans snapped.

"Wrapping the ribs can cause him to have trouble breathing and lead to fatality."

Trey looked chastised. "Then what can we do?" he asked. "He'll make it, won't he?"

"We need to get him medical attention as soon as possible. I have a doctor friend who will treat him and ask no questions," answered Hans. "He lives close by, and his house is still standing. Can we get him in Bruno's car?"

They carried Rickie to the car, drove to the house, and took him inside. The doctor went to work without hesitating. He put a splint on his broken leg and dealt with the cuts on his head and face. "I can't tell if there are internal injuries, other than the broken ribs," he told them. "He needs to go to a hospital, but none are operating. They were all destroyed by the earthquake. Is there somewhere you can take him and watch him? I'll be here if you need me."

"Yes, there is somewhere we can go," said Evan. "Come on, gang. Let's get him out of here. Thank you so much for your help, doctor. Words cannot express our gratitude."

The others followed him. Bruno and Trey carried Rickie.

"What are you thinking, Evan?" Blake was both concerned and confused.

"We need to get him to the Shelter," Evan said.

"How are we going to do that? Come to think of it, how did you guys get here, Trey?"

"I can tell you all about that as we fly home. Rickie demolished the van, but he saved your lives. That's my partner. We have Bruno's car. Is there another vehicle we can drive, too?"

Heidi spoke up. "We can take both of ours."

"All of you need to come with us. You can't stay here now because Messai will have you on his Most Wanted list, like us. We have thirteen of us. I guess that's our lucky number. Forget I said that. This has nothing to do with luck and everything to do with Jesus. Rickie has to lie down, so we'll need all three vehicles. We're heading to Ramstein Air Base and board a plane to the U.S."

"I don't know how you pulled that off, but you can tell us later. Let's go."

Blake was ready to go. He wanted to get Beth as far away from Aissa Messai as he could.

Hans and Heidi rolled in with the cars. They loaded Rickie into the back seat of the largest one.

"Let's try to load all of that stuff we have space for, leave the rest behind, and get on the road." Trey showed that he, the military man, was in charge of this mission until they were back on American soil. He yielded control to Rickie earlier; now it was his turn.

Mila took a moment to bid farewell to her house. She felt sure it was the last time she would see it. Tears flowed for a moment, then she smiled and prepared herself for the journey ahead and whatever the future held.

They followed Bruno as he led them on the fastest route to Ramstein.

"Wow," Trey said to his passengers, "if we had known this route, we would have gotten to you guys a lot sooner than we did."

They arrived at the base. The men who greeted them earlier waited for them. The plane sat on the runway at a point where it would be smooth enough to take off. They helped load their things and get Rickie on board. While they were busy doing that, Blake and Beth hurried around the rear of the vehicle and boarded unseen. They feared someone might recognize them.

One guy said, "We're not asking questions. We can tell the mission was dangerous. Did everyone make it out, or did you suffer casualties?"

"We all made it," Trey answered. "My partner got the worst of it, but he saved the others' lives. No man left behind."

"No man left behind," replied the man, and saluted him. "I suppose the van was a casualty since it didn't make it back. I won't ask about it, and there's no need to explain. We'll take care of the other vehicles. I promise you we won't say a word about this to anyone. Have a safe flight."

"Thank you for your help. We will never forget you."

The runway was bumpy, but after what the group had just been through, it was nothing. They lifted off and flew toward Missouri. They could not wait to get there. It would be Hans and Heidi's first visit, but they believed it would be more than a visit. It would be permanent.

They wished they could call the others and tell them they made it and were coming home. But with communication still out worldwide, that would have to wait until they arrived. *Arrived.* That word sounded better than it ever had. The day was not over yet, but knowing Jesus had been in charge the past few days gave them confidence that he would get them home safe and sound.

CHAPTER 4

The Smyrnians had not only lost touch with each other, they had lost touch with the world. So had everyone else on the planet. Without television, radio or internet, no one was aware of what had happened around the globe. Minus news and social media, they had no way to connect and stay informed. So no one, other than those affected, realized the plague which started in China a few months earlier now touched other continents and was on the verge of becoming a global pandemic.

Ten years earlier, an independent study warned of an incurable disease-causing agent turning deadly and killing tens of millions of people worldwide. Most people paid little attention to it then, but now that day had come.

It spread like wildfire, thanks to air travel and other modes of mass transit. With medical treatment non-existent because of the destruction from the quake, it invaded the planet, moving from one country to another. Many of those who became infected died within days, their deaths excruciating. As had happened in China, it wiped out entire families, and now entire communities perished, too.

The plague had been rural to this point, affecting smaller towns and villages. But within weeks, it would reach metropolitan areas. At that point, it would advance uncontrolled and lead to an exponential increase in the number of deaths. Fear would consume the planet, creating a worldwide panic, leading to mass hysteria. People would turn once again to Aissa Messai for answers, and as always, he would provide them. When he did, something would awaken in him and change everything about the man he appeared to be.

Ally and Miriam sat talking in the Shelter. Their anxiety was getting the best of them as they waited. They hoped their fellow Smyrnians would open the secret door above them and come down the steps to the bunkers any minute. They longed to see their faces and hear their voices. It seemed like weeks since Trey and Rickie flew to Germany to find them and bring them back. The hours crawled by, leaving them with less and less hope of their safe return.

"I wish we had a way to get word of what's going on," Ally uttered. "The wait is killing me!"

"Waiting is all we can do, dear," said Miriam. "We are all eager to see them. I admit, fear has crept into my mind too, but I am trying to fight it with faith. That is true for all of us. I hope they're alive and will return to us. However, every minute that goes by with no word from them causes me to fear something has gone wrong and they're not coming back."

Ally broke into tears, causing Miriam to move over beside her and place her arm around her.

"Ally, honey, I didn't mean to sound so hopeless. They'll come back, and everything will be okay. Jesus wouldn't rescue Beth in such a miraculous way only to let her die, would he?"

"You're right, Miriam," Ally said, wiping the tears from her eyes. "I'm trying to hold on to that hope, but I need to see them. If only we could talk to them."

"I wish we could talk to them too, but we can't. I plan to continue praying for them. Wait and see; they will come down those steps before you know it."

Ally smiled. "You're right, Miriam. I'll watch for them and expect them to get here anytime. We need to get started on that welcome home party. That will show we are sure they'll make it, right?"

"Yes, it will! Let's call everybody in here and start cooking and decorating!"

Faith can be a fickle thing. Sometimes people must act on it before they believe it in their heart and mind. The group decided they would show their faith even when they did not feel it.

•   •   •   •   •

Aboard the military plane over the Atlantic Ocean flew thirteen of the most wanted *criminals* in the world. They had flown six hours and had four hours remaining. Rickie was not in good shape. Hans and Heidi took care of him, as the others stood by to help, if needed. His condition had deteriorated. They feared internal injuries that may be life-threatening. He was experiencing labored breathing, revealing the potential of a punctured or collapsed lung. Internal bleeding meant he would need blood soon.

Hospitals would be closed so there seemed to be little chance of him receiving that. Their only option was to care for him in the best ways they could. He had put his life on the line for them. They would do whatever it took to pull him through this. But there was no stopping until they reached their destination.

One of the injured AMPP men escaped and freed the others. They took a car from a nearby house and drove to Belgium in less than five hours, breaking every speed limit along the way. No police officers were on duty, but none would dare hold them up if they were.

The men had just given Aissa Messai news of the Smyrnians escape, and he was livid. But organizing troops was next to impossible, as was getting word to AMPP forces in the United States. How rescuers came with no flights operating, he could not imagine. But he intended to find out. The moment communication lines opened again, he would place all of his forces on worldwide alert. They would find the leaders of the Smyrnian movement, and every other person in the world who had joined them. Despite what happened, the war had just begun.

New on his list? Bruno and Mila Fromm and Hans and Heidi Meier. Something occurred to him. His former assistant and object of his infatuation hailed from Germany, and her last name was Fromm. Dear sweet Ally belonged to the Smyrnians. Bruno and Mila Fromm were members of the same hated group. It did not take a genius, although he considered himself one, to figure that out. Ally had to be their daughter. She worked as a Smyrnian spy when she was with him! That infuriated him, but it also compelled him to action.

His men who survived drove all the way from Germany to report the events of this day. They said the Fromms had two sons. Thoughts raced through his mind now. The men told of threatening to kill the boys first in front of their parents, causing emotion to rage in the big man. Yes, that was it.

If they find them, the boys will die first. And their precious mom and dad will observe their deaths. They will die next, but not until his forces administer a little torture, trying to get information from them. No, maybe he would try that before killing the boys. Parents will do and say a lot to save their kids. But it will not matter whether they divulge the information. They and the boys will die.

It may be even better if he gets his hands on Ally again. He will force the big man and his wife to look on as he ravishes her, then kills her. Yes, that ought to work. An entire family of Smyrnians wiped out at once and in order. The daughter who made a fool of him will go first. Then a firing squad will execute the boys, and Bruno and Mila will go last. "That will send a message," he growled to nobody but himself.

In that moment, he created a fresh approach in his evil mind: families. "Yes," he chuckled. "That's it! Families." What will bring the Smyrnians out of their holes? Their families hunted down and killed because they harbored criminals or held back information about the whereabouts of enemies of the state. "Brilliant," he said with a sneer.

"I will start in Germany. I am sure many members of Hans and Heidi Meier's family live there, and of the Fromms, too. The same must be true for all of those *Jesus people*. Yes, I will search for their families the minute we can search records. We will flush them out." The look on his face revealed a mixture of anger, hatred, vengeance and glee all rolled into one.

Aboard the plane, Rickie's condition worsened. Hans and Heidi did their best to care for him, but the lack of medical equipment or medications limited their effectiveness. They needed those things for any chance of success.

Hans walked to the cabin and spoke with Trey. "He's losing blood. We must get him somewhere to someone who can help him."

"What am I supposed to do?" Trey asked, with obvious concern for his friend and partner. "We're still over water. Besides, I can't land until we reach the base. I have nowhere else to go."

"Heidi and I are doing everything we can. He may not make it until then, and if he does, I'd say his chances of survival are slim."

Tears welled up in Trey's eyes. "Don't let him die, if you can stop it. I understand you're doing everything you can, and so am I. We'll get there when we get there. I can't speed this thing up anymore. We're flying into a headwind which is normal coming east to west. Rickie did what any soldier would do. He put himself in harm's way to save the rest of you. He didn't stop to consider the consequences when he drove that van into the house."

"I tried to ask him if we had other options, but he didn't hesitate. He told me to grab weapons and meet him there, then floored the van and headed straight into the house without slowing down. He yelled, 'Go!' and I started running, with him driving right behind me. I'm not sure why I'm telling you this, Hans. I suppose I needed to talk. Get back there and take care of my partner."

"I understand, Trey."

Hans spoke English well enough to communicate with the group. He turned and headed back to where Heidi and the others sat with Rickie. None of them would leave him, although they stood back to allow the two of them to care for him. By now, Rickie's heart rate had increased and sweat appeared on every part of his body. His arms and legs became moist with perspiration.

Heidi spoke up. "He's going into shock. His condition has gone from serious to critical."

Anders called the group together around Rickie. "There is a time for medical treatment, but there is also a time when the only answer is prayer. This is the time for prayer. I will call on Jesus to take care of him, and either heal him or keep him alive until we can get him treatment."

While the group held hands and prayed with him, Anders invoked the words of a verse from the Bible. None of them had read it before. He called it a healing verse. His knowledge of the Bible amazed them more each day. He read it at every opportunity. When he prayed, the words flowed from his lips. "Heal him, Lord, and he will be healed. Save him and he will be saved. For you are the one I praise."

An immediate change occurred in Rickie. He did not awaken and sit up, healed and well. But the cold sweat disappeared, and his heart rate returned to normal. They noticed the difference and realized something miraculous had happened.

"His body is no longer in shock," whispered Heidi. "That was amazing, Anders. Thank you."

"Don't thank me," Anders was adamant. "Thank Jesus."

"Where did you find that verse?" asked Blake. "I've never read it. It's perfect!"

"It is Jeremiah Chapter 17, verse 14. I discovered it one day while I was reading the Bible. Jesus told me to open my Bible and he would take me to the place I needed to read. I let it fall open, looked down, and saw Jeremiah Chapter 17. I questioned why Jeremiah?"

"I didn't want to read the Old Testament. I wanted to read about Jesus in the Gospels. But when I looked down, that one verse stood out from all the others. It looked highlighted on the page, so there was no way I could miss it. I sensed Jesus telling me to memorize that verse. He said, 'the time will come when you need it.' It was easy to remember, and I just realized this is the time he told me about. He said, 'Okay, it is time for Jeremiah 17:14.' So I prayed it for Rickie."

The entire group had tears in their eyes now. This journey with Jesus kept getting better every day. It was not an easy one. They had been told in no uncertain terms it would not be. But they had witnessed many rays of sunshine breaking through the darkness at just the right times. On this journey alone, those had been so bright it caused their faith to grow by leaps and bounds.

Even now, on a plane over the Atlantic ocean, they stood together, amazed at an answered prayer. Miraculous deliverance from the hand of Messai and his forces occurred just hours earlier. They knew hard times would test their faith many more times during the remaining six years of Planet Earth. And they would struggle with doubt every one of those times. But they would keep their eyes open and watch for Jesus to show up and do something regardless of those doubts.

They continued to feel certain not all of them would survive to the end of the Tribulation. But they planned to fight and never give up. They hoped Rickie would not be the next to die after Doc. He was not out of the woods yet, by a long shot. He still may not survive till they landed, but his chances had improved after Anders' prayer.

Trey continued his flight toward the base in Missouri, unaware of what took place in the back. He fought to keep his mind off his partner, remembering missions like this during combat. But this one was different, more personal. He felt somewhat responsible for his partner's condition.

He was an experienced combat veteran, too, so *he* should have been the one who came up with the idea to ram the van into the house. It should have been him yelling at Rickie to run while he drove the van. But he hesitated and tried to talk his friend out of it.

Would he have allowed the patrol to slaughter the group? They only had seconds to spare. The captain gave the command and counted down to "Fire!" If Rickie had hesitated, even seconds, every member of the group would be dead, except Blake and Beth.

Blake would have died a far worse death at the hands of Messai. And Beth's fate would have been even more horrific than death. The monster would have enslaved her for the rest of her life. Why did he hesitate? His training prepared him for that situation. But he froze and did not act.

Stop it, Trey. You're beating yourself up for no reason. It happened, and you can't change it, he told himself. *Other opportunities will come. Learn from this and decide you won't make the same mistake again.* He flew on. They were over land now, less than two hours from the base.

Commander Paul Johnson had just put his career on the line for his friends. It was useless to have second thoughts. He made a decision and would live with it. He only knew they were somewhere in the world. His friends didn't even tell him where they were going. And he didn't ask. This may be the most foolish decision he had made in his military career.

Trey was a wanted criminal. Who in his position and his right mind would let a wanted man enlist as a volunteer without taking time to consider it? Then grant him permission to take one of the military's most expensive planes? That momentary lapse in judgment may cost him his career, if Trey and Rickie didn't return.

He chastised himself for failing to arrest Trey on the spot. Following protocol would have required placing him in the stockade, pending further action once they restored communication. But he trusted the guy. Each of them owed his life to the other. He wanted Trey to explain the reason for being on Messai's Most Wanted list. He would do nothing illegal; Paul knew him better than that. But his nerves would stay on edge until they made it back.

Bunker One looked amazing, decorated to the max for the welcome home party. And it smelled of scrumptious food. When, not if, the team arrived, they would greet them with the best of everything. Even suffering from exhaustion, they would still need to eat. Feasting and celebrating would precede sleep. Ally was eager for them to tell about the events of the past few days, including Beth's escape from Messai.

Did they drive to the Fromms' house in Germany, or were they hiding out somewhere? Did Trey and Rickie find them? Were they still alive? Only insane people would plan a welcome home party for people who may never return. But their insanity was the result of being crazy for Jesus, and they were living in faith that he would bring their comrades home.

Ally could hear Evan begging to eat, like he always did. She smiled at her many memories of that. The place overflowed with nervous energy, all of them working hard to keep their minds occupied. Doing that prevented them from contemplating what most would consider the inevitable; that the group would not make it home. Conversation was far less than normal. Fear mingled with faith flooded their minds. But no one would know that if they observed the buzz of activity. They appeared to be a group of people excited about an upcoming celebration.

Trey informed the others he was beginning his descent. He had put a plan together in his mind during the final two hours of the flight. Rickie needed serious medical attention, and the sooner the better. He called everyone to the cockpit, except Heidi, who stayed in the back with Rickie.

"How's he doing?" he asked Hans.

"He's stable, Trey, but still not doing well. He needs help, but no hospital will be open. Heidi and I have done everything we can."

"Is he well enough to travel in a vehicle for an hour?"

"I hope so, but I'm far from being sure about that."

"They can treat him at the base, but they're limited in what they can do. He needs more than they're able to give him. Rickie and I are friends with a surgeon in Springfield. Both of us have been to his home many times. If we can get him there, Steve will help him. I'm not sure I should go to his house, because he knows I'm a wanted man. He saw that all over the news before the quake. But I'll take that chance."

"Here's my plan. We'll go to Springfield, and I'll drive past his house so you can see where he lives. Then I'll park a few blocks away. The rest of you can hop out and hide while I take Rickie back. I have a place in mind for you to stay till I return."

Hans looked confused. "I doubt that will work because the doctor can't do what Rickie needs in an hour or two. He needs ongoing medical attention, or he may not survive. In a hospital, he'd be in a critical care unit for days, or weeks."

"We'll wait and see what Steve says. If he needs to stay, I'm sure Steve will keep him in his home. Prepare for landing and be ready to jump out and go into action the minute we stop."

"Once we land, we'll get on the road ASAP. Paul won't question me any further after I tell him Rickie needs urgent medical care. Once I explain how serious his injuries are, he'll understand that he needs more treatment than they can give him. He'll let us hurry and get on the road."

"My truck only seats five people. The other eight can lie in the back with the bed cover pulled over them. Trust me, others have done it, and they survived. It will be a long drive on rough roads, but I see no other option. If any of you are claustrophobic, ride up front with me."

They settled in as the big plane touched down and bounced up and down on the damaged runway before coming to a stop. Every one of them experienced the roughest landing of their lives. Blake and Anders sat and held Rickie in their laps, off the floor of the plane, trying to shield him. When they stopped, Paul and those who had guided them stood there to meet them. Trey asked the Commander to wait there and ran to get his truck. He returned, speeding up to the plane, skidding to a stop outside the exit, then explained the situation to Paul as the group exited.

"The mission was tough, Paul. We got everybody out, but Rickie sustained life-threatening injuries. He's not doing well, but you'd be proud of him. He threw himself in the middle of a life or death situation to save the others. If he hadn't acted when he did, the group would have been dead within seconds. Without thinking twice, he saved their lives. I can't bear to lose him now."

Bruno and Hans came out carrying Rickie. When Paul saw him he said, "Get him somewhere fast. He's in bad shape and needs more than we can do for him here."

Focused on Rickie, Paul paid no attention to the men carrying him, or the others who left the plane. If he noticed, he would have seen that not all of them were Americans.

"You're right. I would love to stay and talk, and introduce you to everybody, but we need to leave."

Trey told the others, "This is our only vehicle, so four of us, plus Rickie, can ride up front. Everyone else will have to ride back here." He pulled back the bedcover.

"You're not doing that," Paul said. "You can take a van from the base and bring it back when you finish with it. I'll get two radios so you can communicate with each other in case things go bad for Rickie. It will make me feel better if you take them."

"I can't thank you enough, Paul." Trey had tears in his eyes.

The commander embraced him. "Just take care of our comrade, Trey. You know how much I love you guys. We've been through a lot together, and I don't want to see it end like this for Rickie."

Someone had already brought the van, filled with gas and ready to go. The last two to leave the plane were Blake and Beth. Evan and Malachi distracted the men while they exited and jumped into the van. They did not want to take a chance on being recognized. Trey and Evan rode in the front seat of the truck, while Hans and Heidi held Rickie between them in the back seat. The others loaded into the van, and with Blake driving, headed toward Springfield.

The minute they left the base, Trey connected with Blake on the radio.

"Change of plans. Since we're driving the van now, I'll take Rickie to Steve's house by myself. I don't want them to see the rest of you. And there's no use in you sitting parked somewhere, for who knows how long. When we get near the house, we'll stop and let Evan, Hans and Heidi get in with you guys. You and Beth get them to the Shelter, and I'll take Rickie to Steve's house."

"I don't like it," Blake argued. "If Steve turns you in, how will you contact us so we can help?"

"How can he turn me in? He can't call anyone. But if he does, you'll figure it out when I don't make it to the Shelter. Besides, he'll focus on Rickie. He's a close friend, but he's also a brilliant surgeon who will do what he can for Rickie. I'm doing what I think is best; end of discussion."

"You can be stubborn, Trey, but we'll do what you say. I'll follow you until you tell us to pull over. Then you can take Rickie, and we'll go on to the farm."

At the Shelter, Mary had fallen ill. It came on her as they prepared for the celebration. She said she needed to lie down, and they saw she wasn't well. John took her to Bunker Three, where they stayed, and put her to bed. Whatever happened occurred all at once. She became ill, running a fever and vomiting. Miriam walked two doors down to check on her, but John refused to let her in.

"This may be contagious," he said. "No one else needs to come down with it. I'll take care of her, but you *can* bring some medications that might help her. We stocked a good supply of antibiotics. Bring the strongest one we have, something for nausea, and something to bring her fever down."

Miriam hurried back to get them. Ally volunteered to take them and ran back to the bunker to deliver them. John met her at the door, also refusing to let her in. He avowed that they must all protect themselves from whatever Mary had. He could take care of her just fine by himself. If he needed them, he would come and get someone. Ally also agreed and walked back to Bunker One. They prayed for Mary, while waiting and expecting the others to arrive anytime. She must have a stomach bug. It was most likely a 24-hour virus, but none of them wanted to catch it.

A few blocks away from Steve's house in Springfield, Trey radioed Blake to say he was pulling over. Against their wishes, Evan, Hans and Heidi left the truck and got in the van. Trey drove on to the house and pulled into the drive, waving to those in the van as they drove on by.

"We should stay close by, instead of going to the Shelter," said Blake. "What if Trey needs us? I mean, he and Rickie didn't leave us; they came to our rescue. Now they may need us to come to theirs. Remember what they said: No man left behind. What kind of soldiers would we be if we left two of our own behind?"

"You told Trey we would do what he said, honey," said Beth. "He knows what he's doing. We need to go on to the Shelter." She was gentle, but firm.

Blake objected somewhat, but agreed to do what he promised Trey. He drove on through Springfield and turned onto Highway 65 on their way to the farm. In his mind, he was already planning for a few men to return and make sure things were okay with their two teammates. They would get the others to the Shelter first. The drive would not take long.

Trey left Rickie in the truck and rang Steve's doorbell. No one answered for a minute, so he knocked on the door. Still no answer or sound from inside the house. He pounded on the door until he heard someone rustling about, followed by footsteps coming toward the door. Steve had identified him on a security camera.

"Trey, tell me what you want and why you're coming to our house. You're my friend, but you're also a wanted man. I don't want to put my wife in danger by harboring a criminal."

He corrected himself. "I'm not saying you're a criminal. I'm just saying if AMPP is searching for you, those guys mean business. And we would be in danger if they found you here."

"Steve, listen to me. Rickie is lying in my truck over there and he's injured and needs immediate medical attention or he may die. You've got to believe me. I can tell you about it, but right now Rickie needs you. Please help me bring him in. I'm not a criminal, and I've done nothing wrong. I need you to understand that and help my partner because if you don't, he won't make it. I'm serious, Steve. I'll leave if you want me to, but please don't turn Rickie away."

The door opened and Steve stepped out. "Let's get him in. This had better be on the up and up."

"We don't have time to talk right now. When you see him, you'll understand what I mean."

When Steve saw Rickie, his face grew pale. He knew the man was in genuine danger. Trey was telling the truth.

"Quick, let's move him into the house. He's almost gone, Trey. We don't have much time."

The two of them carried the wounded man into the house, and Steve took over. "Let's put him in the spare bedroom down the hallway."

They lay Rickie on the bed, and Steve ran to get his instruments. He hurried into examination mode without wasting a minute. Trey could only stand and watch... and pray.

"He has a broken leg, multiple broken ribs, and internal bleeding somewhere. He's struggling to breathe, so I suspect he has a punctured or collapsed lung. It would take a traumatic accident to cause injuries this severe. I can't go to the hospital. They have no power and no way to do what we need to do there, so we'll do the best we can here."

Before uttering another word, he yelled, "Linda! I need your help, now. Boil lots of water and bring clean towels." He looked back at Trey and said with a serious tone, "It's vital that I set this leg now. It looks like he broke it several hours ago. It can't wait any longer."

The automatic blood pressure cuff inflated on Rickie's arm. "His pressure is low, and his color is bad. I need to do exploratory surgery and find the bleeding. If I don't, he'll bleed to death."

"Can you do that here? Don't you need to be in an operating room with everything sterile and other equipment in case of an emergency?"

"That would be ideal, Trey, but it's not available. Sometimes we do what we can with what we have. That's what I'm getting ready to do now, and I need your help. I'm sure you've seen some gruesome things in the military. I hope you have a strong stomach."

"I can handle anything for Rickie's sake."

"Then you need to sanitize your hands and arms before we begin. Go in that bathroom and scrub with soap and warm water twice. And when I say scrub, I mean scrub, not just wash. I will go down the hall and do the same. Linda will be here with the water and towels by the time we finish. I'll put in an IV and start the anesthesia as soon as I return. Trey, look at me. We don't have a minute to lose. If he has a ruptured spleen, as I suspect, he should already be dead."

Trey understood. He knew their surgeon friend was right. Without waiting for Steve to say another word, he hurried to the bathroom and scrubbed. He hoped he was doing it the way Steve said because sterilization was important for Rickie's sake. He zoned in and got ready for action.

He glanced out the bathroom door and saw his friend's body lying on the bed. Tears welled up in his eyes again. "Hang in there, Rickie. We're coming," he said in a voice loud enough that he hoped his partner heard.

Steve rushed back in. Linda had the water and towels ready. He inserted the IV into Rickie's arm and fastened a bag to it. The man already appeared to be out of it. Why did he need anesthesia? But Trey stayed out of the surgeon's way and let him get to work. Steve's voice rang in his ears. He had no time to worry about whether he could do this. His mind cried, *I'm not ready!* He looked at Steve and realized there was no turning back. It was go time, ready or not.

CHAPTER 5

The group turned on the lane off the side road, which led to the cabin and bunkers. This time Beth prepared the newcomers for what was coming when they made the sudden turn. Hans and Heidi had been through enough in the past few days. They did not need more stress. When they pulled into the clearing, tears poured from several eyes. It was surreal that they were there, because none of them should be. All of them should have died, or at the least, Beth should be Messai's wife by now. But here they were: home.

It was time to get into the safety of the Shelter. Fatigue gnawed at their bodies and minds. The adrenaline rush of the past few days had held it at bay until now. But it was taking control of their senses. They stumbled into the cabin and made it to the closet in the bedroom. When Evan pushed the wall and it opened, Hans' and Heidi's mouths flew open. They saw for the first time the ingenious hidden entrance to the steps leading to their underground home, and it amazed them too. But all they could think about now was getting down the steps and meeting the others.

Indescribable joy filled Bunker One when the group opened the door and stepped inside. If they told the story a hundred times, no explanation would be sufficient. They wept and wept and held each other for what seemed like hours. The time would come for stories to be told, but for now, their joy overflowed, as if it gushed from an endless well within. They thanked Jesus over and over for what he had done. That continued until Evan recognized the smell of some of his favorite foods. And as usual, he turned the moment in a different direction.

"I smell food, and I'm starving! Let's eat!"

"Come on in. We cooked up a feast! We had faith Jesus would bring you home!" said Miriam.

When they moved further in, they saw the Welcome Home banner and streamers and wept again. *Home.* They found it hard to believe they were home. *Different from the suite at the mansion,* Beth thought. She sensed evil there; she felt Jesus here. He was here. Messai was not. This was *home.*

"You guys can stand here and talk all day," said Evan, interrupting the moment. "But this guy is eating, with or without you! It has been a long time since Mila's breakfast."

"We're all hungry, Evan," said Blake. "But let's stop and pray for Rickie before we start."

They took a moment and told about Rickie's injuries and Trey with him at the doctor's house. Then they prayed and cried out to Jesus for him. Anders ended the prayer with the words of the verse he had prayed on the plane.

"Heal him, Lord, and he will be healed. Save him and he will be saved." Then he added the rest of the verse. "For you are the one we praise. Jeremiah 17:14," he said with a smile. "It is one of God's healing verses in the Bible."

Evan added, "Jesus, we thank you for this food. We will enjoy it!" Then he said, "We're eating!" He had a plate and was filling it before the others stepped toward the table. They followed suit. That meal hit the spot more than any meal they had ever eaten. They were glad to be *home.*

Trey, Steve and Linda were in scrubs, along with surgical caps, masks and gloves. Trey had never imagined being in this situation. He froze at first, paralyzed, gripped by panic and unable to function. Steve's stern, yet calm voice snapped him out of it as he took the scalpel from the table by the bedside. Trey had never seen one like it.

"I'll make an incision in the abdomen to get to the spleen. I would love to do an ultrasound or CT scan to confirm the rupture. But since this is an emergency and there's no access to either, there is no choice except to proceed with a laparotomy. Linda, I need you to keep Trey supplied with sponges and towels."

"In case you're wondering, I'm using a harmonic scalpel which will minimize bleeding during the procedure. However, when I get in, if I'm correct about the ruptured spleen, we will see a significant amount of blood. Trey, can you handle soaking up that blood and keeping the area clear while I attempt to repair the spleen?"

"I'll do my best."

"Good, then here goes."

He began making the incision in Rickie's abdomen. He was right; there was very little bleeding as he did. Once he had completed the cut and opened the stomach, what Trey saw amazed him. The ruptured spleen was spurting blood with every beat of Rickie's heart.

"He should not be alive," said Steve. "Something kept him from dying."

Not something. Someone! Trey wanted to say. But it wasn't time for that yet. The group had told him about Anders' prayer and the change in Rickie's condition after he prayed. He knew Jesus saved his partner for this moment with Steve.

"This most often involves removing the spleen, but by some act of nature, I think I can repair it without removing it. I can't believe what I'm seeing. People with a splenic tear almost always need immediate surgery to survive. This tear didn't happen a short while ago." He glared at Trey.

"It has been hours since this happened. I understand hospitals are closed, but you should've gotten him to me sooner." His tone was serious.

I wish that had been possible, Trey whispered under his breath. *If you were in Germany, I would have brought him to you right after this happened!*

"Despite getting to it so late, it appears Rickie has gotten a second chance at life."

He began repairing the ruptured spleen. It did not take as long as Trey had speculated it might. He cleaned blood out of the abdomen while Steve finished the repair. Blood stopped spurting. Their surgeon friend had saved Rickie's life, just as Rickie had saved the others' lives the previous day.

"We'll give it a few minutes to be sure the bleeding has stopped, then I'll close. Outstanding job, Trey. I didn't mean to be hard on you. Whatever happened, and however long ago it was, I could still do the surgery like it had only been minutes. I don't understand how in the world he survived so long. And how the operation was still a success is a miracle."

Trey was certain Steve used the term *miracle* only as a cliche. *I must show him the video and tell him why that happened.* He now saw a golden opportunity to tell his friend about Jesus and hoped for an open door to do that.

"Okay, it's time to close. The bleeding has stopped and the spleen survived. His breathing is back to normal, so he doesn't have a punctured or collapsed lung. The broken ribs will heal on their own. That will be a painful process, but they will heal."

He proceeded with closing the incision. When he finished, he patted the area dry with a clean towel, then applied an antibiotic ointment and dressing. "Finished. Linda, stay with him while Trey and I clean up. We'll be back soon."

Trey followed him out of the room, stumbling along in a fog, dazed and confused. He had witnessed a miracle; not just a miracle in these moments, but one that occurred over a period of almost 24 hours. Rickie should have died in Bruno and Mila's house, not long after he drove the van through the side of their home. At most, he should not have survived the trip to Ramstein.

Even then, it was impossible by human standards to survive a 10-hour flight to the states. But here he was, alive and out of a surgery that saved his life. The result was the same as if it had happened at a house in Germany instead of a bedroom in Springfield, Missouri. This topped all others as the greatest miracle he had witnessed yet.

•   •   •   •   •

In the Shelter, something occurred to Beth when they finished eating. "Where are John and Mary?"

"Mary became ill several hours ago, and John took her to their room in Bunker Three to take care of her. We hope it is only a 24-hour stomach virus. She was very sick," said Miriam.

"I need to check on her." Beth's concern was obvious. She sensed that Mary's condition was far worse than any of them imagined.

"No, dear," Miriam whispered. "John won't let you in. He doesn't want any of us to catch what she has. He fears it may be contagious."

"But we need to care for her," Beth said with obvious concern in her voice. "She may be sicker than we realize. What if she needs medical treatment?"

"Beth, hospitals have been closed since the earthquake," said Ben. "If she needs to go somewhere for treatment, there's nowhere to take her."

"I have an idea!" exclaimed Evan with an excitement that startled them. But it grabbed their attention and caused them to look at him with eager eyes.

"Trey and Rickie's friend, Steve, the surgeon. Rickie is there right now. John and Mary lived in Springfield. If we can get her there, maybe he can help her too."

"That is a great idea, Evan!" Ally loved it. "But I doubt John will go for it."

"We can at least ask him." Evan was not about to give up on the idea. He agreed with Beth, and his heart told him they needed to get Mary help soon.

"Come on, Miriam. You and I will try to persuade him to let us take her," said Beth.

The two of them hurried to Bunker Three and knocked on the door. John opened the door with a look of fear on his face. He would have been overjoyed to see Beth, but his mind was on his wife. Nothing else mattered to him now.

"She is worse," he said in tears. "A lot worse. She needs help."

"Are you familiar with a surgeon in Springfield named Steve? I've been away far too long to know many people over there. We didn't tell you, but Rickie got injured when he and Trey rescued us yesterday morning. Trey took him to Steve's house, but didn't give us a last name."

"Steve Phillips," John said. "He's one of the best surgeons in Missouri. People come to him from all over. He and his wife have been in our shop many times. He'll help her, if he can."

"Do you have any idea where he lives? I doubt that any of us can find his house. Trey pointed it out to us when he stopped with Rickie. But if you know where it is..." John interrupted her.

"I know right where he and Linda live. They've been our faithful customers through the years, and I've made deliveries to their home. We need to get her there right now!"

"Let's ask the others. We need to figure out who should go with you. We can't take a chance on giving ourselves away."

•　　•　　•　　•　　•

Steve and Trey returned to the room after cleaning up from Rickie's surgery.

"How is he doing?"

"He seems to be stable and doing well."

"Good. Trey and I will take over now so you can get cleaned up."

When she was out of the room, Steve looked at Trey. "Okay, talk to me. How did you become a wanted man by Messai? I know you too well to think you would do anything illegal or, as he likes to put it, to interfere with the peace and prosperity of the world." He rolled his eyes when he said that last part. That showed Trey that Steve wasn't very fond of the Secretary-General.

"I want to tell you about that, Steve. But if I do, you must give me your word that you will hear me out. And I need you to promise not to turn me in. I'm not the only one on Messai's naughty list. So is Rickie. And there are others, wonderful people. I need to tell you a lot, if you'll listen. I can do that while we're sitting with him."

"I'll listen to you. We don't have a lot of other things to do, anyway. Since we'll be sitting here all night, you may as well tell me the whole story. I have no clue what happened to Rickie, and I'm not asking. I assume you'll tell me if you want to. But from what I saw, he should be dead, yet something kept him alive."

"Not something, Steve. *Someone.*"

When Trey started talking, they heard a vehicle pull into the driveway. Both men jumped to their feet at the same time.

"Someone is here," whispered Steve.

Linda walked back in. "Steve, a vehicle just pulled into our driveway." The look of fear on her face sent the two men into action.

"Sit with Rickie, and Trey and I will check the security camera." He looked at Trey. "If AMPP knows you guys are here, we may be in trouble."

"What are you talking about?" Linda asked. "What does AMPP have to do with this?"

"I'll tell you in a few moments. Let us check it out first and see what's going on."

He and Trey crept into the living room. Steve checked the camera. "It's a military van."

"A military van?" Trey's expression changed from upset to confused. "That's not AMPP. I hope it's people from the group I told you about. But why would they come here? I told them not to."

"Trey, this is getting stranger by the hour. Why would your group come here, and why would they be driving a vehicle that belongs to the United States Military? You need to give me answers, and you need to give them to me fast."

"It is all part of what I need to tell you. I'll do that, but I need to see what they want. Do you mind if I go outside and talk to them?"

"You can go, but if I see the first sign of trouble, I'll be right here with my Glock in hand!"

Trey opened the door and walked toward the van. He saw two people sitting in the front, but could not see who they were. The passenger side window came down, causing him to freeze in his tracks.

"Trey, get over here. We need help."

He saw Blake. Anders was driving, and someone sat in the seat behind them. Trey breathed a sigh of relief. The side door slid open. John was sitting and holding Mary in his arms.

"John, what's wrong?" Trey asked him. "Why did you guys come here? It's dangerous."

"It's Mary, Trey. She's sick and needs help. We didn't know where else to go. Beth told us you brought Rickie here, and I know Steve will treat her too. Can you help us get her inside?"

"Let me go tell Steve what's going on. When he hears its Mary, he'll let us bring her in."

He walked back inside and Steve opened the door for him, then closed it behind him.

"What is it?"

"It's Mary from the little specialty shop. John brought her and says she is very, very sick."

"John and Mary are two of my favorite people! Get her in here, and I'll take care of her. I must have opened a hospital, or at least an emergency room, in my home. But I'm glad I can help people during this time when there's nowhere else for them to go."

Trey stepped back out and motioned for them to bring Mary, then ran to the van.

"Wait. Blake, you need to stay here. You too, Anders. Let John and me take her inside. I'll tell him you're coming in after we get her settled in. I doubt he will recognize you, Blake. You look nothing like the reporter he has seen on TV for years."

"Anders, you were with us the day we saw John and Mary. You were the one who told them about Jesus. As I recall, your name is Steffen Janssen."

"That's right. Are you sure you and John can get Mary in there?"

John was out of the van now. "Yes, we can, and we need to do it now. Help me carry her, Trey."

Steve held the door open for them as they carried Mary inside. He motioned for them to take her to another spare bedroom. They placed her on the bed and stepped back to let Steve get to her.

"She's burning up with a fever. Tell Linda to bring all the ice she can find. We need to pack her and get her fever down. What else has been going on, John?"

John explained all of Mary's symptoms. His emotions got the best of him, and he broke down and cried. Trey put a hand on his shoulder, and Steve looked at him with compassion.

"I'll do everything I can for her, John. She's a very sick lady."

Steve started working on Mary. He kept the supplies he needed at home to help diagnose illnesses and treat people. Linda often said she lived in a mini-hospital. He drew blood and took it into his homemade lab to test it. He walked back into the room with a serious look of concern on his face.

"This is unlike any virus I've ever seen. Whatever it is, it is attacking all her organs and destroying her immune system. I'll begin an aggressive treatment of the strongest antibiotics I have."

He started an IV and combined the antibiotics with medication to lower her fever and something to help with nausea. Steve was running back and forth between her room and Rickie's room.

Rickie was still stable and sleeping, but it was almost time to wake him. Mary's condition worsened by the minute, and nothing seemed to work. She was violently sick, convulsing and screaming in pain. He had to stay with her, so he sent Linda to sit with Rickie and asked Trey to take John out of the room. He did, although it broke his heart to do it.

"Let's go to the van and get Blake and Anders," he said to John. "It is time for them to come in. You can introduce Anders as Steffen Janssen and tell about meeting him that day in the ruins of your shop. Tell Steve and Linda that Steffen helped you. He told you something that changed your lives and helped you get past the loss of the shop. That will open a door if we get to speak with them later. And it's the truth, isn't it?"

"It is. But I don't want to leave Mary, Trey."

"Steve needs freedom to work with no one else in the room, John. I'm sure you want to be in there, but it is the best thing for Mary right now. He'll let you come back in when it's time."

They walked to the van. Blake and Anders still sat inside, not wanting to get out until Trey gave them the okay. He motioned for them and they got out and followed John and him to the door.

Blake took a deep breath and said, "I'm ready. Let's go in." They walked in and sat down in the living room. Anders sat next to John, trying to console him and give him hope. But he was inconsolable. Nothing Anders said gave him peace about Mary's situation. He sat with his arm around him and held him as he sobbed. Steve walked into the room.

"John, you need to come and be with Mary. I must warn you, she's very sick. Nothing I'm doing is helping her. I've done everything I can, but nothing is fazing this. I've never seen anything to compare it with. None of the common viruses show up in the blood work. Yet her body is shutting down. Her organs are failing. If something doesn't change, it won't be long."

"No!" John screamed as he got up and ran to the bedroom. Trey, Anders and Blake followed him.

Steve came in behind them and asked, "Who are these other two men? Are you the ones who brought John and Mary here tonight?"

"We are," said Blake. "I'm Shawn Smith, and this is Steffen Janssen. We saw that Mary was in terrible shape. John told us about you, so we brought her here. We didn't know what else to do."

"Thank you for helping them. They are precious people. I visited their shop many times, and John even made deliveries to our home. He didn't have to do that, but he did. They are such a sweet couple, and Mary is an unbelievable cook. I wish this wasn't happening to them."

"Isn't there anything you can do for her? Please tell me there is something."

"Trust me, if I could, I would. Whatever this is, modern medicine won't touch it. It differs from anything I've seen or read about in all my years of practicing medicine. She will only be with us for a little while. She can't survive more than an hour in her condition. You guys need to stay with John. He will need you. I'll go back in and try to wake Rickie." He slipped on a mask as he walked toward the room.

They stood nearby as John sat by the bed holding his wife's hand. They did not want to, but they needed to. Moments like this would define the next six years. They were sure of that.

In Jerusalem, Aissa Messai stood atop the Temple Mount before select members of the press, whom he chose for this day and this announcement. These were reporters who would relay the story as he wanted them to. They were not only pro-Messai people; they were reporters who would fall under his spell and be oblivious to any search for truth in his words.

The same was true for the dignitaries gathered, including the Israeli prime minister. They could not show the conference on live television. So, they would record it, allowing for editing, showing only the things the Secretary-General wanted people to see and hear.

"Ladies and gentlemen, it is a pleasure to stand before you today in this most wonderful place. What I and others have accomplished here is unparalleled in all the world. I am sure there are questions, but I will begin with a brief announcement about why I came to Israel alone. You also need to understand why I still came after the worldwide devastation that just occurred."

"First, I want to make you aware that I postponed my wedding following the earthquake. I could not celebrate such a joyous occasion while the world endures terrible suffering. Besides, it was an event my bride and I wished to share with the world, but we could not do that without the benefit of television and internet. I am certain the wedding will happen. However, both Beth and I want to allow the world to recover before we unite in marriage. We have your best interest at heart and will always put your needs above our own. We will delay the wedding until an appropriate time."

He was lying now, something he had not intended to do. His intention had been to explain how the earthquake had led to his wedding being postponed. He never intended to mention Beth or promise that the wedding would still occur at a future date. But the lies flowed from his mouth as he stood before the crowd, as they always seemed to do.

The wedding will happen, he reasoned to himself during a pause. *I will find Beth and bring her back to myself. Then the marriage will take place, and the world will watch it!* A smile crossed his face as the lie became reality in his mind, which now flooded with images of Beth Jennings.

"I am sure you also question why I would fulfill my commitment to come, even though I cannot celebrate my honeymoon. This place and the peace and prosperity happening here are most important to me; so important that I refused to allow anything to stop me from being here today."

"Despite air travel being suspended worldwide, I saw it as urgent enough that we took the chance of getting my private jet off the ground to make the trip. It was difficult and dangerous, but this place means that much to me. The lack of destruction here, compared with the rest of the world, reveals the unique nature of the nation of Israel. In time, the entire planet will experience what you are seeing here. That is the reason I came. Are there questions?"

Half-hearted applause came from the group sitting in a stupor in front of him. They asked no questions as they sat staring with blank faces. He smiled and thanked them for their time. Then he was off to indulge in some Jerusalem nightlife before retiring to the King David Hotel. There he would fantasize about what would have happened had his bride been with him. But he had convinced himself that it would happen. He would relish the time when it did.

• • • • •

Trey, Blake and Anders watched as Mary succumbed to the disease that had taken hold of her. It had ravaged her body in a matter of hours. She no longer resembled the woman they had known for the past several months. John fell across the bed weeping over his wife. The other men wept as they observed the excruciating scene.

"Why?" John asked. "Why would Jesus save others but not her?"

Blake attempted to answer with words that sounded hollow and insufficient. "I don't have the answer to that, John. I wish I did. The only thing I can tell you is that we realize where Mary is. She is with Jesus, and we will see her again in six years."

John rose. "You're right, Blake. I understand that, and it should make me happy for her. But it is so hard."

His tear-streaked face revealed the pain in his broken heart. Anders took a step toward the man he had helped to put his faith in Jesus those months ago. When he did, John collapsed to the floor, his body convulsing and changing before their eyes.

"Steve!" Anders yelled.

The doctor ran into the room and saw John on the floor, convulsing.

"Mary?" he asked, looking toward the bed.

"She's gone," said Trey. Steve walked over and confirmed that.

"Move her to the floor and try to get John onto the bed. But put these on first." He handed them surgical gowns, gloves, and masks. They put them on and moved John to the bed. Steve checked his vitals. "Same as Mary," he said. "I hate to say it, but there's nothing I can do."

"What about Rickie? How is he?" Trey's concern returned to his friend and partner.

"I think he will be fine. He has experienced blood loss and severe trauma to his body. It will take weeks for him to recover. His ribs and nose need to heal. I repaired his ruptured spleen, but it will take some time to heal too."

"He needs to stay here a few more days. This isn't a hospital, but it's the next best thing. Linda and I will take excellent care of him. And you are welcome to stay here with him. Look Trey, I don't know what happened, and I'm eager for you to tell me about it. But I know you well enough to know you're not a criminal."

"Try to help John now. When the time is right, maybe even tonight, I would love for the three of us to sit down with Linda and you and explain everything."

"The three of you? You mean these men are a part of this too?"

"They are, as is Rickie. So were John and Mary."

Blake reached into his pocket, pulled out a flash drive and waved it at Trey.

"Steve," said Trey, "we'll do more than tell you. We'll show you!"

By the time Steve got to John, his body had ceased convulsing and he lay ashen white on the bed. "He's almost gone," Steve informed them. "It's best for us to stay away from him. I fear that whatever has gone on with Mary and him may be very contagious. She got it first, and he caught it from her. This is a deadly and untreatable virus, that much is clear. We can't take any chances, so don't take off the gear I gave you until it is safe."

They looked back at the bed and realized John had died too. Tears filled their eyes. Linda came to the door, and Steve motioned for her to stay away. She turned and retreated down the hallway. Steve took extra blankets from the closet, and they wrapped the couple's bodies in them and left the room. Before they did, Anders whispered to Trey and Blake.

"They came to Jesus on the same day. Now they went to be with him on the same day. They will enjoy his presence, and we will see them in six years."

"Or less," whispered Blake. "Who knows? Any of us may join them before then."

"To be on the safe side, all of us should take hot showers and scrub, just like we were getting ready for surgery," said Steve. "Leave your clothes and the surgical gear outside the bathroom doors, and I'll collect them and take them outside. Linda will get you some clothes to wear. We need to dispose of what we wore around John and Mary. If everybody is clear on that, go to the showers. I will disinfect this room, and every part of the house where they've been, while you do. I will also bring new masks. We must protect ourselves against whatever they had."

The men headed to the showers as Steve donned his surgical gear, collected their clothes, removed the linens from the bed and deposited all of them outside the house. They would burn them later. He then disinfected the house, being careful not to miss a single room or any spot in those rooms.

When the men finished with their showers, they emerged wearing Steve's clothes, looking somewhat funny in things that did not fit. But there was no time for laughter now. They had pressing business to take care of that could not wait.

•　•　•　•　•

"Where are they?" asked Ally. "They should be back by now."

Concern showed on the faces of everyone in the Shelter. They sensed something was wrong, but still did not realize what it was. Without the use of phones or any other method of communication, all they could do was sit and wait for their colleagues to return with news. The wait would prove to be longer than they hoped.

While Steve and Linda showered and scrubbed, Blake, Anders and Trey sat in the room with Rickie. Trey heard his name. Rickie! He was awake. Trey rushed to his side.

"Where am I?"

"You are at Steve and Linda Phillips' house."

"We made it," Rickie whispered. "Did everyone make it?"

"You saved their lives, man. We all made it. And we made the flight and got you here."

"No man left behind," he whispered again and managed a weak smile.

"No man, or woman, left behind," Trey said with tears in his eyes.

The time would come to tell him about John and Mary, but now was not that time.

"Blake and Anders are here too."

The two of them came to Rickie's bedside. Blake touched his arm and said, "You rest, Rickie. We're not going anywhere. We'll tell you the story when you're better."

Rickie smiled and closed his eyes. Rest was what he needed, and strong medication made sleep come. Steve re-entered the room and confirmed that things were going well.

"Now, about the things you wanted to tell me," he said, looking at Trey.

"Get Linda and meet us in the den. It's time you heard the truth."

A puzzled look appeared on Steve's face, but he did what Trey said. He wanted to know the truth, and he trusted Trey Butler to tell him.

•   •   •   •   •

Alexander and Elizabeth Ben Ezra sat reading the New Testament together in their home in Ein Karem, Israel. They could not get enough of the second part of the Bible. They had always rejected it as false, but now it was alive and exciting. When they read John Chapter Three, she spoke up.

"Alexander, we need to pray for someone in the United States. I sense there is someone there who is as Nicodemus was when Jesus spoke to him in verse sixteen. Jesus told him God loved people so much he gave his only son so anyone who believes in him, like we did, will not perish but have eternal life. We put our faith in Jesus and God gave us eternal life. Someone in America is facing that decision, and we need to pray he will do that too. It is very important that we pray right now."

"If you sense that, we will pray. We have said prayers from the Torah our entire lives, but now our prayers are different. We pray in Jesus' name. Power comes through his name, Elizabeth. Jesus told you this, so I will let you pray for whoever that is."

"I will be glad to do that." She did not hesitate.

"Jesus, I sense that as when you spoke to Nicodemus that day, there is someone in America who needs you just as much. It is very important that this person, or those people, put their faith in you. It will be a defining moment of these seven years in which we live. Whoever that is, please draw them to yourself like you drew Nicodemus and us. And please be with whoever is talking to them. Speak through them as if you are there talking to them in person. And Jesus, help them believe in you. Amen."

Alexander placed his hand on hers and smiled, amazed at the person his wife was becoming.

CHAPTER 6

Blake, Anders, and Trey sat on a sofa in the beautiful den of Steve and Linda's home. Both looked at them, ready to hear from them and hoping they would hurry. Trey jumped on the opportunity.

"I could tell you, but I would rather show you. May I put this flash drive into the TV?"

"I wanted to hear it straight from you. Why would you show us a video?"

"This explains it all, Steve. Each of us has seen it, and it changed our lives."

"Does this explain Rickie's injury and why you ended up here tonight?"

"It does... and more. All I ask is that you promise me two things before it starts. One, promise you'll watch it all the way to the end. You may hear some things you don't like, but watch it anyway and don't stop. Two, listen with an open mind. Hear the man out and you will get answers to your questions about the events of the past year."

"Before the video starts, let me ask you something. Did you guys watch Blake Thompson and Beth Jennings' special reports on February 2nd?"

"Nope. We had more important things to do. In our minds, there were no questions about the disappearances. We knew what happened and didn't need to hear anything else. Don't tell me you're showing us a video of that. If you are, I'm not interested."

"You have known me a long time, Steve. I wouldn't show you this if I didn't believe it is the most important thing you will ever see and hear. Please watch it for me, and for Rickie. If he could, he would tell you how what you are about to see changed his life too."

"Okay, okay, we'll watch it. I hope it doesn't last forever. It's been a long day and night."

"Well, it is an hour. But if you will pay close attention, that hour will feel like a few minutes. May I start it now?"

"Please do. The quicker we get started, the sooner we finish."

When the video started, Blake recalled with vivid clarity the first time he saw it in Evan's dorm room in Chicago. He chided Evan for making him promise to watch it after discovering it was a pastor's sermon from four years earlier. His obvious disdain showed when the pastor told how the earth was not billions of years old, as science teaches, but 6,000 years old.

He mocked the man when he said God created the universe in six 24-hour days. Then he stated that according to the Bible, each of those days represented 1,000 years of the history of the earth. But he added that meant history would last 6,000 years, then end. The only thing that kept him from getting up and walking away at that point was his promise to watch to the end.

The tying in of the seven feasts of Israel, saying they foreshadowed the first and second comings of Jesus, left him bored. Until the pastor connected the first three feasts to Jesus' death and resurrection. It intrigued him that Jesus died on the Feast of Passover. That was the day the Jews slaughtered a lamb to remind them how God delivered them from Egypt. The pastor said Jesus was God's Passover lamb who died on that exact day at the same time the priests killed the lambs. Jesus died to forgive our sins, thus God forgives our sins when we believe in him. Blake recalled engaging more at that point.

He paid even more attention as the pastor continued talking about the feasts. That would have been mundane to him before, but he was searching for answers to the disappearances.

The pastor pointed out that the Feast of Unleavened Bread, which began the day after Passover, symbolized Jesus sinless life. And he rose from the grave on the Feast of First Fruits as the first of everyone else who would believe in him and rise too. The Apostle Paul even called Jesus our Passover lamb and first fruit. That was not coincidental!

The middle feast, Pentecost, began the 2,000-year history of the church. It happened on the same day God gave the Law to Moses. God replaced law with grace, allowing us to turn to Jesus and receive forgiveness and eternal life.

That each of the first three feasts occurred on the exact days for the exact reasons in the life of Jesus had fascinated him. And Pentecost occurred on the exact day God gave the Law to Moses in the Old Testament. That was impossible to overlook, too!

But when the pastor reached the fifth feast, everything had changed for Blake. That was the Feast of Trumpets, the day the priests blew the trumpets, calling the people of Israel to the temple to worship. They celebrated a new year and a new beginning. He knew it as Rosh Hashanah.

The pastor said Jesus gave us clues that he would take his people home on a Feast of Trumpets, saying he would come with a loud trumpet blast. But the most important clue Jesus gave was when he said no one knows the day or hour of his coming. He recalled his shock upon hearing the nickname given to the Feast of Trumpets by the Jews of that day. *The feast of no one knows the day nor the hour.* Things came together in his mind at that point.

Based on the timeline of the earth, the pastor said he concluded that Jesus would come 2,000 years after his resurrection, completing the 6,000-year history of the earth. The next impactful thing he pointed out was that Jesus was born in 4 B.C., not 0 A.D., as many people believe. That means the resurrection happened in 29 A.D.

So, he said, if he was right, Jesus would take his people home on a Feast of Trumpets, 2,000 years after that. That would be 2029! He asked Evan what day the Feast of Trumpets fell on that year. Evan smiled and said, "September 11." Blake would never forget the shock of that answer!

The memories returned as if it happened yesterday: the blood rushing from his face, almost as if he would faint. The pastor said Jesus would come with the blast of a trumpet, which he believed would be the loudest sound the world had ever heard. And Jesus told us his coming would be like lightning that flashes from the east to the west. That would also be the brightest light the world had ever seen. Those exact things happened on September 11, 2029!

He would never forget the realization hitting him that what had happened on that day was not an alien invasion, as he believed! The truth smacked him right in the face. Every person taken was a Christian, and everyone left behind was not! That included him, Evan, and Ally.

The other two had already put their faith in Jesus. He had no choice but to accept the truth and do the same. He would also never forget the indescribable feeling when he asked Jesus to come into his life and be his Savior. Everything changed for him in that amazing moment.

Now, as he watched Steve and Linda, he saw the same expressions on their faces that showed on his own face that day. He smiled when he saw them believe, just as he did. Then he listened as both asked Jesus to be their Savior. The tears flowed, as they had from his eyes and the eyes of each of the Smyrnians when they experienced that moment.

While this celebration began, he thanked Jesus that he got to see it another time. Two new believers in Jesus added to the team! They would need Steve's medical expertise many times during the remaining six years until Jesus came again and took them home to be with him.

Then came the hard part as the pastor talked about the seven years of tribulation which would follow the Rapture, the term for what happened on September 11. Steve got it when he heard Jesus' followers would suffer, with many facing death because they believed in him. But if they remained faithful, even if it meant dying, they would receive the crown of life.

Blake heard Steve avow that he now knew Aissa Messai was the Antichrist Jesus said would come. He understood Messai declared war on the Smyrnians and bore responsibility for Rickie's condition. He and Linda were now among their number. Blake saw they were ready to battle evil and tell others the wonderful news about Jesus! He walked to Steve and put out his hand.

"Welcome to the Smyrnians, Steve; you too, Linda. Allow me to introduce myself. I am Blake Thompson." He smiled as he reached for their hands. Steve grabbed him and pulled him into a tight embrace instead.

"I thought I recognized the voice, but I understand why you need to disguise yourself. You are public enemy number one to Messai! It's great to meet you. Trey, thank you for telling us the truth. I don't know how we missed it!"

"Trust me, Steve, we all feel the same way. But we're glad we got it at last!"

"Jesus took my wife and kids home to be with him in the Rapture," Anders explained. "They were Christians. They loved Jesus, went to church, and lived for him. They tried to get me to join them, but I rejected it. When I discovered where they are, you cannot imagine what that did for me! My name isn't Steffen Janssen. I am Anders Norstrom, Blake's cameraman."

"We are thrilled to meet all of you, and be a part of the Smyrnians," said Linda. "I suppose we should celebrate instead of crying because we know where John and Mary are right now."

"You got it!" exclaimed Trey. "It's hard to see them go, but they're with Jesus. We had better check on Rickie. I can't wait to tell him about the two of you!"

Anders and Trey had also relived their own first experiences with Jesus as they witnessed Steve and Linda go through it. But as always, there was little time to celebrate. They had much to do, and for tonight, it began with their comrade lying in the bedroom down the hall.

•　　•　　•　　•　　•

None of them knew what happened to John and Mary was not an isolated occurrence of the flu or any other known disease. It was happening all over the world. People were dying at an alarming rate. The plague had now invaded larger cities, creating panic as hospitals remained closed and there was nowhere to take the sick.

They decided Steve and Linda would leave their home and follow the group to the safety of the Shelter. Clothed in surgical gowns, gloves and masks, they took the bodies of their two friends to bury them on the farm. Steve felt Rickie was strong enough to make the trip. So, trying to stay as inconspicuous as possible, they drove to join the rest of the team. A celebration ensued when they arrived, but it turned to sorrow when the others learned about John and Mary.

The group welcomed Steve and Linda and rejoiced that they had become part of them. The next day they buried the bodies of John and Mary. For two days, they talked and developed a plan of action for when power and technology returned.

On the third day, Ben was recording a teaching he would show whenever internet access became available again. A news alert caught him by surprise when it popped up on the screen. He grabbed his phone and touched Blake's number. In the other room, Blake's phone rang.

"Ben, what are you doing calling me from the next room? All you have to do is walk in here and talk to me. *Calling me!* Ben, you called me; my phone rang! Evan, turn on the TV!"

When the television came to life, the faces of newsmen and women filled the screen. They were reporting as if the earthquake had just occurred the day before. Images of the damage showed on every network. One thing they all talked about was the virus, which was killing people across the planet. When reports came in, the death toll was far higher than anyone could have imagined. And it showed no signs of slowing down.

Medical science would begin searching for a cure, or at least something that would bring it to a halt. The best advice they could give was for everyone to quarantine themselves indoors and away from other people. Businesses and major corporations in every country agreed to close their doors, hoping to stop the spread. The Smyrnians would not leave the safety of the farm.

Communication could now happen via phone, email and social media. Humanity would stay connected, but away from each other. For the team, this brought an opportunity to reach vast numbers of people with their message. Folks could not leave their homes, so they would spend copious amounts of time on computers and phones.

Ben had been in contact with Alexander and Elizabeth. They were ready to do their part to reach the Jews via the secure network they set up. Their identities would have to remain secret, but the website would be their tool. No one could detect their correspondence. It was an open door.

Blake and Beth would reach out to the rest of the world, as they taught those who were already following Jesus. This time of horror for the world would serve as the catalyst for spreading the message of Jesus. It could not have happened apart from the disease that ravaged the planet. Many people were dying, but many others were discovering real life as they turned to faith in Jesus Christ. The Smyrnians would take advantage of every day the opportunity afforded. It would be the single greatest period of growth for the family of believers.

•　　•　　•　　•　　•

Aissa Messai was back in Belgium after a few days in Israel. He had made the most of those days. Treated like the celebrity he was, he basked in the adulation of people who adored him and believed in him. It allowed him to forget about the events of the past few days. He could use a small portion of his mansion for a living space while the rest was under repair from the damage inflicted on it by the quake. Many others lived in far worse conditions.

He called a special meeting with the director and other senior leaders of AMPP for the next day. The latest escape by the Smyrnians had upped the ante. That could not continue to happen. He was eager to tell them his idea about hunting down and destroying members of the infidels' families. His smile was diabolical as he thought about it.

But as he lay down for the night, the other thoughts returned, preventing him from sleeping. Two women. Two *beautiful* women. The first, his assistant who became the object of his infatuation. She jilted him, attacked him, and ran away, leaving him alone, angry, and embarrassed.

The other was the woman of his dreams, the one he had wanted since the day he saw her at the UN meeting in New York. She was to be his wife, despite rejecting him. She too had escaped, causing him even greater angst. *There will be hell to pay*, he said aloud to himself.

Yes, the place from which came his power would bring retribution on them with a vengeance. And Beth would return to him, even if not of her own choosing. With those thoughts in his mind, he slept and dreamed of the day it would happen.

Morning came, and he was up early, ready for his meeting. He sat in what the quake left of his luxurious office building, awaiting the leaders of his security forces. The conference room was in shambles, but he sat at the head of the table as if the room was still its former glorious self. The team entered one at the time and sat around him. He had no time for small talk. This was the time for action. He would make sure they were laser-focused on carrying out his heinous plan.

"Men," he began, "you may wonder why I brought you here today. You know well the Smyrnian leaders have escaped us once again. We have gone too easy on them. They are crafty and have proven all too willing to put their lives on the line for their hopeless cause. But while they may risk their own lives, are they willing to risk the lives of the people they love... their families?"

"We now know their names, or at least most of them. I want you to conduct a search for all their family members and discover where they live, then eliminate them one by one. Make sure the media provides ample coverage of their deaths. I want them to hear it and realize it has only begun. That should bring them out of their holes. When they come to the aid of their families, we will be there waiting for them. Do I make myself clear?"

"Yes sir. We will get right on the search, then eliminate the targets. Does it matter where and with whom we start?"

"I would prefer you begin with the families of Blake Thompson and Beth Jennings."

"You know they are husband and wife, don't you, sir?"

"No, they are not, Captain! No one approved by the state performed their so-called wedding. If there was a *ceremony*, they performed it themselves. So, no, their marriage never happened!"

"I am sorry, sir. I was not aware of that. Please forgive me."

"See that you do not question me again, Captain. Is that clear?"

"Yes sir. It will not happen again."

"As I was saying, I prefer that you start with their families. Start searching and report back to me ASAP. However, I know the families of the Germans will be easier to find. So will the Bartons and Clarkes in England. Hmm... maybe we begin with the members of Parliament who supported Miss Clarke. That will ramp things up."

"Excuse me, Mr. Messai, but as one of your closest advisors, I disagree with that approach. Your popularity in England is strong. The murders of Parliament members could have a negative effect on that, if they discover we killed them. I believe wisdom should prevail over retribution in their case."

"You may be right, Captain. We should not take any chances with that. But as you did in other situations, keep our identity secret, leaving no clue *we* did it. However, I agree with you. Only go after family members. Trace them as far down the line as you can. Leave no stone unturned and no family member alive until the Smyrnians come out in the open and we capture them."

The men left with their orders and would start right away. They must locate family members and dispose of them, while ensuring the Smyrnians were well aware of what was happening.

•　　•　　•　　•　　•

Meanwhile, the plague that seemed unstoppable was showing signs of slowing down, thanks to businesses agreeing to close their doors and society choosing to quarantine themselves until it subsided. Those things prevented the disease from spreading. It had claimed a massive number of lives, but the united effort abbreviated its lifespan.

However, if the world's population thought they would get a reprieve, they could not have been more wrong. What was coming would be far worse than what had been. While the entire earth celebrated the approaching end of the pandemic, a greater enemy lay ominously on the horizon.

• • • • •

"Everybody, get in here!" Evan had paused the TV and rewound a few seconds back. Bruno and Mila were the first in, and he pulled them to the side.

"Before everyone else gets in here, I need to tell you something. Hans and Heidi will need you when I show them what I just saw on the news."

"What is it?" Mila asked with a look of concern on her face.

"Someone murdered Hans' brother and his family in their house last night. No one knows who did it, but the way it happened, there's no doubt it was AMPP. But no one will ever believe that."

"That's not all. It also happened to Heidi's parents. They found them in the yard behind their house. The killings were identical, leaving no doubt the same people are responsible for both."

Mila started crying, and Bruno put his arm around her and held her. "Mila, we need to warn our families. Messai now knows who we are, all of us, so we have to let them know. I wish we had that bunker installed over there."

"We need to find a bunker or get them over here. We can't just let Messai slaughter our families without doing something."

"No disrespect, Mrs. Fromm, but it is too late for that. Before you can get a bunker installed, they'll find them. I guarantee you Messai's men have identified every one of them and know where they live, work, play, whatever. You can bet they know everything about them. They are all meeting with other believers in groups, aren't they?"

"Yes. That means all the others are in danger too."

"More than in danger, Mr. Fromm. Their situations are urgent. AMPP will not kill in the daylight. But by tonight, they will have groups of cold-blooded killers at every house."

The others were all gathered now and saw the three of them talking.

"What's up, Evan? I know you didn't call us in here for no reason," Blake said.

"If all of you will sit down, I need to show you something on the news. I saw it right after I turned on the television."

They all grew quiet. You could hear a pin drop. Every one of them knew this was bad. They had grown accustomed to receiving grim news, but they never got used to it. Bruno and Mila eased over and sat, one on each side of Hans and Heidi. Evan spoke before he hit play to begin the news report again.

"Hans and Heidi, this involves you. I need to warn you in advance, but also let you know we are all here for you. We are always here for each other."

Heidi grabbed Hans' arm and held on. He pulled it away and placed it around her, pulling her close. He reached out with his other arm and took her hand in his.

"We are ready," he said. "Go ahead."

Evan hit play, and the news began in the studio before switching to a field reporter.

"Tragedy struck twice last night in two rural German neighborhoods. Let's go to one of our affiliates for a full report."

The scene came into view, and Hans sobbed. He saw his brother's house with yellow police tape across the front door. Then he watched as replay showed five body bags being carried out earlier that morning. He knew they contained the bodies of his brother, sister-in-law and their three teenage children. His body trembled with grief that turned to rage.

"Messai," he uttered through clenched teeth.

The reporter explained how unknown assailants invaded the home and carried out the attack. They had bound the five family members and tied their hands behind their backs. Then they forced them to kneel and shot them execution style in the backs of their heads. Hans anger overcame him at that moment and he leapt to his feet.

"I will go to Belgium and take him out myself!" he yelled.

Bruno rose and stood beside him. He put his arm around his friend's shoulder and talked to him in a calm voice for the big man.

"You can't do that, Hans. I know you want to, and I want to help you, but we can't. Let me remind you of something. You led them to faith in Jesus a few months ago. Do you remember how happy and excited you were?

Because you did that, they are with Jesus now. And they are with your grandparents. The moment AMPP fired those shots last night, your brother's family saw their faces and the face of Jesus."

Hans looked at him with tears streaming down his face.

"I know you are right, Bruno. I'm just outraged that Messai can get away with this and go on like nothing happened. And the world will never know. Someone has to stop him!"

"Someone will," whispered the big man. "That someone is Jesus. He will stop him and put an end to all of this in a few years."

Hans' expression changed from rage to relief. But before he could say anything else, the picture shifted to another house and a different reporter. The scene was the same. Police had stretched yellow tape around the backyard, and the law enforcement presence was heavy. Heidi gasped as she recognized her parents' house, the place where she had grown up, the same backyard where she had so often played as a kid. A tire swing still hung from a nearby tree in plain view.

"No!" she screamed, as her sobs came so uninterrupted that it seemed she could not breathe.

That brought the entire room to tears, as they wept with her. Mila and Hans wrapped her in a tight embrace, holding her close, fearing she may pass out. She heard none of the remaining report. It broke her heart to what appeared to be the point of no repair. Then the tears stopped, and she sat up, brushed them away, and smiled.

"They are with Jesus," she said, beaming. "They got there before us. Bruno is right; I will see them again soon, and I can't wait! But we have work to do. I know we can't take Messai out, but we can make his life miserable by snatching every person we can away from him and helping them believe in Jesus. Let's get up and get to work. We don't have any time to lose!"

"You're right, Heidi," interrupted Evan. "How many other family members do you have over there? I have a hunch they are Messai's next targets, trying to draw us out. We need to warn them now, because my guess is, AMPP will show up at their homes tonight."

"Hans, we have to call all of them right now! Bruno and Mila, your families will be next."

Both couples got on their phones at once, calling every family member they could. When they got no answer from some, they could not help but think they may have faced the same fate as the others during the night. They had no problem convincing those who had become believers in Jesus, but trying to tell the others was an impossible task.

They spoke to some they had not yet told about their newfound faith. A few listened and agreed to go to the website, watch the pastor's video and hear from Blake and Beth Thompson. They also agreed to speak with the others who were believers and go with them to some place safe. They all had friends with whom they could stay, but they did not want to put them in danger either. Maybe a night or two would not hurt.

They would remind unbelieving friends that Hans and Heidi were on Messai's Most Wanted list and fled the country. They would also point out that the two families murdered the previous night were members of their families. That should be enough to convince them.

Family members who were followers of Jesus would get with members of their groups, which had grown so large, meeting required multiple houses. They may even have to move on from there, knowing AMPP could also track down anyone who had associated with them. They understood the need for a safe place in Germany, but were not yet aware of how or where to find it.

The sad thing was that some family members who had not followed Jesus laughed them off and saw the killings as coincidental. The group knew those would not likely live to see many more days, if any. They prayed that somehow they would put their faith in Jesus, but saw little chance of that happening. They pleaded with them to check out the website or talk to some others, to no avail. They had done all they could do.

• • • •

AMPP did not care whether they were members of the Smyrnians. They only cared about their relationship to Hans and Heidi Meier and Bruno and Mila Fromm. And they would die as the others had. That they would die without knowing Jesus was enough cause for grief, yet they could not allow that to control their thinking. They had tried their best and would now wait and watch the news again tomorrow morning, knowing full well what they may see and hear.

CHAPTER 7

Messai was gleeful as he sat again with the captain of his security forces.

"Well done, Captain!" he gushed. "Last night was a great beginning in Germany. You are sure no one has a clue what happened or associates any of it with me or AMPP?"

"No one, sir. Everyone from police officers to politicians are hypothesizing about who may have carried out the attacks. Most are placing the blame on gangs or drug dealers, assuming the families crossed them and faced execution. They suspect it may extend to other members of the families in days to come."

"Perfect!" Messai almost shouted. "Their speculations play right into our hands. Take out more family members tonight. You have all of their addresses, don't you?"

"All of them, sir. Do not worry. The news will abound with reports of another gruesome night for the families of Hans and Heidi Meier."

"Good, good. Now, have you identified family members of the other Smyrnians?"

"We have encountered some problems with that, sir. Blake Thompson was an only child. His parents died in the World Trade Center attacks on September 11, 2001. He never married before his marriage to Miss Jennings..." His boss interrupted him in a loud voice.

"How many times do I have to remind you, Captain? They are not married! Only marriages licensed and recognized by the state are legal!"

"Yes, sir. I forgot that. Please forgive me. What I meant to say was, he has no children. We have identified maternal and paternal grandparents, but no one else."

"Then take them out!"

"We can try, Mr. Messai. But it seems he spent no time with either and has no relationship with them. I am not sure that will..." Messai interrupted again.

"What does that have to do with anything, Captain? You need to do more than *try*. Do I need to demote you and move someone else into your place?"

"No, sir. I will do whatever you want me to do. I was only suggesting..."

"I don't care what you were suggesting, Captain. Your job is to carry out my orders. If you cannot do that, perhaps *you* should take their place. How do you feel about that?"

"That will not be necessary, sir. We will search for them and take them out as soon as possible."

"That's more like it. How about the others?"

"Beth's parents disappeared in the *Invasion*. She has never married either," (he made sure *not* to include Blake's name this time) "so we cannot identify any children or family members. It does not appear there is anything we can do with her."

"Other than bring her back to me. You can handle that, can't you, Captain?"

"I admit, sir, that will not be easy. These Smyrnians are slippery. Something always seems to happen that allows them to escape our grasp."

"Perhaps that is the lack of your men's ability to do their job, Captain. Are they slippery, or are the men of AMPP just lax?"

"Sir, your men are efficient at what they do. But remember how she walked away from this house the night of the earthquake? The damage was so severe there was no way to escape, yet she did."

"If you value your job and your life, Captain, you will never speak of that night again!"

"Yes, sir. I am sorry, sir," he groveled. "I will not. Don't worry, we will carry out your orders."

"See that you do, Captain. And make sure the media and people of the world keep thinking the same thing about the reasons for the attacks."

"Yes, sir; your will be done, sir. We have identified family members of the others, too, and where they live. I will have our men at those locations beginning tonight."

"I trust that you will accomplish this task, Captain. Doing so will bring a substantial reward. Failure to do so will result in severe punishment. Do I make myself clear?"

"Yes, sir; very clear, sir."

"Oh, one other thing. Keep an eye out for Smyrnians crawling out of their holes attempting to protect their families. When they emerge, do *not* let them escape this time!"

• • • • •

The stark realization hit every member of the group that their families were also targets of Messai's men, at least those known to be part of the Smyrnians. Each spent the day trying to determine anyone they needed to call or if there was any other way to warn their family.

Some had no one to call. Blake had no contact information for either of his grandparents. He only hoped AMMP would not locate them. Beth was not aware of any relatives either. She and Blake helped the others however needed.

Anders, Evan and Malachi were still unknown to Messai and AMPP, as was Rickie, who remained unable to make calls, anyway. Neither was there any concern yet for Steve and Linda. They were new to the team. And while Ben and Miriam had many friends in New York, their family lived in Israel. Messai was not about to take any chances there.

But then there were John, Kathie, Trey, Ollie, and Amelia. All of them were near the top of his list.

John's children had no communication with him or each other. All three lived in other states. He was not even sure the contact information he had for them was correct, but he would try. Messai had people who would track them down. His skin crawled as he imagined them being executed without knowing Jesus. After his calls failed, he sat alone, dejected. Blake came to him.

"I tried, Blake. None of the numbers I have work. All I can do is check the news tomorrow morning, but I fear what they will report. How can I bear it if what I fear happens?"

"John, don't blame yourself. You did everything possible. A man can't do more than that."

"It's not what I can or can't do now that bothers me, Blake. It is what I *should* have done years ago. My children grew apart from me because I was too busy with my work. It was more important than them. So, I spent no time with them, or their mother. I was never there for their important events and left my wife alone many late nights while I worked in my office. I was an influential man. The world depended on my research, and I had to develop and teach young minds things I now know were lies."

"I never cheated on their mom with another woman, but I gave my time to something other than her: my work. She had every right to leave me. When she did, I threw myself even more into my job at the university. I let my children walk out of my life without trying to have a relationship with them, or my grandkids."

"I wouldn't recognize those kids now if I saw them. I haven't seen them many times, and it has been years since the last time. Now AMPP may slaughter all of them tonight, and I will never lay eyes on them again. I will be in eternity forever without them, and it is my fault." He buried his head in his hands.

"John, don't do that to yourself. None of us can change the past. But we can do something about the present and future. I have an idea. Let's check the website for the list of people who have said 'yes' to Jesus and search for their names. Come on, let's try it. You never know, they may be there!" He was trying to give John hope.

When they walked into the next room, they found Kathie frantically trying to call her son and daughter. She had not seen either of them or her four grandchildren since AMPP killed Doc. She called the next day and told them about his death, but refused to tell them where she was, saying it may put their lives in danger. They blamed her for his death and were angry that she buried him without allowing them to say goodbye. It made them so furious they refused to answer any more of her calls. But now it was urgent. Now their lives *were* in danger; perhaps tonight.

"Please answer," she pleaded as she left another voice message. "Julie, please take my call. This phone is secure. You can't call me, but I will call every few minutes. This is urgent. Please, please answer."

She begged her son to do the same. For an hour, her calls went unheeded. At last, Doc Jr. answered. As a boy, they gave him the moniker, Little Doc. But as an adult standing six feet, two inches tall, he chose his given name, Julian. The family honored that, although it took some getting used to.

"You won't give up, will you mom? You disappear, then call and act like nothing happened. Well, it's not that easy. If there is an emergency, tell me about it. But I imagine this is another of your cockamamie ideas, like burying daddy at the cabin and not telling us until after the fact."

"Julian, please listen. I'm sorry about that, but I had no choice. I understand you didn't like it, but it's what your dad would have wanted. Just please call your sister and tell her I will call you back, then merge the calls. She will listen to you. Someone may kill all of you before this night is over, if you don't listen to me! I am telling you the truth. Please call her. I'll call in ten minutes. Do this for me!"

"I will call her... *mom.*"

He said that with clear disdain in his voice. It was a shame that things had come to this. They were such a close family. Trips out of the country together had been the norm every year after Christmas. They lived close enough that spending time with each other was easy. Holidays, birthday parties and any other excuse they found brought them together. It broke her heart.

She did not expect them to understand all of this. Much of it was still a blur in her own mind. But the peace and joy she discovered was greater than any of that. It changed her husband, too. She ended the call and set the alarm on her phone for ten minutes, then paced the floor and waited.

Ollie and Amelia were on the phone with family members in London. Some, including immediate family, had put their faith in Jesus. They met with other believers and told everyone they could what Jesus had done for them. They believed what Ollie and Amelia said and promised to get away from their homes, taking as many things with them as possible.

Others did not trust in Jesus and disowned them after they joined the Smyrnians. Ollie and Amelia embarrassed them with their actions and dishonored their family names, a big deal for folks in England. They pleaded with those family members to go to the website and watch the pastor's video and Blake and Beth's teachings. Some agreed, but most did not. They did everything they could. Now they would wait and see if any of their homes showed up on the morning news.

Trey did not have a large family, but the entire thing was more difficult for him. He was hiding away less than an hour from most of them. The simple thing would be to bring them to the Shelter, but that may put the entire team at risk and leave their hideout open to potential exposure. He may call them, but he could not tell them where he was. As far as they knew, he may be hundreds or thousands of miles away. His secure phone would not show his location.

He told them about Justin, his deputy friend, and how he had put his faith in Jesus the night before his murder. That alone was dangerous information, making them aware he had been in town on that date. They had learned about his association with the Smyrnians. He was a wanted man who had gone into hiding.

Some asked what had changed him so much. When he told them the danger they were in, most agreed to leave their homes before nightfall and check out the video. He warned them that AMPP may have surveillance on their houses already and said he would be in touch with all of them the next day to confirm their safety.

Most important was for them to watch Blake and Beth's video and do what they said. He hoped they would trust Jesus as their Savior and post it on the website. That gave Trey hope, yet left him sad for those who refused to heed his warning. He knew in his heart he would never see them again. AMPP would come calling. Then they would believe him, but it would be too late.

The ten minutes crawled by for Kathie. She had Julian's number already pulled up. The second her alarm sounded, she touched it and listened to his phone ringing in her ear. Her muscles tense, her heart pounding, she prayed for him to answer. Relief flooded her mind when he did.

"Honey, did you talk to your sister? May I call her now, too?"

"You can call her, mom. But I can tell you she doesn't want to talk to you."

She paid no attention to his warning.

"Hold on. I will get her on the phone and merge the calls."

She put him on hold and touched Julie's number. Yes, she answered!

"Mom, this had better be important..."

She did not let her continue.

"Hold on while I bring your brother back in with us. Whatever you do, do *not* end this call!"

Julie's sigh of frustration caused Kathie to fear she may disconnect. She merged with Julian.

"Can both of you hear me?"

"I can hear you, mom," he said.

"Yes, I've got you too." Julie was rude. "Please get on with it, the kids need to eat."

"Just listen to me. Your lives are in extreme danger *tonight.* Get away from your houses and go to a safe place. You have no time to spare."

"Mom, stop it, okay? You're making no sense. How can you know our lives are in danger since you haven't been around for months?" Her daughter's anger came pouring out like a flood.

"Will you both please listen to me? You know I put my faith in Jesus and joined the Smyrnians."

Julie interrupted her.

"Yes, *mother.* I would love to talk to daddy about that, because I'm sure he didn't do it. He wouldn't. Whatever you did got him killed, and I can never forgive you for that."

That cut Kathie to the core. But she would not allow it to interfere with what she had to do.

"If you'll give me a chance, I will explain all of that to you soon. But there is no time for that now. Listen to me: An AMPP patrol killed your dad. They murdered him in cold blood. If you had seen the way he died... He was ecstatic because he had just put his faith in Jesus and wanted nothing more than to go be with him."

"I realize that makes no sense to you, but it's true. We tried to escape. John Baldwin, Doc's friend, put his life on the line to help us. He and I escaped only because Jesus helped us. Aissa Messai is the enemy, the Antichrist. I know you don't understand that either, but I'll tell you all about it when we see each other."

"Mom..." Julie interrupted again.

It did not deter Kathie. She continued as if Julie had not spoken.

"Messai has his men searching for all of us who are part of the Smyrnians, but they can't find us. So he has ordered them to kill all of our families they can locate. They have already begun."

"Mom," said Julian, "just wait. Do you expect us to believe Aissa Messai would do that? It sounds like he's after you and the others, not us."

"He's trying to flush us out by going after our families. Did you watch the news this morning?"

"Mom, I don't have time for this," shouted Julie.

"Did you see the news this morning?" Her screaming caught them both off guard.

"I did," he uttered. Are you talking about the families executed in Germany?"

"Yes! That's what I am trying to tell you! Hans and Heidi Meier are part of our group. They put their faith in Jesus too, and he has changed their lives! They escaped with some of our team and are here with us. Messai started with their families. Our families are next, and it begins tonight! Please get out!"

"Mom, you're scaring me," Julie whispered. "Do you believe that?"

"I don't just believe it; I know it. Leave; both of you. Go to the cabin. It is small, but you will be safe there. I'll come tonight, if I can, and bring John, and a few others, with me."

She heard Julie telling the kids to get some clothes; they were going to Mama and Papa's cabin. Julian was yelling to his wife to do the same.

"I hope you know what you are talking about, mom," he said. "But after seeing the news, I'm afraid *not* to believe you. I can't take that chance with the kids and Joanie."

Kathie was weeping now.

"Thank you, both. It is urgent that you go *now*. I'll call you to make sure you got there. And please do something else. Go to *smyrnians.com* and watch the video on the site. That is what your dad did, and he would beg you to do it, too. Then, while you're waiting for me, watch some other videos. I'll talk to you about them when I arrive. Promise me you'll do that. I love you both so much and can't wait to see you."

"We will be there, mom," said Julie. "And mom..." She broke into tears. "I'm sorry."

"So am I," said Julian, his voice cracking with emotion, too.

All three wept as the call ended.

Blake and John sat in front of the computer searching for the name *Baldwin.* It was there... hundreds of times. They scrolled until they found it:

Johnathan Baldwin! He had put his faith in Jesus! John sobbed, his body trembling.

"My daughters; look for my daughters." He gave him their names, and Blake typed in the search.

Both were there! One must have believed and contacted the others. They followed Jesus and John did not know! He jumped from the chair and ran around the room, then sat back down. The gigantic smile on his face betrayed the joy in his heart.

"If you can find their contact info, write it down. I need to get in touch with them!"

"Here are their email addresses. You can email one and copy the others. Do it!"

John sat and typed faster than he ever had. The email was short and sweet.

Kids, I just found your names on the Smyrnians website. I can't tell you how happy that makes me! Please reply with your phone numbers. Mine is secure, so you can't call me. But if you reply, I'll call all of you. This is urgent. Your lives are in immediate danger!

He hit *Send* and sat waiting for an answer. He would not leave his seat until it came. In less than five minutes, his son replied.

Dad, the news said you died! Is it really you? Yes, I believed in Jesus and have read his Word every day. It tells me I have to forgive you, and I have done that. Please forgive me too. Here is my number. Give me five minutes to call the girls. Jesus has done the same thing in them he did in me. They will be so glad to hear your voice. Five minutes, dad, then call me!

John was lying face down on the desk, sobbing. Blake held him as he did. "This wasn't a coincidence, John. Jesus did it. He's amazing, isn't he?"

John raised his head and started wiping the tears from his face. "He sure is, Blake. Now, if you will excuse me, I have to call my son."

Evan was moving from room to room, checking on each one as they made calls. Seeing they had all finished, he summoned everyone back together.

"All of you give us a report on your calls. What happened, and what do we still need to do? Is there any way we can help you, or you can help each other?"

Hans and Heidi and Bruno and Mila, along with Ally, started. Their stories were a mixture of sadness and relief. More relatives would die that night, but others had heeded their warning and were moving to safe places. They hoped those who had already put their faith in Jesus would convince them to do that too. Tonight they would do all they could do: sit, wait, and pray.

Ollie and Amelia jumped in next. Their stories were like those of the German group, a blend of hope and fear. They were certain to get news of murdered family members the next morning. But they also hoped to discover that others had turned to Jesus. They asked the group to pray for all of them, knowing they did not need to ask. All of them would pray throughout the night.

Trey related the stories of his calls, some being met with rejection, others with acceptance. All the reports sounded the same. The group talked about how their experience was a microcosm of life. Some people believe in Jesus, while others are unwilling to make that decision. But some reject him, regardless of what they see or hear.

Each of them had family members who would die without Jesus that night, or soon, if they remained unconvinced by watching the news. But some would do as they had done: surrender their lives to Jesus and gain eternal life.

John was eager to share his story. It was a miraculous one that led to a celebration in the group. After finding the names of all three of his kids on the website, he called and spoke with them. Not only had they heeded his warning and chosen to get away from their houses, but they had already believed in Jesus. And he had restored his relationship with them. Other than the day he said "yes" to Jesus, this was the greatest day of his life.

They would all find safe places for the night and days ahead. He would stay in contact with them and hoped to bring them to the Shelter soon. This led to a brief discussion of the place being too small for everyone's family and the need to find other locations. They would resolve that issue later. More pressing issues faced them now. One was hearing from Kathie. She held back until last with something on her mind she needed to say.

Kathie cried as she told of her son's and daughter's animosity toward her and how difficult it was to get them to accept what she was telling them. The group sat in silence, feeling her pain as she talked. But then she got to the rest of the story. Her kids believed her at last, after she referred to the news earlier that morning. Her son saw the stories about the murders of Hans' brother and family and Heidi's mom and dad. That had jarred them to reality and caused them to prepare to get away fast. Then she got to the part she needed to tell the team.

"I told them to go to the cabin on our property where John and I buried Doc, and I will meet them there, hopefully tonight. They know it well and can get there soon. It should be a safe place for them. John, I need you to go with me. If others of you want to go, that might be a good thing. Maybe I shouldn't ask this, but Blake and Beth, would you consider going? They promised to watch the pastor's video and as many other videos as they can before I get there. If the two of you can talk to them in person, it may help."

"I agree, but how will we get there? Trey flew me to Wichita before, but he can't do that now."

Before John said more, or Trey volunteered, Kathie spoke up again.

"It would be far too risky for Trey to fly us. We need to travel the old-fashioned way: by car. We can make it in four hours driving the speed limit, if we don't stop or slow down for anything."

"That's just as dangerous, Kathie," said Beth. "Messai has AMPP searching for us everywhere. If they spot us or pull us over, we're goners."

"We can take the military van," Kathie, ever the idea woman, said matter-of-factly. "They won't be expecting it. Evan can drive since no one knows he's one of us, or even who he is. The rest of us can lie down in the seats and stay out of sight until after dark."

"I'm in!" said Evan. "It's dangerous, but it can't be more dangerous than what we just went through."

"Let's go," said John. "We may need to wait until dark. What do the rest of you think?"

"I'll tell you what I think!" The old before Jesus Bruno, *B.J.* as he liked to call it, came out. "You're putting yourselves *and* the rest of us in danger. This trip is not worth the risk!"

"Bruno!" Kathie didn't pull any punches either. "We have to go. I promised them we would be there. Besides, they may need us. If nothing else, we need to tell them about Jesus!"

"They can watch the video," said the big man, not holding back. "A lot of other people have done that. If the cabin is as safe as you say, they'll be fine for now. You can call and tell them you'll be there in a few days. But don't risk our safety, and yours, by taking a foolish trip!"

Mila did what she often did. She placed her hand on his arm and whispered to him.

"Dear, this is not your decision. If Kathie feels like she needs to go and the others agree with her, we have no right to tell them otherwise. Jesus will protect them."

Her husband appeared to feel chastised again. He calmed down and took nearly a minute before he spoke. Everybody else in the room was quiet too, not knowing what to say.

"You're right, Mila, as always. I'm sorry, Kathie. You need to go. We'll be here praying for all of you, and for your family."

"Thank you for understanding, Bruno." In an uncharacteristic move, she walked over and hugged him. Then she hugged Mila and thanked her too.

"Let's get ready to leave," said Evan, standing to his feet. "The only thing we need to pack for this trip is food!"

He grinned as he said that. It elicited a light chuckle from the others, a chuckle they all needed.

Blake, Beth and John started making preparations to leave at once. They would be on the road by 6:30 and planned to arrive at the cabin no later than 10:30. It was too urgent to wait until dark. The group prayed for their safety and for the safety of Kathie's children and grandchildren. They would continue to make calls, but beyond that, their only options were to wait and pray.

CHAPTER 8

Alexander and Elizabeth heard what happened in Germany and realized family members would continue to die. They stayed in contact with Ben, but did not allow those things to deter them from their work. Spreading the word remained their priority. A few Jews in Israel had turned to faith in Jesus because of their efforts. They loved seeing those people register on the website. But the number was increasing slowly. They needed Ben in Israel.

New believers hesitated to tell others about their experience. Once in a while, they sent people to the website to watch the video and listen to Alexander and Elizabeth's story. That and Ben's teaching helped small pockets of Jews believe. Still, most who believed did not speak to anyone about their faith.

Prior to each of Ben's sessions, a video showed the story of Jesus appearing to him and his powerful encounter with him that night in his home. He followed that by telling about his Jewish upbringing, how he had practiced strict adherence to the Mosaic Law and taught his children to do the same.

The passage from Josephus that Blake read to him that night always came next. Then he proved from the Old Testament prophecies how God told the Jews again and again he was sending his son as the Messiah. From the New Testament, he explained how Jesus fulfilled every prophecy. The session ended with telling them how to put their faith in Jesus and invite him into their lives. But as much as he enjoyed that, he wanted more than anything to go speak on site in Israel.

Though few, the stories from Jews who believed brought him great joy. Both he and the Ben Ezras warned them about Messai and the dangers they faced for the rest of the Tribulation. One thing became apparent: Jews seemed to fly under the radar. No networks reported about them turning to

Jesus, or being murdered, like other believers. Ben searched the Bible, trying to figure out why. The answer was there, if he could find it. He needed to be in Israel to reach his people.

Ben did not oppose Kathie's trip, nor the group going with her. That surprised them all. But as the time drew near for them to leave, he insisted on giving specific instructions for staying safe, including what to do in the event AMPP discovered them.

"Ben," Blake said with a reassuring smile, "I don't mean for this to sound bad, but the five of us have far more experience with this than you. I think we can handle it."

"I trust you, but we can't afford to lose you. That would damage the work everywhere."

"Now Ben, should that happen, those new believers around the world wouldn't allow the work to stop. I promise you they won't give up the fight until the day Jesus returns."

Since his warnings were getting him nowhere, Ben gave up and wished them well.

"Stay in contact with us. My one requirement is, call me every thirty minutes. You're leaving at 6:30, so I'll expect your first call at 7:00 sharp, the next one at 7:30, and so forth till you arrive."

"Every thirty minutes? Okay, okay, if you insist, boss. I listen and obey." Blake bowed his head in submission. He was having fun, and Ben went along with it.

"You got that right! I *am* still your boss and don't you forget it!" Ben feigned sternness.

"Enough of that, you two," said Beth. "It's almost time for us to leave. I want to check in with the others one more time before we go."

John said, "Let me go first. I want to share this with everyone. My son and daughters are meeting at a remote cabin in the mountains of Colorado. It belonged to a family friend who sold it, then the new owners deserted it. It has been sitting empty for a few years. Johnathan used it off and on as a getaway spot for himself. AMPP has no way of tying it to him, so they should be safe there."

"It gave me an idea when he told me that. Why didn't we think about the mountains? They offer some exceptional places to hide. AMPP will never find us in a lot of those remote locations. And Johnathan knows the Rockies like the back of his hand. It's something we should consider."

"I love that John," said Ally. "Maybe we can visit. I'd love to see the Rocky Mountains! But daddy, it reminds me of something else." She turned to Bruno. "The Bavarian Alps! Perhaps you need to stop considering a bunker and start looking for a place in the Alps."

"Outstanding idea!" Hans said in a louder voice than normal. "There are places for sale in the mountains that cost far less than a 3,000-square foot bunker. Friends of my grandparents own vacation homes there. If we can arrange an anonymous cash purchase, we can buy one anytime. And you can find them in very remote locations. That's what we need."

"You guys can talk about that," said Evan. "If I'm right, it's time for us to leave. Let's load up."

"Ten minutes," Kathie proclaimed. "We can't be late. By the time we get to the van, it will be time to go."

"Go, and may Jesus be with you," said Malachi. He had stayed quiet. "I wish I could go, too."

"I know you do, Malachi, but your time will come again. Nobody is better than you at what you do. We will need your skills soon. I recognize the danger, but we can't stay holed up in these bunkers. We have to get back out there, and this trip begins that. We'll know more after we see how it goes. Now, let's take off. John and Kathie, you know where we are going, so you can keep Evan straight if he gets lost. Beth and I will gladly bunk down together in the back seat."

"Blake!" Beth said, slapping his arm.

"Look honey, they know we're married. I'm just having a little fun. But I meant what I said, we call dibs on the back seat!"

She slapped him again, winked and said, "You guys heard him. The back seat belongs to us!"

They jumped in the vehicle, with Evan behind the wheel. No time remained to hear how things went with the other families. They took off for Kansas, unaware of what awaited them there.

•   •   •   •   •

"Sir, we have located the addresses of the families of every Smyrnian, except those of Beth Jennings and Blake Thompson," the captain said, speaking to his boss on the phone. "She has no family left. His paternal grandparents died in the earthquake, although I doubt he is aware of that. The maternal grandparents travel the world and are seldom at home. We cannot determine their location."

"Find them!" he roared.

"Sir, we did everything possible, but we will keep trying."

"See that you do, Captain! Are you prepared for another all-out assault tonight?"

"Yes, sir. We have AMPP patrols stationed around the world and ready to move on every single residence at midnight. We will report after carrying out each mission, beginning in Germany again, then in London and moving to the United States."

"Excellent! You will love your bonus. And a promotion is in order for you, Captain. I assure you of those two things. Be sure your men do their jobs and leave behind no evidence of our presence, or survivors who can tell what happened. And remember Captain, Beth Jennings belongs to me."

"As you wish, sir. We will do it just as you command." He ended the call and prepared to lead the mission he most wanted to direct: John Baldwin's son. Baldwin had eluded them more than once, and he had endured Messai's anger, to the point of near execution himself for their failure. They had proclaimed the man dead in Kansas, then discovered later he had somehow survived the truck crash and fiery explosion. So did Doc Sanderson's wife, who was riding with him.

Baldwin was hiding the Smyrnians somewhere. The professor was the one who purchased the bunkers from Sanderson. If he performed this task tonight, it should bring the man out of hiding. He had special plans for the son and his family. It would be like none of the other executions. His men would torture them before they died, video the entire experience, and send it to Messai later. "The boss will love that," he breathed.

Evan, John, Kathie, Blake and Beth were an hour into their trip, which had been uneventful. Blake made the first call to Ben right on time. Now it was time for call number two, but it would be late.

Kathie looked very concerned. She spoke with both of her children right after they got into the van. Julian was ten minutes away from the cabin, and Julie was not far behind him. They assured her they would go straight there, and she told them her next call would come in forty-five minutes, giving them time to make it. That call went unanswered. She had kept trying each of their phones since, but every call went to voicemail.

"Something's wrong. They were expecting my calls, so they would not let them go. You don't think..." She stopped without finishing the question.

"Now Kathie, we can't assume anything." Beth attempted to ease her mind. "Is the phone reception good at the cabin?"

"It's excellent, isn't it, John?"

"It was for us. I had no trouble calling Trey from there."

"It's possible that a tower may be down, or there's some other interruption in service," offered Blake. But he understood that had little chance of making Kathie feel any better about the situation. His concern was greater than he showed.

"I suppose anything is possible, but I have a terrible feeling about this. I'm not sure I can bear losing them now, not after what just happened. Maybe they're safe at the cabin and watching the video right now. That may be why they aren't answering." She tried to force a smile.

"I wish we could get there faster," said Evan from the driver's seat. "But I'm afraid to drive too far over the speed limit. We can't take a chance on getting pulled over because a cop would recognize the four of you right away."

"Just keep driving like you are, Evan. We can't do anything until we get to the cabin." John looked at Kathie with obvious concern for her as he spoke. Then he slid over next to her and held her in his arms. They felt comfortable sitting up now. Darkness had come and concealed all of them as they rode in the van. She snuggled close to him and hung on as if she feared letting go. The next three hours would be the longest 180 minutes of her life.

Blake made the call at 7:40, understanding full well what Ben would say when he answered.

"Blake, you're ten minutes late! Don't do that to us back here. It causes our minds to run wild with all kinds of bad thoughts."

"I'm sorry, Ben, but I need to tell you what is going on."

He told him about Kathie's dilemma, not getting answers when she called her children. He kept the phone off speaker, so Kathie could not listen to their conversation.

"Can Kathie hear me?" Ben whispered.

"No," he breathed, not wanting to give away where Ben was going with this.

"I fear for her family's lives. AMPP is clever. My concern is they will not only send a patrol to their houses but also put one at Doc and Kathie's place.

They may have stayed there off and on in case any of you showed up. If I'm right, you're driving straight into a trap."

"We'll see how it goes when we get there," Blake talked low to make sure Kathie didn't hear their conversation. Then he added, "I hope they've already watched the video and believed in Jesus too! If they have, we'll throw a party! Thank you, Ben."

"Be careful, Blake. Remember, Messai wants Beth. Don't let them get their hands on her, and don't get yourselves captured or killed!"

"Okay, Ben. Will do. I'll call again at 8:30, since it's almost 8:00 now. Perhaps she will connect with them by then." With that, he was off the phone and turning his attention to Kathie again.

"Blake! Blake! Don't do that to me." Ben looked at the others and said, "I'm tempted to call him right back. I can't believe he ended the call like that."

"What did he say?" asked Anders.

When Ben told them about his conversation with Blake, their hearts also told them things were not okay at the cabin. Blake's next call was thirty minutes away. They hoped it would bring news that Kathie talked to her family and all was well. But none of them expected to hear that.

"Anders, I think you and I should go. They'll need backup," said Malachi.

"If you go, I'm going with you!" chimed in Ally.

"We don't know where we're going." Anders was always in, but he wasn't sure about this one.

"Nobody is going anywhere," Ben demanded. "We're all staying right here."

It was obvious he meant business and understood their lives would be in danger if they went. They felt that too, but Smyrnians fight for each other. If the others needed them, they would be there.

"All we need to do is call and ask for directions. And we can come up with a plan as we talk. I'm going," Malachi said with undeterred determination in his voice.

"There's no need to call and ask for directions," said Trey. "I've been there, remember? I went to get John and Kathie and flew them back here. Military guys never forget where we've been on a mission. We commit everything about it to memory in case we need to return later. So, I can get you to the cabin. That means I'm going with you."

Ben was not ready to give up.

"Then, just what do you plan to drive, Trey? The others took the van, and they recognize your truck. They also know the car you guys drove from New York, Anders. You wouldn't even get out of Missouri without getting stopped. All of you need to forget this crazy idea!"

Steve walked into the room and caught enough of the conversation to know what was going on.

"We can take our Navigator, and I'll drive," he said. "They won't do anything to Linda and me. Besides, it will give us room if some of Kathie's family need to ride back with us. I would say that's a good enough reason for us to go. We may be new to this group, but I promise you we're not ones to stand back and do nothing. And we're not leaving our comrades there to fight alone. They told us about Jesus; the least we can do is to be there for them. Ben, I mean no disrespect, but we need Trey if he's the only one who has been to the cabin. He can hide in the back seat."

At that point, Ben gave up. He saw he was losing the argument.

"Well, if you're going, get a move on. You already have an hour and a half to make up."

"Trust me, I can make up time," said Steve. "I always try to drive the speed limit, but when there's an emergency, I can put the pedal to the metal with the best of them. And this qualifies as an emergency in my mind!"

"I promise he's telling the truth," said Linda. She entered the room right after Steve. "You will see when you ride with him," she said, glancing at the other four.

"Grab some food and go to the bathroom if anyone needs to. We won't have time to stop."

"You're a little behind on the food," smiled Ally, holding up two bags. "Time's wasting. Let's roll!"

"Can you guys take care of Rickie until we get back? Steve says he's stable and doing well."

Miriam assured them she was an effective nurse and capable of caring for their fallen teammate. Besides, she had Hans and Heidi to help her. Or more likely, she would help them.

"We can handle that. If you're determined to make this trip, go on!" Ben surrendered, but deep inside he was glad they were going. He feared not only for Kathie's family, but for the others too.

They sprinted out the door, loaded up, and headed down the lane. They wasted no time and were pulling out at 8:00. When they reached the main road, Steve was careful to make sure nothing was in sight before pulling out and heading north toward Springfield. Linda reached into the floorboard in front of her and held up two red emergency lights.

"We'll use these if we need to," she said, smiling. "Cops will never stop us if they believe Steve has an emergency call and needs to be somewhere fast. They know him well in Missouri and Kansas, so they should work in both states. He has performed several emergency procedures at a hospital in Wichita. Even if we get stopped, with hospitals just reopening and running behind on emergencies and overdue surgeries, they won't doubt that someone needs his help. Trust me, they'll let us go. But you guys will need to stay out of sight."

"Cool!" Anders beamed. "I wasn't aware that doctors could use emergency lights. That makes we wish I had gone to medical school. They're not as kind to cameramen."

Now that they were on the way, Malachi called Blake. They had a plan to put in place.

John was trying to keep Kathie calm. She feared the worst, so they could not get there fast enough for her. When Blake's phone rang, it startled her, causing her to jump. Her nerves were on edge.

He looked at it and said, "It's Malachi," then answered.

"What do you mean you're on the way to help us? How are you going to do that if you just left? You're an hour and a half behind us."

"Don't you worry about that. We'll get there as fast as we can. Steve is driving his SUV and has an MD plate and emergency lights, if we need to use them. If you guys are driving the speed limit like you need to be, we can make up a lot of that time. He has the hammer down!"

"I'm glad you're coming, even if I don't think it's wise. Who's with you? If things happen to not be good, we'll need all the help we can get."

"Anders, Ally, Trey, Steve and Linda, and me."

"Ally came? That's too dangerous. She's just as wanted as Beth and me. And Trey? He didn't need to come either. They want him dead or alive."

Ally spoke up. "You guys need us, and Kathie's family needs us. We were not staying behind!"

"And they had to have me," Trey chimed in. "Don't forget, I'm the only other one of us who's been to the cabin! They can't find it without me."

"Well, you're already on the way, so I can't talk you out of it now. Malachi, do you have a plan? You've never been there. John and I have been to PSI, but I've only been to the business. He has been to the cabin, so we need to hear from him, Trey, and Kathie. They all know where the cabin is and how to get to it. I'll put this phone on speaker so we can all be in on the conversation."

"I have an idea," said John. "Kathie, is there a place you and I can drop Blake, Beth and Evan off somewhere near the property that won't be a long walk to the cabin? They can hide in the woods and wait for the others to arrive. If all is well with your family, we can call and tell them so they can come and join us. If that is the case, we'll all be happy!"

"I doubt there's a need for that. Regardless of what has happened, if AMPP sees you and me driving in, I'm sure they'll all head to the cabin to welcome us. The trails in the woods should be unguarded. They can drive to a spot near the cabin, park, and walk in from there."

"I like that," said Malachi.

"You still need to drop us off," said Blake. "We can't go to the cabin with you."

"Trey, you remember how to get to the airstrip you flew into with John, don't you?"

"Sure."

"We'll drop Blake, Beth, and Evan off there. You and Blake can stay in touch so they'll know when you're getting close."

"How far is it from the property?" asked Evan. "We need to get there fast."

"Around twenty minutes, if my memory serves me well."

"That's right, John," Trey agreed.

"If it's twenty, we'll make it in fifteen," said Steve.

"Okay, we agree. We'll leave these three there and head on to the cabin."

"We'll work on a plan," Malachi announced. "It looks like we'll gain close to an hour on you guys. But that still puts our ETA half an hour, or more, after you. It's not safe for Kathie and John to be at the cabin by themselves an hour before the rest of us. AMPP works fast. I hope we're making this trip for nothing and your family is safe, Kathie. But as a matter of precaution, we need to arrive sooner than that. Steve, can you do anything about that?"

"I can try," he said. "But not being on the Interstate, I'm not sure how much more I can do."

"Do your best, but stay safe," Kathie uttered, with a lot of uncertainty.

Both parties drove on toward their destination. Steve looked at the people behind him and said, "Hold on. We need to close this gap all we can." They could tell he was serious, so they held on.

•　　•　　•　　•　　•

AMPP patrols had carried out systematic executions in Germany and London. The news would reach the Meiers, Fromms and Bartons the next morning. They knew it was coming and had prepared themselves as much as they could to receive it.

The news had already reached Aissa Messai. Some parts left him satisfied, while others resulted in rage toward the Smyrnians. Alone in his mansion, the rage spilled out with a vengeance.

They know what we are doing. They are onto us, but it will not stop us! We will hunt them down!

Lightning flashed around the room as it had often done before. Demonic beings flew in and out, screeching and expressing his fury with howls indecipherable to human beings. Hell was raging, but it seemed to appease Messai's anger and bring it under control. After calming down, he picked up his phone and called the trusted captain of his security forces.

"Yes, sir. What is it?"

"It seems we have a problem, Captain."

"Well, sir, I am aware of the executions overseas and of those families who escaped our grasp this time. That is not something I planned to bother you with until tomorrow morning. We have many more missions to carry out tonight. You will be glad to learn I am leading a team so I can carry out one of those myself."

"Be sure you do, Captain. If the Smyrnians got word of planned attacks and warned their families in Germany and England, I feel sure they also warned their families in the United States."

"Do you want me to give the order to move in at all locations, sir?"

"No, just keep guard at every house until midnight and make sure no one leaves. If any of them left, you cannot change that at this point. Which mission are you planning to carry out yourself?"

"I planned to surprise you with the news, sir, but if you insist, I will tell you now."

"I insist, Captain."

"Yes, sir. I am stationed outside the home of John Baldwin's son. Baldwin has escaped my grasp too many times, and I hate him almost as much as you do. I will get him sometime, but tonight I will make him pay with the lives of his son, daughter-in-law, and grandchildren."

"See to it you do that, Captain. And report to me the moment you finish."

"You can count on that, sir."

"I trust you, Captain. Do not let me down. And start searching for those who escaped us this time. Locate them and finish the jobs."

"We will get on that first thing tomorrow morning, sir."

"Thank you, Captain. Do not let them get away. And, Captain?"

"Yes, sir?"

"Keep an eye out for Smyrnians. They will pop up eventually. Make sure they do not escape."

"It will be our pleasure to take care of them, sir. And you will be the first to know when we do."

• • • • •

Julian was the first to arrive at the cabin with Joanie and the kids. Everything appeared normal. They left the brush cleared from the trail that led in so Julie's family would not need to move it again. Joanie unlocked the door and turned on the lights, then went to help carry in their things. Julian put on a pot of coffee. She tried to figure out how eight of them, plus their mom and whoever she was bringing, would all fit in the small cabin. The kids ran outside to play in the woods, as always. She joined her husband in the kitchen.

"Julian, do you think your mom is right about this? She spoke with such urgency on the phone."

"I believe her, Joanie," he said as he poured two cups of coffee. "I've never heard her that upset and demanding before. It's not like her."

"I agree. I could hear her yell all the way across the room. It sent chills down my spine. Julian, this scares me. If she's right, we can only run from AMPP so long. Patrols are located everywhere, all over the world."

"You mean, in places like Germany?"

"Yes! They found those people. Do you really think they know who we are and where we live."

"I'm sure they do. But tonight, they're going to our house to find us. We're safe here, for now. Let's take our coffee out on the porch and wait for Julie and her crew to make it."

They walked outside and sat on the porch swing. It was a beautiful evening, with sunset getting near. Something occurred to him.

"They know about this place too, so now I wonder if we're safe here. I bet mom didn't think about that."

"Stop it, Julian. You're frightening me." She lay her head on his shoulder.

A sudden distraction interrupted the moment.

"There comes Jeff's truck," he said. "No one could mistake it. If anyone is listening, they'll know for sure someone is driving back here. Kids, your Aunt Julie and Uncle Jeffrey are coming!"

They came running as fast as their legs would carry them, excited more than anything that their cousins were there. This was nothing more than a trip to Mama and Papa's house and a night in the cabin for them. Jeffrey pulled up, honking the horn and waving. The kids jumped out and ran toward their cousins, ready to run and play in the woods.

"Kids, all four of you, get back here. We're all going in the cabin right now! You shouldn't be out here by yourselves."

Julie's concern showed on her face and in her voice.

"Now Julie," said Jeffrey, "don't be so strict with them. We've had them cooped up in the truck for a few hours. They just need to romp a little while with their cousins. They're old enough to take care of themselves, so you can't keep treating them like babies at their age. Kids, stay close by so your mom won't worry."

"No, not close by. Get our stuff. We're *all* going in the cabin." Julie spoke in a firm voice.

"Come on kids," said Joanie. "I brought games for you to play inside. Besides, it is getting dark."

They walked inside as Julian and Jeffrey put their bags in the bedroom and returned to join their wives in the living room. The kids had already broken out a board game on the kitchen table and forgotten all about playing outside.

"Mom wanted us to watch a video on that website, *smyrnians.com.* I had trouble accepting that she would get mixed up in that, until she told us about dad," said Julie.

"That reminds me," Julian interrupted. "We didn't look for the place she buried dad."

Julie was demanding. "We can do that in the morning. Tonight, we're staying where we are."

Jeffrey rolled his eyes at Julian and Joanie with his head to one side so she would not see him.

"Okay, since we're inside for the evening, we may as well make it a movie night and watch that video. Did anyone look for popcorn in the cabinets?"

"Jeffrey, stop making fun of this. Mom was dead serious. I believe our lives are in danger, and we need to act like it. Now, I'm getting my tablet so we can pull up that website and see the video. Mom wanted us to watch it before she gets here."

"Why are you suddenly so into what your mom says?" he asked as she walked into the bedroom to retrieve her tablet. "She is the one who went off the deep end, remember?"

Joanie joined the conversation. "We thought she lost her mind, but if what she said to Julian and Julie is right, it sounds like she may have found it."

Julie returned with her iPad, held down the power button and waited for it to come on. She was eager to go online and pull up *smyrnians.com.*

A loud rapping at the door startled them. The kids yelled, "Mama!" and jumped up from the table.

"Sit down," Julie mumbled. She looked at Julian and said, "Mom couldn't get here that fast. She still had three hours to go the last time we talked."

"This is Aissa Messai's Peace Patrol. Open the door, or we are coming in!"

"Kids, come here!"

Julie just got the words out before the door crashed open. The kids ran screaming into their parents' arms. Four AMPP men burst inside, armed and dead serious about their intentions.

"This is private property. I need to see some identification," demanded the leader of the patrol. "Now! All of you!"

The four of them produced their driver's licenses. A member of the patrol took them and looked them over, then walked toward the patrol leader.

"Well, sir, look what we have here," he gloated, handing them to the other to see for himself.

"Call the patrols waiting at their houses. Tell them they need not worry about their jobs tonight. We'll take care of things for them right here. They can take the night off, go out on the town, and have a little fun," he smirked. Then, looking at the four adults and four children huddled with each other before them, he turned his attention back to them.

"We've been watching this property since the night your mommy and Baldwin got away from us. The Boss figured she might show up here again someday. We never guessed she'd be crazy enough to do that, but we've enjoyed hanging out in the house and partying in your daddy's *man cave*." He smirked again. It was clear he wanted to relish this situation for a while.

"Oh yes, your *daddy*." He drew that word out as he grinned. "We have plenty of time to carry out these executions. You're not going anywhere, so let me tell you about that night. Then we'll finish this job, boys, and head back to the house and get some sleep."

The group sneered at Doc and Kathie Sanderson's family, sitting terror stricken before them.

"I wish your *mommy* was here." He drew that word out too, mocking them. When he did, he glimpsed Julie glancing at Julian. "Wait. Is your mommy coming?"

"No," Julie whispered.

"We don't even know where she is." Julian tried to cover for his sister's mistake.

"How about it…" he looked at the identifications again. "How about it, Joanie… Jeffrey? Is she coming? Did she call you and tell you to meet her here?"

The kids started crying. One of them said, "You leave my mama alone!" He tried to pull away from his mom and run at the man.

"She *is* coming!" beamed the AMPP man. "Kathie Sanderson is returning to the scene of the crime. I will tell the boss he was right *after* we finish our job tonight. And you know, I think we will wait for her to get here so she can watch each of you die in front of her eyes, starting with the kids. Besides, this has to happen right at midnight. She and Baldwin made fools of us and almost got us killed for letting them get away. They say paybacks are rough. Well, she will get paid back tonight. The only thing that would make it better would be Baldwin coming with her."

He saw something in their eyes that told him he was right.

"He is coming too! How did we get so lucky? We get to kill two little birdies with one stone, so to speak. Or make that ten little birdies, counting all of you. The boss will reward us big for this night, men." His grin was devilish and reeked of bloodlust and greed.

Jeffrey spoke up as he finished that statement.

"I bet your boss won't pay you as much as you deserve. If you let us go, I'll give you a cool million, and we'll disappear. As far as he knows, we'll be dead, and you'll be rich. All you have to do is let us go. We won't go back to our homes. We'll move, change our identities, fade away, and he will never find out."

One man walked behind Jeffrey and slammed the butt of his rifle into his neck and upper back, knocking him forward, leaving him stunned and slumped over the sofa.

"Jeffrey!" screamed Julie, reaching down to grab him. "Why did you do that?" she demanded. "You're going to kill us, anyway. Why do you have to torture him first?"

"That, my dear, is an excellent idea. Torture. Yes, we will do that. Before your *mommy* sees all of you die, she can watch us torture you until you beg to die."

Julie was crying now. "Please, please let us go. I promise we won't tell."

"Shut up!" the man yelled. "Now sit back and listen so I can tell you a story. It's called, 'The night Doc Sanderson died.' It is a splendid tale of betrayal and murder. And maybe we'll take you out one at a time to look at his grave. We found that when we located this cabin. And yes, we dug him up to confirm it was him, then put him back."

"It gives me great joy to tell you that my men in this group were part of the patrol that killed him. We don't know who fired the fatal shot, but it was one of these outstanding men of Aissa Messai's Peace Patrol. They chased your mommy and daddy and John Baldwin as they tried to escape. They had no choice but to fire at them. I'm sure you understand they were just doing their jobs. We must keep the peace by wiping out those who threaten peace and prosperity in the world. The Smyrnians hide from us, forcing us to take out their families too."

His wicked grin revealed he knew it was all a sham. But it was clear they enjoyed their jobs and were looking forward to taking care of another one tonight. Only pure evil could enjoy killing so much.

CHAPTER 9

The two groups of Smyrnians continued making their way toward Wichita, and the cabin on Doc and Kathie's property. Neither group was aware of what was happening there, though gripped by fear of what may be. Evan was driving along, the cruise control set on the military van to make sure they did not exceed the speed limit. They could take no chances of getting stopped by law enforcement or an AMPP patrol.

But in the Navigator miles behind them, Steve drove at breakneck speed, causing the others with him to hang on for dear life. Anders told them he thought his prayer life was strong until now. On this trip, it had grown, thanks to Steve's driving.

Hour number three of the trip arrived for Group One. Blake placed his *every thirty minutes* call to Ben. Reporting in was a necessity for both him and them. This time Malachi joined the call again so the two groups could try to come up with a plan. But what if their fear of what was happening at the cabin was true? It was hard to grasp how any plan could help them overcome AMPP and save Kathie's children and grandchildren.

And they may as well include the lives of her, John, and perhaps all of them. To make their suspicions seem even more possible, Kathie's continued calls had all gone unanswered until Blake convinced her to stop calling. His concern was, if AMPP was there, her calls would give away that she, or someone, was on their way. She did not want to, but she stopped.

"Hello Ben. Hang on while I bring Malachi into the call."

Ben waited impatiently, as he had not even gotten one word in before Blake put him on hold.

"Malachi, hold on as I get Ben merged back in."

He made the connection, and the discussion began. All three men had their phones on speaker so everyone else could hear. Those in the military van, the group in Steve's SUV, and the ones who remained at the Shelter all needed to give input.

"Where are you guys, Blake?" asked Ben. He was stationed at Command Central, so it was up to him to maintain the contact and location information of both vehicles. Communication was vital at this point. Should either lose connection, the others must know where they were at last contact.

"I estimate we're about an hour and fifteen minutes from the airstrip. How about you, Malachi?"

Trey fielded this question.

"Factoring in the way Steve is driving, I would guess an hour more than that. That means, first, you guys need to pray for us like crazy. AMPP may not get the chance to kill us if Steve keeps driving like this! But second, it means we're gaining ground on you. If Steve can keep this up, we could gain even more time and be only thirty or forty minutes behind you."

"Don't slow down, Steve!" yelled John from the lead vehicle. "We need you there as fast as possible. Kathie and I are going in, no matter what. But we want backup soon after we do."

"Malachi, what are you thinking?" asked Ben. "I can sense those wheels spinning inside your head. Any ideas what you intend to do?"

"We've been talking," Malachi said. "We have some thoughts, but nothing concrete. How about you guys, Blake?"

"Same here. Let's share what we've come up with and try to agree on a plan for when we get to the cabin. We can't hesitate or be in doubt at that point. A strategy must be in place, and we must set it in motion the minute we roll in."

"Some things are obvious," Malachi continued. "We can't just drive in. They would hear us or see our lights. We need to walk in."

John interrupted. "Incorrect, Malachi. We can drive a long way into the woods and park, leaving a five-minute walk to the cabin, with no one hearing or seeing us."

"Thank you, John," Trey said from the SUV, his tone revealing his frustration. "I've been saying that, but no one is listening. They can't understand what it's like until they see it for themselves."

Ben attempted to take control of the conversation.

"I've been listening to what all of you are saying. Based on that, here is what you need to do. I hope things are well with Kathie's family and you don't have to worry about any of this. But we are all aware that you must have a plan, in case you need it. We may have to keep talking until Evan gets to the airstrip, but that's okay. At least we will know what you are doing by then."

"Ben!" John stopped him in mid-sentence. "You haven't even been to the cabin. How do you propose to come up with the plan? Perhaps you should let us handle that."

"I appreciate that, John," Ben shot back, "but I am seeing the property in my mind. It is almost as if I'm on site. John and Kathie, you go on in, but don't be in a hurry. You don't want the others to be too far behind you. Drive all the way to the cabin and go in, like you are just meeting Kathie's family there, with no clue about anything else."

"If all is well, celebrate with the family and tell the others. Then show them the video, and if they say yes to Jesus, bring them back here. But if AMPP is there, Kathie, I hate to say it this way, and your family is still alive, the two of you can serve as a distraction. You can delay them long enough for the others to arrive."

"But we must be prompt and seamless. The executions are being carried out at midnight. That part I figured out. It will be close to midnight by the time all of you arrive. That means every second counts."

"I hate thinking like this, but I just realized Doc has an arsenal of weapons in the house. If AMPP hasn't confiscated them, we need to grab them and plenty of ammo. If we end up being too close to midnight, there won't be enough time for John and me to distract them. I don't want to kill anyone, but if it comes down to them or my family, we have to take them out."

"I can handle that!" Trey said with enthusiasm. "I was a marksman in the military, even though I flew fighter jets. If anyone else can handle a gun, they won't stand a chance."

"Count me in on that," said Steve. "I can hit a bullseye from a hundred yards. It will be no problem to take out a few AMPP guys."

"Everybody calm down," Ben said louder than he intended. "No killing unless it is necessary. If you have no choice, do what you have to do. But if possible, try to get the jump and turn the tables on them. They've burst in on us several times. Maybe it's time we burst in on them."

"Slash their tires before you go in. Disarm them; take their phones. Make sure they understand you could kill them, but you won't because you care about them and Jesus loves them. Then get Kathie's family and get out quick. They can follow you back here."

"I'd love to turn the tables on them for a change, so I like that plan," said Blake. "But it all depends on what time we get to Kathie's place, and on the others making it in time. We can grab the weapons and ammo, walk to the cabin and check things out. If AMPP is there, we will slash their tires and be ready to go. You guys can meet us, and Trey will guide you in."

"I like it," said Malachi. "How many guns can you get, Kathie?"

If Malachi liked it, the others couldn't disagree. It was the best plan they had, so they settled on it.

Kathie answered Malachi's question, sealing the deal for all of them.

"Doc stashed several gun safes in a hidden room off his man cave. He kept them hidden and locked up because he feared someone would break in and steal them. But I can get into the room. Don't worry; we'll bring more than we need. And I can shoot with the best of them too. I just hope we won't need them."

"I hope you're right, Kathie," said John. "But at least we'll be ready if we do."

Plan decided they ended the call and drove on. Shooters among them included Trey, Steve, Evan, Malachi, Kathie, and most surprising, Beth. Her dad taught her well when she was a teenager, and they often had target practice on the farm. If this turned into a shootout, they would be ready.

• • • • •

A loud bang and the van swerved. Evan fought to keep control, jerking the steering wheel first to the left, then back to the right. A tire dropped off the side of the pavement, causing the vehicle to lean perilously to one side on two wheels, feeling like it would roll over. His passengers, tossed around like rag dolls, hung on for dear life. Evan steered onto a small gravel lane and came to a stop one hundred feet down the lane.

"What happened?" yelled Kathie, breaking onto tears. "We don't have time for this!"

"The left front tire blew. Man, I thought we were goners. It took everything I had to keep this thing from turning over."

"You did well, Evan. Let's get out and change that tire. Kathie's right; we don't have time to wait. I hope this thing has a spare." John was up and opening the side door, Blake right behind him.

"The tires on these vans are hard to change," said Blake.

John was at the back, looking underneath at the spare. "How do you get this thing off? And where in the world are the jack and lug wrench?"

"The lug wrench, jack, and rod for removing the spare, are under the passenger seat," said Evan. "My dad drove one of these for a while. I never changed a tire, but I looked it over. I was an inquisitive little guy."

"Stop talking and change the tire!" Kathie yelled. "My entire family is going to die at midnight! We don't have time for you to stand around and talk!"

"Kathie, you can't be sure of that." Beth sat beside her with an arm around her shoulder.

Evan struggled to get the jack and lug wrench out from under the front seat. Blake helped him, but even with both trying, they were almost impossible to remove. John came to assist them too, but the struggle continued. Fifteen minutes later, they figured it out.

Blake and John hurried to the rear of the van to fetch the spare, while Evan began removing the lug nuts from the flat tire.

The two men were now fighting with the spare. Evan finished his job and ran to the back to help them. Another 15 minutes later, they had the spare down, and Blake was running it to the front while John attempted to put everything back together underneath the rear of the van.

Time would not allow them to store the flat tire back where they got the spare. They would throw it in the van and go. Evan and Blake experienced the same frustration trying to get the jack underneath where they could jack up the vehicle. Kathie wept as Beth did her best to console her. Every minute that passed made the possibility of being too late that much more real.

·   ·   ·   ·   ·

"Okay, Julian, Julie, who's going first?" asked the captain. "It's time to go look at your daddy. He's shallow, so it will be easy to uncover him and let you take a peek. I have to warn you, he doesn't look so good. One of you come with me." Neither budged. "*Now!* We need to pass the time till midnight when all of you join him. Pow…" He aimed an imaginary gun at them and feigned pulling the trigger.

Both sat still, not making a move to stand. Neither of them wanted to go outside.

The man charged at Julie and grabbed her by the hair, jerking her to her feet. "I said, come with me!" He started dragging her toward the door as she cried and tried to pull away.

"Leave her alone!" Jeffrey leapt to his feet and started for the man. A shot rang out and he collapsed to the floor, writhing in pain with blood oozing through the leg of his jeans.

"Jeffrey!" screamed Julie.

"Anyone else want to try that?" asked the man who fired the shot.

"As you can see, we mean business," yelled the captain. "Now, you come with me, or a kid gets the next bullet. I wouldn't worry too much about him. It would be a lot better way for him to go if he bleeds to death. He'll die either way." He dragged Julie through the door and onto the porch.

"At least, let me help him," said Julian.

"You'll stay where you are till your sister gets back. Then it's your turn to get a look at *daddy*."

Jeffrey lay in the middle of the room. The kids whimpered as tears streamed down their faces. Joanie sat in shock, her face ashen white from fear. The AMPP men gloated over them all, as midnight crept closer.

•　　•　　•　　•　　•

Forty-five minutes after they began, the three men completed the tire change, threw the flat under the back seat of the van and jumped in, ready to roll. Evan jerked it into gear and spun gravel everywhere as he left the lane bound for the highway. Their ETA was now closer to 11:30 than 10:30. Evan would pick up the speed a little, but they still couldn't afford to get stopped. That would end all possibility of rescuing Kathie's family.

Blake understood he was late calling Ben, but wondered why Ben had not called him. The decision became who to call first: Ben or the group coming behind them, who had, without a doubt, closed the gap now. He decided Ben should be first, so he touched the number; nothing. Still nothing.

"What is wrong with this phone?" he demanded.

Then he saw it: No Service. "Why can't I get service here?" he asked, his frustration showing.

John was just as frustrated. "We are in the middle of nowhere, Blake. It's not all that surprising."

"Evan, get us out of this forsaken place and somewhere I can make a call!"

He floored the van and sped, disregarding the need to be cautious, until Blake said, "Okay, I have it," and called Ben.

Ben answered in the harshest tone Blake had ever heard come from the man.

"Blake! I told you every thirty minutes! It has been over an hour since you called. If you're going on these kinds of trips, you must stay in touch with us! And I don't want any excuses."

"Ben, listen to me!" Blake's tone was almost as harsh. "We blew a tire and came close to crashing this thing. It took us forever to change the tire and get back on the road. We're forty-five to fifty minutes later now, so we have no time to spare!"

Ben interrupted him. "You could have called and told us that!"

"No, I couldn't! We had no cell service where we were."

Ben calmed down. "I'm sorry, everybody. I shouldn't have jumped to such a conclusion. I should trust you. We were just so worried that we were about to lose our minds."

"Ben, I hate to tell you this, but I need to get off here and call Malachi. Plans have to change now. We don't have time to meet at the airstrip, so we need to meet at Kathie's place. They will be right behind us. I have to go."

"Blake! Come on, man. Stop doing that to us."

The entire group at the Shelter sat stunned by the latest developments. But they came to their senses and started praying for both groups on their way to Wichita, and for the safety of Kathie's family.

Blake was already on the phone with Malachi. Both had their phones on speaker so everyone could be part of the conversation. Blake told them about their situation and adjusted timeframe.

"We won't have time to meet before we get there. Both of us need to go straight to Kathie's house. We'll run in just long enough to grab the guns and ammo, then head to the cabin."

"We're less than thirty minutes behind you guys now."

"Make that ten minutes when you arrive," said Steve. "By the time you grab the weapons and get back to the van, you'll see us parked behind it and ready to go."

"The earliest we can make it is 11:30, but we'll get in and out fast. If you are there waiting, follow us to the lane that leads to the cabin. We'll park and sprint the rest of the way. Kathie says it's only five minutes, but we must move quick. It may be five or ten minutes till midnight by the time we reach the cabin. I hope we're doing all this planning for nothing, but we're preparing for the worst and hoping for the best."

"We're with you. If Steve says you'll find us parked outside waiting for you, count on it."

"Okay, I need to call Ben back and tell him what we're doing. We will see all of you in less than an hour." He disconnected that call and called Ben in an almost simultaneous motion.

•　　•　　•　　•　　•

"It looks like the eight of you are down to thirty minutes to live. I was hoping your mommy and Baldwin would get here for the festivities. Don't worry, we'll wait for them after we take care of you. Okay, Julian, it's your turn," the man said as he threw Julie to the floor. "If you hesitate, your precious sister will get a bullet to the leg and join her husband on the floor."

Julian got up and walked in front of him to the door, the gun trained on his back. The pool of blood around Jeffrey had grown as it continued to ooze from his leg. His face was pale, and it appeared he would lose consciousness any minute. In less than ten minutes, the captain returned with Julian, his face streaked with tears after viewing his father's remains.

"Okay, it is time to prepare the prisoners for execution," the captain announced.

One of his men produced a strand of rope and dangled it in front of them.

"If you saw the news about the killings in Germany, you understand how this works. Each of you will kneel facing away from us toward the wall with your hands bound behind your backs. When the clock strikes midnight, we will execute you, one family at a time. It will only take seconds for my men to accomplish that. Do not fear. It will happen so fast you won't even realize what happened. It will be lights out in one quick second. Do you want to say your goodbyes, or maybe give each other last kisses? You have ten minutes. But nobody moves from where you sit."

•   •   •   •   •

The first group of Smyrnians arrived at Doc and Kathie's house and dashed inside to get an arsenal of weapons that would serve them well, if they needed them. Kathie led them as they ran to Doc's secret room. She shoved the wall with a hard punch and the door flew open. They stared in disbelief at the array of cabinets, but were even more in awe when she opened them.

John remembered seeing this man cave for the first time and thinking, *Wow, everything with Doc was impressive!* The man loved the high life. They loaded themselves down with guns and enough ammunition to handle a shootout and sprinted for the steps.

Racing out of the house, they dashed toward the van. Steve's Lincoln Navigator sat right behind it, as promised. They dove into the van and Blake motioned for them to follow. Kathie drove this time, as they sped down the lane. The clock on the dash showed 11:45.

•   •   •   •   •

"Okay, it's time. Two of you do your job. We will make sure none of them try anything foolish. All of you move a few feet away from each other. *Now!*"

"I'm not leaving the kids," said Joanie.

The men grabbed her two children and dragged them away from her as she reached for them, sobbing.

"Do you want us to show you what can happen to them if you interfere? It can be far worse than what will happen in a few minutes."

She wept, gasping for air, as she watched the men tie the kids' hands behind their backs and force them to kneel, looking toward the wall. They cried, calling out for her. Julie's kids were next, then the adults. They bound all eight, hands behind their backs, kneeling, and facing away from their executioners.

"You have ten minutes," said the captain. "Boys, think about the reward the boss will give us for this one." Then addressing the families again, he said, "In case you still don't know, this is complements of Aissa Messai. Your mommy and daddy should have known better than to get mixed up with the Smyrnians. If she and Baldwin show up, they will meet the same fate tonight."

11:50. Kathie pulled up and stopped at the end of the lane leading back to the cabin. They all saw it at the same time. A black SUV bearing the image of a dove and the letters AMPP on the side.

"No!" she whispered louder than she intended, then screamed in a louder whisper, "Let's go!"

They all leapt from the vehicles and began half-running, half-walking back the lane toward the cabin. They followed her in the dark, attempting to stay together. None of them noticed the time, but they knew midnight was near. When they sprinted into the clearing, the sight that met their eyes through the two windows on that side of the cabin sent terror flooding into their hearts.

Four AMPP men stood with guns raised. Weapons loaded and ready, they raced to the windows, where they saw every member of Kathie's family bound and kneeling, with the men standing behind them ready to fire. The events unfolding before their eyes seemed to happen in slow motion. The captain's command floated through the air and entered their ears as if carried on a gentle breeze.

"Ready! Aim! *Fire!*"

In these final moments, Julie was thinking of Kathie. How could she have turned her back on her own mother? She knew her actions had hurt her. Her final wish was to say one more time, "I am so sorry, mom." But that opportunity would not come. Tears ran down her cheeks as precious memories of their family flooded her mind.

Then thoughts of watching the video Kathie had so wanted them to see replaced them. If she had one more opportunity, she would watch it. But that opportunity would not come. She heard the captain's last command, "*FIRE!*" and closed her eyes. The explosive bark of gunfire filled her ears, and her world went silent.

• • • • •

Aissa Messai received reports throughout the night as his patrols carried out their missions around the world. Hour after hour, as midnight passed in different time zones, the reports came. He celebrated each but understood there were far too few. The Smyrnians had warned many of their families, allowing them to escape.

Each of those reports continued to fill him with rage, while each positive report filled him with glee. Rage... glee... all night. The range of emotions made him more determined than ever to rid the world of the Smyrnians. He would be victorious! This battle belonged to him. The other Messiah would bow at his feet and proclaim him lord, as would all people everywhere.

He relished the thought and smiled. But in the back of his mind lived a fear of what the one called Jesus, Son of God, may do to him. No, the events of this night proved he would emerge the victor. Or did they? Fear gnawed at him, but he pushed it back and allowed himself to enjoy this moment.

•   •   •   •   •

When the clock struck midnight at the Shelter, those still present prayed for a miracle. Except for the times during Blake's calls, they had not stopped praying. Midnight came far sooner than they hoped. The hours flew by. No call came from Blake, or the others. Tears flowed from their eyes as the awareness of what had happened to Kathie's family brought a flood of emotions that felt like they would never stop.

But they gathered themselves, also aware that they had to pray for the others. Ben warned them not to go. He told them of the dangers they would face, but they refused to listen. How many of their number had perished this night? They understood they would be with Jesus, but the thought brought little comfort to them now.

What about Kathie's family? They had not believed in Jesus. That awareness tore at their minds even more. Many times had been difficult for them, this was the most grueling time of all.

•   •   •   •   •

Julie opened her eyes. Was she alive? She couldn't be. There must be an afterlife! She had never believed that, but now here she was. No, her hands remained bound behind her back, and she still knelt facing the cabin wall. She looked to each side and saw her family looking back at her, tears falling from their eyes. What happened? The AMPP men fired and her world went silent.

The group of Smyrnians stood outside the windows, staring at the four men lying dead on the floor. Guns in hand, they had raced to the cabin and looked in the windows just as the captain gave the command, "Aim!" There was no time to think. They had to act! Instinctively, they threw their weapons to their shoulders and aimed. When the captain said, "*FIRE!*" they did.

The men inside didn't get the chance to pull their triggers. Bullets from the Smyrnians' guns slammed into their bodies, exploding their hearts and killing them instantly. It required a split-second decision. The group had no time to worry about whether they should take the lives of Messai's men. It was kill them, or see Kathie's family slaughtered before their eyes. They did what they had to do and hoped Jesus would forgive them.

Julie heard voices. Her mother! Footsteps... running. Was she dreaming, or was she dead? Time moved in slow motion for *her* now. She longed for this to be real, but saw no possibility of that. Someone grabbed her from behind, but she could not see them. There was no mistaking the voice. Warm tears wet her cheek and hair. Julie turned her head and stared into the face of her mom, the most beautiful sight she had ever seen.

"Kids... kids... Oh, my children and my grandchildren, all of you. You're alive."

Kathie ran from one to the other and back again. Back and forth, hugging them and weeping over them. When each turned, they saw the room filled with people, men and women, all crying too, and rejoicing at the same time.

Before them lay the four AMPP men dead on the floor, blood oozing from their bodies where bullets from the team's guns had ripped into them. Trey and Evan cut the ropes from their wrists. Their hands hurt and tingled as blood flowed back into them, but they were alive. Nothing else mattered now. They came together, weeping and hugging in the room that should have been their death chamber, but was now a picture of life.

"How...? What...?" asked Julian.

"I am so sorry, mom," cried Julie, remembering one of the final thoughts that had gone through her mind in that agonizing moment.

"It's okay, baby," said Kathie through tears that would not stop. "That doesn't matter now. What matters is that all of you are alive. My family is alive. Jesus has given you back to me."

Jesus, thought Julie. Their family never believed in him. The thought hit her; she had to learn more about him. Jesus... something about that name touched her deep inside.

"Jeffrey!" screamed Kathie, just noticing him in the jubilation of seeing her family alive. He collapsed face down on the floor after Trey and Evan had cut the ropes from his wrists.

Julie almost forgot about her husband in the terror and elation of those few moments. She ran to him and fell down by his side, begging him to speak to her. He was lifeless and pale. Steve raced to him and shouted, "Everybody move away and let me look at him!"

"Do what he says, honey. He's one of the best surgeons in Missouri. He will know what to do."

Steve was already at work. "I need warm water and bandages. Tear some sheets into strips. I must stop the bleeding. Then we need to get him to the hospital. I have performed surgeries at Wesley Medical Center many times. They know me there. I'm sure they know your family too, Kathie. That means you can't go. But Julie can because they don't know she is with us."

"What happened?" asked Julian, coming to his senses. "The captain said, '*FIRE!* and I heard the gunshots. And now the AMPP men are dead, and we're alive. How…?"

"We will tell you how very soon, Julian."

"I'm sorry. Do I know you?"

"My name is Blake Thompson, and this is my wife, Beth Jennings Thompson."

"And I am John Baldwin, the one who came to rescue your mom and dad the night he died. Your dad and I were childhood friends."

"John, thank you! We have heard stories about you all of our lives. And Blake Thompson and Beth Jennings. You are our family's favorite reporters. Dad always made us be quiet and watch when you were on. Thank you, all of you. I want to get to know you, and I want to learn more about Jesus."

"Me too," said Julie. "Mom, you wanted us to watch a video."

"I want you to watch the video too, like we did," said Steve. "But now, we have to get your husband to Wesley Medical."

CHAPTER 10

At 11:45, the captain and his patrol burst into Johnathan Baldwin's house without warning. He wanted to catch the family by surprise. They did not know what was about to happen to them. The men shattered the front door and charged into the living room. No one. Nothing. Quiet.

Where was the family? They searched the house. No way they saw this coming! They must have fled and were hiding in the woods surrounding the house. His team had maintained surveillance all day, making escape impossible. They must be nearby.

"Find them!"

He dispatched his entire patrol in all directions, while he stayed in the house in case they attempted to sneak back in. A voice drew his attention. The TV was on! It wasn't on when they came in. Or was it? It must have been. *More proof they fled*, he thought. He drew his weapon to blast the screen, silencing the man who was speaking. Strange. He had not seen him before.

The man spoke in a way he had never heard a man speak. Something about his words forced him to watch. It was a pastor. He would not listen to the lies of a preacher! But all of his attempts to turn away met with failure.

A video was just beginning. How was that possible, unless the TV came on by itself? *Stop it, Magnus. You are losing your mind.* Those thoughts faded as he stood entranced by what he heard. The man's words seemed to pierce his very soul and enlighten his mind with truths he had never considered. Facts about time and history and the world; about the Bible and God and Jesus. He refused to accept those truths, but then, he could not *keep* from accepting them. Something cut him to the core of his being. A voice boomed.

"Magnus, why are you persecuting me?"

"Who… who are you?"

"I am Jesus, the one you are persecuting. What you do to my people, you do to me!"

"What people? Who are they?" He already knew the answer. *The Smyrnians.* They were the *Jesus people.* Messai had told him it was all a lie, and he believed him. But now he realized Messai was the liar.

The captain's heart softened. His mind changed and tears fell from his eyes. When the pastor invited him to believe in Jesus, he fell to his knees, a broken man, and prayed for the first time in his life.

Brilliant light filled the room. It should have blinded him, but it gave him sight! Something fell from his eyes; a covering that kept him blind to the truth. What he felt at that moment, he had not experienced before. Pure love. Real peace. Happiness like he had never known. The voice came again. He recognized it, though it was the first time he heard it: *Jesus.*

"Stand to your feet, and I will tell you what to do."

He rose, but he did not stand. He ascended higher until his feet floated above the floor. He was walking on air! The weight of his sin disappeared. The hatred, the murders, his allegiance to Aissa Messai, all lifted away within seconds. He now understood who Messai was. The Antichrist. ANTI-Christ: opposed to Jesus. Anti-CHRIST: one who saw himself replacing Jesus. The captain knew that was not possible. *Jesus is Lord!* He listened as Jesus spoke again.

"Follow me, and I will guide you where you must go. You will meet a group of people who will tell you everything you must do and the things you must suffer for my name."

"Where are they, Lord?"

"Missouri. I will direct you to the place where they live underground. Leave now before the others return. They will search for you but not find you. You will be my servant for the rest of your life."

"Yes, Lord. I'm sorry for not believing in you. Now I do! I will follow you until you return to take me home to be with you. Thank you for dying on the cross for me and reaching out to me tonight. I believe it with all of my heart. I love you, Jesus."

He scrambled out the door, got into his black SUV and sped toward Missouri. The Smyrnians. He would find them there and couldn't wait to meet them! But what would they think of him? He had slaughtered some of their own himself and overseen the murders of many more. Would they accept him? None of his questions mattered. He was on his way to Missouri and would find out when he arrived. Now, he no longer drove, but neither did the SUV drive itself, which it was capable of doing. Jesus was taking him where he needed to go. He knew his life would never be the same. For that, he was *forever* grateful.

• • • • • •

The Smyrnians received a much-needed break following weeks of intense action, during which they often stared death in the face. Julian and Joanie, Julie and Jeffrey, and their children believed in Jesus, even without seeing the pastor's video. They did not need to see it after living their own miracle. But when they watched it, they learned things that unlocked their minds.

The group brought them to the Shelter to keep them in *protective custody*. Johnathan Baldwin secured a safe house in the mountains of Colorado that would accommodate many people. Overcrowding turned into an issue at the Shelter. It was impossible for all of them to live there, so they must resolve that situation. But for now, they needed some downtime, even though they were aware it wouldn't last long. The world needed them *out there* more than they needed to be *in here*.

Messai would not take a break in his pursuit of Jesus' followers. AMPP continued to massacre more of them by the day. What a worship gathering that must be in heaven! While they sat together in the bunker, praying for believers everywhere, and reading the Bible, they caught a glimpse of what that is like.

After this I looked, and there before me was a great multitude that no one could count, from every nation, tribe, people and language, standing before the throne and before the Lamb. They were wearing white robes and were holding palm branches in their hands. And they cried out in a loud voice:

"Salvation belongs to our God, who sits on the throne, and to the Lamb..."

Then one of the elders asked me, "These in white robes—who are they, and where did they come from?"

I answered, "Sir, you know."

And he said, "*These are they who have come out of the great tribulation;* they have washed their robes and made them white in the blood of the Lamb." Revelation 7:9-10; 13-14 (New International Version)

They understood they would join them one day. That led to discussing what it would be like for them. None of them knew when their time would come. Many of them had survived harrowing near death experiences at the hands of Aissa Messai's Peace Patrol. How long would they continue to escape before martyrdom caught up with them?

They returned to prayer, so caught up in expressing themselves and lifting their voices to the Lord they did not hear the gentle tapping on the door of Bunker One. But it got their attention when it increased in intensity and volume. They stopped and looked at each other.

"Who is that?" whispered Ally.

"If it was any of ours, they would have called to tell us they were on the way. Or they would just come on in," Evan replied, matching her soft tone. "But we're all here."

Blake took charge. "Evan, you, Anders, and Malachi are the least known. You answer the door. Ben and Miriam can stay here with the other two. The rest of us need to hide down the hallway, out of sight. Kathie, what did you do with the guns? We may need them."

"They're in the van," she said, her fear showing. "We forgot to bring them in!"

The pounding grew louder. Someone wanted in and was not waiting much longer.

"Nobody can find us down here," said Ben. "They may locate the farm and even discover the cabin, but they would never find the secret entrance! The rest of you, hide. We'll open the door and see who's there. Be ready to come if we need you!"

The others ran as the knocking became too loud to ignore. Evan walked to the door, gathered his courage and turned the knob. Outside stood an AMPP man in full uniform and a patch that said, *Captain.* Evan froze. His words came without thinking.

"AMPP!" he yelled, causing the others to rush into the room, joining them and standing together as one. They would not go down without a fight. Where were his men? He would not come alone. His patrol must be in hiding, just out of sight, and ready to charge in any second.

"May I ask what you are doing here?" demanded Ben.

He stepped forward, not flinching as he stared into the invader's eyes.

No others came; the man stood alone. He didn't appear to be like the other AMPP men they had encountered. His appearance showed something different. But none of that changed the fact that he was one of Aissa Messai's thugs. They waited for his patrol to join him. He stepped inside.

"My name is Magnus." He spoke with a slight accent, broken, but excellent English.

"Which one of you is John Baldwin?"

The team huddled around John, refusing to give him away. But he broke through their ranks.

"I am John Baldwin. Who wants to know?"

"I am the captain of an Aissa Messai Peace Patrol. Tonight my men and I waited outside your son's home. You eluded us many times. I wanted to watch my men torture your son and his family and see them die because I loathed you so much. You almost cost me my job, and my life."

John leapt toward the man. "What have you done to Johnathan? I swear, I will…"

Magnus interrupted. "Please, let me tell you why I came. I saw you looking behind me. Do not worry; I am alone. When our group burst into your son's house last night, no one was home. I was sure the family had fled into the woods, so I dispatched my men to locate them and not return until they brought them back. The television was on, and a video was playing."

They glanced at each other, an unspoken question entering each of their minds at the same time. *Is it possible that he was talking about that video?*

"Your Johnathan must have left it playing, hoping I would watch it. I raised my gun to blast the TV, but I could not because something drew me to the man on the screen. When I discovered he was a preacher, I avowed I would not listen to him. But I could not keep from watching. His words pierced my heart. I believed in Jesus and did what he said. I asked Jesus to forgive my sin and come into my life."

"How he could do that for me, I cannot comprehend. After I murdered so many of his followers. Aissa Messai has been my lord. But tonight I realized for the first time Jesus is the real Lord. I am now one of you. Jesus led me here. Otherwise, I would not have found this place."

"He asked me why I persecute him. Then he told me what I do to his people, I do to him. I fell to my knees, but he told me to stand and follow him. I stood to my feet, but I wasn't standing. Something lifted me above the floor. The heavy load that had weighed me down for so long was gone, and I was walking on air! You cannot believe the love and peace I feel. I want to learn more about Jesus. Please help me."

"Saul of Tarsus on the road to Damascus," said Anders.

"Excuse me?"

"Acts Chapter 9 in the Bible. God chose Saul of Tarsus as the one who would go tell the Gentiles about Jesus. Saul was a murderer of Christians, but God selected him. Sound familiar?"

The enormous man broke into tears and collapsed to his knees.

"I am not worthy of such love."

"Neither was Saul, nor any of us," said Anders. "But God often chooses the least likely to be his most powerful witnesses. Jesus met you tonight, Magnus, and called you to be his witness for the rest of your life. If you heard the pastor, you understand that isn't long."

"Yes, I heard that," Magnus said, still on his knees, his head buried in his hands. "I have so much to learn. I know nothing about Jesus or the Bible. Can you help me?"

Blake stepped forward. "Welcome to the Family of God, Magnus, and welcome to the Smyrnians. I am Blake Thompson."

Shock and wonder showed on the man's face as Blake took his hand and lifted him to his feet.

"Mr. Thompson, Messai has taught us you are the enemy of the entire world and we must destroy you. Thank you for speaking the truth, even though it meant risking your life to do so."

"Don't thank me. It all started with this young man who opened the door for you," said Blake, pulling Evan to his side. "He was the first to believe and the one who showed me the same video you saw, allowing me to hear the truth about Jesus."

"Thank you..."

"Evan Ryles." Evan interrupted him with a smile and reached out his hand.

The sizeable man now rivaled Bruno for the largest of the Smyrnians. He disregarded the hand and lifted Evan off the floor, drawing him into a hug so powerful the others feared it would crack his ribs. The rest of the group came to Magnus too, each one welcoming him to the team. It was an awe-inspiring moment, one they had all experienced themselves.

Yet, as with Ben, something was different about his encounter. Jesus called Ben to go announce Jesus as the Messiah to the Jews, God's chosen people. He called Saul to be the Apostle to the Gentiles. Magnus had a special purpose, and the Smyrnians would help him discover it.

They stood amazed at God's miraculous work in the life of a man so high in Aissa Messai's chain of command. But that is how God operates. He chooses the least likely to do the most for him. And Magnus fit the bill. This day would go down as one of the greatest of the Tribulation.

•   •   •   •   •

The dedication of the temple brought with it *Aliyah*, as Jews from around the world immigrated to their homeland. Hanukkah became the first Festival celebration that would include the rebuilt temple. Many would celebrate the Festival of Lights by lighting their candles in Israel for the first time. Anticipation and excitement burned as bright as the menorah itself.

Jews flooded Jerusalem, thrilled to watch prophecy fulfilled before their eyes. It meant the Messiah would appear soon! One year earlier, Aissa Messai stood on the Temple Mount and announced the peace treaty between Jews and Muslims. A part of that announcement included the rebuilding of the Jewish Temple. Much had happened since that time. Most Jews saw this as the climax of the process and were ready for the promised arrival of their Messiah. The time was ripe for sharing the wonderful news of the *real* Messiah.

•   •   •   •   •

Ben and Miriam talked with Alexander and Elizabeth Ben Ezra and made plans to travel to Israel. The day had arrived for them to fulfill their calling. *Go and tell my people.* Those words had remained embedded in their minds since the night they first believed in Jesus. The Lord appeared to them and commissioned them to go tell the Jews that Jesus is the true Messiah.

The rebuilding of the temple and the Jews returning to Israel signaled the time for their work to begin on site. Ben was eager to get there and start working. The Ben Ezras were just as excited about working alongside them. It was about to be *on* in the land of the Bible!

•   •   •   •   •

Aissa Messai was both furious and puzzled. He received word of Johnathan Baldwin's escape from the planned execution. But more than that, his trusted captain was missing. The men of his patrol reported leaving him alone in the house and searching the surrounding area for the Baldwin family. When they returned, he had disappeared, and never returned. Nothing seemed out of the ordinary, nor did they see any evidence of a struggle. They found only an empty house and no sign of their captain.

He could not imagine what may have happened to him. The man was one of his best officers. He had always counted on him to do any job which he assigned to him. Though others had failed him, Magnus never did. A promotion was coming for him following this mission. But you cannot promote someone who isn't there to promote. Perhaps he would call soon.

•   •   •   •   •

While the team prepared to send Ben and Miriam off, Magnus focused on training for his own mission. Anders helped him understand what happened to him in Johnathan's house that night. Then he taught him the *rest of the story* of Saul of Tarsus, alias Paul the Apostle, follower of Jesus Christ. Magnus read the rest of the Book of Acts, beginning in Chapter 9. He then studied the other letters of Paul, from Romans through Philemon. His own mission became clear as he read.

The Smyrnians needed to stay one step ahead of Messai, and he would serve as a valuable resource for knowing what was coming. Because he had been on the inside of Messai's empire, he would give inside information that even Ally could not provide. He was the man for the job.

It was now only three days until the Sanderson crew would leave the Shelter and move to Colorado. Concern existed among the team because of John and Kathie's decision to move with them. "Too dangerous!" Ben warned them. But they had made up minds. Johnathan's safe house in the Rockies provided ample space for both families, and many more, if needed.

The couple surprised the group with another announcement. They wanted the team to marry them before they left! None of them expected that one, but they were happy and excited for them. Both families supported their decision. They knew Doc would approve because he had asked John to take care of her. This would make the third marriage among the Smyrnians.

Another surprise. John's kids came for the wedding. The Shelter ran over with occupants, but they were all good with it for a few days. The group gathered again and performed a simple ceremony. John and Kathie wanted nothing extra or fancy. Their joy following the wedding confirmed their decision was the right one. Kathie reasoned that Doc was smiling too, and the others agreed.

Moving day brought multiple departures, among them Ben and Miriam and their seven children. Nineteen of their number leaving would make the Shelter seem empty by comparison. Jeffrey had healed, although he still walked with a limp. Rickie was thankful to be alive and more than ready to get back in action.

Looking around as the group prepared to leave reminded them of their increase. It began with Evan, then Ally, Blake, John, Anders and Beth. Since then, each came to the team one at a time and in unique ways. Now, here they stood, Jesus' army. They were not a ragtag group. Each brought various skill sets that made the Smyrnians who they were, a formidable foe in the battle with the Antichrist and his evil forces. And they would fight him until the end.

Rickie offered to fly John and Kathie to Colorado. That would keep them out of sight. Flights to and from private airstrips gave him confidence that no one would notice them. His military connections always came in handy when he made these trips, often helping to provide him with secure locations for landing and taking off.

But they opted to ride with family and lie low in the back. All five families would drive separately, staying within range of each other, but far enough apart that AMPP could not stop all of them if it came to that. They hoped it would not.

Rabbi Avraham and Abigail Issacs, alias Ben and Miriam Abramson, flew from Springfield to Newark to Tel Aviv. Alexander and Elizabeth greeted them and whisked them away to their home in Ein Karem. Their residence would be temporary because they needed a safe place immediately. Yet the four of them teemed with excitement, thinking about the massive number of Jews the Lord was bringing to them. The work must not linger. The future of their people hung in the balance.

"Where do we go from here?" Blake addressed those who remained at the Shelter. "We can't stay in here while there is so much work to do all over the world."

"Bruno and I will form an imposing duo," said Magnus. "What do you say, Bruno? Are you in?"

"Bring it on!" announced the big man. "Where do we start?"

"Are you up for Germany? Trust me, I understand how to avoid AMPP. And I am also aware of how Messai operates and his plans for hunting you guys down. Since your encounter over there, Germany is a hot spot on his radar. Do you have a place to hide out as we work?"

"The Bavarian Alps!" shouted Hans. "I have connections who can find us a place just like Johnathan's safe house in the Rockies. I'll call them now, if you are serious and ready to go, on one condition. I will go with you."

"If Hans goes, I go," Heidi said with a determined tone.

"I am going too," proclaimed Mila. "Germany needs all of us."

"I agree with them, Magnus. We all need to go," said Bruno.

"Then make your call... what is your name again?"

"Hans. This is my wife, Heidi. We, Bruno, and Mila, are an inseparable team!"

Hans made the call as he moved to a quiet area of the bunker.

"We are spreading out and maximizing our potential," said Blake. "I think Beth and I may need to stay here for a bit and continue teaching online before we leave again. AMPP may recognize us, regardless of how we disguise ourselves."

"You don't know just how right you are," said Magnus. "Messai created digital images of your faces and distributed them to every AMPP unit worldwide. They have facial recognition technology that can identify you within seconds."

"He has every patrol in the world on the highest alert, which he calls *Code Orange*, meaning they may use the greatest force necessary to take you into custody. Beth, he wants you so much he will do anything it takes to bring you back to him. The two of you must stay in hiding for now. I will listen for the right time for you to go out again."

Only they would remain at the Shelter. The others chose destinations where they would be most effective. The team of Evan, Anders, and Malachi stayed together. Ally was going with Ollie and Amelia, forming a sly team of elusive escape artists. They weren't returning to London. Instead, Israel would be their destination. Ollie's knowledge of the place and his great number of contacts made it the logical choice. They would run interference for the Abramsons and Ben Ezras and help in any way they could. The group gave them their blessing. Danger lurked around every corner for all of them wherever they went.

Steve and Linda returned home, where he would continue his work as a surgeon. Even after their excursion to Wichita, they were not on Messai's radar. Magnus assured them that neither he nor AMPP had heard of them. They would work in the local area for a few months, or until the enemy discovered them. The team would need Steve's medical expertise. He would travel anywhere they needed him, or be available to assist them when they returned home.

Trey and Rickie focused on reaching their military buddies, starting with Commander Paul Johnson. Bradley Rodgers in England was also on their list. A movement in the United States Military would be huge for the cause. But if they found them to be members of the Smyrnians, they may turn them over to AMPP, which would mean certain death. Trey would join Rickie in flying again, as long as he could use only private airstrips, or military bases on occasions.

All of them departed, leaving Blake and Beth behind to work underground. They would be alone for the first significant period since their marriage. That sounded good, but hard work would remain their top priority.

The increase of new believers in Jesus continued to blow their minds. Magnus told them Messai did not understand it either. He had no comprehension of why these *Jesus people* continued to expand. Even when their fellow believers died for the cause, they never stopped multiplying.

The same would soon be true among the group Messai hated most, along with the Smyrnians. It had already begun and stopping it would be impossible. That fact drove them onward in their pursuit of the entire world. But nothing could prepare them for what lay on the horizon. It was coming, ready or not.

CHAPTER 11

Alexander heard the SUVs whipping into his driveway right before he saw them.

"To the attic!" he yelled to his new houseguests, directing them toward a spare bedroom. When they entered, he pointed to a cutout covered with a square piece of wood.

"But what about the two of you?" asked Ben.

"Hurry!" Alexander said, pushing them toward the opening. He used a broom to shove the wooden covering into the attic. "Put the cover back when you get in. We stored piles of old clothing up there. Lie down close together and cover yourselves with them."

Ben had no time to question what he said. The oldest climbed on a chair and went first. They pushed the other children up one at a time. Miriam followed them, and Ben was last. The others walked toward the clothes, using a cell phone for light. Ben shoved the wooden cover back over the hole and ran to join them. Alexander moved the chair and hurried into the living room to join his wife. The pounding on the door had already begun.

"This is AMPP! Open this door!"

Alexander obliged as Elizabeth sat down in her usual chair.

"What do you want? You have no right to come bursting into my home again."

"Alexander, we told you we would return if you messed up again."

"I have done nothing wrong. We have lived in peace since the last time you invaded our home."

"We shall find out if you are telling us the truth this time."

"Why would I lie? I have nothing to hide."

"Oh, Alexander. You are clever with your words. You may have *nothing* to hide. Why didn't you say *no one*? Someone reported you and your wife traveling home in a van loaded with people. You can't hide anything, or anyone, from us."

"I don't know what you are talking about."

"Ah, where have I heard that before? Oh yes, the night you lied to us about taking the fugitives to the airport. We told you if we came back and found you to be untruthful with us again, you would not get off so easy next time. Well, that time may have come. Men, search the house."

"You cannot barge in here like this and go through my house!"

"Did you catch that, boys? He doesn't want us to search his house. That means he has something, or someone, to hide. Search every nook and cranny. Turn everything upside down until you find them. Unless Alexander wants to tell us where they are and save us the trouble."

He glanced at Alexander and got no response, so he went on.

"Elizabeth, do you want your house destroyed? If not, you have ten seconds to tell us where they are hiding."

He started counting down as he had done before.

"Do what you need to," the woman said in defiance. "You cannot find what is not here to find."

His search began with a vengeance. Glasses and plates smashed on the floor in the kitchen. Closets ripped apart with everything dragged out and thrown around the rooms. Mattresses jerked from all the beds and tossed aside. Every drawer in the house pulled out and their contents dumped in piles. One room at a time, they made their way through the house, destroying things as they went.

"Are you satisfied now?" Alexander asked, raising his voice.

"We didn't find anyone, sir," explained one man.

"Sir!" yelled another from the spare bedroom. "We may have something here."

"Alexander..." the captain said his name, wagging his head and shaking his finger at him as he followed his men into the room. The man pointed to a covered opening in the ceiling.

"The attic! I'll bet that's why this chair sits over here. How convenient."

One man produced a flashlight and removed the covering. He stood on the chair and pulled himself up through the opening. Others followed. Alexander took deep breaths, trying to remain calm. Elizabeth did the same. Above them, the men went crazy, turning things upside down again.

"Nothing here, sir," one of them called down.

"Search harder. They must be up there. Guard them," he said to the remaining group in the room. "I will find them myself." He pulled himself up and crawled into the attic.

The couple cringed as he wreaked havoc upstairs too. He screamed and swore and was relentless in his search, but found nothing. He and the men dropped back down into the room, walked back into the living room and stared at the couple.

"I told you I have nothing, or *no one...*" Alexander emphasized that word "... to hide. Now get out of my house."

"We will go, but we will watch your every move. If we notice any sign of others here, you will die with them."

"Leave and do not return. You have destroyed my house, now get out!"

The men left, as Alexander watched to make sure all of them got into the SUVs. He waited until they exited the drive and drove away before walking over and sitting down in his chair next to Elizabeth. Only a small table separated their chairs.

"Alexander, aren't you going to check on them?"

"Not yet, Elizabeth. We need to be certain all of them left. I will go soon."

"I hope they are okay. How did they miss them?"

"I believe Jesus protected them. Remember what he said? He will never leave us nor forsake us. I suppose that includes attics." He smiled to reassure her.

"Alexander!"

"What?!"

She pointed to the door. Two AMPP men stared at them through the glass. He got up and stormed to the door, flinging it open.

"Haven't you done enough? Can't we have peace sitting in our own home? You have torn it apart. Why do you keep bothering us? Get away from our house!"

"We are sorry, Mr. Ben Ezra. We're just doing our jobs. Our captain made us stay behind when the others left to make sure the family he suspected you of hiding didn't come out. I apologize for making such a mess..."

One of the SUVs whipped into the driveway and the captain interrupted him.

"Get in and let's go! Alexander, we will keep our eyes on you. If I were you, I would keep my nose clean. I still don't trust you in the least."

The men obeyed like scolded puppies. They ran to the vehicle, leapt into the back seat and slammed the doors. The SUV sped away, squealing tires as it did. Alexander turned and walked back inside. The covering to the attic slid back and dropped to the floor. He ran to put the chair in place. Ben came down first, followed by Miriam and the children from youngest to oldest.

"Ben, you must come in and tell us what happened. I was sure they would find you when they tore the attic apart. I am so sorry. You have been in our home such a short time and AMPP has already forced you and your family into hiding. I'm afraid we gave you a rude welcome."

"It is all a part of these seven years, my friend. But it tells me we need a safe place as soon as possible. Have you thought about that? Do you have any places in mind?"

"We will talk about that later. But first, you must tell us what happened in the attic!"

"Oh, yes... that. We could hear them tearing things apart down here. But it covered the sound up there and gave us time to hide. Miriam and the kids lay down, and I piled the old clothes, blankets and other stuff high over them. Then I grabbed as many as I could, lay down, and covered myself."

"When they were grabbing stuff and throwing it all over the place, they were right on top of us. While they removed layer after layer, I thought it was over. But they stopped before getting to the bottom. Kids, I give you credit for lying still and not making a sound for so long. I'm thankful we didn't smother under all those clothes."

"Ben and Miriam, it had to be Jesus who stopped them before they found you," said Elizabeth. "We have watched him do many things like that already. I feel sure he did this, too."

"I agree with you, Elizabeth," uttered Miriam, though shaken by the experience. "I could feel their hands pressing down as they pulled off layers, almost down to where we were. One more handful, and they would have uncovered us. Thank Jesus, they didn't."

"That's right, dear. Jesus is the one we must thank," Ben proclaimed. "Some may think it is a coincidence that they stopped right before discovering us. But I give all the credit to him! Now, Alexander, we need to discuss that safe place."

The Baldwins and Sandersons left the Shelter just before daylight. That allowed them to leave the farm without being noticed. They opted to make the fourteen-hour drive during the day, instead of at night. Blending into traffic would provide better cover than driving on deserted roads after dark. The wives drove, with husbands and kids lying down with John and Kathie. They assumed they would appear less suspicious. Only ladies making a trip to the store or driving to work.

Evan provided them with fake IDs, including driver's licenses and passports. Trey and Rickie had started their work by helping another military buddy put his faith in Jesus. The man owned one of the largest used car dealerships in Missouri. He allowed each of the families to trade their vehicles and register their new ones using assumed names. He only had a few years at most to live, he reasoned, so why not take the chance and help the team?

It appeared the Baldwins and Sandersons had vanished. They drove toward Colorado as different people. Their lives had changed, and they would never go back, regardless of what the future held. Blake instructed them to call and report at the top of every hour. "Okay, Ben," said Kathie, smiling. He retorted that at least he gave them sixty minutes between calls instead of thirty. By dark, they should be in Johnathan's safe house in a remote part of the Rocky Mountains. Once there, they would create a plan and begin implementing it.

•　　•　　•　　•　　•

"I have researched many options for safe places," said Alexander, as he and Ben sat at the kitchen table. "But we must find one that allows you to carry on your online work of reaching and teaching the Jews."

"Throw a few ideas at me and let's see if any of them stick."

"We can live in caves in the desert south of Jerusalem. David did so when he ran from King Saul. But that may be different for us three thousand years later." He looked at Ben and smiled.

"That would not be impossible, my friend. Ten years ago, I researched an app which provided connectivity from deep within caves. It was intriguing. But I admit I am not eager to be a cave dweller. I'm sure our wives would agree with that. But the kids would get excited about it." Ben leaned over and whispered, "You and I can pretend we never thought of such a thing and discuss other options."

"I joke about the cave. But I believe you will love my plan. I should have used it instead of bringing you here. I saved this news for your arrival. A kibbutz!"

"A kibbutz! What a splendid idea! But no kibbutzim will allow us to live among them. Most are religious Jews who would never accept followers of Jesus into their community."

"Ah yes, most are. So *was* the one I am speaking about." He emphasized the word *was*.

"Was? What do you mean, *was*? Alexander, are you telling me...?"

His new friend beamed like a kid with a secret he could not wait to tell.

"Yes, Benjamin, yes! I have told many people about Jesus, but few listened. One of those, a dear friend, dwells in an agricultural kibbutz where Elizabeth and I buy vegetables."

Before he could continue, Ben jumped to his feet and ran around the table. He grabbed Alexander, lifted him up and embraced him in a tight hug.

"You are a genius, my friend! A real genius! I would never think of something like that!"

"Not me, Benjamin. Jesus. He opened the door. I walked through it. The credit goes to him."

"Sure! But tell me more. How? When? Tell me all about it!"

"One day when we drove to the kibbutz to buy vegetables, I asked Moshe if I could speak with him about something important."

"Moshe? His name is Moses! This story gets better by the minute!"

"You will find out just how good if you let me finish."

"Yes, yes, of course. I promise to keep quiet until you finish."

Alexander looked at him with a questioning glance, as if to imply he doubted that would happen. Ben moved his thumb and forefinger across his lips, pretending to zip them shut. Alexander appeared satisfied enough to continue.

"I asked Moshe if we could go into his house so I could show him something. He began by watching your story. It touched him and caused him to think. Next, I showed him the pastor's video, and he broke into tears, realizing for the first time in his life that Jesus is the Messiah."

Ben started to speak, but Alexander held up his hand. Ben *zipped* again and sat back to listen.

"He prayed to Jesus right there. Then he brought the rest of his family, and they believed in Jesus too! It was an amazing moment. Jesus appeared and spoke to them. I stood on the outside looking in, a guest at a heavenly meeting."

"That is how Blake described what happened the night I turned to Jesus! He was like a guest… I'm sorry, Alexander. Please continue."

The man feigned frustration, but smiled and picked up where he left off.

"Others will come," Jesus said. "You will give them shelter and protect them from those who seek to destroy them. Do you remember the story of Rahab and the spies?"

He answered, "Yes, Lord. She hid them from the people of Jericho who wanted to kill them."

Jesus spoke again. "You will do the same for those who come, and more will follow. You must protect all of them and join them in their work. And you will begin tonight."

"Moshe wasted no time. He called a meeting of the entire kibbutz that night, and everyone came. He showed them your story. But before he played the pastor's video, he told how he put his faith in Jesus. Benjamin, every man, woman, and child in the kibbutz believed in Jesus!"

"We will travel there tomorrow. They prepared a place for you to stay. You and your family are nothing more than Jews taking part in *Aliyah*, who returned to Israel like many others. But you and I know why you are really here!"

"I must tell Miriam and the kids right now! May I get them and bring them in here?"

"I hate to spoil your moment, but Elizabeth informed them while I told you! Let's go talk to them."

"It matters not who told who. Jesus answered our prayers for a safe place. That's what matters!"

The women brought out fresh baked rugelach, chocolate babka, knafeh, and ice cream. Elizabeth made coffee and sweet tea, much to Ben's delight. The kids had soft drinks and milk. They enjoyed the evening, but ate and drank in anticipation of the coming day.

"We must leave early tomorrow morning. I can't wait to get to the kibbutz! One thing, though; our names aren't Ben and Miriam Abramson. We are Rabbi Avraham and Abigail Issacs."

"But you use your name on the website as you teach. People recognize you as Ben, so I think you should use your actual names."

"He's right, dear," Miriam whispered. "We're Smyrnians. We should not hide our identities."

"Okay! Ben and Miriam it is. Let Messai come after us because Jesus is our protector!"

His phone rang. Ollie. He assumed he and Amelia were on their way to England by now.

"Ollie, old chap. What's going on with you? Have you arrived in the UK yet? You must be very careful there because it is the most dangerous place you can go."

"Ben, or is it Avraham? Your British still needs a little work." He chuckled. "We decided against traveling to Great Britain and chose the second most dangerous place. We will meet you at Alexander and Elizabeth's house tomorrow evening!"

"You are coming to Israel? That is too dangerous. I advise against such a move."

"It matters not what you *advise*. We're coming!"

"Then I say, come on! We need you! But do not come to Alexander and Elizabeth's house. He will give you the address to our safe place!"

"Safe place? He already has a safe place for you?"

"We will tell you the story when you get here. I am thankful for Alexander's faithfulness and Jesus' provision. AMPP tracked us down our first evening at his house and almost captured us, so we will go to the kibbutz first thing tomorrow morning. We cannot stay here another day."

"Kibbutz? You are going to a Jewish settlement?"

"A *Messianic* Jewish settlement, Ollie! The entire community believed in Jesus, thanks to Alexander telling one man. We'll be safe there and can come and go as we please, but we must be careful not to expose them."

"Send me the address and we will meet you there! Oh, Ally is coming with us."

"Ally?!"

That got the attention of the other three adults, their faces showing they had doubts too.

"She can't do that, Ollie. AMPP patrols are all over the place searching for her."

"Sorry, Ben, we're a team. And you never break up a great team! Don't worry, Ally handles herself very well. Besides, what did you say about Jesus protecting us?"

Ben's own words trapped him. He was glad they were coming, even Ally. Together they would build an army of Jewish believers in Jesus in the Holy Land!

• • • • •

Johnathan's wife, Brita, led the way as the Baldwins and Sandersons made their way to the Rocky Mountains. He and a group of kids lay in the back of the Chevy Tahoe. They chose the northern route through Kansas City and Topeka because the southern track would take them straight through Wichita. It was far too dangerous to take that chance.

They did not know if Messai found his men after the group gunned them down at the cabin, but they would stay as far away from Wichita as possible. One of the kids looked through the rear window and yelled.

"Look daddy! Their car is on fire!"

"Brita, stop! They've overheated. That thing is blowing steam like crazy."

"I can't do that! We're supposed to stay apart from each other, remember?"

"Then go to the next exit, and I'll call Julian."

"Looks like the next exit is about five miles."

"Then move on. There's a creek over the hill. They can get water from it."

"Julian, we just crossed a small creek. If you're overheated, you can stop there and put water in the car. I'm glad you let the kids ride with us."

He told Joanie to pull over just ahead and turn off the vehicle. Brita continued to the exit.

Julian had just exited the vehicle when a patrolman pulled in behind them.

"Joanie, stay calm and talk to him," he said over his shoulder as he walked over the embankment carrying two milk jugs. "I'll pretend I didn't notice him." He moved so fast he slid down the hill.

The officer strode to Joanie's window, which she already had down.

"Ma'am, it appears your vehicle has overheated. I saw your husband going over the bank to get water. If you will pop the hood for me, I will see what's going on."

He raised the hood, looked around and using his handkerchief, turned the radiator cap slowly until it was off and steam stopped rolling. He looked closer and stood up just as Julian arrived back at the vehicle, puffing and panting from the lengthy walk.

"Thanks for checking on us, officer. This thing got too hot, and I had quite a hike carrying this water up here." He grinned. "I'll pour it in and we'll get on our way. But I appreciate your help."

"You're not going anywhere, son. Your water hose burst. Pour in all the water you want, and it will blow right back out."

Julian leaned in to look too. Sure enough, the man was right. Now what?

"It's about five miles to the next exit. I can call a tow truck, or if we can carry enough water to fill it, you might make it to the exit. I'll follow you to make sure you do."

He walked back to the patrol car and returned carrying a large can. "I keep this with me for occasions like this," he said with a smile.

Both trekked to the creek and returned with all three containers filled with water.

"When we finish pouring it in and shut the hood, ma'am, take off. I will be right behind you."

By the time they reached the exit, the car was boiling again. Joanie stopped at a garage next door to a restaurant and shut the motor off. The patrolman pulled in behind her and talked to the mechanic. After a brief chat, he took the car in to install the hose. Meanwhile, the others had gotten off the exit and gone into the restaurant. They sat at different tables and pretended not to know each other.

"Ma'am, if you don't mind, I need to see your license, registration, and proof of insurance. How long have you owned this vehicle?"

"We just bought it yesterday." Julian jumped in, hoping Joanie would let him do the talking. Her eyes revealed she wanted that too.

"I thought that may be the case. I ran your temporary tag."

"Sir, we haven't had time to insure the car. I apologize for that. We had to buy it quick so we could get home, but I plan to take care of that right after we arrive. I assume the dealer sent in all the information. He gave us a temporary tag and registration."

They continued the conversation, but he could not convince the officer. While they talked, Julian saw something over the man's shoulder that made his heart race. He hoped the patrolman did not notice his change in expression, even though he tried to stay calm. The black SUV stopped less than ten feet away from them and two AMPP men got out and walked in the restaurant. John and Kathie had stayed in their car. That was a plus.

What if the men or the patrolman noticed that the vehicles all had the same temporary tags and registration from Missouri? In his mind, he attempted to concoct a plan, even as he talked to the officer. In his spirit, he prayed that God would give the others wisdom. He saw them exit the building, one family at a time, get in their vehicles and drive away. Relief washed over him like a flood, causing his knees to weaken.

"Mr. Parker, I cannot allow you to continue without insurance. I can let the registration and tags slide, but the law says you must have insurance."

"If you'll give me a few minutes, I'll call my insurance guy and ask if he'll do that without me there."

He called Blake, who called Rickie, who called the used car dealer. He still carried the car on his insurance. Within minutes, Julian had an email on his phone showing the coverage. The patrolman seemed okay with that but ordered him to insure the vehicle the moment they arrived home. He gave his word.

The police officer left, the mechanic finished installing the hose, and they were ready to go after what felt like an eternity. The two AMPP guys left the restaurant laughing and talking. He saw them look his way and pause, speaking in a more serious tone. He told Joanie to get in the back and jumped in the driver's seat. He jerked the car into Drive and pulled out of the parking lot.

The AMPP men jumped from their vehicle, waving and yelling, attempting to flag him down. He kept going as if he didn't notice them. When he turned onto the Interstate entrance ramp, he saw their flashing lights. They whipped out of their parking space and started for the road.

Julian did the only thing he could do. He stomped the accelerator to the floor.

•   •   ••   •   •

Ben was eager to get moved rather than stick around and take a chance on AMPP returning.

"What time should we leave for the kibbutz tomorrow morning?"

"We will not go tomorrow morning."

"What do you mean we will not go tomorrow morning? We can't sit here and wait for AMPP to return. All of us are sitting ducks! I am sorry, my friend, but I must decide against you on this."

"Then I see that we are in agreement."

"The two of you are making no sense," exclaimed Elizabeth. "I am more confused now than before you started talking."

Alexander explained. "We will go tonight, soon after dark, if Moshe can arrange transportation to the kibbutz. AMPP will not wait until tomorrow to come looking for you again. I suspect they will conduct a raid before the night is over. They must not find us here when they do."

"But if they're watching this house, how can we leave without being caught," asked Miriam. "It would seem that we are sitting ducks in here *or* out there."

"Not if I have anything to say about it. I have a plan, but it depends on Moshe. We can't drive away from this house without being seen. I'm sure AMPP has sentries posted right now watching to make sure we don't leave. If Moshe comes, we can meet him at the edge of a wooded area one mile away. We will sneak out the back, walk through the woods to a narrow street, and meet him there. The sad thing for me is, Elizabeth and I can never return to our home."

"This has been our home for almost forty years," she whispered. "But now, this world is no longer our home, and nothing in it belongs to us. We turned our backs on this stuff and our faces toward Jesus. Make your call, Alexander, and let's get ready to go."

A window shattered and glass bounced at their feet. Before they could run, the front and back doors burst open. They found themselves surrounded by two AMPP patrols with eight men and no way to escape.

"*Alexander...* Did you really think you could hide your guests from us? Mr. Benjamin Abramson, I presume. Allow me to introduce myself. I am Mohammed, Captain of this patrol and Aissa Messai's top man in Israel. You have made quite a name for yourself in the world, and especially here. But few of these Jewish pigs have followed your blasphemous teachings. What? None of you knew that is what he thinks of the Jews? Well, now you do. But you'll never get the chance to tell anyone."

"Yes, we knew," said Ben with unmistakable defiance in his voice. "We too have ways of discovering these things."

Mohammed smiled. "Let us see if you are as brave as they say you are." He slapped Ben across the face, spinning his head to the side. Blood seeped from his mouth, and Miriam ran to his side.

"Be careful how you speak of our leader. Mr. Messai has worked to bring peace and prosperity to the world, and you seek to undermine everything he does. The time has come for you and your family to pay the price for that. It is unfortunate that Alexander and Elizabeth must join you."

"Do you think you can keep this quiet, as you have the deaths of so many others? I think not!"

"You are correct! Mr. Messai has no plans to keep your deaths quiet. Thus, we will not kill you here; I will save you for him. This is one job he wants to handle himself for all the world to see. To do that, he will leave for Israel right after I call him and share this news. It will thrill him to rid the world of one of the top Smyrnian rebels, and his entire family."

He pulled his phone from his pocket and called Aissa Messai, putting it on speaker so all of them could listen. Hearing the voice left no doubt about who answered. They had heard it many times.

"Mohammed, you were only to call if you had wonderful news for me. I trust that is the reason for this call."

"Yes, sir. We captured the targets, have them in custody, and will detain them until your arrival."

"Thank you, Captain! You did well. Mr. Abramson, I assume you can hear me?"

"I hear you loud and clear, Messai. These henchmen of yours have not treated us with respect tonight. You need to train them better."

Mohammed struck Ben across the face again, drawing more blood, and spinning his head so hard to the left it seemed it would fly off.

"Leave him alone!" Miriam screamed.

"Don't worry, ma'am. Regardless what your husband thinks of me, I will not strike a woman."

"Has my captain told you of my plans for you and your wife and children, Mr. Abramson? Now I am forced to include Alexander and Elizabeth, too. Such a shame. But Alexander, you should have known better than to get mixed up with the *Smyrnians*."

"Your plans are no concern of ours, Messai. We worship Jesus and know who you are. You must know you cannot defeat him. In a few short years, he will destroy you and deliver us!"

"You speak with such boldness, Ben. That is an admirable trait. But we shall see how bold you are when the sacrifices begin. Now I must go prepare for my journey to your homeland. Tell them about our plans, Mohammed. It should be quite entertaining!"

"With pleasure, sir," he groveled as Messai ended the call. "Mr. Messai has awaited the opportunity to offer perfect sacrifices in the temple. Since you claim to be pure by the *blood of Jesus*, you are the *perfect* sacrifices! Isn't that exciting news? He will not offer the sacrifices himself, but will instruct his High Priest to do so. The man does the boss's every bidding."

"Mr. Messai will fly tonight, arrive by daylight, and make a special announcement at the time of the morning sacrifice. I'm sure as a good Jew, you know that is 9:00 a.m. The news will concern the evening sacrifice, which will occur at 3:00 p.m. The Priest will offer eleven people on the altar of burnt offering. All you must do is look around you to see who those eleven people are."

"No," breathed Miriam, her eyes showing the fear that lay behind them.

"Yes, Mrs. Abramson. He will sacrifice all eleven of you, beginning with the youngest." He looked toward the kids with an evil grin crossing his face. "The last two will be you and your husband. Apologies to you, Alexander and Elizabeth. You must settle for being numbers eight and nine in the lineup. I confess, watching you die will give me great pleasure. People worldwide will celebrate the removal of people who stand in the way of Mr. Messai's plans for peace and prosperity."

With those words, he collapsed to the floor, blood flowing from his back. The others fell in unison within seconds. The eleven people in the room stood stunned, unable to grasp what had just happened. Twelve men dashed into the house and moved to each of the fallen men, ensuring they were dead. After confirming that, they stood and joined the shocked people whose lives they had just saved.

"Alexander, my brother, are you okay?" He turned and saw Ben.

"They hurt you." Taking a handkerchief from his pocket, he wiped the blood from Ben's mouth.

"Moshe! How… how did you know we needed you tonight?" Alexander stuttered.

"Jesus told me I was to protect you and others who would come, remember? I just did my job."

"My name is Benjamin Abramson, Moshe. It is a privilege to meet you. Alexander told me much about you and your community earlier."

"I know who you are, Mr. Abramson. Thank you for your boldness to share the love of Jesus with your fellow Israelites. Grab only what you need to take with you to the kibbutz and try to hurry. Other members of AMPP may come when they cannot contact their comrades. Alexander and Elizabeth, you will not return here again, but don't worry. We will take care of all your needs. We parked the vehicles up the street. Bring your things, and we will load up and be on our way."

The group grabbed a few things and headed to the door. Ben took the most important thing for his work. His equipment for broadcasting was a must. Elizabeth took one last look at her home, then walked away without regrets. For the next five years, she would live in a kibbutz with a community of people who loved Jesus, if they all survived that long. They would live out their purpose and give their all to help Jews follow Jesus as the true Messiah. She was ready.

CHAPTER 12

Julian descended the ramp onto the Interstate, calling his mom's phone as he drove.

"Julian! Did you get everything taken care of and get away? We saw the AMPP men inside the restaurant and knew they would come outside before you could leave. That worried me."

"Listen to me, mom. They spotted us and recognized who we are, then tried to stop us before we could pull out of the parking lot. I just hit the Interstate and have this car pegged. They're closing fast. We need a diversion. I'm sure they've already called backup, so we're trying to figure out how to get away from them. The only option is to get off the Interstate, so I'm taking the next exit. That will take me toward Wichita, but it's our only chance. Can you guys come back and help us?"

"We're not far ahead of you, and we're all together now. What can we do? *Honey, be careful!*"

"Slow down and wait for me to pass you, then get in both lanes like one of you is trying to pass the other. It will help if the others can fall in there too. Block the lanes so they can't get around. Don't let them pass on the shoulder, or get in the median, if you can stop them. Let me get far enough ahead where they can't see us."

"I'll get off onto 135 at Salina and figure something out after that. If they think I stayed on 70 and keep going, I may have a chance. I'll either take 56 or 50 after I exit, then decide what to do after that. One of us will call and tell you which way we went and where we are."

Up ahead, he saw the others forming a line to allow him to pass. He shot by them, still able to see the lights of the SUV in the distance behind him. When he was past, they formed a two-lane convoy that prevented anyone from passing.

"It looks like there are two or three AMPP vehicles now," said Joanie, turning and looking back, "but none of them have gotten around yet."

"I'm getting close to the exit. Keep me posted on what's going on behind us, and I'll keep this thing to the floor. We're taking 135, so hold on because I need to move fast."

"The others are doing their jobs because I can't see any of them now. Don't slow down!"

The exit came at them in a hurry. He hit the ramp running eighty miles per hour and prayed the light at the intersection was green. It wasn't, but no cars sat waiting at the red light.

"Hold on, Joanie," he yelled and made the left turn onto 135 on two wheels, avoiding oncoming traffic to his right. Horns blared from behind as he sped away, slowing as he encountered heavier traffic. He hoped the SUVs had passed by and continued on Interstate 70.

When the others neared the exit, they cleared the left lane and formed a single line in the right lane, preventing the AMPP vehicles from getting to the ramp. They flew by them, blaring their horns and screaming out the windows. In the lead, Johnathan took the ramp, and the others followed. Kathie was back on the phone with Julian, informing him they had taken the same route and were not far behind. Both agreed on one thing: avoid Wichita.

• • • • • •

The group loaded up in Ein Karem and left for the kibbutz. Each vehicle traveled a separate route to keep from arousing suspicion. When they arrived, the others welcomed them with open arms and showed them to their houses.

"Will this work?" Moshe asked Ben. "It sits in the center of the kibbutz, so all of us surround you should trouble arise."

"It's perfect. Now, I need to set up my equipment. Our people will expect a broadcast at 3:00 p.m. tomorrow, so waiting is not an option. We need to meet with the community leaders in the morning and determine how to proceed. Shall we say 7:00 a.m.?"

"We'll join you in the meeting hall at 7:00. We have work to do, and these people are excited! Nothing else matters to them now that they know the truth. Five years doesn't give us much time to tell our people about Jesus. I look forward to our meeting."

7:00 a.m. Ben had worked most of the night setting up his studio. That was all finished, and the first broadcast would air at 3:00 p.m. Now he stood before a dozen leaders of the kibbutz, witnessing the generals who would lead this army into battle.

"Thank you for joining me this morning, men. We have much to do, and the time is short. Let's get down to business and determine the best way to reach as many of our people as we can. I assume most of you heard my story. Since that night in my home in New York City, the words *'go and tell my people'* have guided me. But it occurred to me in the past few weeks I was now to take those words literally. When Jesus said *go*, he meant *here* in our homeland. Living here provides the best opportunity to tell my people about him."

"Alexander and Elizabeth were the first Jews in Israel to believe in Jesus. A few others followed, but they stayed quiet. However, when Moshe and his family believed, then brought all of you, a movement started. And it's clear that you are ready to do your part. So, it is my joy to welcome you to the Smyrnians! You have a lot to learn, as did I and every other member of our group. Please spend some time on our website, *smyrnians.com*, and watch my videos and the teachings of Blake and Beth Thompson."

"Oliver Barton and Amelia Clarke will join us tomorrow. You may recall their daring escape from AMPP in London. Oliver is a dear friend of the Ben Ezras and is the reason they followed Jesus."

"So, you understand how this works. Oliver told Alexander to watch the video, which resulted in Elizabeth and him trusting in Jesus. Alexander told Moshe, who told all of you. That is how we spread the truth about Jesus. Imagine what will happen when all of us do that throughout the entire country of Israel! And Oliver and Amelia will also bring Miss Ally Fromm with them."

The mention of Ally's name created a murmur among the group. The buzz grew loud enough to prevent Ben from being heard until one man spoke for all of them.

"Do you speak of the same Ally Fromm who was Messai's assistant? We heard the news that she left him, but it is still too dangerous for her to stay in the kibbutz. That will put everyone in danger. She may still turn us in and poses a threat to all of our families."

"She is also the second person after the Rapture to put her faith in Jesus."

The buzz started again as the group talked among themselves. They still had their doubts about Ally, but Ben intrigued them enough to keep listening to what he had to say.

"No one had heard Ally's name prior to her role as Messai's assistant. Although young, she serves as a leader among the Smyrnians and only sought the position to get on the inside and spy for us. Think about it: out of all the ladies in the world who applied, Ally got the job so she could fulfill the role Jesus gave her. Only he could make that happen. Messai attempted to violate her in the King David Hotel that night when she fled from him, but Oliver and Amelia helped her escape and return to us."

"It broke her heart to lose such a golden opportunity to gather intelligence for the team and send it back to us. But she now understands working here with us offers even greater potential to fulfill her calling. Nothing I said could stop her from coming. She will teach us a lot about what we are preparing to do. You will understand that more when you meet her tomorrow."

That appeased them and satisfied their curiosity. They were now eager to meet all three of their new teammates the next day.

"My plan works like this. We will divide the country into sections. Each of you can choose an area where you will work. Why not use God's own map to make those decisions? The boundaries of the land given to the twelve tribes will determine where each of you goes."

"We will stay in the country, not venturing into the territories of Reuben, Gad and the half-tribe of Manasseh in Jordan. But we will still reach those tribes because Jesus is bringing them home in *Aliyah*! You will infiltrate the others as God's spies, telling people about Jesus in all of Israel. Just as Moses sent 12 spies into the land, so will we, except we will *all* go with boldness."

"Give me Ephraim!"

"And you are?"

"Yaakov."

"Ah, Jacob." Ben smiled. "It is good to be in the homeland. Naturally, you want to work in the place where your namesake settled. Who's next?"

"I am Eliyahu."

Ben interrupted, not giving him time to finish. "Let me guess. Issachar."

The man smiled. "Yes, the place my ancestor, Elijah, won a glorious victory atop Mt. Carmel."

"Before we continue, I need to lay claim to my territory. Can anyone guess that one?"

Moshe laughed out loud. "I don't have to guess: Benjamin!"

"Right you are, Moshe! But I will need much help since my primary work will be in and around Jerusalem."

"Ben, they must not see you in Jerusalem, or anywhere near it. I'm not even sure you should leave the safety of the kibbutz."

"Oh yes, I will go. And I will walk and teach in the temple courts, telling our people about the Messiah."

"I will not allow you to go to Jerusalem and die! The cause will die with you!"

"Easy there, Doubting Thomas. Do you think you can stop me from doing what I am called to do? No! I will teach for three days, then go on the Sabbath. Many Jews will be at the temple that day."

Moshe saw trying to talk him out of going was useless. He looked around at the others and asked, "Who will go with him?" Every hand in the room raised. If Ben taught on the website for three days, then showed up at the temple with twelve other men, things may get interesting in Jerusalem on Saturday.

•   •   •   •   •

The Baldwin and Sanderson crew counted it a miracle when they arrived at Johnathan's safe house deep in the Rocky Mountains. After their escape from AMPP, they took back roads the rest of the way and arrived at 4:00 a.m. A fourteen-hour trip turned into twenty after an eventful day led to an additional six hours and a lot of stress.

The enormous cabin sat tucked away deep in the woods, far off the beaten path and invisible to the outside world. At 5,000 square feet and three levels with nine bedrooms, it could comfortably sleep thirty-five people. But it would also accommodate others, if that became necessary. It provided everything anyone could ask for, and more.

When daylight arrived, they discovered a short hike through the dense forest led to a breathtaking mountaintop view. But its most important feature for them was a secret passageway which led to a network of tunnels, each ending in enormous underground rooms... perfect for hiding.

A wealthy recluse built it years earlier as a place where he could escape and live in total privacy. When they checked it out further, they realized it was equal to the Shelter in Missouri. But for luxury, it was far better! When Jesus supplied their needs, he did it right.

"We need to send pictures to the others and make them jealous," chuckled John. "This is almost too good to be true."

He stated the obvious, and all of them felt the same. They stood and stared for a moment before grabbing their things and moving into their new home. This place far exceeded all of their expectations.

•　　•　　•　　•　　•

Blake's phone rang in the Shelter. "Ben, what are you doing interrupting our second honeymoon? We are enjoying having this place all to ourselves."

"I'm sure that's true, but I know you don't like holing up in a bunker. You want to be back in action."

"You know me all too well. We are both going crazy in here. We should be out doing something instead of hiding away, but I fear for Beth. Messai wants her so much that I need to take every precaution I can to protect her."

"Listen, Blake, Jesus said, 'Do not be afraid.' And he told us instead of fearing people, we should fear God. I will cut straight to the chase. We need you here with us."

"You want us to come to Israel?"

"Yes, and the sooner the better. I feel a fresh wind blowing and see it in the faces of the people here in the kibbutz. In three days, I am going to Jerusalem and begin teaching in the temple courts."

Blake interrupted him. "Ben, you can't do that!"

"I not only can; I *will!* Remember how the movement started in the beginning, Blake? Evan Ryles realized the truth in his dorm room and put his faith in Jesus. Then he told Ally, and the two of them told you. The same thing happened here with Alexander and Elizabeth Ben Ezra. They believed, then Alexander told Moshe, who told the people in the kibbutz. Now it is ready to sweep the country, starting with Jerusalem. I can sense that."

"The movement has begun in Israel, and Jesus brought me here to lead it. Blake, the time has come for me to do what he called me to do: *go and tell my people!* Ollie, Amelia and Ally are on their way. Come and get in on the harvest. Don't miss out on what Jesus is doing."

"You drive a hard bargain, Ben. The action in Israel sounds more appealing than life in a bunker. Beth and I could enjoy hanging out in here for the rest of the Tribulation, but you know neither of us wants to do that. Let me talk to her. We may hop a plane to the Holy Land!"

"Now you're talking! Don't waste any time. In three days I will walk into the temple courts and start telling the Jews about Jesus. I don't want you to miss out on that! And that won't be the only place I go. Jesus wants me to follow in his footsteps and teach in places where he taught. He will protect us and allow me to speak without fear of capture or death."

"I'm not sure what the future holds, but the beginning is right here and right now. Where things go after this is unclear. I see persecution coming for my people and the need to flee. We must reach as many as we can before that time and prepare for an inevitable assault. The war is coming to Israel and the Jews, Blake. Of that, I am certain."

"What's your plan, Ben? I know you have one."

"I am dividing the country into areas of the twelve tribes. One of these twelve men Jesus has given me here will lead the work in each of those places. Their first task is to find their *Moshe*. He will then be the catalyst to help spread the news about Jesus to his *tribe*. I don't understand why that's how I'm supposed to proceed; I just know it's what Jesus showed me."

"I love that and want to be a part of it! The people of Israel won't know what hit them!"

"We will have supernatural protection too. I will teach in a lot of places, not just the temple courts. And I want you guys with me to help people when they turn to Jesus. This will be fun, Blake!"

"I won't question you because I trust you, and I trust Jesus. I haven't even asked Beth yet, but you can bet that we are both 100% on board!"

"One more thing: I want the others here too. These twelve men will form the team traveling to the tribes. But I want twelve Smyrnians to walk alongside me."

"You said Ollie, Amelia and Ally are on the way, plus Beth and me. Who are the other seven?"

"Evan, Anders, and Malachi, John and Kathie, and Trey and Rickie. I am calling them as soon as we get off the phone. All of them are battle tested and proven. The time has come to focus on Israel, and we will all go into battle together."

"That works for me! Beth and I will try our best to fly tomorrow. I want to be with you when you go to the temple courts! You *will* need someone to protect you, right?" He chuckled.

"I told you, I already have all the protection I need… supernatural protection! Jesus can handle that part all by himself."

"One question: who can we leave here in the Shelter? I mean, this is Command Central. We can't just leave the place unmanned."

"Get Steve and Linda to come. You can brief them on all the ins and outs of running the place. He can create a hospital there for us when we need it, too. The Shelter is the perfect place for that. Steve can stock one bunker with everything he needs to treat any medical situation that may arise."

"And the farm will continue to be our place of refuge when we need a break. Don't worry, Blake, the Shelter will continue to be our primary location. All or some of us will be back there soon, although, something tells me neither the Shelter nor Israel is in my future. I'm not sure what that means, but it doesn't concern me. Jesus will show me when the time comes."

"Don't talk like that, Ben. You're scaring me."

"Don't be afraid, Blake. Jesus has everything under control."

Blake could see his smile and sense his contentment from 6,000 miles away. None of them knew where the journey would take them next. But they had never known that in the past two years. They were along for the ride, and Jesus was flying the plane. Wherever he took them would be perfect. He walked into the next room to speak with Beth, knowing she would be ready to go.

•　　•　　•　　•　　•

Aissa Messai called another meeting of the UN Security Council in Geneva, Switzerland. The head of his security forces and the Executive Director of

AMPP joined them for this one. They all understood this gathering was urgent.

"Gentlemen," Messai growled in the same low gravelly tone into which his voice transformed at times like this.

"The threat we discussed at our last meeting remains at *Code Orange*. We have yet to capture any of the Smyrnian leaders, although my men have taken out some of their followers. Our intel has slowed, causing us to fear they are planning a major operation somewhere in the world. Neither have we picked up on any chatter since our most recent assault on them and their families in several countries. It looks like they dropped off the face of the earth, but we know that isn't true."

"This is of great concern to me, the directors of my security forces, and the Peace Patrol. If we allow them to get the jump on us spreading their lies in another part of the world, it will damage our goal of worldwide peace and prosperity. We cannot allow that to happen."

"Now something else has come up that may further complicate the situation. One of my most trusted AMPP captains has defected to those rebels. Nothing could have made me believe Magnus would do such a thing, but it is clear now that he has. He is aware of everything about our operations and can give them any information they need to stay a step ahead of us."

"Thus, we must make adjustments to our M.O. That is why we come to you seeking your help and asking for any suggestions you may have. I will now allow Mr. Rossi, head of our security forces, to speak and fill you in on some things that have happened in recent months."

"Good morning, gentlemen. I want to echo the things Mr. Messai just shared with us. The Smyrnians are a divisive group and a destructive threat to everything we desire to achieve. They are very elusive and seem endowed with some magical ability to escape our grasp."

"In the past several months, we have taken several approaches trying to capture them or impede their progress. We apprehended Miss Beth Jennings, one of their leaders, and held her captive in Mr. Messai's mansion. This was an effort to lure the others there to attempt a rescue..."

A member of the council interrupted him. "It is my understanding that she is now Mrs. Beth Thompson, wife of Blake Thompson..."

"Silence!" roared Messai, pounding his fist down on the table with such force it seemed the fixture would splinter and collapse to the floor. "She is not his wife! Any ceremony performed by their group is illegal because it did not comply with the laws of the state."

The man cowered and dropped his head, refusing to look into the glare of Messai's eyes. "I apologize, sir. I was out of line. It will not happen again."

He and the others knew their boss wanted Beth for his own. That much was obvious. But none of them would dare cross him for fear of facing his wrath. To do so may mean more than losing their jobs; it could mean losing their lives.

"You are right. It will not happen again. You may leave the room now because you are not fit to serve on this council."

"But Mr. Messai, I…"

"I said, *now!*" Messai's voice was demonic as the eerie sound erupted into another roar. As the man rose to leave, Messai nodded at the Director of AMPP. The man arose, pulled his weapon from its holster and aimed it at the man's forehead.

"No, Mr. Messai! I said I was sorry! I promise…"

The sound of the gunshot filled the room, reverberating off the walls and causing the others to cover their ears. They watched in horror as the impact hurled their colleague backwards, a small hole in the middle of his forehead. Faces pale, they turned their attention back to Messai.

"Are there any questions?" he asked. None of them spoke, as the room fell hauntingly silent.

"You may continue, Mr. Rossi."

"Thank you, sir. I trust you gentlemen can see how serious we are about this threat. As I was saying, our attempt to lure the others to Mr. Messai's mansion to rescue Miss Jennings was a success. We were aware of their presence and prepared to intercept them the next day. But at midnight, the earthquake struck, allowing her, and them, to escape. We tracked them down at a residence in Germany, only to see most of our patrol killed in reckless fashion."

"In another attempt to draw them out of hiding, we eliminated members of their families. But this time they warned the others after the initial assault, again halting our plans. We continued to pursue them, coming close to capturing some. But their elusiveness and uncanny ability to evade our grasp persists. Now we have no evidence of where they are or their next moves. I reiterate, that is why we turned to you for help. If we roundtable, maybe an idea will come as we talk."

The room was silent, none of them talking as they witnessed the dead body of their fellow council member lying on the floor. A chill crept up each spine and infiltrated their minds, but they were unaware of it as they sat speechless before the most powerful man in the world.

"Speak!" Messai roared once more. "Maybe none of you are fit to serve on this council."

The second those words left his mouth, they started talking, all of them at once and in no particular order. The room sounded like buzzing bees released from their hive. No one understood what anyone else was saying... that is, no one except Messai. He was taking in every word, understanding every statement as if each man addressed only him. The buzz continued until one word, missed by all the others, stood out to Messai.

"*Israel.*"

"That's it!" He stood to his feet, a look of awareness on his face.

"Why didn't I think of that? I should have thought back to the day I saw Benjamin Abramson there for my announcement about the construction of the temple, and knowing he has now returned. It all makes sense, and I believe it is true. They are planning a massive operation in Israel! We will have them cornered in that tiny country, with no way of escape. They have made a tactical error and are ours for the taking!"

He pointed to the man who spoke the word Israel and said, "You sir are the new chairman of this group. That was a stroke of pure brilliance. I need a man like you in charge."

"But sir," the chairman said, turning toward Messai, "You placed me in this position, and I take it seriously. It is an honor to serve you in this role. I would like to continue..."

"You are a disgrace to the entire movement," Messai growled at the man. "You have done nothing since I installed you as chairman." He held out his hand toward the AMPP Director, who placed the gun into his palm.

"No, sir. Please do not do this. I will serve any role on the team you wish me to serve."

But it was too late. When the words left his mouth, the bullet pierced his forehead and he too lurched backwards against the wall, smearing it with blood as he slid to the floor.

"Now, do all of you understand your roles on this council? And are you willing to perform them as I have asked?"

The words, "yes, sir!" came from every seat around the table as the men groveled for their lives.

"Okay, I thank you men for your work and your willingness to serve. I trust you will continue your commitment from this point on, without question."

They all shook their heads in agreement as Messai sat back down, appeased.

"Mr. Rossi and Mr. Abboud, please dispatch one hundred AMPP patrols, and other security forces, to Israel at once. Patrol the airports at all times. Search for traitors who may have joined the ranks of the Smyrnians. And when you find them, hold them until I arrive. I will show the world what happens when people try to interfere with my plans for peace in the Middle East and the world. Ask the police and IDF to cooperate with you. But only do so after you discover those you can trust. This is perfect!" His smile was wide, and his voice returned to normal.

•   •   •   •   •

Ben had now contacted each of those who would come to Israel and informed the remaining group of what was happening. The former were ecstatic and could hardly wait to get there. The latter hoped for the day they would join them, but committed themselves to continuing the work in their current locations until that time came.

Trey and Rickie had accomplished their initial missions. Commander Paul Johnson in Missouri and Bradley Rogers in England had both believed in Jesus. Each had already begun bringing a few of their fellow soldiers to the faith. That would be a tremendous bonus down the road.

Steve and Linda agreed to move from their home in Springfield to the Shelter. Steve was bringing in enough medical equipment to operate a full-blown hospital from there. He had proven he could do surgery in his home without using an operating room. Now he would have the equipment and everything else he needed to perform any needed medical procedures.

The nine who would travel to Israel convened at the Shelter. With Ollie, Amelia and Ally on their way, the remaining group would create a plan for their trip and leave as soon as they purchased tickets. If things fell into place, that would happen in two days.

The only problem with that timeline, in Blake's mind, was missing out on Ben's first trip to the temple. He would love to watch that. He could not imagine what that would be like for the man who had dreamed his entire life of the temple being built and the Messiah returning to it.

But they would be there for every time after this one. Now the team gathered in the underground house they had called home for two years. They were fired up and more than ready to get started. Trey got the ball rolling.

"We shouldn't fly commercial. AMPP security in the airports will be so tight that we stand no chance of getting past them. Our new military contacts can get us anywhere in the world we need to go. They can land at an IDF base to avoid Ben Gurion. American-Israeli relations are good."

Rickie agreed. "We have been there, done that using military planes. I believe Trey is right. Let's contact Paul Johnson right now and set that up."

"Wait a minute, guys," said Blake. "Ben told me something you need to hear. He said Jesus has shown him we will have supernatural protection in Israel. I trust his judgment, so I say we fly commercial and put that to the test."

"No way!" argued Trey. "We could walk into a death trap."

"Listen to what Blake says, Trey." Beth knew her long-time friend would listen to her.

"But, Beth," pleaded Trey, "Ben Gurion will crawl with AMPP men. We'll never make it."

"Trey," she whispered, "do you trust Ben?"

"Sure, I trust him, but why take such a risk?"

"Beth and I will do it." Blake was resolute, and there was no changing his mind. "I hope the rest of you will join us. Ben would never lead us astray."

"I'm with Blake," Evan said with confidence. "Ben Abramson is God's man for Israel. If he says we'll have supernatural protection, I believe him. Who else is with me?"

"I am," said Malachi, followed by Anders.

"Count us in," John and Kathie said at the same time.

Trey and Rickie knew the others outnumbered them. "Okay, okay, we will go with you. But if we get captured in the airport and slaughtered on national television, don't say I didn't warn you. Oh, I'm sorry, gang. I trust Ben. He has never let us down. Let's get our tickets."

The only thing left was coordinating with their other teammates and hearing their plans. John showed them pictures of the expansive chateau in the Rocky Mountains.

"I may go live with them!" Evan chuckled as he spoke.

The others chided him for wanting to live the good life, all in good fun. They knew he was sold out just like they were. None of them had traveled to Israel before, and now they would go for the most important reason of all. Plans made and tickets purchased, they were ready. In two days, they would board a plane and fly to the Land of the Bible. They did not know what awaited them there, but they shared Ben's faith. He had heard from Jesus and believed protection was theirs.

CHAPTER 13

John and Kathie's families remained in Colorado, now left to lead the American movement. They were all new at this but determined to work like seasoned pros. One priority was creating a second safe house for the Smyrnians in the Rocky Mountains. They could not have found a more perfect place for it.

It was difficult to choose a name. They looked for something unique which would set it apart from the Shelter in Missouri. After bantering about names such as Retreat, Lodge and Hideaway, they settled on the *Refuge*. It was not only a refuge above ground, but even more so underground. Should Messai's forces somehow stumble upon their location, it would be close to impossible to find them in the tunnels and hideouts below.

The reclusive former owner even planned for the possibility of someone wandering onto the property by mistake. He created a space for parking over 100 yards from the house that bore a striking resemblance to Doc and Kathie's cabin in Kansas. Downed trees and brush lay to the side of the dirt lane, coming in. They pulled them over the road, making it appear to be nothing more than an abandoned logging road.

The man thought of everything. He wanted people to leave him alone, so he did everything possible to ensure that no one ever bothered him. When the team needed medical care or a technology center, they would go to Command Central, aka, the Shelter. When they needed to escape for a bit and refresh, the Refuge was the place to go.

The temptation to stay and enjoy the last years of the planet was strong, but they understood the urgency of going to battle and telling people about Jesus. Evan gave them new identities for additional protection.

Julian took a full day driving to Albuquerque and trading his car under an assumed name. His purpose was two-fold. First, AMPP now knew the vehicle belonged to him, so he could not keep it. Second, if they discovered he traded it, they would think the group had fled south to Mexico. That would cover their tracks, throw AMPP off, and buy them some time. They tried to take everything into consideration, but during the Tribulation plans were always subject to change.

The morning after his return, they planned their next moves. Johnathan would begin online teaching, sharing the truth about the Rapture and the seven-year Tribulation. But he would take an unconventional approach. He had followed in his father's footsteps, getting his Ph.D. in geophysics. But instead of teaching, he started his own research company. His work included providing analysis for engineering and oil companies, environmental protection groups, and governmental geological surveys. It was a lucrative business.

Now, he needed to use his expertise to help people see the fallacy of their preconceived scientific views concerning the age of the earth. Once he understood that, it opened the door to believing the truth about what happened on September 11, 2029. He would never have believed it himself had he not also followed his father's newfound faith. In reality, scripture proves the earth is only 6,000 years old instead of four billion years, as science teaches. That was clear to him now, but his challenge was helping other people understand it. He would do his best.

The ladies took on Beth's role as Humanitarian Aid workers. They traveled about providing care for anyone who needed it. Their husbands planned to reach people and start more groups of new believers. The kids would play significant roles, too. They all wanted to make a difference in the time they had remaining. In eternity, they would live with Jesus on a new earth that would last forever, instead of 6,000 years. They longed for that time to come and knew it was getting close!

●　　　●　　　●　　　●　　　●

The Sabbath came at last, and Ben was up early to drive to the Temple Mount. Moshe and the other men sat eating breakfast with him, Ollie, Amelia, and Ally and making plans for how the day should go. The latter three had arrived the day before and stayed up late getting acquainted with the others. They would all go together, but drive separate cars instead of taking a bus owned by the kibbutz. Ben must remain inconspicuous during his first trip to the Mount.

Security allowed no one to carry a firearm after they passed through the Dung Gate and entered the Old City of Jerusalem. All the men could do was surround Ben as he walked and taught. But if the Temple Police or an AMPP patrol approached them, that would offer little protection. The mission may end in disaster if Ben was wrong about *supernatural* protection. They would find out when they got there. Until then, it required walking by faith.

The sight of thronging crowds made it clear they would get nowhere near the gate on this day. Parking the cars almost a mile away, they finished the journey on foot. When they ascended the hill to the Dung Gate, elbow-to-elbow with the massive multitude, they sang the Songs of Ascents found in Psalm 120-134. The glorious sound wafted down through the valley, and Ben thought people must hear it from miles away.

He envisioned himself climbing the mount with crowds of worshipers millennia earlier. A slight breeze blowing through his long beard brought a rapturous feeling, causing him to feel as if he floated along on the wind. It carried with it a gentle whisper that did not escape his attention. *Go and tell my people.* He whispered in return. *I will tell them, Lord. I will teach them on your Temple Mount.* Those walking with him sensed something unique taking place. A fresh wind was blowing. And not even the power of AMPP could stand in its way.

They reached the Gate after what seemed like hours, crawling along with the enormous mass of humanity. Ally recalled walking through this entrance with Messai, and a momentary shudder made its way through her body. She soon felt it replaced with transcendent peace. Words could not describe the joy flooding her mind in that beautiful moment. Her companions sensed it too. The singing had stopped; no one spoke. They moved in unison toward the magnificent structure awaiting them beyond the Western Wall.

The group stayed close until they stepped off the bridge and set foot on the Mount. Then ascending the stairs, they hurried around the Dome of the Rock, and entered the Temple's outer court. Ben collapsed to his knees and wept. The others surrounded him, but stood still, and allowed him this moment. They could not fathom what this was like for him. After several minutes, he arose to the sound of excited voices.

"It's him! Benjamin Abramson. He is here!"

The word traveled from person-to-person, and a crowd assembled. Ben did not hesitate.

"Gather around, friends. I have some things to tell you."

His smile betrayed the thrill he felt inside as he started speaking to his eager listeners.

"Brothers and sisters, Ha-Shem sent me here to tell you about our Messiah. His name is *Yeshua*."

•　•　•　•　•

The nine Smyrnians in Missouri knew flying from Springfield-Branson Airport was not an option. A lesser risk was driving to Kansas City, where they booked a direct flight to Tel Aviv, Israel. The military van provided the perfect transport for them and their luggage. Each carried only a duffel bag and carry-on. With no timeline for their return, they could buy clothes and supplies in Israel.

Steve drove so he could return the van to the Shelter. If they arrived too early and sat in the airport for an hour, it would increase their chances of being spotted and captured. But if they arrived late, they risked missing their flight. Precise timing was vital, giving them ample time to get through security and to the gate in time to board. Departure time was 9:00 p.m.

They would still leave early and park near the airport, then sit in the van as long as necessary before driving in and unloading. Curbside check-in would help them bypass the ticket counter and move straight to security. Evan had once again created new passports for each of them. Who could tell how many times their names would need to change?

Their greatest concern was the facial recognition technology Magnus told them about. It was Messai's newest method of identifying them. Fake names and passports would not help them if security used it. But then, there was the supernatural protection Ben had mentioned. How long would it last? Was it only available in Israel, or did it also apply to the United States? So many questions, but no time for concern at this point. They made the trip in good time and parked a mile away from Kansas City International Airport.

"I wish there was a way to get a word on how things go for Ben and the others at the Temple today. But he is asleep now and won't awaken until after we fly out. And we'll be in the air the entire time he is there. Waiting will drive me crazy."

"They will be fine, Blake. Ben was certain he is doing what Jesus told him to do."

"I appreciate your confidence, Beth, and wish I was as sure as you. We can't afford to lose Ben."

"Okay, it's time to head to the airport." Steve sounded less than convinced, too. He would walk them inside and go with them as far as security. "Make sure you get everything and hurry after we unload. Linda and I have flown from here so many times a lot of them know us by name. Maybe that will come in handy."

"If Ben is right, we won't need that," grinned Anders. His faith still never wavered.

Steve parked the van, they grabbed their luggage, and hustled through curbside check-in. Once inside, they saw them. Two airport security workers stood with two AMPP men, there to check everyone who came through.

"What should we do?" whispered Evan. "We can't avoid them."

"All we can do is keep walking, look the other way, and hope they don't pay attention to us." Blake forgot all about Ben's promise.

"Let me talk to them," said Steve. "I'll tell them you're in a hurry to catch your flight. Maybe they'll send us on through."

When they approached the men, one of them recognized Steve.

"Hey, Steve. Looks like you have a late flight tonight."

"Hello, Norm. And it appears they have you working the late shift tonight. What's up with that?"

"Oh, Sam's wife is having the baby, so he and I traded shifts. Covering for him is the least I can do. Besides, he'd do the same for me."

"I don't believe I was aware they were expecting. Please tell him congratulations for me."

Before he continued, telling them the group needed to get to their gate, Norm cut him off.

"Looks like you're flying solo tonight, too. Where's Linda?"

Steve stood stunned, as did the nine people with him. He said nothing, so Norm continued.

"I'm not trying to be nosy. It's just strange seeing you without her. You look lonely walking along all by yourself." He flashed a silly grin.

Steve tried to pull his thoughts together as he answered the man's question. "She's at home. But I'm not flying tonight. I just brought some friends in." Why did he say that? His job was to divert their attention from the others. He wanted to kick himself for that slip-up.

"Well, hurry on and catch up with them. We can let this guy go, men; he's okay. He's a big time surgeon from Springfield. You don't have to worry about him. But if you ever need a doctor who can save your life, he's your man! It's always good to see you, Steve."

"You too, Norm." He walked on, the others following. None of them reacted. This was strange.

"They can't see us," said Trey. "This is crazy!"

"Ben was right, this is supernatural protection. They don't even know we're here." Blake never doubted it was true, but he didn't dream of this.

Leave it to Evan. He walked up to one of the two AMPP men and waved his hand in front of his face. No response. "We *are* invisible!" he exclaimed.

When others came up behind them, Blake grabbed him by the arm and pulled him toward the corridor. "Come on, Evan, let's go. I'm sure everyone else sees us."

When they neared security, Steve said, "I have an idea. Walk around like you all have precheck. Maybe you're invisible to them too. If you make it, I'll leave. I don't think they noticed me, so I'd rather not raise suspicion by walking up to security alone, then not going on through. Go in peace. Jesus is with you!"

The group walked straight through without being seen. They moved on toward the Gate, waved at Steve, and kept going. He smiled and walked away.

"I wonder if the same thing will happen for Ben and his group on the Mount?" Blake pondered. "It will be one of the greatest days of his life, anyway. That would make it even better!"

The call to board came the moment they walked up. The woman greeted them as she checked their boarding passes. "Have a pleasant flight," she said.

This had gotten weird. Who saw them, and who didn't? It seemed they were only invisible to security people, while others saw them, like normal. This was going to be interesting, but fun!

•   •   •   •

Most of the crowd had seen Ben online. Some had watched his daily broadcast. They knew about the Smyrnians and their belief in Jesus. Now they wanted to hear what this movement was all about. Skepticism defined them before, but something, or *someone*, had prepared their hearts for these moments with Ben.

When he spoke, the people drank up every word like thirsty deer panting by streams of water. He quoted Old Testament Messianic prophecies, followed by the accompanying New Testament passages, showing how Jesus fulfilled each one. He considered using the Hebrew Bible or Jewish translation. But as he looked at the crowd, he realized he needed to speak in a modern version.

"Genesis 49, verse 10, told us the Messiah would come from the Tribe of Judah. 'The scepter will not depart from Judah, nor the ruler's staff from between his feet, until he to whom it belongs shall come and the obedience of the nations shall be his.' Luke, Chapter 3, verse 33, tells us Yeshua was 'the son of Amminadab, the son of Ram, the son of Hezron, the son of Perez, the son of *Judah*.' Some people say that proves nothing, but it is only the beginning!"

"The Prophet Micah said the Messiah would be born in Bethlehem. You are familiar with Chapter 5, verse 2: 'But you, Bethlehem Ephrathah, though you are small among the clans of Judah, out of you will come for me one who will be ruler over Israel, whose origins are from of old, from ancient times.' Matthew 2, verse 1, confirms that by saying, 'Yeshua was born in Bethlehem in Judea...'"

"The Gospel of Luke gives us more information in Chapter 2, verses 4 to 6. 'Joseph also went up from the town of Nazareth in Galilee to Judea, to Bethlehem the town of David, because he belonged to the house and line of David. He went there to register with Mary, who was pledged to be married to him and was expecting a child. While they were there, the time came for the baby to be born, and she gave birth to her firstborn, a son.'"

"Joseph lived in Nazareth. But it was no accident that the decree of Caesar Augustus forced him to travel to the town of his family line, to register for the census. God orchestrated the entire sequence of events at the perfect time to fulfill the prophecy!"

"The Prophet Isaiah foretold in Chapter 7, verse 14, the Messiah would be born of a virgin and called *Immanuel*, meaning *God is with us*. 'Therefore, the Lord himself will give you a sign: The virgin will conceive and give birth to a son, and will call him Immanuel.' Luke Chapter 1, verses 26 and 27, tells us Ha-Shem sent the Angel Gabriel to a virgin named Mary, telling her she would give birth to the Messiah. And Matthew Chapter 1, verses 22 and 23, says Mary gave birth to Yeshua to fulfill Isaiah's prophecy. A virgin birth sounds impossible, but we, Ha-Shem's chosen people, know he can do anything!"

The verses flowed from Ben's lips, entering their minds and piercing their hearts as they came. He kept going. "Isaiah Chapter 9, verses 1 and 2 foretold the Messiah would dwell and minister in Galilee. Matthew confirmed that! In Chapter 4, verses 13 and 14, he wrote, '[Jesus] went and lived in Capernaum, which was by the lake in the area of Zebulun and Naphtali—to fulfill what was said through the prophet Isaiah...' The Messiah lived in Capernaum and ministered all over Galilee!"

Ben was just getting warmed up. He had long-awaited this moment, and he could tell his words were hitting home. The others saw it too. But they failed to see the approaching company of men in black suits. AMPP patrolled the Mount, searching for Smyrnians. Some noticed, causing a murmur among the crowd, breaking their concentration on his words. Ben was undeterred.

"Brothers and sisters have no fear of the men from AMPP. They seek me, but Ha-Shem promised me supernatural protection. They cannot harm me. Ha-Shem wants you to know he is Lord, and Yeshua is your Messiah. Stand still and see the salvation of the Lord!"

Ben stepped out in front of the AMPP patrol, facing them as they approached. A gasp spread through the crowd as he faced what seemed destined to be capture or imminent death. Moshe and his men prepared to jump into action, joined by Ollie, Amelia and Ally, to protect their mentor and friend. But Ben motioned with his hand for them to stand down. They hesitated, but obeyed.

When the men came closer, Ben waved his hands, as if trying to get their attention, but they gave no indication they saw him. He yelled, "My name is Benjamin Abramson!" but the patrol continued walking. They reached him, but instead of grabbing or trampling him, walked right through him! Or you might say, *he* passed through them.

They continued on, and Ben still stood. He waved at the men as they walked away, telling them to have a wonderful day. He seemed amused by the entire thing. God's promise to him was true.

"Friends, the protection Ha-Shem promised me came to pass. You saw it with your own eyes! He wants you to know his word never fails. Just as he fulfilled that promise, he fulfilled his promise through the prophets that he would send the Messiah. That came true when he sent Yeshua to the world. Listen, and I will tell you more about him." He held their attention more now than before.

"In Chapter 9, verse 9, Zechariah wrote, 'Rejoice greatly, Daughter Zion! Shout, Daughter Jerusalem! See, your king comes to you, righteous and victorious, lowly and riding on a donkey, on a colt, the foal of a donkey.' Yeshua rode a donkey down the slope of the Mount of Olives and into this city through that gate," he proclaimed, pointing toward the Golden Gate. "Matthew wrote his Gospel for us, the Jews, to confirm that the Old Testament prophecies point to Yeshua as the Messiah. In Chapter 27, verse 37, he said that fulfilled what Zechariah said. And remember, they called Yeshua the *King of the Jews... our* King!"

"But we rejected him and refused to believe in him, just as Isaiah said in Chapter 53, verse 3. John, the beloved disciple, told us 'he came to that which was his own, but his own did not receive him.' We rejected our Messiah and King. But now Ha-Shem has given us a second chance! I ask you to take advantage of that as I did. But there is so much more. I must hurry."

"Zechariah also foretold in Chapter 11, verses 12 and 13 that someone would betray the Messiah for thirty pieces of silver. And he said they would use that money to buy a potter's field. That happened as recorded in Matthew Chapter 26, verses 14 to 16 and Chapter 27, verses 9 and 10."

Ben's words grew in intensity as he moved to the next part. "Isaiah said people would spit on the Messiah and beat him. You have read that in Chapter 50, verse 6. The Gospels tell us after Yeshua's arrest in the Garden of Gethsemane, the soldiers spit in his face, hit him with their fists and slapped him. Then, at the command of Pontius Pilate, they flogged him until it ripped the flesh from his body. Yet, as Isaiah Chapter 53, verse 7 says, 'like a lamb led to the slaughter... he did not open his mouth.'"

Some in the crowd sobbed as Ben's words came even stronger. "Isaiah said the Messiah would be 'numbered with the transgressors.' They crucified Yeshua between two criminals. Psalm 22, verse 16, said they would pierce Messiah's hands and feet. The Roman soldiers nailed Yeshua to the cross with spikes through his hands and feet. Psalm 22, verse 1, tells us God would forsake his Messiah. On the cross, Yeshua cried out, 'My God, my God, why have you forsaken me?'"

The sobbing turned to wailing. Ben did not slow down. "Speaking as the Messiah, David said, 'They divide my clothing among them and cast lots for my garment.' The soldiers gambled for Yeshua's clothing by casting lots as he hung dying on the cross."

"David wrote in Psalm 34:20 that not one of his bones would be broken. John says in Chapter 19, verse 33 of his Gospel when the soldiers came to check Yeshua on the cross, they found he was already dead. They did not have to break his legs, thus fulfilling that prophecy."

"Isaiah said in Chapter 53, verse 9, they would bury him with the rich. Matthew Chapter 27, verses 57 to 60 says a rich man named Joseph from Arimathea took his body down from the cross and placed it in his own new tomb."

"And in the most important verse of all, Psalm 49, verse 15, prophesied that God would redeem him from the realm of the dead and take him to himself. All four Gospels tell us Yeshua raised from the grave! And forty days later, God took him back to himself when he ascended into heaven!"

"It is clear, my fellow Israelites, that Yeshua whom we rejected is Messiah and Lord! Let me tell you my story once again of the night I believed in Yeshua for the first time."

He detailed the events of that night, including his struggle with watching the pastor's video.

"That was hard for me. I became angry and wanted to stop watching. I would have removed the flash drive and destroyed it, had I not given Blake Thompson my word that I would watch the entire thing. The pastor's words pierced my heart and opened my eyes to the truth. But it took Blake reading a passage from Josephus' *Antiquities* for that truth to sink in."

"Our people have overlooked, or denied, that section of Josephus' writing for 2,000 years. We are told Christian sources altered it by inserting the words referring to Yeshua's resurrection. But now I know it is all true. I want to read it for you from Antiquities 18.3.3." He picked up the book and began reading the passage Blake read to him that glorious night.

"Now there was about this time Jesus, a wise man, if it be lawful to call him a man, for he was a doer of wonderful works, a teacher of such men as receive the truth with pleasure. He drew over to him both many of the Jews, and many of the Gentiles. He was the Christ; and when Pilate, at the suggestion of the principal men amongst us, had condemned him to the cross, those that loved him at the first did not forsake him, for he appeared to them alive again the third day, as the divine prophets had foretold these and ten thousand other wonderful things concerning him; and the tribe of Christians, so named from him, are not extinct to this day." Antiquities 18.3.3.

"Now, my brothers and sisters, there is one more verse from Zechariah that I must read to you. Chapter 12, verse 10, foretells this very time. And the prophecy becomes reality today! The prophet wrote, 'And I will pour out on the house of David and the inhabitants of Jerusalem a spirit of grace and supplication. They will look on me, the one they have pierced, and they will mourn for him as one mourns for an only child, and grieve bitterly for him as one grieves for a firstborn son.'"

"God has extended his grace to us, his chosen people. He has not turned his back on us, but has given us another opportunity to accept his Messiah. I point you to Yeshua today and beg you to look upon him and mourn for him. Turn to him, and receive him as I, and the others with me, did."

He did not have time to say more. His hearers collapsed to their knees in unison, weeping, mourning, and crying out to their Messiah. The AMPP men passed by again, paying them no attention. The glory of God came down and covered the mountain. Thunder rolled and lightning flashed. A dove floated down and rested on Ben's shoulder. A voice came from above and said, "I love you, my son. In you, I am well pleased. *Keep going and telling my people.*"

•   •   •   •   •

The plane landed at Ben Gurion Airport in Tel Aviv. The nine Smyrnians exited after a long flight. They did not know what to expect when they left the bridge and entered the airport. They got their answer when they found the passenger line backed up and not moving. They could not even step out of the plane onto the bridge.

The awareness hit all of them at the same time. This was no normal backup. AMPP was searching for *them*. How did Messai know they were coming to Israel? Was he aware that twelve of them were in the country? *AMPP may have us trapped like animals with no escape from those who hunt us,* Blake thought to himself. Would God continue to protect them?

While questions without answers flooded their minds, their discussion was more nervous chatter than anything else. Then it turned to discussing a strategy for getting past them without being captured.

"There's no turning back now, so we need a plan fast," Trey said with urgency.

"Let's not forget the promise of protection God made to Ben," Blake threw in.

"And how he did that in Kansas City. That was fun! Those two AMPP guys didn't see me waving my hand right in front of their faces."

"I'll pass on that kind of fun, Evan. But I have a few ideas that may give us a fighting chance." This situation called for Malachi's expertise. "Let's split up instead of all being lined up behind each other single file. We look a lot less suspicious if we separate from each other. And it will prevent them from capturing all of us at the same time."

"Excellent idea, Malachi. Now, the question is, who wants to go first?"

"Not you and Beth, for sure. Trey, Rickie, and I are the least recognizable. The military taught the two of them how to deal with interrogation, so they can handle it better if they take them in for questioning. I handle that pretty well too, so I'll go behind them. You guys need to come last. The rest of us can fight for you, if we need to."

"I'm not sure how many they have, but there are nine of us! And we've all proven ourselves at least once. I'm ready. Let's get this line moving!" Evan felt invincible after Kansas City.

"Evan, I appreciate your youthful thinking, but we still need to be careful and prepared for what we might face. Because we've all been through this before doesn't mean we will get through it this time. We need that *wise as serpents and harmless as doves* thing again." John continued to be the one who could reel Evan in a bit, likely because of their former professor-student relationship.

"Any suggestion for how to answer their questions?" asked Kathie.

"We're tourists in Israel who came to see the Jewish Temple and the great things Messai has accomplished here," stated Malachi. "Nothing more than that. Whatever you say, just make Messai look good!"

"Excuse us," Blake said to the woman behind him, kicking off Malachi's idea. "I think we forgot something."

Beth saw what he was doing and followed. This would get them in the back of the line and have the order correct. Trey and Rickie were first, followed by Malachi, Evan and Anders, then John and Kathie, with Blake and Beth bringing up the rear. The line moved faster now.

When the first group got close enough to see what was happening, a row of AMPP men met their sight. A biometric face scanner sat between the first two. *Facial recognition*! Magnus told them Messai used this technology now and could recognize them in an instant. Malachi sent a text to Blake, informing him of their plight. Evan did the same with John.

Several people were objecting to the use of facial recognition technology. One man argued and refused to step forward and put his face in front of the machine. A member of AMPP grabbed him, pulled him forward, and held his face still while the machine did its work. When he let him go, the man was much more docile than before. He discovered how Aissa Messai's Peace Patrol conducted their business. Those guys did not mess around.

There were now less than ten people in front of them. With most folks now complying, their turn would come quickly. Malachi and Evan sent another text to the ones behind them. Three to four people separated them from each other. Trey and Rickie arrived at the machine. Trey stepped forward... Nothing. He stood for a few seconds, the AMPP men staring right past him. One growled at the lady behind the two Smyrnians.

"Come on, lady. We don't have all day. Move up and get your face scanned. If you don't, we will assume you are one of the rebels we are looking for and take you into custody right now."

"But what about them?" she objected, pointing to Trey and Rickie.

"We don't have time for games, ma'am. Look how far it is between you and the person who just walked through. You're holding up the line."

Trey and Rickie moved on as she kept objecting. The man ended those in no uncertain terms.

"*Now*, ma'am!" Everyone else heard his yell, and near panic ensued. The next three moved through, leading to Malachi, followed by Evan and Anders. Malachi stepped up to the machine.

"You people stop lagging!" screamed the man operating the machine. "I swear, if I have to tell any of you again, you're all going with us!"

The man behind them did not move. Evan stood in his way and decided it was a good idea to have a little more fun. Normal Evan once again. When the angry AMPP member moved toward the man, his intent clear, Anders shoved Evan from behind.

"Get out of the way! Do you want to get that guy killed?"

"I was just having a little fun."

"Someone dying because of your fun isn't cool."

He was right. Evan moved on while the man tried to explain as he walked to the machine.

"You don't understand. Three guys were standing right in front of me," he protested.

"I don't know what you people are trying to pull, but if you don't stop, someone will die!"

The line continued moving, as the five Smyrnians stood waiting for their teammates to walk through unnoticed too. They had informed them via texts to walk fast, so the people behind them could avoid trouble. No one else caused a ruckus, although they stared at them as they passed by. One intimidating, muscular patron got in their faces just before the other four arrived.

"I ought to beat you guys to a pulp. Whatever you're pulling here is not funny." He grabbed for Evan, who stood closest to him. Two members of the patrol jumped out of line and flew at him, throwing him to the floor, and wrestled his arms behind his back, cuffing them as they did.

"We're not putting up with this anymore," he shouted at the man on the floor. "Causing trouble in line is one thing. Screaming at no one is too much." Two more joined them as they dragged him away. He fought against them to no avail, yelling that he was not crazy and questioning their sanity. Every word that came from his mouth added to the charges he already faced.

John and Kathie walked on, not even stopping at the screen. No problems. After the couple in front of Blake and Beth passed through, the men walked away without a word. It was clear they saw none of them.

"I am living this, but it's still hard to believe," said Blake. "This supernatural protection is awesome stuff! I hope Ben and the others experienced the same thing on the Temple Mount."

"No doubt. I can't wait to hear about it, and to experience some more of it ourselves!" Evan's fun increased with every one of these times. None of them knew how long this would last, but it was theirs for now. Nothing else mattered at this moment. They left the airport unhurried.

CHAPTER 14

Ben watched the words of Zechariah 12:10 come to pass before his eyes as Israelites lay prostrate before him, crying out to their Messiah. They mourned for him and wept for their rejection of him. Each of them begged for his forgiveness and pleaded with him to come into their lives and be their Messiah. God himself foretold this moment over 2,500 years ago.

Ben's colleagues gave each one a card to list their name, the tribe of their ancestors, if they knew it, and contact information. The count was no surprise when they tallied it. 3,000 people of Israel put their faith in the real Messiah on this unforgettable day. Now to mobilize them under the direction of the men from the kibbutz, each in their tribal location.

The movement exploded in one day. Ben was certain this was just the beginning, but time would tell where it led him and these Jewish followers of Jesus. He understood it was not Israel or America. His mind yearned to know their destination and made him eager for that time to come.

Moshe told the families at the kibbutz about the miraculous event they witnessed on the Temple Mount. Ben asked them to throw a party when they returned. This called for a celebration to top all celebrations! He explained the first two parables of Jesus in Luke Chapter 15. A man had one hundred sheep, lost one, then searched until he found it. He brought it home, called his friends and neighbors together and said, "Rejoice with me! I have found my lost sheep!" A woman lost one of ten silver coins. She swept the house and looked for it until she located it, then did the same thing as the man who found his lost sheep!

Both instances pointed to rejoicing in heaven when someone turns to Jesus. He told them how important this day was to these seven years. These were the lost sheep of Israel. The party happening in heaven must be something to behold! Every person in the community would celebrate when they got home. The other nine Smyrnians should be there to join them, and they would rejoice together like none of them had ever rejoiced. It was party time in the kibbutz!

•   •   •   •   •

Aissa Messai sensed something as he awaited word from his top man in Israel, and it did not feel right. Anger stirred inside him, causing rage to consume his mind, though nothing yet justified it. He kept hearing the words, *no victory.* Instead, he sensed defeat, and his fury reached the boiling point, making him ready to explode when word came.

He hoped it was all misguided and the words exploding in his brain were untrue. Perhaps he would receive good news, giving him reason to celebrate. He longed to hear about the capture of Smyrnians and witness the scene as his men brought them before him. He yearned to end their lives himself in front of a worldwide audience, crippling their insidious campaign to defeat him. Yet the rage continued to boil, and he knew no such news would come. His phone rang at last.

"Captain, give me good news!"

"I have no news, sir. Our men covered every port of entry into the country, but there has been no sign of them yet. When they show up, they cannot escape us. We will get them, sir, and bring them to you as soon as that happens. I told the men this is one mission we must carry out."

"Find them!" the man roared. "Do I need to come and handle this myself?"

"No, sir. We will capture them the moment we see them. I understand their elusive ability, but they will not evade us this time."

Messai heard the uncertainty in his captain's voice and doubted the man's words as he spoke them. He needed to go to Israel. It had been a while since his last visit, anyway.

"I will come tomorrow, Captain."

"That is not necessary, Mr. Messai. We…" Messai cut him off with a shout.

"I refuse to allow your men to botch another mission. Meet me at the entrance to the Mount. I will make a personal announcement, enlisting the help of the entire country in our search for them. You will not let me down,

Captain, if you want to keep your job... *and* if you value your life. Their lives or yours; you decide."

The captain knew he meant what he said. His men would feel *his* wrath tonight. He could not allow them to mess this up. *His* life was on the line; not just the lives of the Smyrnians.

• • • • •

Bruno Fromm dreamed again as he slept in Germany. He could not stand being apart from the team, especially with all of them in Israel. He told Mila earlier that day they were the only two original Smyrnians missing in action. The work in Germany thrived and continued spreading, thanks to their efforts.

But he had focused on raising up Hans and Heidi to lead the work there. They identified a safe house in the Bavarian Alps that rivaled the chateau in the Rocky Mountains. Friends of Hans' family who were new believers owned it and were happy to use it for the cause. The number of house churches expanded and spread like wildfire across the country. Many now crossed borders into surrounding nations, too. The movement would continue growing without them.

He found himself in Israel as he dreamed. Magnus walked the streets of the Old City of Jerusalem alongside Mila and him. He and the other massive mountain of a man had formed an unbreakable bond. They referred to themselves as the *dynamic duo*. He saw AMPP patrols everywhere, accompanied by members of Israel's Police Force. They searched for someone, or a group of people. The Smyrnians! He knew they were the target.

The three of them ducked down an alley to avoid them, but met others coming. "Run!" he yelled to his wife and their companion. Before they could make a dash for cover, they found themselves surrounded on every side. Then a strange thing happened. The patrols joined together, discussing their day, and neither recognized nor bothered them. He motioned for the others to follow, and they walked right through the mob of men and down the street. He awoke.

What did the dream mean? AMPP would not allow them to escape in that situation. He considered the impossibility of it. *Jesus.* He was the only answer. Only he could blind AMPP to their presence and give them freedom to walk in Israel unnoticed. No, it wasn't possible. Or was it? It was only a dream.

He got out of bed, shook the cobwebs from his head, and walked into the kitchen. Some milk and a piece of Mila's famous cake should help him. The room was unlit, but he sensed a presence. He flipped on the light, ready to attack whoever it was. Magnus sat at the table drinking milk and devouring two enormous pieces of cake.

"What are you doing, Magnus? You scared me half to death and almost caused me to tackle you!"

"You would have had a fight on your hands," chuckled his fighting partner. "I had a dream, and it woke me up. We were in Israel, surrounded by AMPP, but they didn't even see us. We walked right through the middle of them and kept going."

Bruno stood stunned with a shocked look on his face. He froze and said nothing.

"What's up with you? You don't believe my dream? It's true, but I don't have the foggiest idea what it means."

"I had the same dream," Bruno whispered, still amazed. "Jesus just sent word to both of us at the same time telling us we need to do something. But how are we supposed to know what it is?"

"I think he wants us to go to Israel. I picked up chatter from Messai's security network last night, saying he dispatched an extreme number of AMPP personnel to Israel. He instructed them to join forces with as many of Israel's Police Force as possible. I thought the dream only came because I heard that before going to bed. But now I know there is more to it."

"I'll wake Mila right now. We need to make plans to leave for Israel. Hans and Heidi need to meet with us too, because they will have to take charge in our absence. But to be honest with you, Magnus, I long to be there with the others. Mila and I are the only original Smyrnians out of the action."

"We'll get a report from them in the morning about what went down on the Temple Mount. I also want to know if the others arrived safe and sound. But AMPP failing to notice us in our dreams must have some meaning. Ben mentioned Jesus telling him we will have supernatural protection. Do you think this has something to do with it?"

"Who cares what I think. We have to leave for Israel tomorrow, or as soon as we can get a flight. I'm sure we will find out soon enough when we go."

Bruno called Hans and Heidi and woke Mila. Within an hour, the five of them sat at his kitchen table having cake and milk and discussing their next steps. Sure, he longed to join the others in Israel, but this was about more than his desire. Jesus spoke to both him and Magnus tonight, calling them to go. When they heard the dreams, all five knew they came from Jesus and agreed the call was clear. He would call Ally first thing in the morning and book a flight online at once. The three of them were going to the Holy Land.

•　　•　　•　　•　　•

The darkness of the kibbutz lit up at 4:00 a.m., and the entire community leapt from their beds to a commotion that caught them by surprise. Choppers hovered overhead, spotlights beaming onto the compound below. AMPP squadrons scaled the walls and raced in, weapons in hand. They planned to massacre every man, woman and child, and capture Ben and Miriam Abramson and Alexander and Elizabeth Ben Ezra, along with the leaders of the kibbutz.

Moshe and the men sprinted from their houses, guns in hand, and ran toward the center of the community and Ben's house. They surrounded it and stood their ground, ready to fight to the death. They vowed they would not allow AMPP to capture them alive.

It was still dark, but looked like broad daylight, with lights illuminating the place. The women and children sprinted to the bomb shelters as sirens blared, mothers carrying smaller children and dragging older ones while they ran. Armed patrols dashed past the men and into houses, kicking down doors and racing inside, intent on killing anyone they found. One yelled to the others.

"They deserted the place! It appears they left weeks ago."

"Search everywhere!" screamed the captain. He intended to save his own life. A slaughter of this magnitude and capture of Ben and Miriam Abramson and others would accomplish that, and bring a healthy bonus and promotion with it. They would look until they found them, in case they were hiding somewhere.

"Here we go again," said Moshe. "They can't see us, even though we're right in front of them."

"Let's take them out!" said one man, shouldering his weapon and preparing to fire at the men as they ran from house to house.

"No," said Ben, placing his hand on the gun and nuzzling it down to the man's side. "We only kill when circumstances warrant it. These men don't know we are here, so they pose no threat to us. However, I believe it would be appropriate to mess with them a little." His eyes twinkled.

"What do you have in mind, fearless leader?" asked Eliyahu.

"Go outside the gate and flatten their tires, but don't slash or shoot them. We want them to think we deserted the place so they'll leave us alone after tonight. But a little superstitious fear may be good for them. Let the air out of their tires, but don't harm the vehicles."

The men of the community laughed as they hustled to the gate. They kept their weapons on them, but knew they would not need them. AMPP was blind to their presence, and even to things in their houses. "When Jesus performs a miracle, he does it right!" shouted one as he ran.

The search lasted over an hour, plenty of time to flatten every tire. They returned and celebrated in the street as the AMPP patrol rushed around them, oblivious to their presence. When the men gave up and left the kibbutz, they found the gate now wide-open as they walked to their vehicles.

Moshe and the men gathered outside, watching for their reaction. Most had never heard such language. The men screamed and cursed. The captain placed a call for help to another patrol. When they settled down and leaned on their cars, the gate slammed shut, causing them to dive behind the cars, weapons drawn again. Nothing met their sight except the closed gate.

One yelled, "The gods are against us!"

"There is no god, but Messai," snarled the captain. "Never mention that word again, unless you refer to him."

The men gathered inside the gate looked at one another. Messai's plans went far deeper than they, or the people of the world, realized. Things would soon become much worse.

Ben summoned the men to the meeting hall. Once they arrived, he called them together and asked for quiet. "Gather around. I was just reminded of the words of Jesus in the Gospel of John. 'As long as it is day, I must do the works of him who sent me. Night is coming, when no one can work.' We must remember that because night will come soon, and we have work to do that cannot wait."

"Moshe, how long will it take to drive to the Mount of Beatitudes? I must go there and speak tomorrow. I will put it on the website and announce it on my broadcast today, asking people to bring everyone they can. All of you need to get to your tribal areas today and start the work there. The sun will set on our opportunities soon. Let us work while it is still shining."

When they exited the meeting hall, lights shined through the gate, and someone stood peering through it.

"Not again," said Moshe, shaking his head. "I hope they still can't see us."

Ben heard a familiar voice calling out to him. He looked at his phone and saw a voicemail from two hours earlier. The ruckus had claimed his full attention, causing him to miss the call. He smiled as he walked toward the gate.

"Ben, stop! We must keep you safe!" It was Alexander.

He continued walking as the others followed. Nine people stood waving from outside.

"Open the gate."

It sounded more like a command than a request. Moshe did as he asked. Ally sprinted toward Blake, Beth and the others, grabbing Evan in a tight embrace, Ollie and Amelia joining her. Ben spoke to the group watching the reunion.

"Members of the kibbutz, let me introduce you to these Smyrnians. Blake and Beth Jennings Thompson, Evan Ryles, the one who began our movement, Anders Norstrom, Malachi... I'm sorry Malachi, I don't know your last name." He smiled and continued. "John and Kathie Baldwin, Trey Butler and Rickie Cruz; the original Smyrnians, minus two. I wish Bruno and Mila Fromm were here. Jesus called us together to do his work in Israel before the night comes. It will come soon."

Dawn had broken over the kibbutz. None of them noticed it until this moment. Ally's phone rang, garnering their attention. She stepped away to answer the call. In a few minutes, she returned and interrupted their conversation.

"That was daddy," she whispered. "He and Magnus dreamed the same thing last night. Jesus showed them they need to come here. They booked a flight and will arrive late tomorrow."

"That makes all of us," said Ben. "We have seen this happen before. It is no accident. He showed us last night, the time is short. Our focus must be on this place. Things will change fast."

• • • • •

Aissa Messai's private jet landed at Ben Gurion Airport. He stepped out with a stern look of determination that faded into a smile when he encountered others. He came here for a purpose, to ensure the capture and elimination of his hated enemy... the Smyrnians. They were here; he smelled them. His men would find and apprehend them, then bring them to him.

They would incarcerate them until everything was prepared. Then he would watch them meet their fate, as the people of the world looked on. Their public demise would discourage others from rejecting him. The Jews would soon join them, while the rest of the world bowed to him.

This was his hour, and the power of darkness would consume the earth. What was coming next would rock the planet, but it was only the beginning. He could hardly wait for the grand finale!

He called a meeting with the leaders of AMPP for later that afternoon. His captain had not reported since their previous conversation. Surely he would bring good news this time. If not, the meeting would not go well for the other men. But the capture of their prey remained an inevitable thing. The only uncertainty was when and where. *Let the fun begin!* he mused.

• • • • •

Johnathan finished setting up his studio in Colorado. He spread the word on social media, understanding the danger of doing so. He prepared well and was ready to tell the masses the truth about the actual age of the earth. He did not believe such a thing before either. But his eyes now open, he saw it. His story should speak volumes to anyone still clinging to the old earth theory. That included everyone who did not belong to the Smyrnians. Tomorrow the world's population would hear truths which would challenge things they had held as reality their entire lives.

• • • • •

Bruno, Mila, and Magnus boarded a plane for their flight to Israel. Unknown to Messai, Magnus continued to intercept messages between him and his inner circle, to which he had once belonged. Sown inside the lining of his jacket, he carried a notebook filled with written pages explaining several of AMPP's upcoming plans. He knew Messai sensed the Smyrnians move to Israel and intended to trap and destroy them there.

The preceding night he got wind of an attack on a kibbutz where they believed them to be located. It came too late to warn them. The raid was already in progress by the time he heard about it. Ally told Bruno the entire group survived once again. But it happened only because Jesus intervened. He wished he knew the name of the tipster who worked on the inside, gleaning such information. Perhaps he could discover that after they arrived in Israel.

Magnus was now one of the most wanted men in the world to Messai. He wore that as a badge of honor and prayed for the ability to help the cause of Jesus and the Smyrnians for the remaining years of Planet Earth. Jesus brought him to the faith for such a time as this, and he was determined to fill his role. But one bit of chatter continued to elude his grasp.

The nature of the communication made it clear this was something enormous, bringing devastating consequences to the earth and its inhabitants. He tried hard to decipher the messages, but they scrambled them or made them so vague he could not understand the transmission. The urgency of the correspondence told him it was coming soon.

Bruno and Mila slept as the flight continued while Magnus pored over his notes in his mind. He could not remove them from his jacket, but he knew them from memory. Words like invasion, eruption, and destruction came across. But where? When? How? Who? Answers to those vital questions remained hidden from him. Even though he had no exact date, he understood one thing. It would happen soon. Apart from that, the rest was anybody's guess. The others would join him trying to figure that out when they reached their destination. For now, he should sleep.

•　　•　　•　　•　　•

In Israel, Aissa Messai sat with his team in a remote location. Discussion centered on capturing the Smyrnians and on how they continued to elude their grasp. He knew they were there, but his men had not found them. His anger with his captain and the patrols had subsided. They had done everything they could, but the rebels stayed out of sight. That is one reason he came. Another reason was just as important, but he could not allow it to distract from this one. He must eliminate the Smyrnians. They stood in the way of all he must accomplish in a brief amount of time. The day drew near for his plans to unfold. He addressed the group.

"Thank you, men, for your diligent efforts to locate the rebels. I realize the failure does not lie with you. Some responsibility falls on me. But most of the blame lies with them and the strange magic they use each time they escape us. They are here; I can feel them and smell them. Their odor is like a stench in my nostrils. I cannot find peace until we destroy them and unleash our worldwide mission."

"However, I need you to hear me loud and clear. Nothing will interfere with carrying out that mission, not even them. The time draws near, and preparations have begun. We are gathering resources and mobilizing armies. The world will soon *see that which they have long feared* and *feel the sting of all it brings.* Let us continue our search for the enemy as we await the greatest invasion of all time!"

The room filled with applause and shouts of affirmation. The chill was colder than usual, and it drew them to follow their leader. His expression of gratitude this day compelled them to push on, do more, try harder than ever. They would enforce his agenda, complete the mission, then reign with him forever as he ruled the world.

Under his spell, they continued to believe in his cause and would never break free. If they only understood the outcome of it all, but they did not. So they readied themselves to charge from their meeting place and search for the Smyrnians until they emerged from their hiding places. They felt sure they would find them soon.

•　　•　　•　　•　　•

Magnus awoke and sat straight up. He nudged his partner awake, taking care not to disturb Mila.

"What Magnus? Can't a man get a little shuteye while he has time? Leave me alone and let me sleep." He turned back toward the window and lay his head on the small pillow that came with the flight.

The man shook him again until Bruno surrendered and sat up, laying the pillow aside and rubbing his eyes. "Okay, what is it? You won't let me sleep until I listen, so tell me before I fall asleep again."

"I was just in a meeting with Messai and the leaders of his security forces!"

"Magnus, look me in the eye. We are 35,000 feet in the air on a plane traveling to Israel. Messai is not on this plane, and we don't know where he is. You were dreaming. Now, go back to sleep." He rolled over again, but Magnus grabbed him by the shoulder and prevented him from staying there.

"Bruno, listen to me!" His voice was much louder than he intended, causing the people sitting near them to shush him. "I'm sorry," he apologized. "I didn't intend to speak so loud." He leaned over toward Bruno and whispered in his ear.

"I was not dreaming. Something transported me to a meeting somewhere in Israel. Don't ask me to explain and please understand I am not crazy. I heard everything he said and need to tell you before it escapes my mind. Write as I talk. It will come verbatim, in the exact words he spoke."

Bruno pulled his phone from the seat pocket in front of him, opened his notes app and prepared to type. "Go ahead. Are you sure this is on the up and up?"

"Yes! Now, here goes, before I forget. He said, 'The time draws near, and preparations have begun. We are gathering resources and mobilizing armies. The world will *soon see that which they have long feared* and *feel the sting of all it brings*. Let us continue our search for the enemy as we await the greatest invasion of all time!' That's all. I have heard recent chatter I cannot decode. This time I saw it and heard it firsthand and understood every word! Now to figure out what it means."

•   •   •   •   •

The sun rose on another crucial day for Ben's ministry. Yesterday had turned into a busy one following the nighttime AMPP invasion. He spent the day promoting and planning for today's appearance on the Mount of Beatitudes. His army of Smyrnians contacted every person who had believed in Jesus on the Temple Mount the preceding day, letting them know what time to arrive.

The twelve men from the kibbutz traveled to the lands of their tribal ancestors to enlist attendees. Ben aimed his online teaching at the importance of the day. Then he went to bed early to get plenty of rest so he would stay alert. Now the time came to drive from the kibbutz past the shore of the Sea of Galilee to the mountain where Jesus often addressed the multitudes.

When the sea first came into view, it blew the minds of those who had not seen it. Few things awaken the visual senses like viewing that for the first time. After people put their faith in Jesus, looking down on the sea before beginning the descent from above is an overwhelming experience. It stimulates their spiritual senses to the point they can envision him walking on the water through eyes of faith.

"Wow," whispered Beth.

"I don't know why, but that makes me think of my Angie and our three kids," uttered Anders.

Moshe signaled to the other van traveling behind them and pulled over to the side of the highway. "Take a moment to enjoy this," he said. "Get out. Take some pictures. Let Jesus speak to you as he did when you first believed in him. Can you see him walking on the water, or riding in a boat with his disciples? Perhaps he is strolling on the shore and teaching the crowds. I see him. This was my favorite spot before I said yes to Jesus, but now it does something for me it never did before."

The group spilled out of the van, phones in hand, taking pictures almost as soon as their feet hit the ground. Ally had her camera, so they would all expect digital photos from her.

"Time's up, people. Get back in the van. I have thirty minutes to be on the mountain greeting those who arrive. We must go... *now.*"

None of them wanted to leave, but they knew Ben was right. The people would come to hear him teach, and he could not take a chance on running late. They loaded up and left, driving past Tiberias and nearing the left turn that would take them to their destination. The sight that met their eyes spoke volumes about the importance of this day. Traffic came from three directions, creating a logjam and stopping them cold.

"I will never make it on time." Ben's frustration showed, as did his disappointment.

"Don't worry, Ben. If I can get around on the right side, I know a place where we can leave the vans and climb the mountain. Staying in such excellent physical shape will pay off for you now."

Both vans worked their way around traffic and reached the parking area. No one had stopped there. They followed Moshe up the mountain and arrived at the top ten minutes before the time to begin. But he would not start on time today. He must allow the people to arrive.

And arrive they did, en masse, as cars and buses grew tired of sitting in parked traffic. Realizing they had no chance of parking on top, many pulled over anywhere they could, left their vehicles behind, and climbed the rest of the way on foot. Others followed the same trek Ben's group took. They came from all sides until Ben found himself surrounded by a sea of humanity, as he stood in the middle. The smile on his face revealed his pleasure at what he saw.

"Fellow Israelites, it warms my heart to see all of you here today. Who discovered the Messiah during our time on the Temple Mount?" His voice carried from the mountain to the valley below.

Hands went up throughout the crowd. Many stood, waving their hands back and forth.

"And how many of you invited or brought someone with you?"

From Ben's vantage point, every one of those hands appeared to raise again.

"Now," Ben asked, "tell me which area you come from? I will go from the eldest to the youngest."

He asked about each of the twelve tribes, beginning with Reuben and ending with Benjamin. Many came from each tribal land, some more than others, but a good representation from all twelve. Ben estimated the number to be at least fifteen to twenty thousand, possibly as high as twenty-five thousand. People packed the natural amphitheater overlooking the Sea of Galilee from top to bottom, even surrounding Ben too. He could not escape if he wanted to, but leaving was the last thing on his mind. When he held up his hands, the multitude quieted.

CHAPTER 15

The plane carrying Bruno, Mila, and Magnus landed at Ben Gurion Airport. Excited about their arrival in Israel, they grabbed their carry-on bags and stood close to the front of the line, preparing to exit the plane and enter the bridge. Magnus, now using the German name, Max, secured seats just behind first-class, making that possible. The line moved at a steady pace until it came to a sudden stop. After moving only a few feet, they saw what caused the logjam. AMPP men stood at a biometric facial recognition machine, scanning each passenger as they walked through.

"They won't need that thing to identify me!" Magnus whispered. "I recognize one guy. He served in one of my patrols. They will seize me in a heartbeat."

"I won't let them take you without a fight!" exclaimed Bruno. "That machine will tell them who we are, too. But unless they brought a bunch of guys, you and I can take them!"

"I know how Messai operates. You can bet they have full patrols stationed at every gate, exit, and entrance of this airport. We can't escape them."

"Do you have a better idea? I say we fight!"

"If we fight, we will die."

"If we don't fight, we will die! I'd rather go down fighting! Besides, I plan to protect Mila at all cost." She stood beside him, squeezing his arm in a tight grip, her fear obvious.

"We must keep moving with the line. I'm not sure what I will do until they try to grab me. But when my survival instincts kick in, I'm sure I won't go down without a fight either. I saw that among the believers in Jesus we murdered when I did what those men are doing now. The quiet ones died peacefully, but others fought, even though their deaths were inevitable. Let's go," he said with only two people remaining in front of them.

Each of those stepped in front of the machine with no fear of being recognized. It was Magnus' turn. He stepped up and spoke to the man in front of him.

"Hello, Liam. It is good to see you, my friend. You know me, so there is no need for this machine. Because of our friendship, I hope you will let me pass." He extended his hand in a gesture of peace.

"Next!" the man yelled in an impatient voice.

Magnus looked at him stunned, then back at Bruno and Mila, with a shocked look on his face. He shrugged his shoulders and walked on, passing by other security personnel as he went, thankful that Liam had let him go.

"Hurry!" shouted Liam. "We don't have time to stand around here waiting for you." He pointed to the man behind Bruno, and glaring at him, said, "You, come, or we will come and get you!"

Bruno grabbed Mila's arm and pulled her past the men with a yank that caused her to stumble.

"I'm sorry, dear, but we need to hurry. I don't understand what's happening, but we're not sticking around to find out."

"Don't worry about me. Let's go! I can't believe that just happened! What is going on here?"

They hurried past the men and joined Magnus. The man behind them protested as he walked to the machine. He saw them, but something hid them from the eyes of the patrol.

"What the...?" Bruno asked his new teammate and fighting partner.

"Supernatural protection!" Magnus beamed. "Ben said Jesus promised it to us, but I didn't understand it until now. We are invisible to them! Watch this."

He walked back to three of the AMPP men standing near them.

"Magnus," said Mila. "What are you doing? Come on. Let's get out of here!"

The giant of a man who could never hide because of his stature and enormous frame remained undeterred. He stepped in front of the man and waved his arms back and forth.

"Come, get me!" he said, making a crazy face.

His two companions had not seen this side of him. They took him for the serious type. But it now appeared he loved to play as much as he loved to work.

"Okay, let's go. But I had to do that. It was fun!"

"I assume going to baggage claim is okay, too," said Bruno. "If we're invisible, they won't see us there either. I want to watch their faces when our bags lift off the carousel and walk away!"

"More fun!" laughed Magnus.

"You two are like big kids," Mila said, shaking her head and rolling her eyes. "They didn't notice these carry-on bags, so I doubt they will spot us, or our suitcases, either."

"Now, you're spoiling our fun, Mila." Magnus feigned a pout. "I suppose you're right, but I wish you weren't. Let's go find out."

The two men appeared disappointed when they retrieved the bags. Other people saw them, but the AMPP men were oblivious to them, and the suitcases. The man who had stood behind them in line exiting the boarding bridge walked up to Bruno and glared at him. He started to speak, but the giant of a man stepped closer and sat down his bags. He towered over the man, like Goliath standing before David. This time, Goliath won the battle as the man ran, almost dropping his bag.

"Even more fun!" laughed Magnus. "I hope this supernatural protection stays with us for a while, because I could get used to it! How about you, Bruno?"

Before her husband responded, Mila interrupted their amusement. "Come on, children. We need to leave here and get to the kibbutz."

Both appeared chastised as the two hulking men followed her like little puppy dogs. Passing every AMPP patrol, they secured a rental car and drove away. They would sleep in the kibbutz tonight.

●   ●   ●   ●   ●

When Ben started speaking, the crowd of thousands was silent, soaking up every word.

"Friends, today we gather at the place where the Messiah delivered his most well-known sermon. For centuries, people have called it the Sermon on the Mount, an appropriate name, don't you agree?" he asked, motioning all around with his hand. "Here where he spoke, I remind you of one thing he said. Matthew recorded it in Chapter 5, verses 17 and 18. *Do not think that I have come to abolish the Law or the Prophets; I have not come to abolish them but to fulfill them.*'"

"Most of you have viewed my teachings online. Some of you listened to me speak two days ago about how Yeshua fulfilled all the prophecies concerning the Messiah. For 2,000 years, we have believed he came to nullify the Torah and vilify the writings of the Prophets, but he did neither. He fulfilled everything they taught and foretold! The word *fulfill* is best understood by reversing it. The good news is, Yeshua *filled full* the prophecies. They all came true in him!"

A buzz spread through the crowd, as it had two days earlier on the Temple Mount. Ben calmed them again with an extended hand.

"In verse 18, Yeshua told of the importance of the Law. 'For truly I tell you, until heaven and earth disappear, not the smallest letter, not the least stroke of a pen, will by any means disappear from the Law *until everything is accomplished.*' My brothers and sisters, we now live in the time he spoke about!"

"Yeshua took his people from this world and home to be with him on September 11, 2029. Ha-Shem announced through the prophets that only seven years of time remain after that event. We call it the Tribulation. The prophets proclaimed it to be both the time of his wrath, and a time for us, his chosen people, to turn to him by accepting our Messiah. That occurred on the Temple Mount, and I expect many more of you to join us today!"

He wanted to say much more, but what happened next took him by surprise again. Thousands of Jews fell on their faces, wailing, and crying out for forgiveness. No one remained standing or sitting. They lay prostrate on the grassy slope before him and everywhere around him, declaring their faith in Jesus as their Messiah and Lord.

Ben collapsed to his knees. The sight overwhelmed him to the breaking point of spiritual ecstasy. His helpers filled their roles, handing out cards and collecting all the information they could. Gathering it from such a massive number of people was an impossible task. Ben regained his composure and addressed the crowd again.

"Please give me your attention for five more minutes. In one week, we will meet again in the Valley of Armageddon. I expect our numbers to more than double after today. Meet me in the plain of Megiddo at noon. Bring your family, friends and neighbors to learn about the Messiah. Nothing else matters at this point. I will put out a call on the website for the Jewish people from around the world to come to Israel and meet with us."

"Let us work to fill the valley with our people. In the meantime, your leaders will communicate with you and help you connect with one another. I will introduce them and what tribe they are from, in case you fail to recognize them. They have scattered throughout the area. Try to meet with them and the other people from your homeland before you go. Then, as Jesus said to me, *go and tell our people!*"

The leaders stood as he introduced them and pointed out where they were located. The sight of his fellow Jews rushing to join their groups again overwhelmed him. He regained his composure this time and turned to leave. Members of the Israeli Defense Force approached him as he did.

"Mr. Benjamin Abramson?"

They saw him! Had Jesus' protection left him? He stood alone, seeing his Smyrnian teammates and the men from the kibbutz immersed in the sea of people on the hillside. Left with no choice, he stepped forward and walked toward the soldiers. Courage surged inside him as the powerful presence of Jesus drove him on. *Go and tell my people.* The words came crystal clear every time he heard them. With each step, they came again. *Go and tell my people... I am going, Lord.*

"Yes, I am Ben Abramson. Thank you, men and ladies, for coming today and for serving in our country's military. How may I help you?"

"Sir, you need to come with us." They approached him, and two of them grabbed each of his arms, pulling him to the side and into a small grove of trees.

"You need not pull me. I will comply with your wishes and come with you. May I ask what you want from me?"

Once out of sight in the trees, one young woman spoke on behalf of the group.

"Mr. Abramson, we saw the crowd gathered and came to find out what brought such an enormous group together. This most often spells trouble. We watched the people's response but saw no one speaking to them. Then, as if our sight returned, you appeared before us. We know who you are and what you did here today. Sir, we want to see Yeshua, the Messiah."

Tears flowed from Ben's eyes as he drew the young soldiers close and told them about the Messiah. They believed and prayed to receive Jesus too. The glory of the Lord shone around their circle, and Ben praised Jesus for this moment as he instructed them on their next steps. These young men and women would play a pivotal role for the Smyrnians. The group finished their work and drove away, stopping for one more view of the sea before continuing. Another miraculous experience lay behind them. This day convinced them that many others lay ahead.

• • • • •

Their three teammates arrived at the kibbutz before the group made it back. When they drove up to the gate, the men who now stood guard drew their weapons, demanding they get out of the car. They jumped into action when they saw Magnus, recognizing him at once. The news showed his face every day. He once served as an AMPP captain, but was now wanted by Aissa Messai.

"State your purpose for being here," one of them demanded.

"I am Magnus Larsen. I can tell by your actions you recognize me. I led groups that slaughtered believers in Jesus and thought I did the right thing. Then Jesus spoke to me and told me to follow him. He led me to the Smyrnians and now I serve him. You and I are brothers in him."

"He tells the truth," Bruno spoke up. "I am Bruno Fromm, and this is my wife, Mila. You have met our daughter, Ally. Jesus told us to come and assist Ben Abramson and you with the work in Israel. So, here we are! May we please come in?"

The men hesitated, but after asking a few more questions and looking at their identification, they opened the gate and welcomed them in. Two led them to a house where they would stay. After settling in, Bruno called Ally. She filled them in on the events of the day, leading to a kibbutz-wide celebration. They were eager for the others to return and hear it from them, but even more to get in on the action themselves.

• • • • •

In Colorado, Johnathan Baldwin was now going strong with his online young earth teaching. His initial session began with introductory remarks, followed by the pastor's video, explaining how the earth's 6,000 year history revealed the date of the Rapture as September 11, 2029. His passion spoke volumes about what he believed.

He concluded with a few more brief remarks and announced the next session would include his story of how he came to believe what the pastor taught. That one drew lots of comments, both positive and negative. People clamored about him telling how he, a geophysicist, came to renounce everything he held as true about the age of the earth. The views for his third session grew by the thousands. The topic was *Point of Origin.*

"Two primary points exist from which views concerning the age of the universe originate," he began, "science and scripture. I am a scientist. Thus, my point of origin was always science, and I accepted its axioms as fact, without questioning them. For many others, their point of origin was scripture. I accepted the axioms of science, but they believed the teachings of the Bible."

"The first verse in the Bible says, *'In the beginning, God created the heavens and the earth.'* That was far too simplistic for me to accept. In fact, I flat out rejected it. Now, I understand why. Hebrews 11:3 says, *'By faith we understand that the universe was formed at God's command, so that what is seen was not made out of what was visible.'*"

"I discovered that faith works in the opposite manner of science. As a scientist, *believing* required *seeing.* But faith required me to *believe* before I could *see.* Once I believed in God, it all made sense to me. But the pastor's video you watched in my first session was quite persuasive too." A smile came to his face.

"Some would argue that since no one was present when the earth came into existence, no one can determine its age. I would argue someone *was* present: God! Since God was present when the earth originated, the record of events provided by him should be our point of origin. We find his account in the Bible. When you read it through a new lens, as I did not so long ago, the facts become apparent. God created the universe in six literal 24-hour days."

"Science denies that fact. Even those who attempt to combine science and scripture claim each day of creation must have been millions of years. Both miss the boat on that point. The Hebrew word used for day in Genesis Chapter 1 is *yom.* Other Old Testament writers used that word several times with different meanings."

"But anytime a number accompanies it, such as 1, 2, or 3, or the words first, second, or third, it *always* refers to a literal 24-hour day. Genesis 1 clarifies that even more. Of each day, it says, 'And there was evening, and there was morning—the first day, the second day, etc. through the sixth day.'

What does a 24-hour day require? An evening and a morning. No one can misinterpret that."

"But some of you may question the integrity and accuracy of the Bible because it places the order as 'evening and morning' rather than 'morning and evening.' The answer is simple. The Hebrew day begins at 6:00 p.m. and ends at 6:00 p.m. Thus, when Jews observe Shabbat, the Jewish Sabbath, they start at 6:00 p.m. Friday and end at 6:00 p.m. Saturday. That is a 24-hour day."

"*Day* means *day*. And God created the entire universe, including our planet, in six days and rested on the seventh. When you add the generations of the people in the Bible, combined with other internal evidence, you arrive at 6,000 years as the age of the earth. I understand this teaching to be simple and true. You should too. We will dig deeper next time."

•　　•　　•　　•　　•

Messai could not allow those teachings to go unchallenged. Johnathan hit his radar as a dangerous perpetrator of lies. If the earth is only 6,000 years old, it made the pastor's explanation of what happened on September 11, 2029 true. And it dealt a crushing blow to the Secretary-General's reputation, based on his denial of those facts.

Many people believed after watching the video, including all the Smyrnians. Messai must squash Jonathan's teaching before it infiltrated society and spread lies which further increased their numbers, threatening his own position and power. The world needed to hear from him again, requiring another press conference to address the threat. He stood before the cameras on the Temple Mount, with the Jewish Temple serving as a backdrop.

"Good afternoon, ladies and gentlemen. I remain humbled by your trust in me and amazed at the things we have accomplished together. One of the greatest examples sits behind me. It shines as a beacon of hope for peace and prosperity in our world. The credit belongs to you for working so hard to help make that dream a reality. I stand before you again to say, thank you."

"However, one threat to our cause continues to rear its head, seeking to divide us and disrupt our progress. The Smyrnian rebels persist in promoting their falsehoods. Johnathan Baldwin, son of the rebel John

Baldwin, has arisen as a voice for their divisive cause. While we seek to bring peace, he threatens to destroy it. He denies scientific proofs concerning the universe which we know are true. I feel certain his views came from the bizarre and senseless ravings of his father."

"Such things are not only laughable lies; they also undermine undeniable facts. I can tell you with absolute certainty the earth is four and a half billion years old. That truth alone destroys their entire movement, which they base upon the absurd theory that the earth has only existed for 6,000 years. That leads them to believe some *unseen god* created it. No such being exists. Do not accept their lies. You and I exist as the gods of this world who have achieved greatness through our unified efforts. *God* is nothing more than a figment of the imagination for weak minds."

"So, I come to you seeking your assistance once again. Please help me put an end to this threat before it disrupts the goal we have worked so hard to attain. If you know or learn the whereabouts of Johnathan Baldwin, call our tip line. I will honor any tip that leads to his capture with a significant reward. I expect a rapid response to my request. You have never let me down. We could not achieve our goals without your help." He ended abruptly and walked out of view.

After the conference ended, he placed an additional bounty on Johnathan Baldwin's head. He offered this reward only to his Peace Patrol. It appealed to them far more than the one presented to the public and would propel them into action. It would also strengthen the teamwork among each unit and create a little competition. Nothing fires up a group of guys like competition. And the promise of a reward doesn't hurt. All members of any AMPP patrol who took Johnathan alive and delivered him to the world leader, would receive immediate retirement and a life of luxury for as long as they lived. The search was on! But how can one find that which he cannot see?

$\bullet \quad \bullet \quad \bullet \quad \bullet \quad \bullet$

When the group returned from the Mount of Beatitudes, Bruno, Mila and Magnus greeted them. Bruno and Magnus grabbed their Smyrnian brothers one at a time and lifted them off the ground with tight bear hugs. Neither realized his strength, so crushed ribs were not out of the question.

"I have struggled to keep these two under control all day after our experience at the airport," said Mila.

"You don't need to tell us," smiled Evan. "We all experienced the same thing. It *was* fun!"

"See there, Mila," chuckled big man number one. "I told you nothing is wrong with having a little fun at others' expense. We men like to enjoy ourselves at times like that."

"I am all for having fun," Ben interjected. "But we have work to do, too. So, we must balance the two. Busy days lie ahead for us and time is flying by. Almost three years of the Tribulation have passed. Our work and trying to stay a step ahead of Messai and survive must be our priority. One thing I know is this: my people in Israel depend on us.

• • • • •

Johnathan Baldwin refused to allow Aissa Messai to intimidate him. He cared more about telling the truth to an unbelieving world than he cared about his own life.

"In my last session," he began, "I said only two points of origin exist for what we believe about the age of the earth. One is science, and the other is scripture... the Bible. As a geophysicist, I believed in an *Old Earth*. I stood entrenched in the scientific camp, believing the earth is four and a half billion years old. The Bible teaches that the earth is only 6,000 years old. I saw that as absurd, as did others in my profession and with my educational background. I took the Bible to be a book of fables, with science presenting the facts."

"But something changed my beliefs and turned my search for truth from science to scripture. I now refer to myself as a Creation Scientist. Scripture has the answers to every question about the creation, history, and future of the earth. And those answers are far different from what they taught me in the classroom. I realized that I had somehow missed it my entire life. It began with understanding a fundamental fact of the search for truth about the universe. Science does not present verified facts. It gives hypothetical presuppositions to unanswered questions and bases its theories on observable phenomena, things we can see."

"But I will say this: science and scripture are not altogether exclusive. We trust some scientific research and observations. Let's talk about two types of science: operational and historical. Operational science conducts experiments to discover things, such as cures for diseases. Historical science uses observations of things in the present to develop *theories* about the unseen distant past."

"I found major fallacies in those *theories* I had overlooked my entire career. I will cite one example: the lack of reliability in radiometric and radiocarbon dating. Scientists say radiocarbon survives *only a few thousand* years. If that is true, how is it found in *all* diamonds, which scientists say are *billions* of years old? You can't have it both ways. Or as the old saying goes, 'you can't have your cake and eat it too.' Try to connect these contrasting *scientific* dots in your mind."

1. They say radiocarbon can only survive for a *few thousand* years.

2. However, *all* diamonds contain radiocarbon.

3. Scientists tell us diamonds are *billions* of years old.

"Somehow, I refused to consider the fact that those dots will not connect. If Carbon-14 only survives a few thousand years, diamonds cannot be billions of years old. And obviously, the earth must be thousands of years old, not billions, proving the biblical explanation is true. Millions of others and I overlooked the obvious fallacies and clung to a *theory* sustained by our trust in Carbon-14 dating. That trust was misguided. I overlooked facts and accepted *theories* as truth. I urge you to not make the same mistake."

"When you accept that the Bible contains absolute truth, you understand things that have happened during the past three years and what is coming during the next four years. You cannot afford to get this wrong. Tune in next time, and I will give you an example of another false scientific teaching which people accept as truth without examining the facts. Thank you for watching. I look forward to our next session. Invite some friends to join you."

•   •   •   •   •

Time flew by as the Tribulation moved at warp speed now. With Ben and Miriam joined by their teammates and the people of the kibbutz, the Jewish movement thrived in Israel. The effect of Ben's first teaching on the Temple

Mount was enormous, but it was only the beginning. Jews nationwide continued turning to Jesus. Israel was now the hotbed of Smyrnian activity in the world and picking up steam every day. God's chosen people were discovering their Messiah!

Jesus spoke directly to Ben these days. He promised him supernatural protection, and it came to pass. After the call to speak in the Temple courts came the call to speak on the Mount of Beatitudes, then the plain of Megiddo. His obedience led to thousands of Jews believing in Jesus. Yet, he knew many more would follow. The time for his people to accept the Messiah grew shorter. He did not know how long it would last; it was drawing to a close.

Now something even more unique started in Israel, all part of God's Masterplan. The movement took another turn, catching them by surprise. When word spread of the events taking place there, *Aliyah* became a movement of its own. Descendants of the so-called Ten Lost Tribes of Israel began coming home. It had been 2,750 years since the Assyrians conquered the Northern Kingdom and carried its inhabitants away as captives. They disappeared from records of human history, unheard of since that time.

Most people denied their existence. But God knew who and where they were. And now, he began bringing them back to the country in a mass migration. Members of the Tribes of Judah and Benjamin followed suit. Ben discovered why *Aliyah* was happening now as he prayed and read the Old Testament prophecies. He would share it at the next large gathering. But first, he needed to tell his teammates. He sent a message calling them to the meeting hall that evening.

•　　　•　　　•　　　•　　　•

Aissa Messai received a summons to meet with a solitary figure whose power was greater than his own. He drove to the deserted site. Once known as Caesarea Philippi, then Banias, it was now a scene of utter desolation, a demonic, godforsaken domain of evil. He ascended the steps and walked onto the stone platform. A large niche dominated the side of the immense stone wall at the base of the mountain. Smaller niches adorned nearby areas. Messai stepped up to the giant opening where a statue to the pagan god Pan once stood and knelt before it. He sensed his master's presence, refusing to lift his head or open his eyes. The voice that often became his own spoke.

"Raise your head and look at me, Aissa."

He obeyed, remaining low to the ground, paying homage to the beast.

The sight that met his eyes brought a chill, causing him to shudder with fear. But he always gained strength from the creature during these meetings. The gigantic red dragon hissed, then threw back his head, opened his mouth and let out a loud roar. Flames spewed forth, hot enough to incinerate anything in their path. Messai wondered how such heat could erupt from one who brought such cold when he appeared. The presence of pure evil that gave him his power engulfed him in a ring of deep darkness. He dared not speak, so he waited for the voice of the creature. He did not have to wait long.

"Aissa, I empowered you and sent you to conquer the world, clearing the way for me to rule. When that happens, you will sit enthroned at my right hand. Sometimes you have excelled and performed well. Now, it almost appears that you are failing."

"The Smyrnians are a sly group, Master..."

"Silence!" roared the dragon. "Did I give you permission to speak?"

Messai remained silent this time. He knew the creature would not kill him. Doing so would stymie the mission and leave the world in a state of hopeless chaos. He waited for what felt like hours before the hissing voice came again.

"These *Smyrnians* continue to slip through the fingers of your men. Can you tell me why?"

His tongue stuck like glue to the roof of his mouth. He tried forcing it to move, to no avail. Words refused to come. His knees throbbed from the pain of bowing bone upon stone.

"Speak!" the dragon bellowed, fire shooting from its mouth.

The heat burned down upon him. His mouth flew open, and he knew words would come now.

"Your Majesty, I have stationed many AMPP patrols in Israel, but none have seen them. It is impossible to catch that which we cannot see."

"Impossible? You dare say anything is impossible for me? I will rule the world!"

The hissing overwhelmed him as it grew in intensity and amplification. It rendered him mute and unable to speak again. He understood what that meant. It happened every time, and in an even greater way when the beast got angry. He lowered his head once again and placed his hands on the stone altar, paying homage to the dragon.

"Do not concern yourself with them for now. Their day will come, and you will triumph over them. The time for phase two of our mission draws near. Do you understand?"

The creature's breath reeked of sulfur, almost causing Messai to gag. His head raised as he sensed himself lifted to his feet, standing paralyzed before his master. He faced the dragon, eye to eye, inches away from its scaly body. Fear seized him, but with it came the strange peace he experienced during each of these encounters. The odor now mesmerized him instead of sickening him. He waited for the eerie hissing which would give him the next steps of the mission. The creature seemed to enjoy these moments of anticipation combined with trepidation. The words came at last.

"Stir up the nations. Bring division and rage. The time draws near to unleash the long awaited *infernal chaos* on the earth and its inhabitants!"

His body sank back down to the stone floor. It felt cool on his hands when they touched it, but warmer than the chill that consumed him moments earlier. He rose to leave, but the hissing voice interrupted him, whispering into his ear. The creature's breath stung his face like heat from a furnace.

"If you carry out this phase of the mission to my satisfaction, I will return your most cherished prize to you. She awaits you, Aissa. Obey me, and she is yours."

He knew what the dragon meant. She would belong to him at last. Thoughts of Beth Jennings filled his mind, bringing an evil smile to his face. *Infernal chaos.* Is that what the dragon called it? The time had come. *They will pay*, he said to himself. *And she will be mine.*

•   •   •   •   •

Blake and Beth sat in their temporary home in the kibbutz, awaiting Ben's meeting. Their curiosity about his news caused time to drag by. Beth suddenly started shivering. Goose bumps broke out on her arms. She could feel them covering every part of her body. Her chair began moving, the legs sliding around on the wooden floor of the house. The shaking that started with her hands now moved through her arms and into her legs and feet and became uncontrollable.

Blake leapt to his feet and ran toward her. "Beth, what's wrong," he screamed. She looked at him through eyes of fear, not knowing what was happening. Blake reached her, but before he could take her in his arms, something hurled him backwards. He slid across the floor to the opposite side of the room, his body slamming into the wall with a thud.

He sat dazed for a few seconds, then pulled himself up and charged toward his wife again. Two feet before reaching her, he crashed into an invisible wall and slumped to the floor. He watched helplessly as she sat shuddering and twitching for a full minute before it finally stopped.

"It was him, Blake. He spoke to me, and the chill consumed me. It was frigid. I am so afraid. Please keep him away from me; I cannot bear the thought of him taking me again."

The fear in her eyes crushed him. "I will never allow that to happen, Beth. He will not get his hands on you again, no matter what I must do to stop him. I will protect you and stay by your side every minute." He knelt before her and wrapped his arms around her, pulling her close.

"You said the same thing before."

Her voice did not sound right. Something was different about it, but Blake did not notice the low tone. He only heard her words. They cut like a knife to the depths of his soul. To be honest, he had not forgiven himself for allowing Messai's men to abduct her before. He should have listened to her and left instead of entering the house in Tehran. They should have driven to the airport and fled Iran. But he refused. The tears poured from his eyes as he collapsed his head onto her shoulder and wept.

"I am so sorry, Blake. I didn't mean that. The cold took hold of me again, and I couldn't stop the words from coming out of my mouth. I heard them, but it wasn't me who spoke them. Please believe me, Blake. It wasn't me; it was him."

"Your voice, Beth! The words cut me so deep that I paid no attention to the voice. It *wasn't* you. It was *him*! He tried to gain control of your mind and drive a wedge between us. You must stay here with the men of the kibbutz guarding this house. Then we need to leave Israel as soon as we can and go back to the Shelter. That is still our safe place for these seven years, and we need it now more than ever. I will go with Ben and the others to the Temple on Saturday, and we will fly home the next day. We will book a flight today and I will let Ben know after our meeting."

"Blake, I am ready for the Shelter now. I don't want to wait. Book a flight for tomorrow and let's get out of this place. Messai plans to stay in Israel searching for us, and I can't bear the thought of being anywhere near him. Please Blake, please, let's go home tomorrow."

"I love going with Ben when he speaks, Beth, but I love you more. I will find a direct flight right now before the meeting. The men will post a guard tonight and I will hold you close as we sleep, if I can sleep. This time, I promise, he will not get his hands on you."

CHAPTER 16

The time for the meeting arrived and Blake left, appointing a security force of men and women from the kibbutz to guard Beth. It was impossible for anyone to get near her, but then, Messai was no normal foe. After what he witnessed earlier, Blake refused to leave anything to chance. The women sat with her in the house, while the men stood guard around the outside.

Ben stood outside the meeting house waiting to see how many would come. If the number was greater than the house could accommodate, they would move out to an open space large enough for everyone to sit. That proved to be the case, so they chose an expansive grassy area not far away. When everyone sat, Ben stood to speak.

"Fellow Smyrnians, followers of Jesus Christ, and believers in the true Messiah," he began.

"Come on, Ben, that is way too serious," chuckled Evan. "We've all been together a long time."

"Okay, Evan, I will save such formalities for speaking to the masses." Ben smiled.

"Friends," he started again, "in studying the Old Testament prophecies, I discovered the reason for the sudden rise of *Aliyah*."

Evan poked Anders and said, "He can't help himself, can he?"

Ben cleared his throat and continued after shaking his head at him. "All of you have read Ezekiel's vision in the Valley of Dry Bones. When I read that earlier, it occurred to me that we are witnessing the fulfillment of that scripture right now! Listen and you will understand." He began reading Ezekiel Chapter 37, verses 15 through 22.

"The word of the LORD came to me: "Son of man, take a stick of wood and write on it, 'Belonging to Judah and the Israelites associated with him.' Then take another stick of wood and write on it, 'Belonging to Joseph (that is Ephraim) and all the Israelites associated with him.' Join them together into one stick so that they will become one in your hand."

"We call that an object lesson with a visual aid depicting what God says he will do in the last days. I need not remind you that we live in the final days of history. The midpoint of the Tribulation draws near, and God must bring his people home. Listen, and it will become clear to you."

'This is what the Sovereign LORD says: I am going to take the stick of Joseph—which is in Ephraim's hand—and of the Israelite tribes associated with him, and join it to Judah's stick. I will make them into a single stick of wood, and they will become one in my hand.'

"For years, people have believed the ten tribes of the Northern Kingdom disappeared from the historical record. They refer to them as *lost*. But God's chosen people have endured to this day, including those tribes. Because the world did not recognize them, does not mean the same was true of God. He has always known who they are and waited for this time to bring them home. The next verses refer to *Aliyah*."

'This is what the Sovereign LORD says: I will take the Israelites out of the nations where they have gone. I will gather them from all around and bring them back to their own land. I will make them one nation in the land, on the mountains of Israel.'

"I see by your expressions you do not need me to explain further. We must remind our workers in the lands of all twelve tribes to expect many fresh faces moving in! God is bringing them to us, and we must tell them about the Messiah!"

Ben finished, but the meeting was far from over. The excitement caused by this revelation turned into jubilation. Each of them understood they were living in the last days. They knew it before, but God's message to Ezekiel confirmed it. Moshe walked away and returned carrying two sticks bearing the names Judah and Joseph. He joined them together and proclaimed, "*Aliyah!*" A cheer erupted from the group. They rose in unison and joined him in the cry: "*Aliyah!*" It rang throughout the kibbutz: "*Aliyah!*" Their time had come.

While the celebration continued, Blake pulled Ben aside and told him about Beth's experience.

"We are leaving tomorrow. Beth must get away from Messai, and I refuse to make that mistake again."

"I agree with your decision, Blake," Ben reasoned. "But remember, as we have supernatural *protection*, Messai has supernatural *power*. Ours comes from Jesus, but his comes from an evil source. I'm not sure how long our protection will last. It seems to be with us wherever we go for now. I hope it stays with Beth too, but Messai's ability to affect her like that concerns me. That came from someone other than him, and we both know who that is. Watch her closely, Blake."

"On another note, I think it is time for the others to go back with you. They have stayed here a long time. During that time, Jesus raised up an army of Jews and prepared them for *Aliyah*. Now they are ready to introduce the masses who return to Jesus. The number of new Messianic Jews has already exceeded 40,000, but as amazing as that is, it has just begun."

"I will call everyone together tonight and encourage them to go with you. Something bad looms on the horizon. I can't figure out what it is, but every day it gets closer. Do you remember how we felt after the eclipse? We knew something happened that night, but the next morning it appeared nothing happened. The world was at peace as it was before the *invasion of darkness*. We expect that again, but also know utter destruction will follow. I don't know what that means either, but I am convinced it is true."

"I feel it too, Ben. I didn't until today, but watching what happened to Beth and not being able to do anything about it stirred something in me. Maybe I got comfortable, or even cocky, with our supernatural protection from AMPP. Then being here and witnessing such a movement among your people gave me so much joy that I forgot about the enemy for a while. But he's on my mind again now! It fired me up again when all of that went down today."

The two of them walked away, knowing in their hearts another all-out assault was coming soon. The midpoint of the Tribulation crept closer and closer. They dreaded whatever was coming, but they would face it head on, as they had everything else the enemy threw at them.

•　　•　　•　　•　　•

Johnathan Baldwin's teachings on the age of the earth had already changed how many people thought about the subject. The number of viewers for his previous online session increased exponentially. The debates raged, but more and more people bought into what he said. Many others stood on the fringe, needing very little to push them across the line from evolutionism to creationism. Johnathan accepted the challenge and met it head on.

The more effective he became at changing people's minds, thus turning them to faith in Jesus, the more intense Messai's verbal assaults turned. The reward for any tip leading to Johnathan's capture increased to a million dollars for the public. He added the million dollar reward per man onto the already promised immediate retirement and life of luxury for any AMPP patrol who captured or killed him. That led to what amounted to a treasure hunt, with AMPP patrols and people everywhere getting in on the chase.

Johnathan remained undeterred and took his teachings deeper each time. He knew his time for continuing was drawing to a close. Conversations with his dad, Ben, and Blake confirmed that. All of them believed Messai would catch up to him soon. If he did, Johnathan maintained he would die for his faith and never turn his back on Jesus. But even if that did not happen, they determined what was coming soon would put an end to all their online activities.

The topic for today's video was *Deep Sea Diving: The Truth About The Ocean Floor.* He moved it up to 7:00 a.m. so folks could watch before they left for work. A quarter of a million people tuned in for this one. None of them realized it would be his last.

"In my work as a geophysicist," he began, "I have joined oceanographers in performing extensive research dealing with the ocean floor. It remains one of the favorite parts of my former job. Now, I often reflect on questions that bothered me then, but whose answers I chalked up to unexplainable phenomena. Let me give you one example."

"I could never account for the thickness of the sediment at the bottom of the ocean. The average for all seafloors is about 1,500 feet. To help you understand what I mean by average, consider the Pacific and Atlantic oceans. The sediment in the Pacific runs about 1,000 feet deep, some would say up to 2,000 feet, while the Atlantic is closer to 3,000 feet."

"Granted, one-third of a mile of sediment sounds like a lot, and it is. If you or I sank into that like quicksand, we would be in *deep* trouble, no pun intended." He smiled, having become much more comfortable with these sessions. "However, when you take into account the fact that 20 billion *tons* of sediment accumulates on the ocean floor each year, the numbers do not add up. Estimates point to 1 billion tons being removed because of the shifting of tectonic plates. That leaves nineteen billion tons remaining every year."

"You do not have to be a mathematical genius to understand that is a lot of sediment! *But*, even at that rate, the current average of 1,500 feet would take around *eleven million* years to accumulate, *not billions* of years. 'Okay,' you say. 'You just proved the earth is at least millions of years old, even if it is not four and a half billion years old.'"

"Not at all. Let's take that a step further. Science teaches that the oceans have been around for 3.8 billion years. If my calculations are correct and that much sediment accumulated over 3.8 billion years, it would equal around ten miles of sediment, give or take a mile or two. Once again, mathematical genius is not a requirement to understand that 1,500 feet is far less than ten miles." He smiled again.

"The only explanation science can muster up to account for *only* 1,500 feet of sediment in 3.8 billion years instead of ten miles is this. Sediments *must* have deposited at a very slow rate early on, then increased over time to the rate we see today. Pardon my simplistic response, but that is *hogwash*. How did I ever buy into such a laughable theory? But that is how science often answers questions about things for which they cannot account."

"So, how can we make the numbers work? We don't have to; *God did!* They work perfectly when we see them through the correct lens: a *biblical* lens. Based on the above figures, there is only one logical answer for a mere 1,500 feet of sediment accumulating, rather than ten miles of sediment. A cataclysmic event during the 6,000 year history of the earth deposited it there in a brief period."

"The Biblical account of Noah's flood occurred around 4,500 years ago. When the floodwaters receded rapidly from the earth, a massive amount of sediment poured into the oceans. The remaining amount has accumulated over the last 4,500 years. Boom!" His comfort level showed again. He would have never used that word to say, *Yes!* or *Gotcha!* Now it came naturally.

"So, there you go, folks; another of the mysteries of our wonderful world explained. But science does not answer it. We find the answer in the Bible, given to us by God so we can understand how the world came into being and how it has developed. But he also tells us how it will end, and shows us we are living at the end right now. In a nutshell, the earth is 6,000 years old.

God created it all in six twenty four-hour days. The Bible says a day with the Lord is as 1,000 years and 1,000 years as a day. The Apostle Peter wrote that within the context of Jesus' second coming."

"Jesus himself told us he would come with the blast of a trumpet and as lightning flashes from the east to the west. He hinted that would occur on the Jewish Feast of Trumpets. That should come 6,000 years after the most pivotal event in history: his crucifixion and resurrection."

"The Feast of Trumpets in 2,029 fell on September 11. The deafening sound we heard was the blast of an angelic trumpet. The blinding flash we saw was the lightning he described. On that night, he took his people home to be with him in the blink of an eye. We call that the *Rapture*. The Bible teaches that only seven years of history remain after that. We are moving through that time at a rapid pace. That means Jesus will come again in less than four years!"

"There is only one way you can be ready to meet him and go live with him forever. Put your faith in him and ask him to come into your life and be your Savior. I did that, and I can tell you it is the best thing I have ever done. Don't miss it! The same video that helped me understand will show right after I finish today and will continue showing throughout the day. Please do what I did. None of us know when our time will end. Do it while you can! This is Johnathan Baldwin, telling the truth for such a time as this. Thank you for watching. I will see you again next time!"

When the last words escaped his mouth, the sound of voices filled his ears. He dashed from the room, screaming at the others as he ran.

"Go!"

All of them understood what he meant. They had held the drill more than once, as schools hold storm and fire drills. Hidden entrances to the underground passageways and spacious rooms below lay scattered about the chateau. He could hear the pounding of their footsteps as he raced to join them. The front, back and side doors all crashed open at the same time. AMPP patrol members sprinted through each one. When he rounded a corner and headed for the next room where an entrance to the tunnels was located, they saw him.

"Stop, *now!*"

A warning shot slammed into the wall ahead of him. He faced a choice: continue and lead the men to the secret entrance where his family and the

Sandersons had just fled, or surrender. He could not lead the men to them. It forced him to make a split-second decision. The options ran through his mind: give himself up or give them away. Johnathan made the choice any husband, father, and friend would make. He stopped and put his hands in the air.

"Johnathan Baldwin, you are under arrest. Put your hands behind your head and don't move."

Thoughts flooded his brain. He had declared his allegiance to Jesus and proclaimed he would die for his faith, if that became necessary. Would he do that now that the time had come? Pictures of his family flashed through his mind. Memories of happy times washed over him. His childhood, his father and mother, followed by a lost relationship with his dad and the anger and hatred he had harbored against him.

The disappearances. The eclipse and invasion of darkness. Blake Thompson's special program. Truth! Turning to faith in Jesus, experiencing the overwhelming joy so many others had discovered. A message from his dad. Happiness! Restoration!

The Shelter in Missouri, purchasing the chateau in Colorado, fleeing from AMPP, arriving here and finding it more than they could have imagined. The perfect place! No one would ever find them here. But they had! How? Someone called Messai's tip line. But who? No one knew they were here. Yet it happened.

How would they kill him? He pushed that thought from his mind. Peace rushed in to replace it. He smiled inside.

His teachings. The incredible response. People turning to Jesus! He would teach for four more years! Not now. Those thoughts showed up one at a time within a matter of seconds, as if he watched them on a gigantic movie screen. The scenes stopped playing when the men grabbed his arms, jerked them down behind his back and secured them with zip ties. Pain. Too tight! They would cut off his circulation! Peace again replaced the pain, and his mind returned to Jesus.

He would not shed tears. If he did, they would fall for his wife and kids. He refused to give these men the pleasure of seeing him cry. Silent prayers flowed from him to the God he now loved with all of his heart. The prayers carried the names of his family, but also went up for these men who needed Jesus.

Forgive them, Lord, he pleaded in his mind. *If only they knew the truth...*

The men dispersed throughout the house, searching for the others. They returned with news that he was alone. They found no one else in the house. The voice of the Patrol leader jarred him back to reality.

"We got him, boss." A brief pause. "No sir, there is no sign of the others. He is alone."

The man put his phone on speaker. Johnathan recognized the voice of Aissa Messai. Fear seized him, catching him off guard. He expected a surge of strength and boldness. He prayed for faith.

"Bring him to me. Tell me about the house. Is it as luxurious as our source claimed?"

"Oh, yes, sir. It is a mansion in the mountains. And it is stunning."

"Then it is all yours, men! I believe all of you are single, is that correct?"

"Yes, sir, every one of us."

"Fantastic! Make it your home, or the place where you come and go. Enjoy it!"

"Thank you, sir. I promise we will take advantage of all it offers. The opportunity to retire here seems like a dream come true. We are grateful to you, sir."

"Not retirement. That reward only stood if you found Johnathan yourselves. The money goes to the couple who gave the tip. The chateau and property go to you. Send two of your best men to deliver him to me. Leave today. This cannot wait. Those men who attend him here will receive a full year's pay for their sacrifice, in addition to their regular salaries. The others of you may stay and enjoy yourselves. I want you there in case his father or others show up to attempt a rescue."

"I will accompany him myself, sir, with two of my men. When do we leave?"

"We booked a direct flight to Brussels, leaving Denver at 4:00 p.m. I will leave within the hour and meet you there. That gives you time for a little fun before you leave, if you get my drift."

"I do indeed, sir. I promise we will enjoy ourselves." He sneered at Johnathan.

"One more thing, Captain. Record a few videos of the infamous Mr. Baldwin and send them to me. They will show on the morning news, and I will follow up with an announcement when they end. We will execute him as an enemy of the state at 6:00 p.m. so the world can witness it."

"That sounds perfect, sir. And the videos should arrive in your inbox within two hours."

"Very good. Search every square inch of the place. The source who submitted the tip was certain there are others with him. Comb the entire property, to be sure. If you find them before you leave, bring them too. The more the merrier! And Captain, make sure your men do not leave the house unattended. Stay on high alert and keep watch for Smyrnians. When they cannot contact him, I feel sure they will come to his rescue. Capture *them*, and the ultimate reward is yours!"

•　　　•　　　•　　　•　　　•

Fourteen Smyrnians arrived in Kansas City, and Steve picked them up at the airport. There was no opportunity to test their supernatural protection because there was no sign of AMPP. Messai's search for them now focused on Israel. They drove back and arrived at the Shelter, oblivious to what was happening in Colorado.

Being home and safe felt good to all of them, but none more than Beth. Her fear remained, causing her to jump at even the slightest sounds. Could Messai reach her here in their safe place? Would his icy presence consume her as it did in Israel? Blake refused to leave her side, and she clung to him every minute.

In Colorado, John and Kathie's families sat trapped underground. The AMPP patrol above them blocked their only avenue of escape. Brita was distraught because of her husband's capture. The soundproof room where they fled yielded no sound from overhead. Johnathan had not come. That meant only one thing: AMPP had captured him. And they were powerless to do anything about it.

They needed to get out, but feared the patrol had not left. Julian decided he would confirm that, but could not take that chance yet. They checked their phones; no service. The tunnels and rooms were so secure that cell phone use was out of the question. They could not call and inform the others, nor could they emerge from their hiding place. The group discussed their options. But if Julian confirmed their fears, they may all die down here. They waited for daylight to come.

Above them, Johnathan sat bound in a chair while the patrol enjoyed themselves at his expense.

"What happened on September 11, 2029, *Johnathan*?"

"Jesus took his people home in the Rapture."

Smack! An open hand crashed across Johnathan's face so hard it almost toppled the chair. He winced from the pain, but remained undaunted, staring straight ahead.

"How old is the universe?"

"6,000 years."

Whop! The other cheek. His head whirled to the left, blood dripping from his mouth.

"These are simple questions, *Johnathan*. You're a sharp guy. What do you call yourself? A geophysicist? Let me help you out. On September 11, 2029, aliens abducted millions of people from the earth in the *Invasion*. The universe has existed for fourteen billion years. As a scientist, you should know that. Now, let's try another question. How did the earth get here?"

"God created it in six days."

Thunk. A punch to the stomach would have doubled him over if they had not cuffed his hands behind the chair, holding him straight up. He gasped for air as the blow knocked the wind out of him.

"You can save your life, if you just admit that Messai is lord and bow to him. Look into the camera and say it. We will send him the video, and he will pardon you as soon as he sees it."

Johnathan now realized what was coming. He already knew, but hearing those words confirmed it. Messai would soon proclaim himself lord and demand that people worship him.

"Jesus is Lord. In four years, he will return. Every knee will bow to him and every tongue will confess that he is Lord, including Aissa Messai and all of you!" Speaking had become difficult.

Thud. A kick to the shins with a steel-toe boot sent his head back, his mouth twisted from the pain.

"I think that's enough fun for tonight. We need to save some for the boss. Clean up his face and make him presentable for his special appearance on the news."

"Johnathan isn't answering his phone, and neither are the others," said John, his brow wrinkled from worry. His wife stood by his side, with the same look of concern on her face.

"I need to get to them. AMPP must have caught up with them and may have already murdered all of them. Trey and Rickie, how soon can we fly to Colorado?"

"*We* can't, but the military can! Paul Johnson and several others believed in Jesus. They're ready to do whatever it takes to help the cause. I'll call him right now!"

"Who is with me?" John asked. He issued a challenge to all of them, and they understood it.

"I want to go, John, but I can't leave Beth. I'm afraid she isn't safe from Messai, even down here."

"I understand that, Blake. Who else is with us?" he asked, raising his voice.

"Count us in," said Evan, Anders and Malachi standing with him. Bruno and Magnus joined them.

"You know we're not missing this!" proclaimed Ollie, pointing to Amelia and Ally.

"You need me," said Steve. "But Linda will stay here." She agreed. Bruno insisted that Mila stay too. Blake needed her help with Beth, anyway, and she wanted to be there to provide that.

"That makes thirteen of us. Let's roll! It's over an hour to the base, a two-hour flight from there to the base in Colorado, and another hour to the chateau. I'm afraid we're already too late."

They ran out the door, jumped in the van, and drove away toward the military base. They weren't aware that by the time they landed in Colorado, a flight would leave Denver bound for Belgium.

•   •   •   •   •

Aissa Messai arrived in Brussels and paced the floor. If his captain carried out his mission, tomorrow would go down as his most colossal day yet. When the world finished watching the execution, he would tell of the couple who just received a million-dollar reward for the tip that led to Johnathan

Baldwin's capture. That should lead others to follow their example. People would turn in their family for a million dollars, he reasoned.

The captain must get this done. He checked his email. There they were! The videos of Johnathan. Excellent! They captured the *fun* and sent several others of him seated in the chair with his hands bound behind his back. He planned to send those to the news networks who would show them three hours prior to their arrival time. He had plenty of time to watch the videos before he retired for the night. He planned to replay them several times, then sleep like a baby.

•   •   •   •   •

Commander Paul Johnson had everything prepared and ready for the team to exit the van and board the aircraft the minute they arrived. While the plane climbed into the air, bound for Denver, four men sat in the airport there waiting for their flight to leave. It was on time. The captain cuffed Johnathan to himself to prevent any attempted escape.

Messai booked their seats in economy class so two could sit with Johnathan between them. He thought everything through in advance and took no chances. The call came to board, and they found their seats. When the military plane carrying the Smyrnians landed at a base in Colorado, another plane left Denver bound for Brussels.

On board, Johnathan Baldwin sat between two AMPP men, cuffed to one. All possibility of escape had disappeared. When the plane reached cruising altitude, two military vans drove away toward the chateau where John and Kathie's families were imprisoned below with an AMPP patrol stationed above them. This stood the chance of being the bleakest day in the brief history of the Smyrnians.

Johnathan sat between the two men, his mind on his family. He fought back tears as the faces of his wife and kids flashed through his memory. Did selfishness cause him to put his life in danger, risking their lives too, or create the possibility of dying and leaving them behind, mourning his death? No, he knew he had taught the truth for the sake of the cause.

Thoughts of how Messai may execute him haunted him. He wondered what Jesus looks like, knowing he would see him when he took his last breath. Most portraits depicted him in similar ways, but no one knew how he looked. A slight smile crossed his face as he considered seeing him soon. Conflicting thoughts led to a restless spirit that plagued him as they flew.

Somehow, he fell asleep and dreamed. Messai's face loomed before him as he stood in front of him. Members of AMPP demanded that he bow down to him. He refused, saying he knelt to no one but Jesus. The verdict came quickly: guilty of crimes against the state and interfering with the peace and prosperity of the world. Messai sentenced him, then they dragged him away and prepared him for execution.

He could not determine how they carried it out, but just prior to dying, he awoke and sat straight up in his seat. His arm flew up, as if to shield himself, jerking the arm of the captain with it. The man growled and glared at him, pure hatred covering his face. *You can't touch me on this plane*, Johnathan mused. He allowed himself a moment of pleasure at the thought.

The flight continued as both men settled back in their seats. The dreams continued, but Johnathan learned to maintain more control with each one. He was powerless to change the outcome, anyway.

His dad and comrades in the faith arrived at the chateau. John directed the driver to the parking area. They would walk in from there. Another van parked behind them, and a squadron of soldiers from the base jumped out. They wore full combat gear and followed John and Kathie as they led the way.

Every member of the Smyrnian party was armed and ready for whatever they may face. When they neared the house, two black SUVs sat outside. They understood what that meant. John and Kathie's reaction expressed everyone's feelings… fear and dread at what they may find inside.

Paul Johnson led this mission himself. He motioned for the infantrymen to follow him and instructed the others to remain outside, stationed at each entrance. They must stay prepared for action at a moment's notice. The doors stood open with damage pointing to forced entry.

The soldiers crept inside, listening for voices or sounds that would lead them to AMPP's location. When they went further, sounds came from straight ahead and to the left. The men laughed and talked in loud voices. They were celebrating a victory and partying with gusto. When the unit reached the entryway to the spacious living room, they saw the group for the first time.

Alcohol flowed as they waved bottles of whiskey and vodka in the air. They were drunk, but each had his weapon by his side ready to stop anyone from escaping or entering. When the soldiers burst into the room, catching them by surprise, the men began firing.

The squad returned fire, dropping all of them where they stood. They rushed to check them and confirmed that none survived. Paul motioned to his men, sending them to search the rest of the house for any remaining AMPP personnel or members of the Baldwin and Sanderson families.

The group outside heard the gunfire and dashed in, racing toward the sound. They entered the room and witnessed the scene. Seven members of an AMPP patrol lay dead on the floor. Paul's squad returned, saying they had searched the property and found no further sign of enemy troops.

One pointed to an overturned chair lying near the wall a few feet away. Moving closer, the scene that met their eyes showed signs of torture. Splatters of blood stained the wall and floor. Magnus lifted the chair, pointing to scratches up and down the back.

"I hate to say it, but someone sat in this chair with his hands cuffed behind it. These scratches came from the cuffs sliding up and down. This is the work of AMPP," he said, laying the chair down.

Kathie wept, and John shook all over, his face pale. The group remained silent, taking in the scene and sensing the pain of their teammates.

"They took all of them," John said, his voice quivering.

"We don't know that, John" said Malachi. "Didn't you say the previous owner dug hidden passageways and built secret rooms underneath this place? If the group made it to the tunnels before AMPP found them, we might find them alive."

A partial resurgence of hope filled the group. John and Kathie led them to an expansive master suite and left them there as they walked into the adjoining bathroom. They heard a creak and froze in their tracks.

Without time to run, both watched as the medicine cabinet moved and the wall holding it cracked open. John yelled and prepared to attack in case the intruder turned out to be a member of AMPP. Julian's face peered out as the secret door opened more. Kathie screamed and ran toward him, nearly knocking him back down the stairs. She embraced him, weeping.

"Julian, where are the others? Are they safe?"

Both families started spilling out of the door when she asked that. Kathie wept and hugged her children and grandchildren as each came into sight. The soldiers and Smyrnians celebrated behind her. Brita was the last to exit. She walked to John and embraced him, tears pouring from her eyes.

"Johnathan?" he asked.

She shook her head, trying to speak amid the tears.

"They took him, John. Just as he finished his broadcast, they burst in, and he yelled at us to run. We made it, but he never came."

John broke into tears, his entire body convulsing. Brita held him in her arms as Kathie came and embraced him from behind, her tears soaking his shirt.

"The chair," he finally got out. "It was him."

"The chair?" Brita questioned, still sobbing.

He led her to the living room, and the others followed. When the sight of the overturned chair and blood spatters on the wall and floor met her eyes, she collapsed to her knees, screaming, "No!"

Her wailing reverberated through the house. John fell beside her, grieving with her. The group fell silent, tears streaming down their faces at the thought of what happened to their colleague. Johnathan was aware this may happen, but continued his teaching despite the danger to his life. The troops removed their helmets and stood at attention beside them.

Silence filled the room for several minutes, the only sound coming from the grieving family. John finally stood and broke the silence.

"They took him to Messai in Israel," he whispered. "He will do what we have often said and make an example of him to the watching world. Someone call Blake and fill him in."

"I can do that," offered Evan. "Maybe Ben and the others in Israel can help. There are thousands of them. I'll ask Blake to call him and fill him in. You never know..." His voice trailed off.

Evan left a somber room and walked out to make the call. They estimated the plane carrying John's son had a three to four-hour head start. Ben was their only hope.

Blake put his phone on speaker so Beth and Linda could hear the conversation. The mood there became just as somber soon after Evan started talking.

"I will call Ben," Blake said. "Maybe the young IDF soldiers who joined us can do something. Perhaps they can get the military involved. Or if Ben puts the word out, a bunch of people may turn out. Imagine if they all show up in force at Ben Gurion. That may be all we need!"

"I wish you guys were there too. Hey, I wonder if the military can fly you to Israel? You're already several hours behind, but depending on what happens at the airport, and Messai's plans, you may still get there in time to help. Why don't you ask Paul Johnson if that's possible?"

Evan ran to Paul, telling the others to gather around.

"Paul, can the military fly us to Israel? If the IDF will let us land at one of their bases, maybe we can do something. I know we're a few hours behind, but we may still have time."

"Evan, I want to go more than any of us," said John, "but they likely flew three or four hours ago. By the time we get back to the base and make the fourteen hour flight, Messai will have Johnathan. Ben and his group have a better chance of helping him than we do. They can get to the airport and wait for them to arrive with him."

"I'm not trying to be negative," said Magnus, "but Messai won't wait. He instructed us to bring you guys to him when we captured you and promised to move fast after we did. He knows how elusive you have been in the past and doesn't want to take any chances of you escaping."

"Let's go anyway," said Ollie. "I'd rather be there trying to do something than standing around here wishing I was."

"I'm willing if all of you want to go," said Paul. "We can be back at the base in an hour and have the plane ready to go. But it will take us at least fourteen hours to fly to Israel. The time difference is nine hours, meaning it will be 4:30 a.m. in Israel by the time we depart. That will put our ETA at 6:30 p.m. Say the word and we will leave for the base right now. A van will drive the rest of you there, then fly you to Missouri. Another van will take you on to the Shelter from there."

"Let's go, John," said Kathie. "We can't just give up."

"I'm going too," insisted Brita.

"Brita, you shouldn't do that," said John.

"We need to go, and I'm going." Her tone made it clear there was no changing her mind.

While they talked, the van from the base drove up.

'That's our sign!" Trey shouted. "Load up everybody. We're flying back to Israel!"

They hustled into action. Neither clothes, nor anything else, crossed their minds. They had only two thoughts: Johnathan and Israel.

CHAPTER 17

Johnathan sat awake now less than halfway into their flight. Both AMPP men slept on each side of him. The snoring of the one on his right made it impossible to sleep. It annoyed other passengers too. All they could do was listen to music and hope to drown it out.

Johnathan prayed silently. He asked Jesus to give him strength for what he was about to face. Prayers for his family poured from his heart to the throne of God. Protection for the Smyrnians and success in their efforts spilled out too. While his prayers continued, he fell sound asleep and dreamed again. Jesus stood before him.

"Johnathan, you have served well. Many people believed in me because of your teachings. The seeds you planted will continue to reap a harvest, as many more will turn to me. I come to you with this word: even though you walk through the valley of the shadow of death, fear no evil, for I will be with you. I will comfort you and give you the strength to bear what you are about to face."

"You have fought a good fight and will now finish your race, having kept the faith. Do not worry about your family. My angels will surround them and protect them. When they witness your courage, their boldness will arise too. Do not be afraid, Johnathan, for you are getting ready to cross the finish line. And I will be there waiting for you."

He awoke from the dream. An epiphany! Was it real? Yes! Jesus came to him and spoke to him, as real as any experience he ever had. Peace flooded his body, filling his heart, soul, and mind. The voice of Jesus was unlike any he had heard. It drew him in, strengthened him, and created a longing to be with his Savior. Jesus' appearance was more amazing than he could describe. But there was no one to describe it to. Or was there? Without giving it another thought, he yanked his handcuffed wrist, jerking the captain's hand into the air. The man awoke and glared at him again.

"I just saw Jesus, Captain! He appeared to me and talked to me. I wish you knew him. He is pure love and peace. Let me tell you about him, sir. Jesus came to give you real life, and to give it in abundance."

"Captain, God loved you so much that he gave his only son to die on a cross for you. If you will believe in him, you will never perish but will have eternal life! He wants to forgive you for all the wrong you have done, including what you did to me. And sir, I forgive you too. Because he forgave me, I can forgive you. Please turn to him before it is too late."

"The man you serve is the Antichrist. He is from Satan and will lead you down the path to hell if you follow him. Turn to Jesus, Captain. His arms are open wide! He took his people home on September 11, 2029. Don't believe the lies you were told. Believe in Jesus! He is real, sir."

"I lived my life not believing in him until I saw a pastor's video. I'm sure you are aware of it too. Watch it. Trust in him, open your heart and life to him, and ask him to come and live inside you. Please captain, do that before it is too late. He loves you, and I love you. I want you to know him."

The man stared at him as though he was a madman. He yanked his arm down, and Johnathan felt the cuff dig into his wrist. He smiled at the captain with a look that touched the man deep inside.

"Do this for me, sir. Look at my face when I die. See the peace I feel and the way I go. Jesus said we can be where he is. I will be with him Captain, and you can join me there one day. Trust in him. He is real and he lives in me. He can live in you too."

The man sat and looked at him through questioning eyes. *What is wrong with this man? Doesn't he know he is about to die?* He broke his trance and spoke.

"I *will* watch you die. We'll see how you feel when you face the squad. Where will that peace you speak of be then? Bow to Messai, deny the one you claim to worship, and he may let you live."

"I bow to only one: Jesus. Bow to him, Captain, and call out to him. He will give you eternal life!"

The man said nothing else, but for the rest of the flight, he pondered those things in his heart. When he slept, he dreamed of Johnathan before the firing squad. When they prepared to fire, he wanted to rush forward and stop them, but knew he could not. He would watch him die, but he feared it would haunt him for the rest of his life. Asleep... dreaming... awake, until they arrived in Belgium.

Beside him, Johnathan Baldwin slept peacefully, not waking one more time. Every time the captain awoke, he looked at him again and saw the smile on the face of a sleeping man. What was it about the words he said to him? He could not get them off his mind. Asleep again... dreaming again... awake again. *Please, let us get to Belgium and get this over with.* For the first time in his life, he experienced empathy for another human being. His heart went out to the man sitting beside him.

•　　•　　•　　•　　•

The group of Smyrnians were now on their way to Israel. Paul Johnson had conversations with his connections in Israel as they flew. The commander was a well-rounded man with friends in *high* places, in *many* places. One Jewish friend who held a prestigious position in the Israeli government became his liaison on this important day. The man got permission for the American military plane to land at Ben Gurion Airport, an unprecedented move, but it happened.

Everyone on board tried to sleep, but found it impossible with Johnathan on their minds. So they came together and sought a plan to free him. Ben agreed to meet them at the airport with the men from the kibbutz. As far as he knew, their supernatural protection still worked, but they would not know until they tried it out. That would happen when they walked into the airport and faced what was sure to be a massive AMPP presence.

None of them understood why it hadn't worked for Johnathan until Ben told them it was now only good inside the borders of Israel. And he believed less than a week remained before it disappeared altogether. Its purpose was to protect them until the movement spread throughout Israel and *Aliyah* started. That had happened.

With both planes in the air, Ben, Moshe and Eliyahu sat in Ben Gurion Airport waiting for Johnathan's flight to land. They could not confirm a gate for their arrival, so Ben called for more volunteers to cover all the gates in Terminal 3. It served as the major gateway for international arrivals into the country and had forty gates divided among the B, C, D, and E concourses.

Ben wanted ten people at each gate, or four hundred total. Others would stand guard throughout the airport, including the primary entrance and exit, along with security and shopping areas.

What seemed to be a major *ask* turned into a minor *situation*. Ben asked for five hundred volunteers, but well over a thousand reported for duty. So many begged to help that it forced him to turn hundreds down. He settled on seven hundred. That allowed for three hundred patrolling every part of the airport, with ten watching each gate. Every man and woman held pictures of Johnathan Baldwin and watched for his arrival. If he walked through any gate in Terminal 3, they would know.

•   •   •   •   •

The plane carrying Johnathan landed in Brussels as seven hundred men and women moved into position in Tel Aviv. It taxied to the gate and stopped. Passengers got up from their seats, opening overhead compartments and removing carry-on bags. The captain looked at the man in the seat next to him, still cuffed to his wrist, and still sleeping and smiling.

This man knows he will face a firing squad before this day ends. How can he have such peace? He longed to save Johnathan, but knew he could not. He wanted what the peaceful sleeper had. *Is it possible that he is right about Jesus?* He nudged him to wake him up. No jerking of the cuffs or shoving, just a gentle nudge attempting to awaken him from his deep sleep.

"Hello, Captain," Johnathan smiled. "I hope you slept well."

"I did okay." He tried to sound gruff, but he knew it didn't work. Johnathan still smiled at him with that peaceful smile. Instead of annoying him as it should, it made him feel warm inside. They exited the airport and got into a black limousine which drove away to the mansion. When they arrived and walked inside, Messai greeted Johnathan with an evil grin. *What a difference between the boss's grin and Johnathan's smile*, the captain thought.

"Johnathan Baldwin. I am pleased to meet you at last. We have an exciting day planned for you!"

Johnathan should have feared him. The chill should have consumed him, turning him into an icy puppet. But neither happened. Instead, he smiled at Messai with the same smile the captain had witnessed for the last several hours of the flight.

"Aissa Messai. At last I stand before the Antichrist, Satan's man, the epitome of evil. You, sir, may win this battle, but you will lose the war to Jesus! *He* has an exciting day planned for *you*!"

Messai's face changed, along with his voice. The low growl returned and the grin turned into a glare. "We will see if your attitude changes when you face the firing squad at 6:00 this evening. That's right, Mr. Baldwin. You will die today, and for what?"

"Oh no, I will not die; I will live! And you will help me do that. For that I say, thank you!"

"Take him away and get him out of my sight! Prepare him for execution. The world will watch at 6:00. Let this be a lesson to all of them!"

•　　•　　•　　•　　•

The expected arrival time of 3:00 p.m. for Johnathan's plane came and went. Ben checked with every member of their group, but no one saw him. They continued waiting and watching, but still no Johnathan. AMPP patrolled the airport, but remained oblivious to their presence. Did they take Johnathan somewhere else in the country? No, they would have flown to Ben Gurion. Maybe the flight got delayed. They would stay at their posts until they saw him exit a bridge and enter the airport.

•　　•　　•　　•　　•

The captain treated Johnathan with kindness, a far different man from the one who brutalized him less than a day before. He fed him and cared for him as if he was part of his family.

"Johnathan," he asked, "can you tell me more about your peace, and the Jesus you serve?"

He talked to the man until 5:30. Then it was time to parade Johnathan in front of the cameras while Messai denounced him as an enemy of the state. The Secretary-General would give his usual spiel about the Smyrnians seeking to destroy the peace and prosperity of the world.

Then they would lead Johnathan in front of the firing squad, his hands cuffed behind his back. They would not blindfold his eyes because Messai wanted the condemned man to see everything that took place. It would end within seconds. The world would celebrate the execution of a rebel while the captain mourned the death of a good man. But how could he mourn when he knew where Johnathan had gone?

•　　•　　•　　•　　•

The plane carrying the group of Smyrnians landed at Ben Gurion Airport. They exited quickly, and Ben, Moshe, and Eliyahu met them when they entered the gate. AMPP could not see them, so there was no need to stop at the scanners. Others protested, but to no avail. When they walked into the terminal, they saw people crowded around TVs, captivated by something. They pushed their way in and a brutal scene met their eyes.

Messai was speaking and telling the world AMPP would execute one of the rebel Smyrnians in a few minutes. They came to the wrong place! Messai took him to Belgium! Johnathan appeared on the screen. John collapsed to the floor. His body grew weak and his legs would not support him. Evan caught his former professor just before he crashed onto the hard surface. Brita screamed and pleaded with God to stop her husband's murder.

Though AMPP neither saw nor heard them, others did and turned to see what caused the commotion. While they led Johnathan to the place of execution, some wept with her, while others applauded and jeered. His fellow Smyrnians watched in horror as the squad leader gave the commands.

But as the camera panned in on Johnathan's face, they noticed something that amazed everyone watching, including the Smyrnians. A smile. Not just a smile, but peace like none of them had ever witnessed. He gazed toward heaven. John and Kathie recognized the look. It was the same one they saw on her husband's face just before AMPP shot and killed him as they tried to flee.

They knew Johnathan was looking at the same thing: the face of Jesus. And he wanted to go and be with him. Brita saw it too. Kathie had told her the story. The same peace that filled Johnathan now rose up in them. It was the most wonderful thing they had ever felt. "Go see Jesus, Johnathan," she whispered. John stood and held her as the squad leader gave the final command: *"Fire!"*

Johnathan heard the crack of the guns and felt the bullets riddle his body. Darkness engulfed him, and he dropped to the ground. The darkness immediately changed to brilliant light. He stood and walked toward the light, then saw a figure coming to meet him. Johnathan knew who it was: *Jesus!* He ran as fast as he could and leapt into the waiting arms of his Lord. His smile had not changed.

"Welcome home, Johnathan."

It was the same voice he heard in his dream on the plane. No voice ever sounded sweeter. And now he saw the face! Pure love. Perfect peace. He was *home*, home to stay.

"You did well, my son. Come and let me introduce you to some people who believed in me because of your words. I want you to meet many others too. Come on, let's go. I'll race you!"

Off they went, racing through the light, laughing as it turned to green grass and beautiful flowers. Johnathan ran like the wind, not out of breath, never growing tired. He had never felt so alive, so vibrant, so... perfect. He wished for his family to be with him. They would come soon enough.

Only a few years remained for Planet Earth, but here time did not matter. He caught up with Jesus, and they rolled in the grass laughing. Others came to join them. He had known some of them in his life before the Rapture; others had heard his teachings and believed. They all celebrated together. He hoped his family and the others knew he was okay. A nod from Jesus told him they did. His smile grew wider. This was home...

The captain stood staring at the dead body on the ground. Johnathan Baldwin was no longer there. He had gone to be with the Jesus he spoke about. A smile came to the captain's face. This man was a true child of God, a follower of Jesus.

He fell to his knees and prayed, "Jesus, I want to know you like Johnathan did and have the peace that he had. I believe in you. Please come into my life and by *my* Savior, as you were *his* Savior." The moment was glorious. In heaven, the smile on Johnathan's face exploded with joy! He endured this for one man, and it was worth it all.

Things had now changed for the Smyrnians. They were more serious than ever about their seven-year mission. They wanted to tell the truth about Messai to everyone they could and convince them to turn from believing in him to faith in Jesus. But while Johnathan's execution increased their faith, it dealt a blow to the potential for that to happen.

Messai's plan to make an example of Johnathan for the rest of the world worked to perfection. People still believed in him and supported his so-called mission of bringing peace and prosperity to the world. But now they also feared the most powerful man in the world.

The one place where the movement had not diminished was Israel. Ben continued teaching enormous crowds of Jews in widespread outdoor spaces, which would support the massive crowds that gathered for each event. The plain of Megiddo became his favorite spot. Jewish believers now numbered well over 100,000. *Aliyah* had not slowed either, as Jews from all over the world kept returning to their homeland.

Alexander and Elizabeth, Moshe, Eliyahu and others from the kibbutz devoted themselves full-time to spreading the word. People from every one of the original twelve tribes of Israel now claimed the Messianic faith. Messai knew something was going on, but could not put his finger on it. Despite all of that, the prospect of one catastrophic world-changing event excited him more each day as it grew closer. He would unleash it soon.

Ben knew in his heart the supernatural protection was ending. Its expiration date lay on the horizon like a dark cloud. He expected AMPP to discover them any day and feared a massacre of his people. But something kept gnawing at his mind. A plan. Not his plan, but Jesus' plan. He could not grasp it, and Jesus had not revealed it to him yet. Something about it caused him to feel safe, but it was not the same supernatural protection they enjoyed now. His eagerness for it made him almost giddy. *I love this journey with Jesus*, he thought, with a smile.

•   •   •   •   •

The others returned to the Shelter, joining John and Kathie's families who had arrived just in time to watch Johnathan's death on the news. All of them both mourned and rejoiced at the same time. Seeing the smile on his face, and knowing the reason behind it, helped. Any of them may follow him before this seven years ended. None of them relished that thought but knew the peace that filled him would be theirs too, if they did.

The midpoint of the Tribulation drew near. They had survived to this point, but understood what was coming would be the worst yet. Things would then steamroll downhill into absolute devastation. Who would live, and who would die? No one knew.

•   •   •   •   •

Peace like no one ever saw suddenly covered the earth. The entire planet exchanged chaos for calm overnight and felt as *eerie* as it had prior to the darkness that invaded it during the lunar eclipse. It bore a resemblance to the calm before a storm. One could describe it as not a leaf moving on any tree. War and violence ceased worldwide. People lived at peace with one another. A moment of silence... quiet... solitude... peace... *eerie*...

The group housed in the bunker in Missouri battled confusion once again. It made no sense, unless fear related to Johnathan's martyrdom brought it on. However, they lived through this before and knew what to expect soon: the return of chaos. What they did not understand is this time that chaos would be *infernal.* The globe would turn into a hellish place where the fight for survival would be more intense than ever before.

A throng of Jews covered the Plain of Megiddo on Sunday morning. Messianic Jews now worshiped on the first day of the week celebrating Jesus' resurrection. Those who believed in Jesus as the Messiah brought others to hear Ben Abramson speak. The event was a sight to behold.

Jumbotron screens adorned the valley. Huge speakers boomed sound to the farthest reaches of the estimated 125,000 attendees. Concession stands offered free fish and loaves, mirroring one of Jesus' most prolific miracles. The festive mood and air of anticipation was the greatest yet at these events. Miracles would occur today!

Messianic hymns and worship songs rang out in a crescendo of praise, reaching to heaven. The stories of Alexander and Elizabeth, Moshe, Eliyahu, Yaakov and others followed the music. Then the climactic moment arrived as Ben stood to speak. The valley reverberated with thunderous applause, far greater, Ben thought, than Messai received when he spoke. That brought a temporary smile to his face as he raised his hands, signaling for the crowd to quieten.

The power of his words penetrated every heart. When he asked the crowd to respond to his message, 125,000 people covered the ground lying prostrate on their faces crying out to their Messiah. The wailing pierced the air, and celebration followed as people rejoiced with the new believers. The sound of rejoicing was greater than the wailing. Laughter, shouts of joy and praise, and clapping drowned out every other noise.

No one saw or heard the choppers flying overhead and black SUVs speeding up from every side. Hundreds of AMPP troops raced toward the crowd, firing their weapons as they ran. The helicopters hovered low overhead, their whirring blades creating even more havoc. Panic spread like wildfire through the sea of people as hundreds of AMPP men turned into thousands.

The sounds of gunfire, combined with the *thwok, thwok, thwok* of the rotors, deafened Ben's audience. People attempted to flee, but the surrounding AMPP army made escape impossible. They drove them back toward the center, crowding them into each other like sheep trapped in a pen. The Supreme Commander of Aissa Messai's Peace Patrol and security forces strode to the platform.

"Silence!" he yelled into the microphone.

With a wave of his hand, the choppers lifted higher, easing the overwhelming sound and wind. The troops formed a circle around the entire valley surrounding the crowd. They were serious about this mission. Blood may soon flow on the Plain of Megiddo, where it had often run before during the valley's many wars.

"This is an unlawful gathering, in direct disobedience of Aissa Messai's orders," the commander continued. He turned toward Ben. "Ben Abramson, you are under arrest for spreading the lies of the rebel Smyrnians and inciting riots. We had peace in Israel until you came and turned things upside down. Aissa Messai will no longer tolerate your divisive behavior!"

Four men rushed the stage and grabbed Ben, throwing him to the floor. They jerked his hands behind his back and placed him in handcuffs. Then pulling him to his feet, two of them placed leg irons around his ankles, preventing him from moving. He stood undeterred by their attack, then bellowed in a voice that needed no amplification.

"Brothers and sisters, do not fear the enemy. Stand still and see the salvation of the Lord!"

His words propelled Moshe and Eliyahu into action. Both leapt onto the stage at the same time. Moshe stood to the left of the commander as the troops continued to hold Ben captive. Eliyahu stepped directly in front of the man, confronting him to his face. Fire exploded from his mouth, engulfing the commander in flames, igniting his clothing, and turning him into a human torch. He ran toward the end of the stage but collapsed before he reached it. His screams filled the air as his body burned until death silenced his cries.

Eliyahu now moved toward the men who still held Ben's arms. When he got closer, they turned to run, but it was too late. Fire again roared from his mouth, igniting them and leaving them to die in the flames without leaving the stage. The handcuffs and leg irons fell from Ben's wrists and ankles, setting him free.

The crowd watched in awe as Moshe raised his hands to the sky. Tornadic winds attacked the helicopters, driving them back, and throwing them into frantic spins and turns. Pushed farther away from the crowds, the entire fleet nosedived to the ground exploding in balls of fire.

Moshe turned his attention to the armed men surrounding the crowd. Swarms of locusts descended upon them, covering them as they dropped their weapons and tried to run. Swinging their arms at the locusts, they desperately tried to remove them from their bodies. Darkness covered the plain at midday. Once again, Ben's voice thundered from the stage.

"The battle is not ours; it is the Lord's. Again I say, stand still and see the salvation of the Lord!"

Darkness continued for several minutes then gave way to brilliant sunshine once more. The scene that met the eyes of the people left them stunned. Bodies of AMPP personnel littered the valley floor. None escaped the fury of the locusts. The people burst into raucous applause.

They watched as Moshe raised his hands again and a powerful wind blew the SUVs into a mountain of metal far away from the crowd. One breath from Eliyahu's mouth ignited them in a blazing inferno. An explosion rocked the ground as flames hit the gas tanks. The crowd cheered again. Ben stood before them, Moshe and Eliyahu at his side.

"What you witnessed today is the almighty power of Ha-Shem!"

Thunderous applause echoed through the valley.

"But," Ben went on, "we also witnessed the end of our supernatural protection."

The people grew silent, knowing this was a pivotal moment.

"From this point on, we can no longer meet out in the open like this." He held up his hands to silence a murmur spreading through the vast number of people. "Form groups in the areas where you live. Continue to worship Yeshua! After today, all of my teachings will be online. I hope you will tune every day." A cheer told him they would.

"Something is coming soon. I do not know what it is, but it will be devastating. Let us prepare ourselves and allow Ha-Shem to show us the way we should go. I believe he will reveal that to us soon. Stay safe and connected with each other. Only four years remain until our Messiah will defeat the enemy and we will live with him forever!"

Deafening cannot describe the sound that filled the plain. The celebration started again and continued until evening. Then they left and returned to their homes, not knowing if they would see each other again on earth. But they would fight as long as they lived. And they would turn as many fellow Israelites to the Messiah as they could.

•   •   •

A blood-curdling scream erupted from the mouth of Aissa Messai. He had just received word of the catastrophe in the valley. Over 1,000 of his troops died, including his Supreme Commander. Demonic creatures flew around the room amid flashes of lightning and crashes of thunder as they had done at prior times like this. His rage persisted for thirty minutes without abating.

Then, out of nowhere, he found himself face-to-face with the dragon. The heat from the beast's mouth and foul odor of its breath drove him to his knees.

"Master..." he began.

"Aissa," the dragon interrupted. "Calm down. Who needs security forces when armies await at your disposal? It is time, Aissa. Release my infernal chaos on the pathetic inhabitants of this filthy planet. Let them destroy themselves. Then we shall reign. The earth will belong to us!"

With that, the beast was gone. Messai knew what he had to do. The time had come. His rage subsided as he thought about the millions who would die in the approaching storm. An evil grin formed on his face. Then one thing took it away: the Smyrnians. Others would die, but he *must* destroy them!

•   •   •   •   •

While he traveled back to the kibbutz, ever alert to the possibility of any AMPP vehicle along the way, Ben got Blake on the phone.

"The protection left us, Blake. But you must hear what Jesus did today."

He detailed the events of the day. Blake took them in as the entire group at the Shelter gathered around to listen. This day signaled a turning point in the Tribulation. Whatever was coming would hit any day. They must be careful now that the enemy could see them again.

All of them, from Israel to Missouri to Germany, wanted to prepare for the coming attack on the earth. But how do you prepare when you are unsure of what lies ahead? Their only choice was to wait and pray. When it came, they would face it head on, as they always did.

"I wish I understood what I heard in Messai's meeting." Magnus held the notes from that night in his hand. "I wrote what he said word for word. Jesus transported me to that meeting because he wanted me to hear what they said. But now we need to interpret it."

"Read it to us again," said Blake. "Maybe we can figure it out together."

"*We are gathering resources and mobilizing armies. The world will soon see that which they have long feared and feel the sting of all it brings. Let us continue our search for the enemy as we await the greatest invasion of all time.* It is clear that he refers to war."

"We know war is part of these seven years," said Beth. "And we really haven't seen it yet. Violence, brutality, killing, yes. But not war between nations."

"But what did he mean by *the world will soon see that which they have long feared and feel the sting of all it brings?* The earth has survived many wars, including two World Wars. History has no recorded time without war somewhere on the planet."

"That line bothers me," Blake mused. "*The world will soon see that which they have long feared and feel the sting of all it brings.* We are missing something."

Magnus sat straight up. "No..."

It hit the others at the same time. Their faces said it all.

CHAPTER 18

22,000 miles above the earth, simultaneous explosions occurred in space. Within minutes, the attack wiped out the entire SBIRS constellation. The purpose of the United States Spaced-Based Infrared System was to alert the country to incoming nuclear missiles. They scheduled the entire system for replacement by 2029, but September 11th of that year put the decision on hold.

For a few years, the U.S. suspected the Russians' real purpose behind launching the Kosmos 2543 satellite. The Kremlin maintained they created it to inspect their own equipment. But it also packed the capability of launching projectiles aimed at destroying other satellites. And on this day, at this critical juncture in history, the 2543 caught America by surprise.

Impossible on a normal day? Maybe. But prophecy announced it would come just before the mid-point of the last seven years of the Earth. Jesus revealed it to John, one of his apostles, over 1,900 years earlier. John recorded it in Chapters 8 and 9 of the biblical book of The Revelation. And today, it happened, leaving the United States of America under-protected against Intercontinental Ballistic Missiles launched from four of its most ruthless enemies.

Two world powers, Russia and China, joined forces with North Korea and Iran to destroy Israel's number one ally. An ancient proverb fit the coalition: *The enemy of my enemy is my friend.* All four were enemies of America and Israel. Now they joined as *friends* for one purpose: to annihilate the world power standing between them and their primary target. The attack was swift and 2-fold: eliminating SBIRS, followed by nationwide Hypersonic Intercontinental Ballistic Missile attacks.

Blake Thompson sat at his workstation in the Shelter, speaking to believers around the world. In the middle of his presentation, a news alert flashed on his phone. He stopped speaking and ran. He and Evan narrowly avoided a collision as each sprinted toward the other.

"Did you see what I just saw?"

"We were right. He did it. He unleashed it on the world, and on America."

The others joined them, coming from all three bunkers after seeing the same thing. They stood in silence, looking at one another. None of them could fathom that it happened, but it did.

Undetected Hypersonic ICBMs carrying nuclear warheads hurtled through space at 20,000 miles per hour bound for the United States. In fifteen to twenty minutes, they would re-enter earth's atmosphere and plummet toward their targets like blazing torpedoes. Unsuspecting cities lay in wait for imminent destruction.

The Hypersonic boasted the newest technology in missile development, traveling at twenty-seven times the speed of sound. In the past ten years Russia, China and the U.S. had perfected these ICBMs, along with their ability to carry nuclear warheads. They proved to be undetectable and unstoppable. The Russians ensured that by taking out America's SBIRS constellation. Still, no one thought this day would come.

At mid-morning on the East Coast, New York City bustled with activity. The coalition planned the attack and carried it out with precision timing to result in the most catastrophic damage and maximum number of deaths. People outside watched in horror as the missiles appeared and blazed toward them at speeds of 2,000 miles per hour. Panic ensued as they attempted in vain to run for any place of refuge they could find. But nothing could save them from the inescapable disaster which would hit them in seconds.

The first bomb slammed into Times Square, exploding on impact. An incendiary fireball reaching millions of degrees vaporized everything at Ground Zero. Intense thermal radiation created a firestorm engulfing bodies and buildings in a blazing inferno. Raging fires spread quickly through midtown Manhattan, filling the air with smoke and ash and burning everything and everyone within a one-mile radius.

Gas lines, fuel tanks, and power lines erupted in one explosion after another. People five miles away experienced third-degree burns. Most of those proved fatal. First-degree burns occurred as far away as seven miles.

Up to twenty-one miles away, flash blindness rendered people sightless for several minutes.

A colossal shock wave spread in all directions, generating five hundred mile per hour winds. It demolished every structurally unsound building and ripped roofs and walls from stronger ones, leaving only twisted shells of metal. Utility poles snapped like toothpicks. Trees uprooted in Central Park, ripped out of the ground by the winds.

Bricks, glass, wood and metal flew with deadly force. Few buildings remained standing. Collapsing structures buried any survivors under mountainous piles of rubble. The force of the wave ruptured eardrums and burst lungs. The electromagnetic pulse knocked out computers, cell phones, and communication towers for miles.

A huge plume shot upward, leaving behind a 50-foot crater where Times Square once stood. It rose as a red ball of fire, then morphed into a white mushroom cloud carrying the vaporized material sucked up by the powerful updraft. The material then bonded with the radioactive particles inside the fireball. Within minutes, radioactive dust started falling from the sky onto the city.

By the following day, those affected by the dust experienced itching and burning. In a few weeks, the itching and burning would turn into lesions. Anyone who inhaled or swallowed the dust exposed their body to an ongoing source of radiation.

The fallout would travel for miles, dropping radioactive dust and affecting people, homes, crops, animals and water sources, resulting in more deaths. Over one million people died in New York City alone. Another two million incurred injuries, with an additional half-million killed or injured by the fallout.

People exposed showed immediate signs of acute radiation syndrome: headache, dizziness, nausea, and vomiting. Some died within hours. Those who did not would develop more symptoms. Diarrhea, fever, seizures, and bleeding in the mouth and under the skin would bring horrific suffering. Many became emaciated and delirious, and some even incapacitated.

The intensity of their suffering left them begging to die. Death came when their immune cells were depleted to the point they could no longer fight off infections. For others, the radiation damaged their digestive system so badly it no longer functioned properly. Both led to agonizing and torturous deaths.

New York was not the only city hit by the attack. In Washington D.C., Secret Service agents saw the flaming projectiles just in time to hustle the president into the White House bunker prior to impact. The explosion and shock wave that followed rattled the underground shelter. They knew the devastation was extreme but had to remain underground for 24 hours before emerging to survey the damage.

The house no longer remained above the bunker. The blast obliterated it and destroyed everything from there to the National Mall. When the totals came in, 120,000 people had died, with another 170,000 injured. The Capital of the greatest nation on earth lay in a pile of rubble.

Over 150,000 perished in Chicago. 200,000 more suffered critical injuries. The blasts annihilated downtown. The initial bomb set its sights on Willis Tower, the perfect location for widespread death and destruction. The Los Angeles explosion killed at least 100,000, with over 150,000 hurt. Houston saw 90,000 deaths and over 60,000 injuries. San Francisco lost less than 65,000, but experienced nearly 175,000 injuries. Those numbers would skyrocket as the fallout continued to spread.

The coalition targeted other heavily populated cities around the country, aiming to cripple the nation. They hit military bases and nuclear storage facilities. Nukes landed in the oceans off each coast, damaging marine life. Sources for drinking water and fishing became targets, too. America lay in ruins from border to border. But the country had not lost its ability to respond.

The word went out and nuclear weapons launched from multiple U.S. locations, at home and abroad. America had restored the sea-launched cruise missile program. It now stood ready to join the fight. Missiles fired at once, aimed at strategic locations in each of the four nations. As explosions rocked major cities in Russia, China, North Korea and Iran, *World War III* had begun.

U.S. allies, France and the United Kingdom, quickly fired warheads at Russia and China. India, another U.S. ally, embroiled in a decade-long feud with neighboring China, joined the fray. India's mortal enemy, Pakistan, retaliated with an assault against them. The world could only watch as nuclear holocaust wreaked havoc on three of its seven continents. But they knew it would have a major effect on all of them. Israel was the only country believed to have nukes, who stayed silent.

•   •   •   •   •

Ben sat in the kibbutz talking with his leaders. They understood that the supernatural protection had left them, but that was the least of their worries now.

"We are well aware of his goal, men. This is not a battle between nations; it is a precursor to the ultimate battle between good and evil, between Ha-Shem and Lucifer. And in four years, Jesus will ride out of heaven and end it once and for all! But the question is, what do we do *now*?"

"He will turn on Israel soon," said Moshe. "When we see the war subside, that will come next."

"I want to welcome our newest members to the group. This is Michael and Hadassah. Ha-Shem brought you to us *for such a time as this*." He smiled at the girl. "That day on the mountain when you sought me out, I knew. So, tell me about your work with the IDF."

The young soldiers believed in Jesus when Ben taught on the Mount of Beatitudes. He recalled his shock when they saw him and the fear that they came to capture him. Those feelings turned to joy with their next words: *We want to see Yeshua.* Now they were a valuable part of the team in Israel.

"We have shown your testimony and the video to a few of our comrades, Rabbi."

"Michael, I told you to call me Benjamin, or even Ben."

"I'm sorry, Rabbi, but that does not seem right to me. You are my elder and our leader."

"Are you saying I am old, Michael?" Ben asked with a twinkle in his eye, then burst out laughing.

"Of course not, Rabbi. But you are much older than us." Now it was Michael's turn to smile.

"How many of your fellow soldiers have believed in Yeshua?"

"Only eight. But now they are telling others, too. However, two of them are pilots and very important pieces of the puzzle for you. Their names are Ezra and Shimon. Hadassah is sweet on Ezra." He looked at the girl with a mischievous grin.

"I am not!" she exclaimed, punching his arm. "Rabbi, I am ready to do anything I can for the cause. What do you need from me? Please tell me, and I will do it."

"Not yet, Hadassah, but Yeshua will reveal that to us in his time. Be patient, young one."

•   •   •   •   •

"We can't sit in this Shelter while the world needs us so much," Blake began. "The minute it becomes safe to leave, we have to go. What do you say, Beth?"

"I agree. Fear has kept me cooped up in here for too long. I am ready to go, and I know where."

"New York, right?"

"Yes! We are going home to help in any way we can. I recall us wondering if we would ever return and saying it would look far different if we did. Well, that time has come."

"Count me in!" Anders jumped out of his seat.

"You're not leaving me behind," proclaimed Malachi.

The four New Yorkers understood where they needed to be and how dangerous going there would be. But their former home called out to them, and they would heed the call.

"I'm going with you!"

"No, Evan." John spoke with a firm voice. "Think about it, and you'll know where we need to go."

"Chicago," whispered Ally from across the room.

"Back to where this journey began for all of us," Evan agreed. "Bring on the Chicago pizza!"

"You may not find any of that. I doubt that we will even recognize the city when we arrive. None of us have seen what it's like out there. We don't want to, but people need us."

"It is too dangerous," said Steve. "Radiation levels may still be too high. You don't want to find out what Radiation Sickness does to the human body."

"We have four years left on this earth, Steve," Beth stated. "What do we have to lose?"

"I suspect we have less time than that to act. The time to bring people to Jesus has almost passed. With nuclear war going on, this may sound crazy, but I believe we have yet to see the worst of things. What is happening now pales compared to what is coming." Blake was serious.

"I understand how Messai thinks and how to get into his mind," said Magnus. "I would love to infiltrate his inner circle and get some intel that will help us stay a step ahead of him. But I don't think Jesus wants me to go to Israel, New York, or Chicago."

"What are you saying, Magnus? We're a team. Where one of us goes, the other goes. Wherever you go, I'm going with you. Whatever you're doing, I'm doing too."

"I would never go without you, Bruno! Few men are brave enough to mess with us." He smiled, but he was dead serious about what he said. "I understand the danger, but I think we need to infiltrate the central figure of this war: China. I haven't mentioned this before, but Messai has focused on them for a while. He plans to use them. It didn't surprise me when they led this charge. If we're there, we should be able to learn things about his next moves. I'm going to China."

"Then I'm going to China! But Mila, I can't put you in that kind of danger. You need to stay here at the Shelter or go home to Germany and help there."

"I'll go back home, but I won't stay long. The boys have begged to join us, so I'll bring them back with me. We can go to Chicago. They love that pizza too. But I am sure they are ready for this."

"Now, Mila..." She cut him off.

"Bruno, they have begged to do this. I cannot say what will happen, but neither can I hold them off any longer. They only have four years left to do something important for Jesus. Hans and Heidi can lead the work in Germany."

The big man gave up, although the fear showed on his face. He was glad of one thing: at least Ally would work in Chicago, thousands of miles away from Messai.

"Trey and I will pass on New York, too," said Rickie. "We believe Ben needs us, so we will take your Israel trip, Magnus. We don't know why, but we're sure that's where Jesus told us to go."

"Then you need to go! If the radiation levels are down, I say we all leave day after tomorrow." Blake looked at Beth, Anders, and Malachi and asked, "Are you with me?" In two days, they would drive back into their old home. They all nodded in agreement, except one.

"I hate to leave you guys, Blake," said Malachi, "but Magnus spoke my language. My gig is infiltrating inner circles and getting information. You understand that. Evan and Anders saw it firsthand in Belgium. I need to go with Magnus and Bruno to China."

Evan and Anders shrugged and nodded. They had seen the man in action. No one was better.

"Go where you feel you need to go, Malachi. I support whatever decision you make. Ollie and Amelia, you two have stayed quiet. What's on your minds?"

"We have to go home to London, Blake. They are in the thick of this war too. I doubt anyone will expect us to show up there again, but even if they do, that is where we need to be."

"I get that, Ollie. Let's take this a little at a time and meet back here in a month, but stay in touch every day till then. Any of us can come back earlier, if we need to. Is everybody good with that?"

They were, but others remained: The Baldwins, Sandersons, and Steve and Linda.

"We have stayed in here long enough when so many people out there need medical help. Linda and I would like to join you guys in New York, if that's okay."

"We'd love to have you! Does that mean the rest of you are staying here to run this place?"

"Not me," said Brita. "I'm going to fight for Johnathan. I have a score to settle with Aissa Messai."

"You can go with John and Kathie," said Blake. "The rest of you need to stay here with the kids."

"I agree. It's probably not going to be safe out there for a long time, but people need Jesus. I say we go now. You said it earlier, Beth. What do we have to lose?" John wanted to get to Chicago.

Everyone was ready and would leave in two days. Preparation and prayer would fill the hours until they left, but it was time, and they knew it. They would leave the safety of the Shelter and go back into the thick of battle.

This time it was war. Each of them would put their lives on the line by going, but they wanted to make the most of the time they had left.

$$\bullet \qquad \bullet \qquad \bullet \qquad \bullet \qquad \bullet$$

In the outside world, the war raged as the U.S. and its allies continued their battle with the coalition. Bombs flew and people died in nine countries. Charred remains of burned cities dotted landscapes. War continued from land, sea, and air in North America, Asia, and Europe. Smoke rose from burning ships, joining the smoke from flaming cities. Nukes that exploded in the water contaminated it. Beaches and lakeshores lay littered with dead fish and other marine life.

Radiation affected every part of life on the three continents. The fallout continued to spread and fall back to the earth, poisoning water, land, and people. When people drank the water or ate seafood, they consumed radiation, and many died. Crops containing lethal levels also killed those who ate them. It forced farmers to destroy the source of their livelihood. And there was no letup as the war continued to rage.

However, things would soon take a different turn and threaten the entire world. The timing would align perfectly with God's plan for these seven years. Not all the Smyrnians would be around to see it, but none of them were aware of that. For now, they must continue their fight against Aissa Messai as they told everyone they could about Jesus.

But even as nukes flew to its north and east, Israel seemed immune to the battles of the outside world. All of its inhabitants, except the Jews who believed in Jesus, accepted the false propaganda being spouted by Aissa Messai. *The man of peace protected them*, he said. The Messianic believers knew that was a lie. Their protection came from Jesus. He had a plan, and they trusted him.

The same held true throughout the Middle East. Iran remained the only rogue Middle Eastern nation to join the nuclear fray. They were the gateway to opening up the way for the world's greatest army to make its march to the Holy Land. China used Iran to get what they wanted, but Iran would also get their greatest wish when it all went down. That time drew near.

Ben Abramson sensed something in his spirit. God's supernatural protection had returned. Something changed for those who believed in

Jesus. They were no longer invisible, but they felt invincible. Neither Messai nor AMPP could touch them, for now. That was a part of whatever Jesus had in store for them throughout the next four years. They would soon be halfway through the Tribulation. Ben felt sure the second half would be even more difficult than the first.

While waiting, they continued telling Jews about the Messiah. Some believed, although that number was slowing down. Ben and Miriam sat with Alexander and Elizabeth, Moshe, Eliyahu, Michael, and Hadassah. They talked over coffee after dinner.

"The best I can count our number totals around 140,000 now," offered Alexander. "But the work has almost ended since we stopped the large gatherings."

"We couldn't put the believers in danger after the protection left us," Ben answered. "But they're still getting it done. The war may or may not reach us, but something bad is coming. We must prepare the believers for it when it does."

"Rabbi?"

"Yes, Hadassah?"

"I have discovered my purpose."

"You have? How did you figure that out?"

"Jesus told me."

"Well, don't keep us waiting. Spill the beans! I'm sorry. That's an American expression. It means..."

"I know what it means, Rabbi," she said, a shy smile pursing her lips. "I must convince the *Aluf* to use military equipment and personnel to support our cause. We will need his help soon. And I hope I can convince him of the truth about our Messiah too."

"You know the Major General?" Moshe seemed shocked.

"Yes, sir. He is my uncle."

"And she's his pet. He will let her get by with anything. Everybody sees that."

"Stop it, Michael. Yes, he keeps up with me and likes to hear how I am doing, but he does not play favorites. And he has never given me any special favors."

Michael rolled his eyes and turned his head. "Sure... Oh, come on Hadassah, I'm only kidding. I love your uncle. It still blows my mind that I have met him and eaten in his home."

"And you have me to thank for that! The Aluf, my uncle, has no children, and I am his only niece. But I am more like his daughter. My parents died in an accident when I was a young girl. He and my aunt took me into their home and raised me. He was so excited when I came of military age. I am sure he will help us. He is a wonderful man. His name is Mordecai."

Now it was Ben's turn to look stunned. "Only Jesus could bring pieces of a puzzle like this together. Your name is Hadassah, and his name is Mordecai. He is your uncle, your parents died, and he raised you. He is in an influential position, and you will ask him to help us. You're not pulling my leg, are you? I'm sorry, that's another American expression."

"I am aware of that saying too, Rabbi. It is all true, and I believe Jesus has brought me to himself during the Tribulation *for such a time as this*. I don't understand what it all means yet, but he will show me when the time comes. He has already shown Michael what he is to do."

With all eyes now on him, Michael got serious.

"My parents named me for the archangel. Like Hadassah, I believe God brought me to Jesus for this time. The Bible often depicts Michael as the great warrior angel who fights for the people of Israel. I understand my young age, but Jesus has called me to organize and lead an important part of the upcoming movement. Communication has already begun with those God has given us. The pilots will serve an important role when the time comes. None of us are aware when that is, or what their role will be, but it is never too early to plan!"

"The two of you are a blessing to me! The Chief Prince, Michael, plays a significant role in the last book of the Bible. It foretells these exact days in which we are living. And that part of the story is getting close. That is why I knew Hadassah and you were special when you came to me seeking Jesus that day. You are not here by accident!"

The day came for the Smyrnians to depart for four different locations. The New York five and Chicago five would drive, while the others flew overseas. It was their first time to emerge from the Shelter since the war began. Each of them dreaded what they might see. But they realized this was what they had to do, so they pressed on.

Blake, Beth and Anders took the same route back to New York they had taken when they came to Missouri. This time Steve drove his SUV, and Linda sat in the front with him. The other three stayed out of sight in the back. The trip was smooth, and in time, they rolled into the city. But the shock set in well before they arrived. No TV images could do justice to what met their eyes.

"Oh, Blake, this is worse than I imagined." Tears rolled down Beth's cheeks.

Smoke still rose on the horizon as they saw the city for the first time since the nukes demolished it. The Skyline looked nothing like the city they knew and loved. Gone were the Freedom Center, from which they had observed the eclipse, the Empire State Building, and Statue of Liberty.

Nothing appeared to remain in or around Times Square. The Rockefeller Center, St. Patrick's Cathedral, and many others, were absent. When they drew closer, the utter devastation took their breath away. So did the AMPP patrol guarding the entrance into the city.

"You guys still look nothing like yourselves, but you had better get down between the seats and stay out of sight, just in case." Steve's SUV made hiding a lot easier than did the car they drove before. He pulled up to the checkpoint and put his window down.

"Thank you, gentlemen, for being here doing your job today. I'm guessing you have been here for quite a while. Sad time we're living in."

"Cut the small talk and tell us your reason for entering the city. They allow no one in except approved personnel. Turn around and leave or we'll take you into custody."

"I am a surgeon. My wife and I came to help with medical needs. Here are my credentials. Go ahead, call and check me out."

"Pull him up on your phone, Andre. We don't have time to call in about everyone. A quick search ought to tell us if he's legit."

"Got him right here. Dr. Steve Phillips, Springfield, Missouri. You came a long way to help, didn't you, Doc?"

"New York needs us more than any place in America. That's why we're here."

"Go on in and do what you can. But two warnings before you go. It's an ugly mess in there, and radiation levels may still be high."

"We brought masks and protective gear. We'll take our chances."

They drove over buckled roads and got as close to Manhattan as they could. It required a hike from that point. They stood and stared, speechless upon arrival. Times Square no longer existed. No evidence remained of the luxury high-rise apartment where Blake and Beth lived prior to leaving. They saw no signs of life. No one needed their help here.

They made their way back to the SUV, ready to head to Anders' former home in Brooklyn. The destruction was indescribable, but signs of life remained. A few people walked the broken streets, careful to avoid the cavernous holes and debris. The government had sent in additional Law Enforcement and the National Guard to protect against looting and violence. One policeman stood off to himself, leaning against the twisted post of a streetlight. Blake sprinted toward him.

"Malik! Malik, is that you?"

The man turned as he approached, reaching for his weapon.

Blake slowed to a walk as he got closer and lowered his voice. "Malik, it's me, Blake Thompson."

The officer looked closer, then grabbed Blake in a tight hug, lifting him off the ground. They were two friends who had met for a brief time, but neither would ever forget the other. Beth and Anders had reached them now. A grievous day gave way to a glorious reunion.

"Step into the alley so nobody will get suspicious. They brought us here to guard the place, but there's nothing here to guard. It's a waste of my time, but it pays well. I wish I was home with my wife. New York has nothing for us now. And Jesus' coming is still four years away."

"Get your wife and come with us, Malik. Maybe you are the reason we came."

"I would love to, Blake, but I must stay. This place needs Jesus, and I can tell them about him."

"You're right. Maybe you can assist us while we're here. Can you show us where people need our help? This is Steve and Linda Phillips. He is a surgeon. People must need him."

"Yes, sir. They set up makeshift hospitals all over the place. Follow me. I'll take you to one."

They swung by Anders' place first. He wanted to see if it was still standing.

He shed tears when he found his former house, now only a pile of ashes. The tears didn't last long. They followed Malik to a colony of temporary hospitals. Nothing could have prepared them for what they saw when they walked inside. Burn victims lay scarred over most of their bodies. Many raw, open wounds had become infected. Their pain was almost unbearable.

Others, deafened by the blast, lay in silence. Blind eyes stared straight ahead with hollow looks from eerie white pupils. Many people suffered from continuous vomiting and diarrhea, brought on by severe radiation sickness.

When people died, volunteers in protective gear carried them to makeshift morgues. Blake thought he would throw up. But they soon settled down and went to work caring for sick and dying people who they felt certain had not trusted in Jesus. That part was more heartbreaking than any other.

John, Kathie, Brita, Evan and Ally found the same in Chicago. The university was missing, with little evidence it ever existed. Makeshift hospitals also gave them opportunities to serve. They worked as a team and did their best, but they could only do so much.

The world had changed to the point they no longer belonged in it. Every believer in Jesus shared their thoughts. Had Satan taken over the planet? They understood Jesus was still in control, but it took strong faith to *keep* believing that.

Mila found Germany to look much like it did before. The war touched it very little. Fallout affected a small percentage of the population, but things appeared to be normal. When she got to her boys, she embraced them and held them close for a full five minutes.

In those few minutes, she re-thought her words about taking them with her into battle. Even she wanted to stay in the safety of her home country, hiding away with friends and family. But she and her sons were Smyrnians, and followers of Jesus in the Tribulation never play it safe.

Ollie and Amelia arrived in London to a city they almost did not recognize. It bore the brunt of the coalition's attack on the UK. Gone were the Tower Bridge, St. Paul's Cathedral, Big Ben, both Houses of Parliament, Buckingham Palace, and Westminster Abbey. The couple stood and gazed for the first time at a war zone of the worst kind. But this was not just some place they toured as correspondent and official; this was home. At least the government took steps to protect its leaders.

Prior to joining the U.S. in the war, they whisked away the Queen and Royal Family into hiding in an unknown bunker. Members of Parliament moved into a separate bunker. None of them had a place where they could return.

Ollie and Amelia made their way to her friend's house in the country where they went when they fled from AMPP a couple of years earlier. It now sat abandoned and would make a perfect hideout during their stay. They searched for friends to see if they were okay and looked for places where they could help. But they still needed to lie low.

Trey and Rickie arrived in Israel and joined Ben and the others at the kibbutz. They found a joint air of celebration and preparation. Neither understood what was coming, but the two pilots from America were sure they fit in somewhere. It gave them time to get acquainted with Michael, Hadassah, and the others and become part of the group. All four believed they would work together, if only they could figure out what that meant. They would know when the time came.

Bruno, Magnus, and Malachi would face the greatest threat in China. None of them understood the danger that awaited them there. But they sensed it the moment they stepped onto Chinese soil. An overwhelming awareness of pure evil penetrated their minds. The nuclear explosions caused extensive damage, but the country stood armed and ready for war.

They had their minds set on utter destruction and worldwide domination. And they would eliminate anything or anyone that stood in their way, including the three Smyrnians who had just arrived. Things were about to get real for the spy and the two hulking men who would face a fight for their lives.

CHAPTER 19

Blake and Beth walked outside the tents that provided housing for volunteers in New York City. They used flashlights, even though it was mid-afternoon.

"Why is it getting dark so early, Blake? It's 2:00 in the afternoon and pitch-black. I can't see anything. And have you noticed how dark it is the last few hours before sunrise?"

"I wonder if it's like this everywhere else, or just here where the nukes wiped everything out?"

"Why don't you call the others and ask?"

Only one small area provided cell phone service. People had already packed it trying to call home and check on their families. Blake edged into the outer fringe. Two men yelled at him and shoved him out of the group. He glanced at his phone. *No service.* His anger flared up, and for a moment Beth thought he would charge both. She rushed to his side and grabbed his arm.

"Blake, it's not worth it. What would Jesus do right now?"

"He would grab a whip and drive them out!"

"Blake! You know better than that."

"I do, Beth, but my nerves are shot. First, we come back and see our city in ruins and deserted. Then we come to this so-called hospital and work all day with mangled, sick and dying people. And now the darkness. It's driving me insane."

"I understand that, but we're all going through the same thing. The only one who seems comfortable with it is Steve. He has worked in these conditions before and never lets up."

"We've been here three weeks. Maybe we should go home. I don't know how much more of this I can take. None of these people listen to us when we tell them about Jesus. Even the dying ones tune us out. Their hearts are so hard we can't get through to them. It may be like this for the rest of the Tribulation. And we will stay on the run for our lives."

"Settle down, Blake, and make your calls. You can crowd in right over there."

He called Ben first, then pulled everyone else together on a conference call. Hearing was difficult with people all talking at the same time. He focused and finally blocked them out. The darkness was the same everywhere in the Northern Hemisphere, and it grew worse by the day. Even the daylight hours were hazy, like fog covered the sun.

A lull came in the nuclear attacks, but it felt like being in the eye of a hurricane. The calm would pass and the storm rage again, but no one knew when that would happen. They decided the American contingents should return to the Shelter, while the overseas groups stayed put, except Mila. They would communicate with each other by phone. A critical time was coming, and they wanted to be ready.

Mila booked a flight from Germany for her and the boys. John, Kathie, Brita, Evan, and Ally left Chicago the following morning. Blake, Beth, Anders, Steve, and Linda departed from New York that evening. Their 20-hour trip required driving through the night to arrive near the same time as the others. Each trip was smooth, and they arrived at the Shelter in the unusual darkness of late afternoon. Julian picked up Mila and her sons at the airport in Springfield with no problems.

Exhaustion claimed their bodies and minds after the long hours of the previous weeks and lengthy trips back to the Shelter. Steve gave them sleeping medication to ensure that they rested. All of them slept through the night, without moving, until the smell of food awakened the group in Bunker One. Julie, Joanie, and the Baldwin girls got up early and cooked a huge breakfast.

Evan woke the others in Bunkers Two and Three, yelling he refused to wait for breakfast! They had worked long hours, and none of them had eaten as they should. The good sleep and best meal they had eaten in weeks, refreshed and restored them. They were now ready to plan, prepare, and go wherever necessary.

"I believe everything is getting ready to go down in Israel," said John. "Ben will need us soon."

"And we need to go. But we should stay here at least a week and rest up, so we'll be ready. We must all be at our best because we don't know what we'll face over there." Steve took control of those decisions, being the medical expert in charge and their resident physician.

Beth spoke up. "The darkness is bothering me a lot. It's affecting my mind and how I think. Are any of you experiencing that?"

It bothered all of them when it started, but now it was only affecting her.

"You've gone through a lot of trauma in the last couple of months, Beth. I think the darkness is compounding that and hindering your recovery. You need something to help clear your mind. You slept well, but you need to rest today."

"I don't know. Have you noticed how much colder it has gotten, too?"

They sat without saying a word. The looks on their faces showed none of them had noticed cooler temperatures.

"It chills me to the bone. I freeze and shake all over. Are you sure none of you feel that?"

Blake edged over and put his arm around his wife.

"I love you, Beth. Maybe you need to stay here when the rest of us go to Israel."

"I am going where you go, Blake. I can't spend the rest of the Tribulation sitting in here. I'll be okay. Steve is right; a few more days of rest will take care of this. I think I'll go lie down." She smiled as she got up to leave, but everyone else saw the anxiety on her face.

•　•　•　•　•

It was midnight in China, and as Magnus slept, he dreamed again. The room appeared to be underground and dimly lit. Messai sat at a conference table with ambassadors from the four nations of the coalition. At first, Magnus could not make out what he was saying, then it became clear.

"Gentlemen, our attack accomplished its purpose. You sustained heavier losses than I hoped, but we also moved closer to our target. We brought the Great Satan to its knees. Another barrage of nukes will finish it. They think it is over, so we will take them by surprise."

Magnus understood the reference to the United States. More nuclear attacks were coming against the country! He must warn them, but for now, he needed to hear everything said in this meeting.

"When we finish them, we will also defeat their allies who join them in their useless efforts to stop us. France and the UK must go. They are like pesky flies we can destroy with one swat. We must also annihilate India. They should have stayed out of the conflict, but they attempted to interfere. I assume China will be happy to get rid of them." He smiled at the Chinese ambassador, and the man returned his smile as he nodded his head.

"Good, good. The time for peace in the Middle East to end is coming soon. In the upcoming attack, we will now weaken Israel so they cannot stand against us when we launch the final battle. Then we will destroy the Little Satan once and for all! When we finish, the world will be ours!" The ambassadors applauded his proclamation.

Israel was next! The coalition was far too powerful. They would demolish the tiny nation! Magnus' mind raced with thoughts of warning the U.S. and Israel. He needed to leave, but he must stay until the end of the meeting.

"In the last battle, the Arab nations will join our cause as we march against Israel together. Afghanistan, Egypt, Gaza, Iraq, Jordan, Lebanon, Saudi Arabia, Syria and Turkey will join the Iranians and form an alliance to strengthen our efforts. Our friend from Iran," he said, glancing at the man, "has guaranteed that."

"Yes, I have! They can't wait to help us rid the world of the Little Satan forever!"

They also met his words with applause and stood to shake his hand.

"Outstanding work, my friend. I will reward your faithfulness. The leader of Pakistan will join our group for the next meeting. Although his country is not an official part of the Middle East, they have proven themselves worthy. They will march with us against Israel in the great final battle, and I assure you the other Muslim nations will join us, too!"

As far as the Chinese, Russian and North Korean men knew, Messai was leading them to world dominance. They would eliminate him and the Arab nations and assume control, if that became necessary. Their power was now unmatched on the planet. The Iranian was thinking the same about them.

Magnus thought he recognized questioning looks on the men's faces as they glanced at each other. Then he saw Messai turn to *him*, and it brought him back to reality. He froze in fear.

"Magnus, my former trusted captain. It is good to see you again, old friend. I did not want to believe you would join the Smyrnians. The time always comes to pay for desertion, and it is always punishable by death. You are well aware of my plans for the future. Perhaps I should let you be the first to test my little capital punishment device. Can you imagine what will go through your mind right before your head gets severed from your body, *Magnus?*"

When he attempted to run, Messai stretched out his hand and his feet left the floor, leaving him dangling in mid-air. He grabbed at his throat, thrashing, struggling to breathe, and fighting in desperation to escape, but to no avail.

Just before he blacked out, Messai lowered his hand and Magnus dropped to the floor with a thud, still trying to draw air into his restricted airway. AMPP men rushed in and surrounded him. He looked into the faces of his former patrol. They pulled him to his feet and cuffed his hands behind his back.

"Bring him to me, men."

They dragged him across the floor toward Messai. Fighting to free himself was useless. The men held him face-to-face with his former boss and forced him to look into his eyes.

"But then, why should we wait, huh, Magnus? I cannot take the chance of you escaping and returning to the Smyrnians with information from this meeting. Give me your gun," he said to one man, who handed it to him without questioning.

Messai put the end of the barrel against Magnus' forehead. He jerked his head back as the cold steel pressed against it.

"Goodbye, Magnus. I wish you would have remained loyal to me. That is too bad."

Magnus heard the explosive sound of the gun discharging and awoke with a start. Sweat poured from every part of his body and soaked the bed. He shook all over. It took a few moments to realize it had only been a dream. His fear subsided.

But, wait! The meeting was real, and he was there. He stood in the room and listened to every word. Jesus had once again showed him Messai's plans, and each step as it would take place.

The last part was a nightmare. He was still alive. Perhaps it foretold what would happen to him. He couldn't worry about that now. He leapt from the bed, racing toward Bruno and Malachi.

•   •   •   •   •

Beth walked into the bedroom alone, while Blake worked on the computer in the other room. She closed the door and lay on her back, staring at the ceiling and drawing in deep breaths, trying to calm her mind.

Get ahold of yourself, Beth. You are letting little things get to you. A chill filled the room.

She closed her eyes and pulled the blanket up to her neck. Memories of lying in another bed two years earlier flooded her mind, taking her back to Messai's mansion and the private bedroom where he held her prisoner. A wedding. No! She would never marry the Antichrist! The door opened. Blake was coming! She needed him to hold her. A wave of relief washed over her, but the cold intensified.

"Hello, Beth. I know where you are now. You cannot hide from me any longer."

She recognized the voice. Evil... alluring. He stood before her, looking down on her lying on the bed. The chill ran down her spine as the room turned icy. Her body shivered, increasing until the entire bed shook. A powerful impulse to run consumed her, but she could not move. His presence paralyzed her.

"You belong to me, Beth. He cannot protect you. I take what I want, and I want you. I have always wanted you."

She saw him, but it was only in her mind. Or was it? His smile was as charming, as seductive, as ever.

"Plans are falling into place, Beth. Soon you will join me and become my wife. When I rule the world, you will be by my side. Now, let me touch you so you can feel my love."

His hand came down toward her in slow motion, bringing with it both warmth and coolness. She screamed and Blake came running into the room.

"What is it, Beth? What's wrong?"

"It's him, Blake; he's here. We have to get out of this room. Please, Blake, please. Let's go."

He saw the goosebumps covering her arms and the look of panic on her face. The chill consumed him now, shooting up his spine and spreading through his arms and legs. His entire body started shaking. He understood what was happening.

"Come on, Beth. Let's go! *Run!*"

He pulled her up, grabbing her hand, and sprinted toward the open door. Just before they reached the door, it slammed shut. Blake grabbed the knob and pulled with both hands. It would not budge. He turned to Beth, but she was not there. She stood across the room beside the bed, her body trembling, the fear in her eyes begging him to rescue her.

He ran toward her, but something stopped him in his tracks, immobilizing him. His legs and arms froze. He stood staring at her standing there, her entire body shaking.

"You left her again."

It was the same gravelly voice as before.

"You promised you would never leave her side but would protect her. See, Beth. I am the one who cares for you. He is not the one you need. Come with me."

Blake grabbed at his throat as a hand tightened around it. His feet lifted from the floor, leaving him suspended in the air, unable to breathe. Beth screamed his name but could not come to him.

"Listen to me, Blake Thompson. She will be mine soon. You cannot protect her. I will have my bride. And remember, I know *where* you are now, so you can no longer hide from me."

The voice returned to normal. "The Smyrnians will now *feel the sting of all I bring.*"

Blake dropped to the floor with a thud, holding his throat and gasping for air. Beth ran to him and held him. He would never leave her again. When he got his breath, they walked out of the bedroom, shaken by the encounter, and called for the others to come.

•   •   •   •   •

"Bruno! Malachi!" Magnus yelled as he ran. "Wake up! I need to talk to you!"

The two men came to meet him, rubbing their eyes and yawning.

"This had better be good, Magnus," said Bruno. "I was out of it."

"I was in a meeting with Messai and the coalition ambassadors!"

"Stop it. You haven't even left here. Now, what is going on?" Malachi was grumpy.

"Let him talk, Malachi. He did this same thing before, and he was right!"

"Listen to me! They're hitting the U.S. and its allies again, then going after Israel! This attack is to weaken Israel so they will not have strength to fight the final battle. Then they will demolish them once and for all. We have to warn them!"

"Ollie and Amelia are in London! Someone needs to call them!" Bruno ran for his phone.

"I have Ben's number," said Magnus. "I'll call him. Malachi, you can call Blake. I doubt any of them can do anything about it, but they need to know what's coming." He called Ben's number as he walked away, and Ben answered on the first ring.

"Ben!" yelled Magnus. "I had another vision. I was in a room, and Messai was meeting with the coalition ambassadors. They're hitting America and her allies again, then coming after Israel. You guys are next. Make sure everyone is ready to get to the shelters in a hurry. Can your two soldiers alert the IDF? Someone must tell the military, and you guys have to be prepared! Bruno and Malachi are calling Ollie and Blake."

"Slow down, Magnus. Are you certain about this?"

"One hundred percent certain! I was there just like the vision on the plane and heard everything. The rest is true, Ben, I promise!"

"With peace in the Middle East, won't the Arab nations join sides with the Jews and fight against the coalition?"

"No! They will align with Messai and turn on the Jews."

"Sounds like the *man of peace* is getting ready to reveal his true self."

"He isn't just revealing his true self *now*; it's who he has always been. I understood how much he hated the Jews, but he even fooled me at first with the *peace in the Middle East* thing. However, I was sure this day would come. The Arab nations won't help Israel. They'll sit back and watch, then join the fight against them when the time comes. I'm telling you, Ben, it's days at most. Please warn the people; warn the military! Don't let the coalition take them by surprise."

Ben knew Magnus was right. There was no mistaking his sincerity. He did not understand how these visions came about, but they did. And they always occurred just as he described them. He could not sit back and let Messai slaughter his people and destroy the country. The four nations were the ones doing it, but Messai controlled them. And Satan controlled Messai. The others would warn the U.S. and the UK. He had to focus on Israel and the Jews who followed Jesus.

He called Michael and Hadassah as soon as he got off the phone with Magnus. They left for the kibbutz at once. She called her Uncle Mordecai as they drove, certain he would take her call. He always took *her* call. The Aluf would know what to do. He would put the IDF on high alert, and their lives would be on the line. The worst part of the Tribulation was beginning.

•   •   •   •   •

Ollie and Amelia were so connected they could get the info into the right hands. But they would need to be careful because they were both wanted by AMPP. The wrong person may turn them in to the authorities in a heartbeat.

When the bombing stopped, the royal family and Parliament members emerged from their bunkers and returned to London. Amelia called former colleagues from the House of Commons until one answered at last. When she told him what was coming, he did not question her. He contacted the Queen and Prime Minister right away, and they called an emergency meeting for all government officials with the Royal Family in their bunker.

Blake reminded Malachi of his relationship with the Senator from New York. Both Blake and Beth had contacts in government that got them through to the President. Within an hour of their calls, the President called a meeting at Camp David for that night. Members of Congress and the Joint Chiefs of Staff, who survived the initial attack, convened. None of the Smyrnians would be present. They trusted no one and could take no chances on being captured.

Malachi's senator friend did not reveal his source who gave him the information, but assured the president he was 100% certain the man was right. Leaders discussed a plan to defend against the new wave of missiles. That part remained difficult, so they decided attacking first was their best option. The entire United States military prepared to move into action at once.

The President and Congress ordered a preemptive strike against the four countries. U.S. allies joined them, and missiles flew toward China, Russia, North Korea, and Iran before the latter four could initiate their attack. The coalition intercepted and destroyed some missiles, but many found their mark, hammering away at their major cities again.

·   ·   ·   ·   ·

In Israel, Aissa Messai raged for the first time since the war began with the assault on the United States. His most trusted advisors sat in the room facing his ire, yet none dared to challenge him.

"How do they stay a step ahead of us? Who gave them the information about our planned attacks? We have a mole among us whom we must root out and remove!"

"Sir, if I may, I believe Magnus somehow infiltrates our ranks and discovers our next moves. He knows everything about how we operate."

"Magnus?!" Messai screamed as lightning flashed in the room. "How can he infiltrate our meetings and overhear our discussions? Have any of you seen him?"

"No, sir. But I have sensed his presence." The man spoke in a fearful tone.

"Absurd! If he attended a meeting, do you not think I would know he was present?"

The room turned cold, and the entire group fell under his spell. When they did, he let go in all of his fury. Throwing his head back, he roared at the top of his lungs, as demons screeched around the room, expressing rage, too. Fire darted through the air until it appeared the room was ablaze.

"Show me, master," he screamed.

The creature entered and ambled across the room until it stood face-to-face with him. Its fiery breath burned his cheek as the foul odor entered his nostrils. He waited for the instructions to come.

"Do not respond to their strikes in kind, Aissa. Instead, unleash the nuclear arsenal at Israel. It is time to weaken them and prepare for the great battle. Their allies leave them unprotected while they focus on the coalition now. They will not notice until the major cities and IDF bases are ablaze and many Israelis have died. Then lead the PLA to begin its march toward Israel."

"Yes, master!" Messai laughed hysterically. "That means the time is getting close. I will do as you say!" The room returned to normal, and the men snapped out of their trances. Messai ended the meeting and left to carry out the creature's orders.

•　　•　　•　　•　　•

Ben called the kibbutz together as soon as he got off the phone with Hadassah and shared everything Magnus told him. Michael and Hadassah arrived minutes after the meeting began.

"We must now prepare for the war to come to us. Messai has controlled everything that's happened over the past few weeks. He holds power over the leaders of the coalition. They are under his spell, and all four will soon send nuclear weapons against Israel. The Arab nations will not join Israel against them, but will be silent at first, then join the coalition later."

"How can Israel survive? We are so small. There must be something we can do," said Alexander.

"Michael and Hadassah can do something," Ben said, his eyes zeroing in on the two.

"Tell us, Rabbi," said Michael, rising to his feet.

Hadassah joined him. "Yes, Rabbi, we are ready."

"Hadassah, did you talk to your Uncle Mordecai? He must get the military on high alert for the attack that is coming. Magnus believes it will happen soon."

"I tried, but he did not answer my call. That is very unusual. I know he will alert the IDF as soon as he hears my message. He hasn't believed in Jesus yet, but he will believe me and take action."

"Michael, tell us what has happened with your pilot friends."

"Ezra and Shimon have developed a squadron of pilots who stand ready to do anything they can. I continue to believe we need them, although I still do not understand why."

"Neither do I, Michael. Whether we need them now or later, they must be prepared when the time comes. You are in charge of mobilizing them."

"That is an honor, Rabbi. I will not let you down."

"Hadassah, you must convince your uncle to supply us with planes for every pilot we have. This is where you come in, Trey, and Rickie. We need your expertise."

"We will work with the IDF pilots, if they will allow us to," said Trey. "I'm eager to get in the air again. It has been too long. But I'm not sure I understand what our role will be."

"Neither do I, but get ready because we will need you soon. However, right now, we must make sure the IDF is aware of the coming attack. Hadassah, call your uncle again. Michael, call anyone you can."

Both stepped out to make calls. But the next moment proved they were too late.

Sirens wailed throughout the kibbutz. Men, women, and children raced for the bomb shelters. Ben hoped Hadassah had gotten word to her uncle in time, but knew in his heart that had not happened. While he ran with the others, he prayed for Jesus to protect his people this night. With nuclear missiles flying at the country, nothing else could save them now.

Men hurried their families into the shelters. They designated one for Ben and the leadership. From the safety of that underground bunker, they would plan their next steps. It felt like home to Ben. He knew he would not see the Shelter in Missouri again. But he trusted Jesus to supply all their needs during the four years remaining until he returned to take them home.

•   •   •   •   •

Israel's Iron Dome and Arrow 3, parts of the most effective missile defense system in the world, sprang into action, intercepting incoming missiles. But they did not intercept them all. The attack came hard and fast, and caught the IDF unprepared. Hadassah's Uncle Mordecai moved the status of the entire military to high alert immediately, but not soon enough. Nuclear missiles got through to many military bases, demolishing them and wiping out entire units.

More flew toward the three largest cities in Israel: Jerusalem, Tel Aviv, and Haifa, plus others. Again, the system picked some off, but several struck their mark. Each detonated as an *air burst*, miles above the surface of the earth. They chose the altitude of the blasts to cause maximum injury and death.

The attack came so fast that much of the population did not make it into shelters. Some sat in their homes or ran outside trying to make it to safety, but failed to get there in time. Many outdoor groups left themselves exposed. The coalition selected the time to ensure a massive number of casualties and carried it out to perfection.

Jews spilled out of their homes at 6:00 p.m. Saturday evening, following twenty-four hours of quiet Sabbath observance. Shoppers, diners, and revelers filled the streets, while others took walks or stood around talking. At 8:00 p.m., sirens sounded just as the sky lit up with exploding nuclear missiles.

Screams filled the air as the blasts caused massive damage and injuries. Severe burns seared exposed skin. People were fully or partially blinded on the spot. Acute radiation sickness plagued most. It was a devastating night for the nation of Israel.

While Mordecai Chaim observed the attack at IDF headquarters, he sat in shock at what he saw and heard. He never believed this day would come. How had the enemy caught the nation and its military by surprise? It was his responsibility to keep the military prepared for these attacks. Yet, that was not the case on this night when it mattered most. He did not realize a certain red creature ensured that. What now? The coalition destroyed much of the country he loved, G-d's nation and people, in one night.

A thought hit him out of the blue. Hadassah said something about the Messiah. Had the time come? It made sense. The Jews had rebuilt the temple on the Mount and restored worship. Every Jew learned the prophecy as a child. She was right! The Messiah would soon defeat their enemies, come to his temple, and reign in Jerusalem! Tonight's nuclear attack by the coalition must prove that, too. He would talk more to his niece about that when this night ended.

When the barrage finally stopped, he picked up his phone to call her. His eagerness to learn more could not wait until daylight. He longed to see the Messiah come and bring victory to his people, especially after what just occurred. That brought a small sense of relief to the horror of the night.

•　•　•　•　•

Coalition leaders celebrated their success. With Israel crippled, they now turned their attention back to the United States and its allies. Missiles flew toward those countries in an overwhelming show of force. While each intercepted some, most found their mark. A trail of destruction lay in the attack's wake, incapacitating each country.

After this latest barrage, little doubt remained that the coalition sustained far less damage. And their ability to continue fighting far outweighed the others. The United States mainland looked like a wasteland. News channels that remained operational provided aerial views from throughout the country. The assault ended the nation's ability to continue fighting. It appeared the greatest nation on earth was finished. And the Chinese would soon ensure that was the case.

The Smyrnians watched helplessly from the Shelter. They could neither do anything nor leave their place of safety. TV cameras showed what was happening outside their walls. Nuclear Holocaust would now give way to a post-World War III apocalyptic earth.

Nuclear firestorms burned hundreds of thousands of acres in each of the affected countries. A thick plume of smoke created by 150 to 200 million tons of soot rose into the stratosphere. The soot cloud spread until it covered the entire Northern Hemisphere in black clouds of ash, blocking the sun's rays.

A black barrier formed between the sun and earth, transforming almost half the planet into a place of darkness and despair. The sunlight at noon was sixty-six percent less than before the war. An ebony sky swirling with dark clouds covered the area, entombing it in a black shroud of gloom. In the stratosphere, above cloud level, the rain could not wash away the soot and smoke.

Temperatures cooled by twenty to thirty degrees north of the equator. The rapid onset of winter promised to bring frigid weather to colder climates and freezing temperatures to others. That would make survival difficult. Widespread nuclear fallout, pollution, and a toxic radioactive environment increased the potential for death and destruction. The number of people who would die from these aftereffects of the war remained to be seen. The likelihood of numbers climbing into the millions again remained high. But as horrific as things were, the worst was yet to come.

CHAPTER 20

On the outskirts of Beijing, China, Malachi lay flat on his stomach in a heat and air duct, peering down at the room through a return air vent. This was his specialty. He often boasted that he could find his way into any place and get any desired information. His left leg cramped. He attempted to shift it without making a sound. He was well aware of the danger involved, but the believers in Israel depended on his success.

The door opened below, and the group paraded in. The President led the way, followed by leading members of the Chinese Communist Party. They moved to a huge circular platform with seats around the perimeter. A chair reserved for the president sat at the head, with an opening at the other end. After being seated, he called the meeting to order, then sat in silence, waiting for someone else to enter.

The silence created angst for Malachi as the men would hear even the tiniest sound from above the room. He lay still, denying the pain in his leg and the claustrophobic anxiety brought on by the cramped space. The doors finally flew open and the awaited guest arrived. Malachi recoiled at the sight, forcing himself to remain prostrate and motionless. His mind pleaded with him to back out of the duct and flee. He steeled himself against the fear and refused to move.

The enormous red creature strolled through the opening and stood in the center of the circle. He turned all the way around, allowing his fiery breath to touch each face. Malachi could feel the heat from above the room. His nostrils burned from the putrid odor coming from the mouth of the beast.

Why hadn't he thought of that before? The Chinese Red Dragon. Anders spoke of a giant red dragon in The Revelation proclaimed as Satan himself. He was looking at the devil directly underneath him! Every fiber of his being pleaded with him to run. He fought the urge and lay still, watching the men under him pay homage to the creature stalking them from inside their circle.

"Gentlemen," he hissed, sparks floating from his nostrils. "The *beast of the east* has prevailed over the *beast of the west* and its allies. Congratulations! You now reign supreme as the new world power!" His voice sounded high-pitched and raspy.

"The time draws near to proceed with eliminating the one who has always stood in our way. You know of whom I speak: *Israel.*" He said the name with scorn. "They are too weak to stop us now."

Malachi cringed, panic-stricken, his body cramping. He prayed for the meeting to end.

"You must start your march of destruction while the smoke rises. Let it begin!"

The beast turned his head upward and roared, flames shooting from his mouth toward the ceiling. Then he turned and left, exiting the room within seconds, almost as if he disappeared. The others filed out next, without saying a word. They understood what they had to do.

The flames poured through the vent, hitting Malachi's face. He closed his eyes and turned his face upward to protect himself, but the fire scalded his face, neck and chin, searing them red, and blinding his eyes. He gritted his teeth to endure the pain. When the lights went out, the darkness left him lying in the duct, unable to see, his face burning from extreme pain.

Outside, Bruno and Magnus feared for their partner after watching the men leave the building. Racing to the area where Malachi entered, they crawled inside. Distant sounds came from overhead, telling them their comrade was backing out of his crawl space. They waited for him to reach the opening where he had climbed in.

•   •   •   •   •

Residents of the kibbutz left the shelters and returned to their homes. Everything they heard said the attack devastated the country. The missiles had hit their targets. Yet, inside their walls, no radiation tainted the air. Why had the kibbutz gone unscathed? God's protection? Perhaps. But in the morning, the same dark skies and cold air that greeted everyone else would greet them, too.

In Missouri, the group saw enough news to understand what happened. But they still did not expect what they would see with their own eyes when they walked outside. They longed to be with their teammates. They had no way of finding out how they were, or if they had survived. Getting to them was impossible, unless...

They must find some way to contact Paul Johnson. Perhaps he could do something. Ollie and Amelia shared the same thoughts in London. The UK held nothing for them now.

• • • • •

Bruno and Magnus waited, listening to sounds coming from the duct, afraid to speak. Scooting, stopping, scooting again. They could tell he was getting closer now. Groans. He was in pain.

"Malachi," Bruno whispered.

He was attempting to speak, his voice trembling with pain and fear. He sounded different.

His feet appeared in the opening, and they each took hold of one to lower him to the floor. When his feet touched the floor, he turned to face them. Both gasped.

"What happened to your face?!" Magnus' voice was full of shock and louder than he intended, prompting Bruno to jab an elbow into his side.

Malachi collapsed to the floor, pulling his knees against his chest, his breathing shallow and rapid. It took a moment for him to speak, but both big men sat beside him, waiting.

"Red dragon... *f-f-fire*... Satan...," he finally stammered.

"What are you talking about, red dragon and fire? *Satan?* What happened in there?"

"I know what happened, Bruno," Magnus said in a soft voice, laying his hand on Malachi's arm. "Messai told me about a creature that gives him his power. I never saw it and didn't want to believe it was real, but now I understand. He said it was red and breathes fire. It sounded like mythical stuff to me, but he was sincere when he talked about it."

Still in shock and sitting in the same fetal position, Malachi looked toward the men through hollow eyes. They knew he was blind. He whispered, "Anders said… *The Revelation*. Satan, red dragon…" He breathed two more words: "*Red China*."

"Red China? What does that have to do with…?" Bruno leapt to his feet. "The Chinese symbol! A red dragon! Satan! This is about China, isn't it, Malachi? They are Satan's tool to destroy Israel!"

Their partner nodded his head and spoke again, his voice growing weaker.

"*Beast of the east*… new world power… *Beast of the west* gone." He struggled, but managed a few more words. "Time to rid the world of *the one who stands in the way*…"

"Israel," Bruno muttered. "What else, Malachi? Did he say anything else?"

"Begin your march of destruction… *while the smoke rises*…"

"While the smoke rises… The smoke from the war! It is rising and blocking the light of the sun! The darkness and cold temperatures make this the perfect time for an army to march! We must tell the others!" They needed to move fast.

Malachi's hand moved toward his face. "Fire… *breathing fire*. The vent… can't see…"

"You're badly burned. We need to get you help," Magnus said, leaping back to his feet.

Malachi tried to stand but fell backward, hitting the floor with a thud.

"We have to do something quick. The fire blistered his face, and it is no normal burn. If we don't move fast, he won't make it!" Magnus went down to one knee beside his fallen comrade. "Grab his feet, Bruno. I've got his shoulders. There must be cold water here somewhere."

They lifted their partner and carried him toward a door straight ahead. The outside door handle turned, making a sound loud enough to attract their attention.

"Under here!" Bruno yelled in a voice not much louder than a whisper.

With Malachi in their arms, they dove under a metal staircase to their left, sitting there, afraid to breathe, peering through the perforated risers between each step. The door flung open. Magnus held Malachi in his arms as they knelt, expecting Chinese soldiers to burst in. They would discover them in this hiding place. It provided little protection.

Nothing could have prepared them for what they saw. The door slammed into the wall behind it and bounced back. A scaly red foot with short, pointed claws reached through the opening and caught it. They saw the creature for the first time as he entered and stood just inside the door.

Bruno and Magnus cringed and grabbed each other. Magnus almost dropped the man he held in his arms. Now, they understood his terror. The giant red dragon threw back his head and let out a deafening roar. The stench of his breath repulsed them. Flames poured from his mouth, racing toward them in milliseconds. The perforated metal provided little protection.

Throwing up their hands and covering their faces, they fell to the concrete floor, trying to shield themselves from the blazing inferno. Magnus covered Malachi's body with his own to protect him from more burns. Fire penetrated their dark hoodies, singeing their hair and searing their scalps. It was all they could do to keep from screaming out in pain.

The beast stopped and spoke in a much deeper voice than before.

"Tell your friends they cannot win. I know where all of you are, and you will all die. The Smyrnians cannot hide from me anymore than you can hide behind those steps. Inform them I am coming for all of them. No kibbutz in Israel, remote house in London, or bunker in Missouri can protect them from my wrath. They will not escape! Go ahead, warn them. I will enjoy the game, but it will not last long. All of you will die!"

The roar came again, accompanied by the stench and flames. They turned their backs toward the dragon as the searing heat penetrated their clothing again, burning their backs this time. Pain racked their bodies, and chills sent shivers over them from head to toe.

"I am coming for you. The wretched souls of the nations will do my bidding, and you will die like many others have died!" He turned, his long tail dragging across the bottom step in front of them. Without another stride, he vanished from their sight, leaving them lying under the stairs, overcome by pain and fear.

"We have to warn them," Bruno groaned, pulling his phone from his pocket. *No service.* "I'm going outside and try to find a place where I can make a call."

"Not without us," Magnus groaned through the pain.

They carried Malachi and left the building, walking toward the vehicle hidden almost a mile away.

•   •   •   •   •

It was mid-afternoon in Missouri, although the darkness made it feel like early evening. Blake, Evan, and Anders climbed the steps to the cabin. Steve told them it was safe to go outside now. They reached the top and walked through the closet door into the small building. What they saw caught them by surprise. At 2:00 p.m., the cabin was dark.

When they looked out the windows, they saw the same. They stepped out onto the porch, using their phones for light. When their eyes adjusted, they could see more, albeit very little. The cold air hitting their faces felt like they had wandered into Antarctica. An eerie chill pulsed through their bodies, and an undeniable sensation rushed over them.

Something was wrong. The wintry air did not cause what they felt standing outside the cabin. This sent fear deep into their souls and penetrated their minds, warning them of impending danger. They rushed back to the bunkers to tell the rest of the team. Something horrendous was coming. If only they knew what it was.

•   •   •   •   •

Nuclear winter spread across the entire Northern Hemisphere. Darkness and much colder than normal temperatures covered the land, even as the dread of winter lay on the horizon. Ben and Alexander sensed the same foreboding danger as the group at the Shelter. They had tried to call each of the others, but cell phones were now useless. The four groups lost contact with one another, neither knowing if something had happened to the others.

A storm brewed in China as the new world power prepared to take control of Israel. The crippled nation lay powerless to do anything about that following the nuclear assault. With its allies also weakened beyond the point of posing a threat, the Chinese leadership prepared to make their move. Less than five months remained now until the midpoint of the Tribulation.

• • • • •

Bruno and Magnus walked a mile to the car, carrying their friend, while fighting their own agony. Trying to call anyone was useless. They drove to the run-down hotel where they stayed and tried to determine what they could do to help him.

"Both of us need to take cold showers right away," said Bruno. "But Malachi needs help first. We can't take a chance on taking him to a hospital. Let's soak towels in cold water and cover his face. When the towels get warm, we'll keep replacing them. I wish we had antibiotic ointment, or something else we might use to soothe the burns."

"Cold water is all we have. We'll do that, then one of us can shower while the other sits with him."

They brought a cold towel and laid it over Malachi's face. He did not respond. He took slow and shallow breaths, his chest rising and falling with several seconds between. Sometimes they thought he would not breathe again and shook him until he did. Magnus sent Bruno to the shower as he sat with his new friend. They had not known each other long, but his heart broke for him.

He showered after Bruno. Their burns were not as severe as Malachi's. Still, the cold water brought only slight relief to their heads and backs. The hoodies had provided just enough protection to spare them the most severe burns. They continued doing everything possible for him, but without medical help, his chances of survival were slim. *If only Steve was here...*

• • • • •

China had extended its economic and political influence using the Belt and Road Initiative. The New Silk Road spanned seventy-one countries in Asia, Europe, and Africa, where half of the world's population lived. People in those areas trusted the Chinese government and believed its leaders had their best interest at heart.

The *Beast of the East* prepared for this moment by building military bases along the road. They kept friendly relations with Middle Eastern countries who benefitted from the superhighway. What they did not know was that the Belt and Road Initiative served a greater purpose than the Chinese revealed. They planned it with military domination in mind. Now, those plans were about to pay off, as attack helicopters and bombers prepared to fly from some of those bases bound for Israel.

The smoke and soot from the nuclear holocaust rolled through the Middle East, bringing even darker and colder conditions. Dense smoke filled the air, making it appear that hell had unleashed its fury on the land. It would soon conceal the aircraft coming toward Israel. The country struggled with the extreme conditions, just like every other nation in the Northern Hemisphere. However, they fought for survival, unaware that yet another storm was on the way.

But Israel was not the only target. Military jets and helicopters also flew toward their unsuspecting allies, who they had already ravaged with nuclear attacks. China's military genius built bombers capable of making international flights, increasing their superiority even more.

Nations turned their heads and allowed it to happen, closing their eyes to what was going on. While they did, China became the most powerful nation on earth with the most advanced and dangerous military on the planet. The world would now witness that force in action.

•   •   •   •   •

Some bombers flew for the United States, or at least what the coalition left of it. Two of them carrying bunker buster bombs headed for Ozark, Missouri. Meanwhile, the group of Smyrnians remained in the Shelter, clueless to what was coming. Bruno and Magnus could not warn them without a computer and no cell phone service. They battled a crisis of their own, which would soon claim one of their lives.

The People's Liberation Army Air Force assembled first in Iran. They would do this alone. China must rule Israel, but make them think they ruled in peace until the last battle. When that came, they would annihilate them once and for all. Iran waited in the wings in case they needed them, but they would not.

North Korea bore the responsibility for finishing India in their depleted state and unable to defend themselves. They assigned the role of taking care of the battered U.S. allies in Europe to Russia. The other European countries along the New Silk Road would not interfere. Their economic success depended on China, and they understood who was behind the attacks. The Chinese planned to demolish America themselves. With everything in place and plans made, the day came to set the plans in motion.

Aissa Messai upheld his part of the plan. Most media outlets in Israel still broadcast, and electronics functioned, although the news could not reach the rest of the world. He spread word that he planned to speak from the Temple Mount about the current crisis. News crews scrambled to get there and provide coverage. Messai always had answers. Amid death, despair and agonizing pain, he would tell them what to do.

"Ladies and gentlemen of Israel, I stand before you with a broken heart. Your pain is my pain. I have rejoiced with you in the past, and I grieve with you today. Hospitals are functioning in a limited capacity, but we are trying to get volunteers out to help people. You are my primary concern at this point. I believe it was for this reason that I stayed in the country instead of returning home."

"I spoke with the Chinese president about their grievous attack on your nation. He assured me they will not attack again, although their military will arrive soon to maintain peace. Please do not fight back against them, but do what they say. Your survival depends on that."

"Trust me as I work to restore peace with those who have become your enemy. I will provide updates at noon each day. The IDF remains on high alert but will not retaliate. This temporary setback will not impede our goal of peace and prosperity. Please believe that and keep your faith in me."

•   •   •   •   •

The group at the kibbutz had just finished watching Messai's announcement. Ben called the leaders together again.

"Gentlemen, I have no words for what I feel right now. Neither can I explain why all of us remain unaffected by the nuclear missiles and radiation. My heart tells me the other believers in Israel have come through unscathed too. We need to pray and ask Jesus how we are to respond and to show us our next moves."

"I also want to welcome our newest member and follower of the Messiah to our group: Mordecai Chaim. You know him as the Aluf, Major General in the IDF. Hadassah knows him as Uncle Mordecai. He became a believer in Jesus after the nuclear attack. Mordecai, please share your thoughts with us."

"Thank you, Benjamin. I sit with you today, feeling like a man who let my country down. My military was unprepared, and the blame for that lies with me. But from what my sweet Hadassah tells me, it may all fit into Ha-Shem's plans for these seven years in which we live. And now that I know the real Messiah, I am ready to join *his* army for the next four years."

"What if they attack again? Are we prepared for that possibility? We believe nothing that comes out of Messai's mouth."

Moshe and Eliyahu had become warriors for the cause. They grew more bold in their faith every day, after their destruction of the AMPP forces on the Plain of Megiddo. There was something unique about them the people of the kibbutz had never noticed. Normal men could not do the things they did that day. Yet, the others had not spoken about it since.

"Our security noticed movement by the PLAAF, Moshe. They are mobilizing in Iran, and I am certain their plans are not for our good. But I must tell you, we are powerless to stop them, anyway. We will depend on the Messiah to give us victory when the time comes."

"Well, just in case..." Eliyahu interrupted him.

"Eliyahu, trying to stop them now would bring death to our country. I believe the prophecy that says the Messiah will rule on his throne in Jerusalem. We await that day and trust that it will come."

It was clear his answer did not satisfy the two men. Before either responded, Michael spoke.

"Ezra and Shimon have joined forces with Trey and Rickie to bring other IDF pilots to the faith. Together, we are preparing for whatever Jesus has in store for us. I seek him daily, trying to discern what that will be. He has yet to give me an answer. All I understand is that his plan involves pilots. And they must be ready to swing into action at a moment's notice when the time comes."

"I trust you will take care of that Michael."

"We are working with them every day, Ben," said Trey. "I assure you, we will be ready."

"Thank you, men. We must stay prepared to move at a moment's notice. I only pray that what is coming will cause our people to turn to their Messiah and trust him, instead of Aissa Messai."

The meeting ended with more questions than answers. None of them saw what was coming next.

•　　　　•　　　　•

Malachi's condition worsened by the hour. Bruno and Magnus did everything they knew to do, but nothing worked. They also tried to care for their burns at the same time. Theirs would heal, so their concern was for him. They continued applying cold towels, but the burns seemed to penetrate his face. Flesh was coming off in chunks as they removed the towels. He was now unrecognizable, not just as himself, but as a human being. This was no normal burn, and it came from no normal foe or earthly source.

They watched as their friend and comrade succumbed to his injuries. Both wept when he took his last breath, even though they knew he was with Jesus. That comforted them, but still did not ease the pain of losing a dear friend and capable warrior in the fight against Aissa Messai.

The seven years of the Tribulation were not yet half over. How many more of them would die before it ended? They remained unable to contact the group at the Shelter and were unaware that Chinese bombers were on their way to Missouri at that very moment.

•　　　•　　　•　　　•

PLAAF bombers and choppers flew from Iran to another base along the New Silk Road during the night. From there, they would fly to Israel the next day. They would bring a powerful show of strength and domination that would drive fear into the hearts of every citizen of the doomed nation.

Yet, the dragon made it clear they must obey Aissa Messai until the day of the great battle. "Victory will come through him," the dragon said. Messai demanded they kill no more Israeli citizens, but allowed them to enforce their will. Many would die from radiation poisoning. They relished that thought. That would further weaken the already disabled nation and set the stage for China to stand alone as the ruler of the world. The dragon assured that. They would follow him.

People in Israel sat and waited for the Chinese military to arrive. The wait was grueling, but they could do nothing else. Businesses closed across the country bringing the nation to a standstill. All eyes looked eastward, as they listened for the sounds they knew were coming. The smoke would obscure them until the last minute when they appeared like a sudden storm. Many hid in bomb shelters, but had too few rations to survive long. Others stayed indoors, clinging to the false hope that the walls would somehow protect them.

• • • • •

Evan led an emergency meeting of the Smyrnians hunkered down in the Shelter. All of them sensed the angst of impending disaster, but none could decide what it may be. They had no way to know, but still needed to prepare, whether that meant fight or flight. None of them wanted to leave the place they called home. However, if evacuation became necessary, they would go.

"Maybe we're just anxious because we don't know if the others are safe," suggested Beth.

Mila started weeping. Beth walked over and put her arm around Bruno's wife.

"Mila, I wish we could get in touch with them. Blake keeps trying, but neither they nor we have phone service. All we can do is pray and ask Jesus to protect them."

"But they are in the most dangerous place in the world. Why did they go to China?"

"They believed Jesus called them to go there. Bruno and Magnus are big enough to take care of themselves." Her forced smile as she referred to the men's size did little to make Mila feel better.

"Malachi is the best at getting in and out of places when he needs to. I'm glad he is with them." Blake tried to reassure Mila, but his words were empty, too. He knew the three men were in grave danger and only Jesus could protect them. But he wanted to hide his feelings from her as much as possible.

"What should we do?" asked Evan. "How do we prepare for something when we don't know what it is, or if it's even coming?"

"Our best bet is to stay in here and wait until things calm down."

"I agree with that, John, but we need a plan in case trouble arises. Perhaps we should look for a temporary place to go, for now. We can come back when it is safe."

"I agree with Blake." Steve entered the conversation. "We need to protect ourselves. Linda and I talked about this, and we want you to come to our house."

"Now everybody," Anders spoke with a reassuring look on his face, "the most important thing is to trust Jesus. We need to pray and decide based on what we hear from him. If all of you will join me, I am going to pray!"

They surrounded him, grabbed each other's hands, and prayed the most powerful prayer they had ever prayed. They believed Steve and Linda's place was the right choice.

•　•　•　•　•

Nothing could have prepared the people of Israel for what they heard. The sound of thundering hooves from a thousand horses above the smoke, accompanied by the unmistakable buzz of planes. Dread seized the hearts of those who heard them. The first choppers burst through the smoke, flying in formation. They kept coming until it seemed there would be no end. The sound even deafened people inside their homes to the voices of the others with them.

The choppers flew low, an obvious attempt at intimidation, and it worked. Anyone who was outdoors ran for cover, fearing an attack from above. At last, the rows of choppers ended. When they did, fighter jets broke through the smoke, flying at a higher level. PLAAF aircraft carriers entered the Mediterranean Sea via the Suez Canal. China's military ties with Egypt were strong.

People feared bombs dropping any minute. But Aissa Messai promised that would not happen. No more killing; only maintaining the peace.

However, it did not feel like peace as the choppers hovered overhead and jets threatened to unleash another barrage of missiles.

They would soon learn the aircraft arrived in every part of the country, with a focus on the cities that already lay in ruins. Yet, less populated areas did not escape the threat. From the Golan to the desert, the scenes were the same.

Messai said hospitals operated in a limited capacity, but no one could get to them now. Those battling radiation sickness, blindness, and severe pain from the earlier nuclear attacks had to fight the pain and illness without medical attention. The suffering was extreme throughout the country. Many begged to die, but death would not come.

The Chinese military ordered people to stay in their homes. Anyone caught outside would suffer the consequences. The nation was under siege. Most families had supplies to carry them through a few weeks. But they did not realize this would go on for five months. Every day the choppers and planes flew overhead, as if daring people to leave their homes. Those who ran out of food had no choice except to emerge. Messai promised no one else would die at the hands of the Chinese forces. But some things are worse than death...

●　　●　　●　　●　　●

Bruno and Magnus sought answers for their predicament. Still grieving Malachi's death, they needed a plan to escape China. But after much discussion and prayer, they concluded no such plan existed. They sat trapped in the country with no way out.

Jesus must have a purpose for them being here. But if that was true, why did he allow Malachi to die at the hands of the dragon? Wasn't Jesus more powerful than the creature? They knew the answer was yes, but doubts still flooded their minds amid their heartbreak.

They could no longer stay in the seedy hotel where they had lived the few days since coming to Beijing. But Malachi may still help them. Nobody was better at finding places and discovering information than him. The three of them had discussed this dilemma not long after they arrived and checked into the hotel.

Malachi had insisted on going out alone in search of a safer place. He returned with what he called the *perfect location* in mind and a map drawn on a piece of paper detailing how to find it. It was a cave with a hidden entrance covered by bushes and rocks. He had worked his way in and scoped it out. That's how he rolled.

They checked out of the hotel, using their assumed names, and left in search of their new hideout. The map worked better than any GPS and led them straight to the dense forest where they located the cave.

Malachi had mentioned a grove of trees not far away he believed the car could squeeze into. They found it and discovered a narrow opening between two trees. Bruno pulled one back just enough for Magnus to drive the car through.

Then they carried the body of their fallen comrade to the cave, along with their things. Malachi was right; this place was the perfect hideout.

After settling in, they buried their friend in the depths of the cave. The real Malachi was with Jesus, but this seemed to be the perfect resting place for his body. Then they hunkered down and prepared the place, enabling them to survive as long as they needed.

China would be their home for a while. Their size may make them more conspicuous, but they must do what Malachi would have done. They must serve as Smyrnian spies in the most dangerous nation on earth, until the military captured or killed them, or they escaped the country, whichever came first.

•   •   •   •   •

Ollie and Amelia had a plan to get out of the UK: Bradley Rodgers. Trey's military buddy flew them to the U.S. when they were in trouble before. Perhaps he would do the same for them this time, especially since he was now a believer in Jesus. They drove to the military base to see if they could sneak in and find him.

The base survived, but the latest attacks created severe damage. Gaping holes riddled fences and went unguarded. Runways looked too damaged for planes to take off or land, and personnel were at a minimum.

What are the odds that one of them would be Bradley Rodgers? Slim chance under normal circumstances, and these circumstances were dire.

But the odds always seemed to be in their favor with Jesus! They heard voices and ducked into a hangar, listening for them to pass.

"I'll see what I can do about that. Maybe one of us can come up with an idea before our meeting at 0900 tomorrow morning."

It was him! Bradley Rodgers! How lucky could they get? It was not luck, and both of them knew it. Jesus kept doing things like this for them. Bradley walked into the hangar, and they stepped out to greet him, catching him by surprise. Trey wasn't running interference for them this time, but they trusted their new comrade.

• • • • •

The Chinese military in Israel had something some may consider worse than death. Their long-range pain beam worked like a microwave, burning people from the inside out from over a half-mile away. It functioned by heating water molecules in the body, causing overwhelming pain. They called it a non-lethal weapon, but most said victims wished it had killed them.

China attached the system to planes and helicopters. It looked like a smaller version of a satellite dish. When pilots spotted people coming out of their homes, they zeroed in on them and zapped them with the beam. The victims screamed, feeling like it ignited them on the inside. Those hit attempted to escape the torture, eventually forced to run back inside their homes or find other shelter. Israel's cities had become dystopian societies with little hope of future restoration.

The siege reached a point of desperation. Food shortage and starvation spread throughout the country. Israel's population may not die from more nukes, but how many would survive a five-month siege? The human suffering reached a level seldom seen in the modern day. And the Chinese military showed no signs of letting up.

Aissa Messai's promised daily updates went by the wayside. Would Jesus intervene? Or would God allow his chosen people and other residents of the country to perish at the hands of a brutal enemy? Would Messai have an answer? The people still believed he would save them. They waited for a miracle that seemed less likely by the day.

The followers of Jesus remained the one group unaffected by the suffering. If there was a saving grace for the nation, it was them. Now over

140,000 strong, they went out every day, providing care for those in need. An invisible shield seemed to surround them, causing the pain beam to deflect away. The Chinese soldiers could not touch them.

The believers told people about Jesus and shared his love with them. Moshe and Eliyahu were the most bold. But despite their efforts, no more turned to him. They continued living their lives as though he did not exist. It frustrated Ben and the others, but did not stop them from caring for those who suffered. If only they would believe in Jesus, but they would not.

It seemed their number had reached a limit that it would not go beyond. They knew the *shields* were temporary. Jesus revealed to Ben a frightening vision of a day when they would flee for their lives. And it was coming soon.

●　　　●　　　●　　　●　　　●

At the Shelter, the group reached a decision. None of them wanted to do it, but all of them believed they must. Whether it was instinct or something that came from Jesus, they could not deny it. So, they decided and wasted no time acting on their decision. Sometimes prudence does not allow for delay.

"We have to go, at least for a little while," said Blake. "We all sense something bad is on the way. We can't just ignore that. I hope nothing happens and we're back here in no time. But for now, we're not taking any chances. Let's get packing."

"Okay Blake, I'm with you," John said with confidence. "It's the right thing to do."

"I'll bring the vehicles from behind the barn," said Anders.

"No, let's leave them till we're ready to load up and go. Steve, are you guys up for this?"

"Yes, sir! AMPP still doesn't know who we are, so our house will be a good safe place until things settle down. We have a big house, but fitting all of us in could get interesting. You'll be up close and personal with each other for a while, but we can make things work."

"Up close and personal is fun. I enjoy hanging out with you people!" Evan tried to bring his usual levity to the situation. He saw it wasn't working.

"Come on, everybody. I hate leaving this place as much as anyone. We're just going on a mini vacation. We'll be back." A silly grin covered his face, but no one paid any attention. He shook his head and shrugged his shoulders.

"We will enjoy the vacation, even if they don't," said Ally, grinning back at him. She needed something to help keep her mind off her dad in China. "That's what Jesus wants us to do! Bet I can beat you, Evan!"

The two of them ran to get some things like two kids racing each other. To some others, they were still kids. But in reality, they had proven themselves as two of their top warriors for Jesus.

"Okay, it's time. We need to go *now!*" The urgency in Blake's voice shocked them.

They jumped to their feet and followed his lead. Unhooking electronics and gathering clothes, they carried them out of the bunkers to the automobiles. It took over an hour, even with everyone helping.

The steel structures they had called home for three years looked like the empty shells they buried there in the early months of 2030. It was especially sad for those who had worked to install them. But they all thought of this place as home.

"There isn't much left," Steve said. "Let's grab the food and water. We don't want to leave them."

They filled the vehicles until there was barely room for everyone to sit and stored the rest in the barn. They would return for it later. With everything loaded, they stood for a moment, taking one more look at the Shelter. The reality hit them that this could be the last time they would see it.

CONCLUSION

"Wait, the external hard drives with all of our information. I left them in the safe in our room. We can't leave them. It will just take a moment for me to run back down and get them."

"Hold on, Blake, let me go. I think I'm a little faster than you." Evan ran toward the cabin, glancing over his shoulder at Blake and laughing as he ran. Through the window, they saw him disappear into the bedroom. It would only take a few minutes for him to open the safe, grab the hard drives, and run back.

"The rest of you load up," said John. "We need to roll as soon as he gets back."

Then they heard them: planes. Nothing unusual. But something sounded different about these. Military planes! All of them saw it at once. The bomb released and descended rapidly toward the cabin.

"Evan!" Ally screamed and made a break for the cabin. John grabbed her and held her back as she fought to free herself.

"Run!" Blake screamed, shoving Beth toward the barn.

The last thing they saw was Evan standing in the cabin, smiling and waving, with the hard drives in his hand.

Beth screamed this time.

"Evan, get out!"

Just as he turned from the window, the bomb plowed into the cabin, burrowing into the ground. The building erupted in an explosive fireball, debris from the bunkers underneath hurled with it into the air. The others raced toward the barn, while Ally stood screaming.

"Evan! No! Please Jesus, no!"

Anders ran to her, scooped her up in his arms, and sprinted after them. The force of the explosion knocked him to the ground. He threw himself on top of Ally, shielding her from the debris raining down on them, burying their bodies under a mountain of rubble. While rocks, wood, and steel pummeled his body, Anders' thoughts turned to Angie and his kids. The din that filled his ears slowly turned to silence. He heard their voices just as he lost consciousness... then slipped from this world to the next.

OTHER BOOKS
BY DAVID O. BULLOCK

How can the world change in 26 minutes and 51 seconds? But it can, and it does, just as it did 100 days earlier on September 11, 2029. A worldwide blackout brings a fiery darkness that invades the earth with pure evil directly from the pit of hell. Blake and Beth Jennings Thompson fire the first shot in the battle against Aissa Messai and his forces. It begins a war that will rage for the remaining six and half years of Planet Earth. It will lead to worldwide death and destruction. The fight for survival becomes real. As Messai increases in power, his hatred for the Smyrnians intensifies.

When a supposed alien invasion suddenly takes billions of people from the earth, a band of warriors arise to battle an insurmountable foe in Episode One of this thrilling series. Join them as they face the fight of their lives that will become a fight for their lives. When you enter the struggle with them, you will find your own life being challenged and changed as you read.

ABOUT THE AUTHOR

David O. Bullock was raised on an egg farm in rural Kentucky with 10,000 chickens. Really! He left the farm to become a pastor at age 20. He holds Bachelor's and Master's degrees. David is still happily married to his high school sweetheart, Glenda. They have two daughters and six grandchildren. He's still a pastor, loves writing, and drinks lots of Diet Rite and coffee. He's also up for the occasional round of golf.

Email: davidobullockwriting@gmail.com
Facebook: facebook.com/david.bullock.376
Twitter: twitter.com/bullockwriting
LinkedIn: linkedin.com/in/david-o-bullock

NOTE FROM THE AUTHOR

Word-of-mouth is crucial for any author to succeed. If you enjoyed *Infernal Chaos*, please leave a review online—anywhere you are able. Even if it's just a sentence or two. It would make all the difference and would be very much appreciated.

Thanks!
David

Thank you so much for reading one of David O. Bullock's novels.
If you enjoyed the experience, please check out the beginning of the
series!

Rise of the Smyrnians by David O. Bullock

Blake Thompson is the top reporter for a major television network. When up
to one-fourth of the world's population suddenly disappears, it appears an
alien invasion has finally taken place. As the world deals with the devastating
loss, Blake sets out to discover and report the truth and also help prepare
humanity for possible future attacks.

As facts unfold, an unlikely band of warriors known as the Smyrnians arises.
These include Blake's cameraman, Anders Norstrom, his rival in the news game,
Beth Jennings, college students Evan Ryles and Ally Fromm, professor John
Baldwin and others. Together they will battle what appears to be an
insurmountable foe. They will face not only the fight of their lives but a fight
for their lives.